A FAREWELL TO
WOODMYST

A Farewell to Woodmyst

THE WOODMYST CHRONICLES BOOK X

Robert E Kreig

WHITEKEEP BOOKS

For my family, friends and supporters.
Thank you.

The Realm

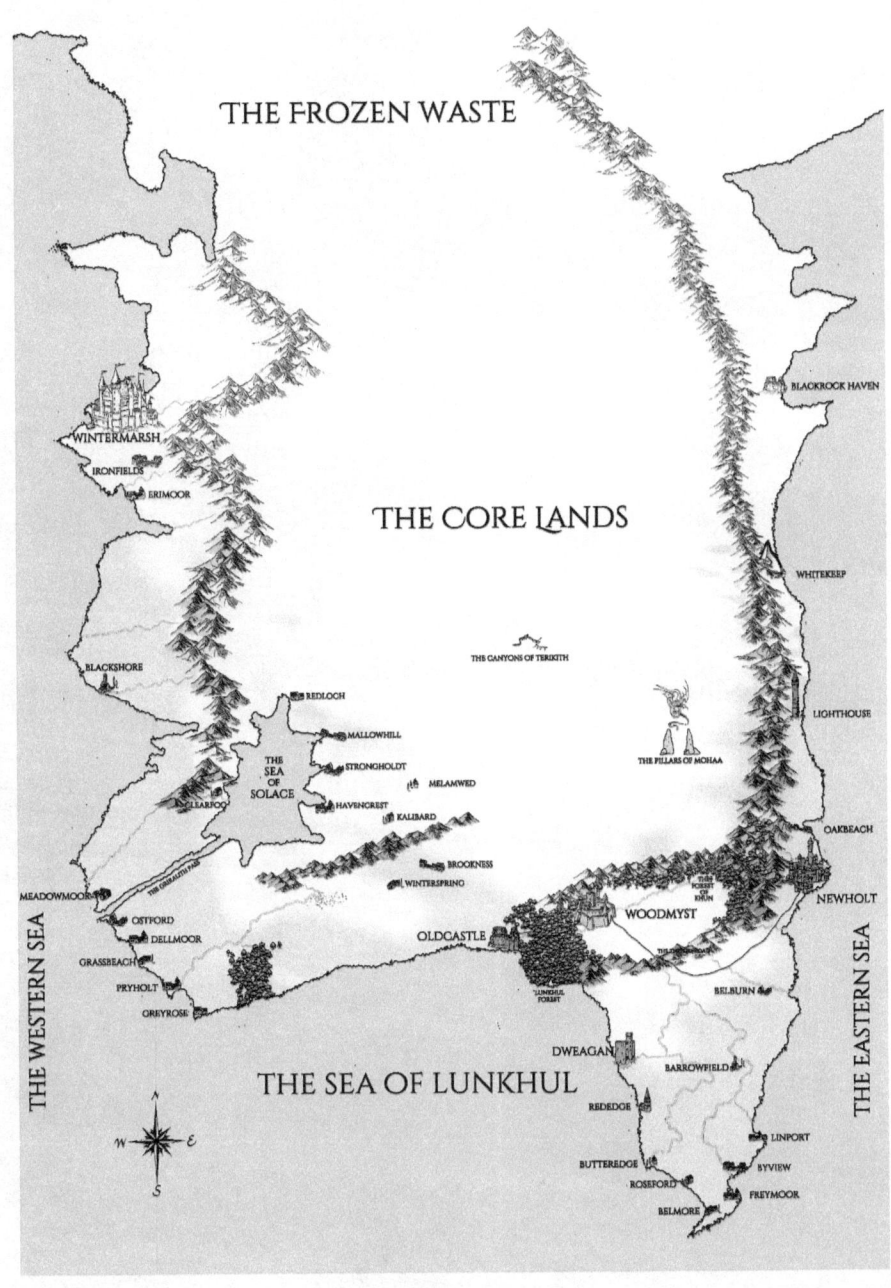

Prologue

A chill wind suddenly flooded into the campsite, intensifying rapidly.

The tents shook violently, rocking this way and that to the point where anyone inside leapt to their feet and rushed into the open, fearing the shelters would collapse. Others, seated by fires, raced to the nearest tent to keep the poles and ropes in place before the canvas toppled.

Gruloch charged to the dragons, leaving the warmth of the flames so he could settle the nervous beasts. They chirped and groaned, twisting their necks about, seemingly in search of what caused the sudden change in weather.

"What is wrong with them?" one of the Kazrekh riders asked, rubbing the underside of his dragon's neck. The beast stared at the open plains north of their position.

"I don't know," said the Lord of the Haigok, squinting as he peered into the oncoming wind. His face felt the sting of speeding sleet attacking his skin. "Perhaps they see something we can't."

"There is nothing but snow and wind," another Haigok shouted.

Haildur, the leader of the Traruk Clan, stepped to Gruloch's side.

"There is something," the clan leader said. "Listen."

Gruloch tilted his ear, hearing the howl of the wind and the patter of snow smacking against his flesh. He shook his head.

"Listen," Haildur pointed into the gale.

The Lord of the Haigok tried again. The wind howled and howled. It sang melodically, harmoniously, with notes that would rise and fall.

But amongst it, deep within, the noise of something else. Something strange.

It reminded Gruloch of a dragon's wing upon the air as it glided through the sky, or of a giant piece of fabric hung out to dry.

"Listen," Haildur said again. "Can you hear it?"

The sound moved far to the left, back across in front of them and far to the right.

It was coming towards them.

"I can hear it," Gruloch told him. "Over there." He pointed to the northeast. It continued to move farther and farther to his right.

"It makes its way around us," the other clan leader announced. "You should tell the man soldiers."

Gruloch turned and raced back towards the camp, shouting to the men fighting the wind to keep their tents upright. "Something is coming. Something is coming."

The soldiers left the shelters be as they reached for their swords and bows. Some tents toppled over. Others continued to sway and shake in the strong windstorm.

The howling wind sang loudly as the strange sound whipped around to the east of the campsite.

"Can you see anything?" one man hollered.

"Nothing," another replied.

The Lord of the Haigok scanned the ground beyond the light of the campfire as best he could, but he too could see nothing but snow.

The sound moved by, farther to the south and around the edge of the encampment. Some panicky archers fired arrows into the darkness, hoping to hit the source of the terrible noise.

"Cease fire," an officer called out. "Could be friendlies out there."

The bizarre noise continued around them before starting for the top of the ridge to the west. Gruloch raced in the direction of the sound, not knowing what he should do.

"A shadow," a man called. "I see a shadow."

By the time the Haigok reached the soldier, there was nothing to see. Even the odd sound had silenced.

Only the howling wind prevailed.

"It's gone," the soldier said, looking at Gruloch.

"Where?" he asked, a heightened urgency in his voice.

The soldier pointed to the ridge.

Gruloch charged up the small embankment, several men and Haigok on his heels.

Upon reaching the top, they scanned the scene below them.

Houses and structures lined neat little streets far below them. Warm candle and lantern light emitted from small windows dotted throughout the township.

There was no sign of a shadow.

No strange sound carried upon the wind.

Nothing.

Only Erimoor and the ships floating upon the bay.

"What was it?" one of the Haigok riders asked.

"A trick of the brain," another answered, dismissing the event as he turned away. "The wind playing games."

Gruloch wasn't so sure.

As the crowd disbanded one by one, he remained upon the ridge. His eyes combed the streets in search of something. Anything.

But from so far away, his eyes couldn't see anything unusual that would explain the sound that they all heard. That they all thought they had heard.

A light flickered to life from the streets. He focused, squinting his eyes tightly, and saw a figure, dark and tall, cloaked and moving strangely.

Could this be the thing that gripped our fears so tightly? he wondered.

The figure reached out with a long rod, a small flame upon its end. It touched the flame to a lantern hanging from a post outside a storefront.

Just a man, Gruloch thought. *Just the town's lamplighter. Nothing more.*

After a while, he too, gave up and returned to the camp.

The wind subsided.

The dragons settled once again.

The Lord of the Haigok sat by the fire and reached out his hands towards the warm flames as a soldier across the hearth from him stoked the embers with his sword.

"Might put the pot on," the man said. "Fancy a cup of tea, Mister Gruloch?"

The Haigok replied with a smile. "Thank you, yes."

One

Alice stayed by the beacon tower until the fire inside of it had completely died away.

Her eye occasionally drifted to the harbour, watching Zakhar riding a longboat to the docks. Eventually, he reached the shore and marched along the pier before disappearing between some buildings by the waterfront.

When only thin ribbons of smoke wafted through the windows and the last of the orange glow emitting from the tower's top faded, she lifted herself from her place upon a rock a few yards away.

The walk back to the township was long. She held her cloak about her tightly. The thick leather material kept the biting draught at bay. Secretly, internally, she thanked the Agrodien women for making such a gift for her. She didn't believe that her regular cloak would have been of as much help against such weather.

Her boots crunched the snow noisily as she followed the road. As she took in the view of her surroundings, she could see beauty here.

Erimoor looked to be a quaint and well-protected village. The high-ridge that surrounded the township shielded it from the onslaught of the northern winds. The sheltered bay offered a safeguard against any unwanted visitors that may approach by the sea.

All in all, she surmised that Erimoor would have been a peaceful place to live, if it wasn't for the intervention of the Mirikin and, more recently, the Maji.

By the time she reached the edge of town, she could barely make out the dark form of the beacon tower in the distance. Its shadow loomed against the night sky, smoke still rising from its crown, drifting away upon winds sweeping down the hillsides.

She turned to walk along the street, moving into the town, passing houses and storefronts, including a certain cake shop she had visited earlier that day. She peered into the window as she strolled by.

The store was empty.

Amma Gertrude, the proprietor, an old woman with kind features, was nowhere to be seen.

A flickering light emitted from under a doorway to the rear of the shop. Alice surmised that the woman had retired to her private quarters for the night.

Although she had a bad feeling about the old lady, she still wanted to properly thank Amma Gertrude for sharing her knowledge about the tower.

Alice approached the door, intending to knock.

She stopped herself before her knuckles touched the timber frame.

Slowly, she retreated away from the store, thinking it best to let the old lady alone for the night.

After all, it was cold and by a fireplace was where anyone should be on a night like this.

Someone ahead of her, moving about on stilts, drew her attention.

It was a strange oddity to perceive.

The figure was lighting lanterns that hung upon tall posts by the storefronts lining the street, using a long rod, about the length of her arm, with a small torch sticking from its end.

The figure, hunched over a little, wore a long cloak that hung past their feet so that Alice could see only the thin timber struts they walked upon beneath them. At certain angles, when the lamplight hit it just right, the cloak appeared to have a purplish tinge to it. At other moments, when the wind blew a little, it bore the glow of the flickering lanterns and looked dark, almost black.

"Hello, young mistress," the figure said from beneath his hood as she drew nearer. The voice sounded old and raspy.

"Uh." She was taken aback. The sight of an old man stepping about on stilts amazed her. But something made her feel uneasy. "Hello. I'm Alice."

"I know who you are," he said. There was a hint of playfulness in his voice. He moved towards another lantern, holding the candle out to light it. "We all saw what you and your dragon did to that tower out there. Shame the blasted thing is still standing."

She turned to peer over her shoulder as the man on stilts lit another lantern. She could still just see the silhouette of the beacon tower rising from the rocky point far away.

"Yes," she replied.

"Do you think the curse still holds?" he asked.

"I don't know," she said, looking back at him. He was staring at her. Although she couldn't see his face beneath his hood, she could feel his eyes on her skin.

"You are a pretty one," he said, his gaze lingering a little longer.

Alice felt her stomach tense. The man-made her feel a little uncomfortable. The stilt man let out a soft chuckle as he started towards the next lantern.

"I told you who *I* am," Alice said, moving after him with an inquiring look.

"Must get the street all lit up," the other muttered as he walked on.

"Won't you tell me who *you* are?"

"No one else will light the lanterns," the stilt man continued.

"What's your name?" Alice pressed, her voice composed and gentle.

"All the men have gone away," he said, his voice almost melodic and changing. "Only girls are here today."

"What?" She stopped in her tracks and stared after the stilt man.

He turned his frame slowly, lifting a finger to the shadow of his hood.

"Shhh," he hissed. "Hopeful children sup on bread. But, soon their fathers will be dead."

"Who are you?" Alice reached over her shoulder for one of her swords. "Stop this game."

The stilt man giggled.

"Who are you?" she barked.

"No more games," he told her. His voice was familiar, young. She recognised it immediately.

"Takmel."

"I'm going to destroy you, Alice," he told her. "But not until I have slaughtered all the ones you love first. Your mother. Your sister. Your precious Arthur. All of them."

"Face me now," she growled, pulling a sword free of its sheath. "Let's get it done right here."

His head tilted to the side teasingly, still covered by the shadow of his hood.

"No," he laughed, his face still hidden from her. "I only came to see how you were faring after such a significant loss at the Griralith Pass. I saw your men on the hill. I saw your dragons on the snow and your horses in the stables. I saw your mother and my beloved Catherine in the manor.

"Now, I know your numbers. Now, I know just how pathetic you are."

"Fight me here, coward," she barked. Her teeth gritted so tightly that she could hear them grinding in her ears. Her heart raced so intensely she could feel it in her throat and temples.

"They will all die for you. Because of you. But… you can save them."

"I'll have your head on a spit," she snapped.

"Become my wife," he offered. "Become mine and I will spare them all."

"I'll tear you to pieces, pig," she huffed, stepping towards him.

"Not today," he replied. His hands turned dark and lost their form. "I'll be ready for you when you reach Wintermarsh." Thick strands of black smoke seeped from his limbs. The cloak itself transformed into a cloud of blackness. "If you reach Wintermarsh."

The stilts fell to the street, crossing over one another when they landed.

Alice watched the cloud of dark vapour rise into the night sky, moving against the wind at tremendous speed.

***

"He was here," Alice told them.

Her hands were holding the dining-room door open, and she peered around at all the faces gathered at the table. Brondt and Amicia were seated at one end, their grins dying upon their intimate conversation being interrupted by the girl's announcement. Ursula had a hand on Thornton's arm, no doubt consoling him after his encounter in the beacon tower. Commander Zakhar sat next to them. He had been engaged in a discussion with Catherine. And Emily, seated by her daughter's side at the other end of the table, jolted from her discussion with Akasati, Schoenbach and Karlena, who had their backs to the Alice.

They all offered her the same puzzled expression.

"Who was here?" Emily questioned.

Schoenbach was already on his feet and moving for the fireplace to the side of the room.

"Where are you going?" Karlena asked.

"To get my sword," he replied. Alice noticed their weapons resting against the wall beside the stone hearth. Her mother's and Karlena's swords were side by side. Akasati's bow and quiver rested next to her short, curved blade in its sheath. Brondt's long sword and Thornton's blade lay on the floor.

"He's gone," the girl called after him. Schoenbach halted by the door and looked at her.

"Who?" Emily asked again.

"Takmel!" Catherine gasped. "He was here?"

"Just now," Alice answered, peering to the food laid out on the table; roast chicken, potatoes, green beans and steaming carrots. "What's all this?"

"Dinner," Amicia answered. "The servants here offered to prepare this for us."

"In our honour," Ursula added.

"In honour for what?" Alice asked. Fine silverware and gold embroidered dishes adorned the bright, white tablecloth that stretched over the long surface of the table. "All we have done is arrive in their town. Have you eaten any of it?"

"We were waiting for you," her mother replied. "It's just been served up."

"There was the incident with the tower," Commander Zakhar offered. "Perhaps they made it in gratitude of…"

"That only just happened," Thornton put in. "Not less than an hour ago. This meal would surely have taken longer than an hour to prepare."

Alice peered around, leaning back and forth to look along corridors leading off from the sides of the room. A plump servant woman was standing just inside a passageway to her left.

"You," Alice called to her.

The woman, plump in appearance, looked about nervously before smiling with a clumsy curtsy. "Yes, Mistress," she said cheerily as she entered the room.

"Did you prepare this fine meal for us?"

"No, Mistress," the other replied with a quick shake of the head. Her behaviour seemed odd to the girl. The woman's grin was too broad, and the little giggles she gave after each sentence made Alice grow rapidly suspicious. "I oversaw the preparation."

"The cook," Alice moved towards the fireplace, passing Schoenbach, who watched on warily. "Is he a man of good morals?"

"She," the other corrected. "And yes. She is the finest chef I know, and a good and honest person." More giggles.

"Then, you, and she, wouldn't mind taking all of this fine food and offering it to some of the more needy people of the town. Would you?"

Alice positioned herself near the fire, stretching her hands out as if to get warm. Schoenbach, however, noticed that she had positioned herself near Akasati's bow.

"We don't want to offend these people," Amicia said. "They were kind enough to prepare this fine meal and…"

Schoenbach shot her a harsh stare.

She understood the silent message and closed her mouth.

"I don't understand," the servant woman said, her grin widening beyond what Alice thought possible. She appeared to become increasingly uncomfortable, both with the girl's requests and questions, as well as the sudden tension and silence that had filled the room. "Is it not sufficient? Would you prefer something else?"

"Would you?" Alice asked.

"Mistress?"

"If I offered you this meal," Alice started, "would you prefer something else in its place?"

"It looks delicious," the woman replied with a giggle. The sound was setting Alice's teeth on edge. "Smells delightful. I don't see how I could refuse something so delectable."

"Perhaps a piece of that nice hot chicken, then?" The girl gestured to the table. "Or some of those sweet carrots?"

"No. I must decline." The woman chuckled politely. There was a hint of fear growing in her voice that Alice detected immediately. Catherine must have noticed it as well.

"You should join us," the older sister implored. "Please. You must be famished. Overseeing the preparation and all must be a most tiresome duty, I assume."

"No." The other laughed nervously. "Thank you, but no. I always eat with the other servants in the quarters to the rear of the manor."

"Let's bring them in here," said Schoenbach jovially. "Let them sit at the big table and eat the fine food with the expensive knives and forks for once."

The woman turned to see all the faces about the table peering at her. She suddenly felt like prey being surrounded by a pack of wolves. When she heard the bowstring creak from across the room, she understood her predicament. They trapped her.

She was their prey.

The wolves had her now.

"Did you see him?" Alice asked, levelling an arrow directly at the servant woman's head.

The woman's chin quivered as tears spilled over her cheeks. She nodded timidly.

"What did you do to the food?"

"Puh, puh, poison," she whispered. "I laced everything with it. He asked me to, and so I did."

"The other servants?" Alice queried. "Were they privy to this deed?"

"Yes," the other replied. Her knees were shaking, causing her whole body to tremble. "All of us. Everyone. The whole town."

"Even the cake woman? Amma Gertrude? The stableboy, Warren?"

"Not the children." She looked at Alice with pleading eyes. "None of the children knew."

"Are all the women and men in Erimoor loyal to the Maji?" Alice pressed. "Are there none that would help us? Are there none who will turn from him?"

"There are none here that will help you," she replied. Her voice was bitter and full of fear at the same time. "We all serve him just as we served his mother. And we always will.

"I hope he causes each of you terrible pain," she continued, her voice growing angrier and louder with each word. "I hope he tears your flesh from your bones while you still breathe. I hope I live just long enough for him to burn you alive. I hope he—"

The arrow whistled through the air and pierced through the servant woman's right eye, breaking through the back of her skull to stick out the other side.

The woman collapsed to the ground in a lifeless heap.

"Alice?" Amicia gasped, offended by the girl's action. All who sat at the dining table were now on their feet.

"You heard her," Brondt said to his wife, pointing to the body on the floor. "They're all loyal to him. They want us dead."

The girl placed the bow back on the floor by the quiver.

"We're losing our bond," Alice said, looking to the other three of her coven, seemingly changing the topic suddenly. "Have any of you looked into a mirror of late? The change is occurring more rapidly. Your hair is almost back to how it was before. I can see the colour returning in your eyes.

"I feel it in me, too," she continued. "I couldn't sense him when he was right in front of me. And, now he knows that, along with the numbers of those travelling with us."

"We were caught off guard," Akasati put in, attempting to defend their actions.

"Yes, you were," Alice replied sternly. "Did you not even wonder why there was no seat for me?"

The others looked around the table, alarmed and stunned. They hadn't even noticed.

"He has a plan," she reminded them, looking at Catherine, Ursula, and Amicia deliberately. "Tonight, it was to be your demise. With you gone, I would be alone." She looked to the ground and emitted a deep sigh. "I can't defeat him without you. I can't win if I am to fight his army and brides on my own. I need you all.

"The closer we get to him, the stronger his influence will become. We need to be better prepared."

"Eat nothing here," she instructed them. "Take nothing from the stores. Burn it all. We can't be sure what else they have tampered with." She moved towards the passageway that led out of the building.

"Grab your belongings and move back to the camp," Alice said, looking at Brondt and Thornton. "Tell our people not to eat anything that they have not hunted or prepared themselves. Then, inform the good people of Erimoor that they have until first light to leave this township once and for all. I will spare them if they heed my words. After that, we bathe their homes in dragon fire and they will never get the opportunity to leave again."

Two

Arthur peered into the heavens.

He saw stars reaching over the sky as far as he could see.

The snow had ceased and he could see not a single cloud.

Still, a chilly breeze swept down from the north, leaving him without a doubt that the snow would return soon enough.

He wondered how Alice fared.

Did she cope with the chill air as badly as he when she slept alone, without her beloved husband to snuggle up to? He smiled at the thought, hoping she did. He knew he was having trouble sleeping without her by his side.

He found the whole concept quite odd.

Until Alice and he had made the choice to be husband and wife, he had always slept well, on his own, in his own bed. The moment they had joined, something beyond explanation had transpired.

They had become one.

He needed her, and he knew she needed him.

As the stars twinkled brightly, he wondered if she was peering up at them as well. He hoped she was.

He hoped that she and he could at least share this moment, so far away from one another.

"I love you, Alice," he whispered to the sky.

"Hurry boy," David called through the open door, ruining the moment. "It's freezing."

"Sorry, Papa," Arthur replied, bending down to load the pail with firewood piled against the wall by the door.

"I'm making tea," Becka called past the big man. "Would you like some?"

"Yes, thank you," the boy replied as he quickly filled the bucket.

David and Becka had moved away from the door by the time he had completed the task. He lifted the pail and started back.

His gaze returned to the heavens.

"I miss you," he whispered to her.

He moved inside and closed the door.

***

The *Gypsy* rocked side to side, gently, almost soothingly.

Stalekk Rank'sku sat at his tiny desk tucked against a wall in his small quarters as he read through the manifest. His massive frame hunched over, knees almost touching his elbows as he lifted the parchment closer to the lamp resting on the back corner of the table's top.

The first officer didn't even consider asking his captain for a larger desk. He was so used to the small furniture used on most ships that he always had felt uncomfortable when he took a large bed and room from a tavern or inn when they were at port. He couldn't remember the last time he had done that, stayed on shore, preferring to sleep onboard even if all the other men didn't.

Besides, he wouldn't have the space for a larger desk. His room, deep in the belly of the *Gypsy*, pressed to the aft of the gun deck, comprised of the table he worked at, a trunk for his belongings and a cot. The walls surrounding all of this were just big enough to fit it all in.

The captain's quarters were two decks directly above his. Storage for sails, ropes and such lay between them. He knew that area was designed for him, or at least one performing the duties of first officer. A larger room with a wide window, instead of the tiny porthole he had.

But he had chosen to be down here, of his own free will.

He wouldn't know what to do with such a large space all to himself.

His whole life, for the most part, he had spent at sea. His early days as a sailor saw him share cramped, sweaty areas with many men, packed in together on cots lying directly on the floor, swinging hammocks layered and levelled above in twos or threes until they almost touched the ceiling.

It was during those days that he learnt to sleep in the hammock closest to the deck. Never sleep on the floor where the rats would climb into your bedding to keep warm with you, and never in the top bunk where you could knock your head against the rafters just by trying to get comfortable.

Somewhere in the middle was the best.

The worst that could happen is you could bump into the one above you or the one above you could fall onto you during your rest.

There was also the fact that bodily functions could get the best of someone after they consumed a rum barrel or two. He smiled at the thought.

But those occasions were rare.

Still, years of living in such a way had made him accustomed to small confinement. So, when Captain Staiger had promoted him to the position of first officer, and when she showed him his quarters, he accepted the job but turned down the room. Instead, he opted for the tiny space that he occupied, which was intended for storage.

He read through the manifest carefully. Most of the non-perishable items had been purchased and stowed on board. There were still quite a number of things that he needed to get.

A knock at his door brought a small sense of stress.

He was certain that most of the crew had spread themselves amongst the few taverns still standing in Newholt, leaving only himself and a few men who stood watch on deck. He immediately assumed the worst, thinking a watcher had come to report bad news.

"Come," he said, turning to face the door.

"Are you decent?" Staiger's voice called softly from the other side.

"Yes, Captain," he replied, standing to open the door.

She gave a smile as she scanned the room quickly.

"How are you?" she asked.

"Fine, Captain." He gestured to his cot. "Would you care to sit?"

"No," she answered, peering at the parchment on his table. "I won't stay long. I'm staying on shore tonight. In the palace, if you need me. I just thought you should know."

"Thank you." He smiled.

"The manifest?" She jutted her chin to the list.

"Yes." He turned to it briefly. "I think we have done well. Water barrels are loaded. Powder kegs are stowed. We have new ropes and some rigging equipment we acquired for replacement if we need to make repairs. Pulleys and tackles mostly. I got them from a few different merchants in town, but several shackles look worn. They probably salvaged them from old vessels. We should consider purchasing new equipment. Replace the lot."

"We'll need to wait until we reach Dendadia to do that," she replied. "I need the *Gypsy* to go at a moment's notice. Besides, none of the equipment for ships here is in great condition. With the trade routes closed and most of the stores destroyed, there isn't much that we can do regarding repairs or upgrades. We'll have to make do with what we have for now."

"Aye, Captain." He looked at her questioningly.

She could obviously see something troubled him. "What is it?"

"I am just wondering when we plan to go," he said. "We haven't heard from anyone. They could be dead for all we know. Why are we waiting? All I need to get is the salted meat, a few more supplies for the galley, and we'll be set. I can have that by tomorrow."

"We are waiting because I promised them I would," she reminded him. "Landon won't step down from his position until they have relieved him of duty, and it will take either the queen or Commander Brondt to do that. Or news of their demise."

"I'm sorry, Captain," he said, lowering his eyes. "I didn't mean to question your orders."

"I understand, Stalekk." She placed a comforting hand on his shoulder. "You want to sail. Sitting at a dock, waiting by the shore, is not what the *Gypsy* was made for, or you either. I promise, we'll sail again. But, we may be here for a while before we do."

***

Sarah sat in front of the looking glass, a woman peering back at her with sad eyes. A woman she almost didn't recognise.

The same features she bore were all there. The same golden hair. The same brown eyes. The same lilac gown.

But it wasn't the woman she wanted to be.

She didn't want to be sitting in that seat, before that mirror, in a palace far away from her home.

She wanted to be Sarah Fitzwillyam.

She wanted to be in her little house, in Woodmyst, with her husband Stephen.

She wanted to be held in his arms and told that everything was fine, and that she was loved, and that she wasn't alone.

But she was alone.

There was no love here.

As she stared at her reflection, she understood that all of those things were gone now. She could never get them back.

Woodmyst was far away.

They would never let her return.

What she had done for the Maji had made sure of that.

What she had done to her beloved Stephen had hindered any chance that she could have had at redemption.

And, just how was she to get redemption anyway, if she could not forgive herself?

And why would she forgive herself?

Stephen was dead.

She wiped the tears from her cheeks.

Part of her wanted to simply drop upon the bed behind her and sob until she could sob no more. But, another part of her wanted to be held tightly, and spoken to, and loved.

She had hoped by her coming here, Takmel might have visited her. Instead, he had barely acknowledged her. Barely even looked in her direction.

She hated him for that.

If he wouldn't love her, she thought, then she should find someone who would.

She needed to be loved.

She wanted to be touched.

She didn't want to be alone.

A sudden and strange sensation filled her as she entertained her thoughts.

An odd tingling moved through her legs and into her loins.

She wanted to be loved.

She needed to be loved.

Looking to the door, closed and latched, she considered how she could fulfil her desire.

She pushed her thoughts of sorrow away and gave in to those of carnality.

Just for one night.

Just this once.

She rose to her feet, crossed the room, unlatched the door, and opened it.

Braden was there, guarding her room dutifully.

"My queen," he said, brushing his long, dark hair from his face.

She looked at him for a long time. Part of her was telling her to shut the door and go to bed. She considered obliging the little voice, backing away as she pulled on the door, closing it slowly.

"Come in," she heard herself say.

The voice inside her head questioned her.

What are you doing?

"My queen?" he asked, perplexed by her instruction.

"Come in, Braden," she told him casually. "I need you."

"Of course, my queen," he replied, bowing slightly before stepping through the door.

She shut it and latched it behind her, pressing herself against it as she devoured him with her eyes.

He was peering about the room, looking for anything that needed his attention.

"What service do you require from me, my queen?" he asked.

She started unlacing her gown.

"Take off your clothes, Braden," she commanded.

Three

The pale morning light had just illuminated the clear sky, casting faint pinks and yellow streaks from the eastern horizon. The sun was still resting below the mountains in the east, yet it was alive enough to cast its radiance over the land and sea by Erimoor.

Alice sat on Liana's back, resting atop of the hill overlooking the manor. It was already ablaze, flames and smoke billowing through its windows and doors. To her left and right, the other dragon riders waited for her order to strike the rest of the township.

She intended to give the people enough time to evacuate.

"First light has come, Kayl'sro," Nola'ee said from behind her. She and Nakrah had stayed behind, seated upon their steeds behind their leader.

The girl nodded as she fondled the iron claws hanging from her neck.

"You should leave," she told them, using their tongue. "Catch up to the others."

"As you wish," Nakrah grunted. He pulled his horse away.

"Wait," a faint voice cried from below.

Alice peered down the side of the hill to see a tiny figure climbing towards them in haste.

A few dragons emitted deep growls as the youngling drew nearer.

Fear-filled eyes stared up at them as the figure froze in place.

"Warren?" Alice called to him. "Why have you come? You should be far away from here."

"I want to go with you," he answered, starting his climb again.

"You can't come with me," she informed him. "We're going into dangerous territory."

"Everywhere is dangerous territory," he said, clambering over slippery stones and soggy snow.

Alice pursed her lips and looked about, frustrated. The army was already marching northward. The fleet had already pulled up anchors and was sailing out of the harbour.

As if to signal, three cannon blasts rumbled through the air. Each projectile fired hit the base of the beacon tower on the point.

Warren turned around in time to see the great structure tumble into the sea. A brilliant explosion of white spray erupted from the shoreline as the tower smashed into countless pieces before disappearing beneath the waves.

"The ships are the safest place for you," Alice told him. "And they are beyond the point of being summoned back. You should go with your people."

"They're not my people," he said. "I hate them all. My parents are gone. I have no one here. The stable master made me sleep in the stable house. He doesn't care about me. Look at my clothes." He held his arms out to display the torn and tattered rags on his back. "As long as I kept the troughs full with grain and water, and the stalls clear of shit, I might get a meal here and there.

"I'm not allowed to talk to anyone unless they speak first. I'm not good enough for them. The only friends I have are the horses that were taken away. And, maybe you. I think.

You are the only person I know who cares for them as much as I do. Please, take me with you. I'd rather stay here and wait for your dragon fire than go with any of them."

Alice's heart sank. "Is the town empty?" she asked him.

"Don't know," he said, shaking his head. "Don't care. I saw some heading south during the night. More earlier on when your men were clearing the stables."

She let out a long sigh and turned to Nola'ee.

"Can you take him?" she asked.

"Yes, Kayl'sro." The other smiled.

Alice looked at the boy. "You ride with her," she told him.

Warren appeared apprehensive when Alice gestured to the reptilian woman. He saw enormous claws on the ends of long, leathery fingers. A thick tail draped over the side of the horse she sat upon, poking out from beneath a long cloak. He saw sharp rows of teeth in a wide mouth, big enough to fit his entire head into. Or, at least, he thought so at that moment, in his heightened state of anxiety.

"Is she safe?" His voice trembled slightly.

"No," the girl replied. "And, that's why she is my personal guard. She will protect you better than any soldier I know of."

The boy looked at Alice questioningly.

"You need to trust me, Warren," she said, looking back to the town below. The streets looked to be empty. The houses and stores were silent and still. Only the manor provided any sign of movement, and that was because it filled with fire and smoke. "Do you trust me?"

"Yes," he immediately answered.

"Then ride with Nola'ee," Alice instructed the boy.

Warren climbed past Alice, shrinking slightly to the side as Liana moved her snout to inspect the newcomer. The dragon offered a friendly chirp as he moved by briskly.

Nola'ee held out her hand, which the boy took apprehensively. She hoisted him onto the back of her steed.

He placed both of his hands on her waist nervously. Her tail lifted over his right thigh and wrapped around the small of his back before sagging limply off the left side of the horse. She grabbed his arms in her leathery fingers and pulled them all the way around her waist, forcing the boy to press his body against her back.

"You hold tight like this," she commanded. "You no be scared. I no bite you. Unless you want me bite you." She gave a playful smile to Alice. The girl tried to maintain a stern composure, but found the corners of her mouth rising slightly. Gruloch snorted back a laugh, covering it by pretending to blow an obstructive morsel from his nose.

"No biting," Warren replied timidly. "Please, no biting."

"Catch up to the others," Alice instructed the Agrodien warriors in their tongue. "Place him into one of the wagons and keep an eye on him."

"You don't trust him?" Nakrah questioned.

"I don't know who he is loyal to yet," she explained.

"And if he is one who follows the Maji?" asked Nakrah.

"We need to be certain," Alice said. "If he is, and there is no question about it, kill him."

"Yes, Kayl'sro," he replied.

"Yes, Kayl'sro," Nola'ee repeated. Both reptilians kicked their heels into their steeds' sides and raced away to the north.

Alice returned her gaze to the ships leaving the harbour. The last frigate flying the Dendadian flag had moved beyond the point. The fleet was turning north to follow the coast all the way to Wintermarsh.

"After losing Erugoth," Gruloch began, "I have often wondered why we did not see Ganda and the Nrarukh again. I fear we may have lost them too."

Alice recalled the leader of the ice lands clan. She remembered the stories associated with his people and the dark creatures they called Khadzh. Part of her surmised that, if Takmel had anything to do with it, then the Nrarukh had probably met an ill fate. That there had been no word from them during all of this time told her they had indeed been prevented from joining the fight. Alice couldn't be certain, but something inside of her believed there was nothing but death on the lands of ice and snow.

"It doesn't matter," the Haigok said. "Not right now. But when this is over, I will go to the Nrarukh Clan with Tarnas and Haildur and find out why they didn't return."

Alice looked to both the leaders of the open plains clan and the northern tablelands positioned proudly on their dragons further down the line.

"Would you like me to accompany you?" she asked the other.

"No," he replied with a grateful smile. "I think this is a task for Haigok only. You should return to your husband as quickly as you can. I'm sure he is lost without you."

Alice felt a lump form in her throat.

"And I without him." She looked to the snow-covered rooftops of the quaint buildings of Erimoor. It truly was a beautiful town. "Shame," she said upon reflection.

"Shall we begin?" Gruloch asked.

Alice nodded.

A Kazrekh rider blew his horn, signalling the riderless dragons in the air first. Alice urged Liana off her perch and into the sky. The others soon followed.

Within moments, thirty-two dragons swooped over the township of Erimoor and let loose a barrage of fire.

***

A great, thick cloud of dark smoke rose into the sky far behind them. Emily had tears welling in her eyes as she watched it rise slowly into the air. Before long, she returned her gaze to the road ahead. Her countenance was empty and distant as she tried to bury her emotions.

"What troubles you?" Akasati asked quietly, noticing her friend and knowing her all too well.

Emily's chin quivered as she tried to find the words.

"My daughter is a monster," she replied, attempting to keep her voice soft.

Akasati peered around. The others were riding far enough away so that they couldn't hear.

"You used to think that of this one," she said, gesturing to Catherine a few yards away in deep conversation with Ursula. "Remember?"

"I know," Emily answered. "And to some degree, I was right then. What she did with Takmel... for Takmel, is unforgivable."

"But you forgave her."

"She's my daughter." Emily looked at her friend sorrowfully. "What else was I to do?"

Akasati nodded silently before peering back to the cloud of smoke rising in the distance.

"She's doing what she thinks is right," the Erilian woman said.

"She killed a woman with your bow," Emily reminded her. "An unarmed woman."

"A woman who tried to have us poisoned," Akasati said. "A woman who was in league with Takmel. Your daughter, the monster, is destroying anything that could harm unsuspecting passers-by. Think of it. What if some poor nomads come into that town and raid the supplies, only to be poisoned by whatever it was they put in our food?"

"That's pretty long odds," Emily said with a smile. "Unsuspecting nomads?"

"You know what I'm trying to say," the other told her. "Besides, so what if your daughter is a monster? She's our monster."

Emily met Akasati with a perplexed look.

"I can't believe that you accept what she is becoming," Emily said. "I want both of my little girls back. I want to be home with them in my arms. I don't want any of this."

"Neither do I," the Erilian replied. "I trained her from a very young age. I never expected it to lead to this. But it did.

"She is the monster we need to defeat the monster that Takmel has become. Perhaps when this is all over," Akasati continued, "we can all return home and you can hold both of your girls in your arms again. Perhaps the monsters will simply go away."

Emily wiped tears from her cheeks.

"I hope so," she whispered.

***

The Lilac Queen opened her eyes. Her head rested upon her personal guard's bare chest. She looked up to his face and saw that he still slumbered.

He breathed slowly, deeply, strongly, his chest rising, lifting her head with it before it fell slowly. She ran her fingers through the thick hair covering the skin there, eventually tracing a bare line that ran across the right side of his breast. A scar from an old wound.

Following it with her finger, she tracked it to his collarbone, below his jaw. There were no marks on his neck, but the line continued from his jawline where it met with three others that ran parallel to it all the way over his face to his forehead.

There, she used all of her fingers and lightly ran them over the marks and through his long hair.

He stirred, opening his eyes and peering at her.

"Morning, my queen," he mumbled.

"Good morning," she smiled, planting a kiss on his cheek. "Did I wake you?"

"No, my queen." He smiled, looking to the light emitting through the window. "I should have been up a long time ago."

He rose, but she urged him back down, pressing her hand against his chest softly.

"Stay," she told him.

"I should be at the door, guarding you," he contended.

"You should be where I tell you to be," she corrected him. "And, right now, I'm telling you to stay."

"Yes, my queen," he replied, relaxing.

"You pleased me last night," she told him, running a finger over his skin, twirling it over his nipple. "I hope you feel the same?"

"You were most pleasing, my queen," he answered.

"Then," she said, moving her hand beneath the covers, running the tips of her fingers across his abdomen, "perhaps you would like to please me, and let me please you more often?"

"Indeed, I would, my queen," he said, tensing slightly as she moved her fingers lower and lower.

She slid her thigh over his waist, climbing onto him. She brought her hands up to his face and pressed her lips to his.

He held her there as he moved into her.

She moaned, arching her back slightly.

Her lips touched the scars on his jaw as she slowly moved upon him. "How did you get these?" she queried.

"A bear," he told her. "When I was very young. My first proper fight."

"How did you win?" she asked, moving faster.

"I didn't," he answered. "I neither won nor lost. I was only nine. The bear was still young, too. Not a cub, but not old either. We both walked away, each with scars to show for it. But it was a good fight. It lasted a whole day."

"A whole day?" she questioned, thrusting faster and harder, breathing deeper and louder. "You lasted a whole day fighting a bear?"

"Yes, my queen," he said.

"Let's see how long you can last with me," she said in between breaths, "doing this."

The bed creaked as he turned her onto her back.

She called out involuntarily as he pushed into her.

The sound resonated through the door and into the corridor, where it echoed over the stone walls along the passage to the bed chambers.

A figure stood there, listening, his damson cloak draped about his frame, his hood over his head.

His fist tightened so that his knuckles cracked, but he didn't approach.

He didn't play to his fury.

In his mind's eye, he saw himself ripping the two of them limb from limb.

He imagined their blood spraying over the walls of the room, soaking into the bedding and pooling on the floor.

But, no.

There would come another time to exact vengeance.

Instead, he simply leered at the door and listened.

Four

The journey lasted most of the day. The troop paused, only to give the horses and infantrymen enough time to rest their legs before moving on again.

It had been several hours since they had seen the dragons pass overhead, gliding towards the north. Since then, they had marched through woodland and waded through snow piled as high as the soldiers' knees.

The carts had become bogged occasionally. One had a wheel that came loose as they descended a gradual slope covered with many loose rocks hidden beneath the frosty surface. Each time that something like this occurred, they slowed down somewhat, which made the travelling more arduous and hard going.

Eventually, they came to a stream that snaked from the mountains, across a wide plain and into a thick forest of pines to the west. The Western Sea was in that direction, but they could not see it. The land had expanded farther away towards the ocean the more they journeyed into the north. There wasn't even the slightest hint of salt in the air any longer.

It took a long time for them all to cross the stream. Its water was icy, and the horses were just as hesitant to step through as the rest of them. The wagons needed the extra assistance of foot soldiers on either side, pushing and pulling with all of their might to get the vehicles over large boulders and through deep divots concealed beneath bubbling rapids.

By the time the army was on the march again, the sun was already dipping towards the western horizon. They continued over hills and through long shallow vales, trudging onward through dense snow and tiring rapidly.

"That's it," Brondt said after some time of listening to men grumbling behind him. "We haven't seen Alice all day. I don't know how far she intended for us to travel. The men are weary and the horses need to rest."

"And you're getting grumpy," Amicia said, smiling playfully.

"Indeed, I am," he returned with a grin. He pointed to a low ridge ahead of them. "We climb that rise and find a suitable place to make camp on the other side."

"Sparrow," Thornton barked.

"Sir?"

"Ride ahead and see what lies beyond that hill."

"Sir," Sparrow acknowledge, giving his steed a swift kick with his heels. Snow exploded around the horse's legs as the soldier charged towards the rise. Some of it splashed over Brondt and Thornton, a little of it hitting Amicia and Ursula softly in the face. Catherine was spared, but giggled at the sight of the others brushing the slush from their cheeks and noses.

"Bastard," the captain growled, glaring after his man.

They continued forward as they watched Sparrow manoeuvre his charger up the embankment. When he neared the top, he dropped from his horse and crouched low. He was almost on his belly, crawling when he neared the summit.

He froze in place.

Thornton watched him curiously.

"Come on, man," the old man grumbled in a low voice. "It doesn't take that long to see what's on the other side."

It amazed all of them when they saw Sparrow stand to full height, still facing away from them, and wave his hand in a friendly gesture.

"What in blazes is he doing?" Brondt questioned, giving Thornton a sideways glance.

"No idea, sir," the other replied.

Sparrow turned and beckoned to the others excitedly.

"They're here," he shouted down to them, pointing over the top of the ridge.

"I hope he means our friends and not the enemy," Karlena remarked.

***

They had created a long trench in the snow. By the time the soldiers had set up tents, they put timber and kindling in place and lit it. Resting over the fire, set upon simple spits, were many deer, sheep and a few heifers, which the Haigok carved into portions before tending to their dragons.

They placed great canvases over the giant creatures to offer some protection against the weather during the night ahead as others piled more fresh animal carcases in readiness for the hungry creatures.

"Where did you find such bounty?" Schoenbach asked Alice. Brondt was standing by his side, looking about at the encampment.

She was rubbing Liana's snout after covering the creature's body with a thick fabric sheet made of many different coloured blankets, crudely sewn together and barely large enough the drape over the dragon's body completely.

"And where did you get that thing?" Brondt enquired, pointing to Liana's new gown.

"Gruloch and I saw a village in the mountains," she explained. "There was a tremendous amount of livestock up there, but no people. It's as if they just left without a trace.

"There were barns and open stores with these sheets." She pointed to the covering on Liana's back. "They were being used to shelter bundles of straw, some of which we brought here." She then gestured to a tall pile of neatly packed stubble placed by the horses. She could see Warren, the stableboy, tending to the steeds under the watchful gaze of Nola'ee.

"I would have come back to tell you earlier in the day," Alice said. "But we have been busy. We sent scouts to the north. There is a large town not too far from here, but the riders informed us it appears to have emptied recently as well.

"I rode out to the fleet about an hour ago," she continued, "and found them on approach to Wintermarsh. They still have a long way ahead of them, and they can barely see the city. But, they could be there within a day.

"I ordered Zakhar to take refuge until we signal them to continue. It will take our people here more than a day or two to get there. I thought it would be best if we strike at the same moment."

"Did you look at Wintermarsh?" the Commander of the Newholt forces questioned.

"Two of the scouts did, from very high above," she reported. "There are catapults and cannons lining the waterfront. No ships that I could see, so I believe our fleet will be safe for the time being.

"The palace has high walls," she informed him. "Not as tall as those surrounding Woodmyst, according to the scouts. They're fortified, with men occupying four towers, one on each corner. But there was no way for them to count all the men on the ground."

"Let's assume that the Maji has many soldiers at his disposal," Brondt said. "Probably far more than we have."

"The village in the mountains and the town just to the north of us," Schoenbach put in. "Why would they have been emptied of people? Why would they leave all of this behind for the taking? Could they have poisoned the straw and the meat?"

"The meat was alive when we found it," Alice answered. "It was also eating the straw. I don't know why the village had been deserted. There was no sign of struggle. No blood. I can't speak for the town to our north. I haven't seen it for myself."

"I think I have a theory," Brondt interjected. "I believe that they may have all been called to service."

"Farmers?" the old seafarer enquired. "Women and children?"

"Think back to Captain Thornton's account of what he saw in the beacon tower," the commander replied. "There were children amongst the dead."

The colour in Schoenbach's face drained away.

"He wouldn't," the old man groaned. "Surely. Would he?"

"He has his mother in him," Alice answered. "I still have dreams about the night my father died. I saw the bodies of fallen men rise under her command."

Schoenbach shook his head in disgust.

"Two scenarios present themselves," Brondt said to them both. "Either, everyone in Wintermarsh is alive and they are all willing to fight to the death for the Maji. In which case, he brings them back to fight on until none of us remain. Or, everyone in Wintermarsh is already dead. In which case, he brings them back to slaughter us all."

"You can't kill what is already dead," Schoenbach remarked. "Just how can we defeat such a foe?"

Alice stroked Liana's snout. The beast offered a soft, friendly chirp before emitting a deep purr.

"I have an idea or two about that," the girl replied.

***

Takmel drummed his fingers on the armrest of his throne.

His eyes moved between the three women seated by the wall to his right, particularly the Lilac Queen, and the guards by the inglenook, particularly the one with long hair and four scars that marked his face.

All he had to do was give Commander Versel, standing by the door at the other end of the room from him, a simple look and she would have the bastard's head. A quick flash of the blade, and it would all be done.

Or, he could take power from his two young brides, seated on both sides of him, and hurl him into the flames. Watching the dog burn alive, flailing and screaming, appealed to him far more than a simple lopping of his head.

But no.

Time would present itself for vengeance.

He drummed his fingers on the armrest over and over.

"Ironfields," he said, calling on Versel to report.

"Ready, my lord," she replied. "We followed your instruction and the men you sent me carried the task out."

"Where are the men now?"

"In stations around the city," Versel answered. "We have also established four command centres, one in each of the quadrants. They will report to the base command centre, which will station here on the palace grounds, my lord."

"Your captains will command these command centres?"

"I was considering placing two of my men into each, keeping one here with me," she acknowledged. "If you wish for others to command in their place, I can find other assignments for them, my lord."

He looked to the scarred man again. The long-haired guard was standing by the fire, oblivious to Takmel's glare.

Sarah noticed. And she was becoming terrified for her personal guard.

"Place who you wish where you wish, Commander," the Maji replied. "I trust your judgement in such matters."

"Yes, my lord," Versel said, bowing slightly.

Takmel placed his attention on the woman dressed in dark armour.

She was indeed as beautiful as he had heard many men say she was. Her blonde hair draped over her shoulders. Even with her battle-worn attire, he could see a woman's body beneath it all.

He had heard the talk of how many men had tried to bed her, only to end up bested by the woman by a reply of a gauntlet to the face or painful knee to the groin. The stories that he had heard whispered amongst the guards were that she chose her partners impulsively, sometimes stealing women out of the clutches of her own men, so as to claim them for the night, leaving the poor sod to entertain himself.

Takmel found this information somewhat exciting, arousing. He had considered taking Versel for himself, knowing that she would let him without a fight if he commanded it.

If he commanded it.

After all, she was a soldier, and she only responded to him because he commanded her.

Let her lie with women.

Let her lie with men.

As long as she didn't question his commands, and followed them to the fullness he expected, he didn't care what she did or who she did it with.

He was tempted, though.

Why not?

I am the Maji.

But she served no purpose except to be a soldier.

She had no power for him to extract.

There was no need for him to claim her in such a way.

"The docks?" he asked.

"Cannons are ready," she reported. "We have surplus stores of black powder kegs stashed along the waterfront with plenty of ammunition. We'll have them if they try to run their fleet at us, my lord."

"Tell me about these ballistics weapons," he insisted, turning his gaze to Sarah. The Lilac Queen was looking at him, flashing her eyes to the floor when he met hers.

"The catapults are standard projectile weapons, my lord," the commander said. "We have placed them more to the southern edge of the city and compiled enough material to—"

"Not the catapults," he interjected, holding up his hand to her. "The other ones. The..."

"Scorpions, my lord?"

"Yes." He sounded intrigued as he leant forward in his seat. A smile stretched across his face. "Tell me about these scorpions."

***

She had picked the leg bone clean, finishing what little meat had clung to it after everyone else had their fill. With a hefty toss, she threw the bone into the fire. It kicked up a few sparks as it settled upon the red-hot embers beneath a burning log.

Leaning back against her saddle, which she used as a backrest, she placed her hand on her stomach and rubbed it with her hand in small circles. She could feel the swelling. Not from the meal she had ingested, but because of the life growing inside. It was still too little for anyone to notice with their eyes, but she could feel it all the same. The thought made her smile a little as she watched the flames dance about.

Her mind turned to home. She pictured Arthur sitting in a chair by the fire in the Woodmyst house, reading a book of some sort. She could see shadowy forms of David and Becka there, too. Others sat around the table. Uncle Lor and Aunt Linet. Her cousin, Alan. Sevrina and Andris. Ruttger and Courtney.

She couldn't be certain, but she believed she was seeing home as it was at that very moment. Arthur appeared to her as clear as day. As real as the fire flickering brightly before her. He appeared sad and distant as he turned the page of his book. She could tell that he wasn't really reading it, not fully taking it in. Instead, his mind was elsewhere. His gaze moved to the fire before him now and then instead of following the print in the book.

Is he thinking of me?

She tried to call to him through her vision, but he didn't seem to hear. He simply stared blankly into the hearth before him, just as she did, so many miles from home.

"What are you thinking of?" Emily asked, sitting beside her.

"Home," Alice replied, watching the image drift away like a cloud upon the wind.

Emily looked at her daughter's hand, still making circles on her stomach.

"Are you bloated?" she asked. "Feeling like you could burst?"

"No." The girl smiled. "I'm full. Contently so. It's the baby."

"Is something wrong?" Emily asked, a little concerned.

"Not at all," Alice answered. "I just feel more connected with him when I do this."

"Him?"

Alice met her mother's eyes and nodded.

"Him," she said.

"How can you know this?"

"I don't know how," the girl replied. "I just do."

Emily felt shame. She had called her daughter a monster earlier that day. Now, she was thinking of how wrong she may have been. Her daughter was carrying her grandson.

Part of her, from deep in the back of her mind, reminded her of the White Mistress and the boy she had carried as well. That part of her remembered the lad she had let into her home and raised as one of her own. She recalled how he had grown to fool them all, secretly stretching his influence across the land to build his empire.

Could this unborn boy be something like the Maji?

Could he be something worse?

Emily pushed her feelings away. She didn't want her daughter to sense any misgivings towards the child. Instead, she smiled, appearing happy for the girl.

"Who else knows?"

"Catherine presumed he was a boy," Alice told her. "Amicia too. Ursula thought he would be a girl. I wasn't sure until today."

"When you were flying around with Liana?"

"When I was burning the main street of Erimoor," the girl informed her. Emily looked at her, an expression of horror flashing upon her face. Alice noticed and cried. "He didn't like it, Mama. I thought I was going to be sick, but it was him. I put my hand on my belly like this, and then I knew."

"There were people in Erimoor?" Emily said softly, sympathising with her daughter. "People inside their houses?"

Alice nodded.

"Most had gone before we started," she sobbed. "But there were still some hiding away. Mama, I could hear them screaming."

She fell towards the auburn woman, her face landing on Emily's chest. As she started crying uncontrollably, her mother wrapped her arms around the girl.

My daughter is no monster, she thought, her hold tightening around Alice's shoulders as she started rocking the girl in her arms. *A monster would not have this much remorse.*

Five

"This must be Ironfields," Brondt said from atop of his horse.

The sun was high in the sky. They had journeyed since first light and reached the top of a long ridge that overlooked the township just before noon. Dark clouds had gathered on the horizon to the north, slowly making their way towards the assembled army.

"It looks quiet," Amicia observed, moving her gaze along the empty centre street.

There was no sign of life. No man or woman. No horse. Not even the sound of dogs barking.

Liana gave a soft chirp as Alice shifted her weight in the saddle.

"We should use it to our advantage," the girl told them. "We could shelter here, but I fear it is a trap."

Thornton tilted his head this way and that, peering to the buildings on the outskirts of town.

"There's only one way to find out," he said, urging his steed down the hill.

"Where are you going?" Brondt called after him. By then, Brook, Jendryng, Sparrow and Vawdrey were trailing their captain.

"Going to search through those houses and stables," the other replied. "Could be something worth our while. Could be filled with food and supplies."

"Could all be poisoned," Gruloch offered from the back of his dragon by Alice's side.

"Could be." Thornton smiled. "We won't know anything until we look."

"Commander," Alice said, turning to face Brondt. It was more than just a call to him. He could hear the instruction in her voice.

Turning to some cavalrymen grouped behind him, he gave his own orders.

"You lot, take a look at those building out to the edge of town there." He pointed to a small collection of timber structures to the east. He then looked at another group of horsemen. "And you go and search those a little farther to the north."

Yuri started down the hill after Thornton and his men. The other Agrodien warriors followed closely. All except Nola'ee, who remained by her Kayl'sro's side, seated upon her steed.

"Be careful," the young reptilian female called after one of them in particular. Nakrah returned a smile to her.

"We should send the rest of the men into the town itself," Alice told Brondt. "The sooner we make sure it is clear, the more at ease I will feel."

"Agreed," he replied. "Where will you be?"

"I'll remain here with the Haigok," she answered. "The ladies and Captain Schoenbach too." She looked to the three others of her coven, as well as her mother and the Erilian warriors. "And you."

He was content with all the others being listed. Not so when he heard himself amongst them.

"I should be with my men," he contended.

"You should be where I say you should be," she told him. "And right now, you should be by your wife's side.

"If my men fall into peril down there while I remain safe up here..." he began.

"Then you will remain safe," she interjected, watching the men riding down towards Ironfields. "Amicia will be happy that you are alive and you will get the opportunity to throw whatever form of insult you can muster at me. It will be my fault if anything happens. Not yours." She looked at the commander sternly. "Now, order your men into the town."

His face was flustered. He looked to Amicia beside him, the Queen of Newholt. She offered no comfort. Her expression remained neutral.

"Alice is my prime," she reminded him. "I answer to her. Her command would be as if I have given it myself. Order the men into the town."

He felt small, like a disciplined child being put in his place. The worst part about the entire exchange was that the girl was right. Amicia would be of no use to Alice if he were to perish. She would definitely withdraw into herself to grieve for him. This, he knew in his heart of hearts, because it would be what he would do if she were taken from him.

Reluctantly, he turned and signalled for the soldiers to move over the rise.

"Search the village," he shouted.

The soldiers and remaining cavalry marched forward.

"And what do we do in the meantime?" Gruloch enquired.

"Tell the others to keep watch on the town's borders," she replied. "If there is a sign of movement, raise the alarm. There may be enemy soldiers hiding in wait where we cannot see them."

***

The Assembly Hall's doors were wide open. A small gathering of seven people had collected around a long table on the platform.

Arthur sat at the head, his father to his left and Becka to his right. His gaze fixed upon the surface of the table, his eyes were distant and he appeared not to be listening to the words spoken by the young bookkeeper, Gilbert Obelyn.

"All walls have been inspected and appear to have suffered no major damage," he said from the farthest seat along the table on the boy's left, reading from parchments bunched in his hands. "Some doors and bars in the prison will need to be replaced." He looked at Andris, who sat to his right. "I can get the specifics to the blacksmiths when you are ready."

"I'll have someone pass on the measurements as soon as I'm able," the other assured the bookkeeper.

"Very well." Obelyn nodded. He rifled through his papers. "Ah. Oh. Some good news. They left the grain stores untouched and with the loss of the prisoners, we have more than enough food stores and blankets to last out the winter. Perhaps we can spare more for the lizard people living in the caves?"

Arthur looked up from the table and glared sourly at the bookkeeper. David growled as deep anger stirred from inside. Even Becka pursed her lips and shook her head upon hearing the young bookkeeper's words.

"Agrodien," Arthur retorted.

"Beg pardon," Obelyn replied, seemingly oblivious to the minor offence he had committed.

Through his rising irritability, Arthur could not tell if the bookkeeper was apologising for the slur, or if he hadn't heard the boy's words completely.

"Agrodien," he repeated a little louder. "They are Agrodien. They are our friends. As close to us as family for my wife and me. Never refer to them as *lizard people* again. Not in my presence. Definitely not in earshot of my wife."

"I'm sorry," Obelyn said quietly, the colour leaving his face as he sat down, clearly demonstrating that he had no intention of insulting anyone.

"Forgive us, Arthur," uttered Stephen Latham, the elderly magistrate from Oldcastle. "We have not yet had time to get to know these people as you have."

The boy looked at him. Latham's face was empty. Sad.

"I should ask for your forgiveness," Arthur said after a short time. "I miss my wife and the others of my family she has taken with her. My temper has been short of late and I've been distracted."

"She'll return, Arthur," Becka told him, reaching her hand out to his.

"I hope so," the boy replied, looking at his father.

"She has to," David agreed. "They all do."

Ruttger, seated between Becka and the old magistrate on the boy's right, waited for them to have their moment. When he felt the time was right, he spoke up.

"Master Bookkeeper Obelyn has a point," the old soldier said. "We have provisions. Enough to comfortably share with those at the glade. Should we do so?"

Arthur looked around the table.

"We should move them all into the city," he said. "Or, at least offer that choice to them."

"The Agrodien here?" Andris enquired.

"You have something against them?" David asked, a hint of crossness in his voice.

"No," the other answered. "Not at all. I just wonder if they would want to live amongst us. Perhaps, they would prefer to stay out there."

"That's why we offer them a choice," Becka told him.

"The city offers better protection," Arthur put in. "If those creatures return, they would be safer behind our walls rather than out there in the open."

"From what Glaun and Lilen say, those creatures didn't stand a chance against the Agrodien younglings," Ruttger offered.

"I would feel better knowing that they were here," the boy added. He placed his attention on the young bookkeeper. "There are houses available, are there not? Emptied since the Seven left Woodmyst?"

"Many families of the soldiers who went with them have moved out of their homes, yes," Obelyn answered. "A large proportion of the men did not return, leaving their wives and children behind."

"Where have they gone?" Becka asked.

"Some of the older wives have joined with others and share accommodations," he replied. "Some of the younger have returned to their parents. Some have moved out of the city altogether, possibly making their way to Newholt for a new beginning, or are in search of lost husbands."

"Or, to the Maji if they are loyal to him," Andris added. "And many soldiers were. So, I assume their wives would be as well."

"That doesn't matter. Empty dwellings are my concern," Arthur said. He placed his attention back on the bookkeeper. "Would there be enough for the people at the glade?"

"I would need to know their numbers," the other told him.

"Thirty-two Agrodien women," Ruttger answered. "Around sixty children. I couldn't tell you which infant belongs to what adult. They appear to share the responsibility of raising their young. There are also four human families. No children yet."

Arthur looked at the old soldier, impressed with his summation. Ruttger noticed the boy's stare.

"I used to command the forces of the Lilac Mistress." The old soldier grinned. "Observing and remembering details is an excellent trait to have if you are going to spy out enemy territories."

Arthur looked to Obelyn for a response.

"We can accommodate them," the bookkeeper said. "Quite easily. There are currently over fifty dwellings that are unoccupied, for certain. I suspect there are more."

"Good," Arthur said, seeming to relax his composure. He looked to Andris. "Send an envoy to offer an invitation to the people at the glade."

"Of course," Andris returned, standing.

"I'll go," Ruttger interjected.

All eyes moved to him questioningly.

"We have people who are ready to ride out there on a moment's notice," Andris informed him. "They can be there and back before the day's end."

"I think they will respond better to a familiar face," Ruttger replied. He looked at Arthur. "Courtney and I will take a ride out today. If you don't mind, we will stay in yours' and Alice's cabin overnight."

"Of course," Arthur agreed. "Could I ask you a favour?"

Ruttger nodded.

"I still have things in the cabin that need to be brought here," the boy told him.

"Say no more." The old soldier smiled. "Courtney and I will bring everything back. I'll just need to borrow a wagon before I leave."

"I'll help you with that," David said, pushing his chair back and rising from the table. He then looked along the table. "I assume the meeting is over."

All eyes moved to Arthur.

"I've nothing more to add," he told them. He waited for someone to say anything. No one else spoke. "Meeting adjourned then."

***

Commander Willard Zakhar lay flat against the bowsprit of the galleon. The fleet had anchored in a cove several miles south of Wintermarsh and was, for the best part, well hidden from line-of-sight to the city. Only the galleon had manoeuvred into a spot where Zakhar could try to keep watch.

He hoped the lookouts in Wintermarsh did not have scopes like the one he used, and that they remained unseen. He rested his elbow against the very end of the protruding section of the ship to steady his long spyglass. It was something that was more akin to a large telescope that wise men and scholars might use to observe the stars. Something he kept locked away in the officers' quarters for just such an occasion.

"I see one of them," he called to First Officer Grady, who was watching on from the edge of the foredeck.

"Near the big warehouse to the left?" the other asked.

"No," Zakhar replied. "I didn't see that one. I was referring to the one just near the windmill on the shoreline, a little farther to the north. It's positioned under a canvas cover they've propped up on poles."

Grady unfolded his own spyglass and lifted it to his eye. It was much shorter than the contraption his commander was using.

A wry grin appeared on Zakhar's face when he heard the shorter scope clicking as he extended it.

"You won't see with that," the commander told him, rolling onto his back and holding the larger piece out for Grady. "Here."

The first officer folded his scope away and put it back into his coat pocket. He carefully took the large spyglass from Zakhar and, using the banister that hemmed the ship's deck to rest his arms upon, looked through the contraption to the northern end of the city.

The haze caused by long distance made everything unbearably hard to see. With intense focus and time to adjust, he found the windmill and saw the temporary shelter to the side, set above a mechanical device that brought dread to his heart.

It looked like a large archer's bow, resting on its side with two wagon wheels joined on either side.

"That's two ballistae," Zakhar said, lifting himself to his feet. "I guarantee there will be more. Can you see the catapults and cannon hatches along the waterfront?"

Grady moved the scope.

"Yes," he replied. "Seems like they are expecting us."

"I think they were expecting their fleet to hold out at Blackshore and Erimoor," the commander surmised. "These defences were to be the last resort, I guess. But, there are some fortifications being constructed by the docks. They either know we are here already or that we are coming."

"No ships," the first officer observed as he scanned the docks.

"Not one," the other acknowledged, stepping from the bowsprit and onto the foredeck. He rested his hands against the guardrails and peered out towards Wintermarsh. It appeared as nothing more than a strange blur, far away on the edge of the water. He saw some shapes resembling structures. In particular, the large white palace perched high on a hill overlooking the city. "They positioned those cannons and catapults for us," Zakhar said to the first officer. "I presume there would be infantry in position, ready for a ground assault to the south. Perhaps catapults and cannons there too. Those other ballistae are for what might come from the sky."

"Should we send a team ashore to sabotage them?" Grady questioned, lifting himself to full height and lowering the scope from his face.

Zakhar shook his head slowly.

"We can only see two," he replied. "Who knows how many are scattered about, or where exactly? We can't risk sending anyone in there just so they can get captured or tortured. We are to sit here and wait for Alice's signal."

A long, frustrated sigh escaped the first officer.

"We can't even get word to our people that they will be walking into a trap," he grumbled, scratching at his beard.

"Or flying into one," the commander added.

Six

The cavalry positioned themselves along the streets of Ironfields, spreading out to keep watch as the infantry moved through yards and entered huts and structures throughout the township.

Unlocked doors and open shutters informed the soldiers that there wasn't time enough for the inhabitants to ensure that their property was secure before abandoning their homes.

The searchers employed swift kicks or hefty shoulder barges to doors in order to gain access into the buildings. The sweet, sickly smell of death met them in every case.

"Blood in here," a soldier shouted to three others gathered near the door. He was standing in a small room with three beds lining the walls. Each of the cots contained a large, dark, crimson stain in its middle. The floor brandished long streaks of blood leading from each bed and out the door, where they vanished beneath the freshly fallen snow. "No bodies," the soldier informed them.

The rider, seated on his steed just outside the hut, overheard the infantryman reporting what he could see to the three nearby. He turned to see another rider a few yards away, watching another group of men coming out of another small house.

"Oy Kristoph," he called.

"Yeah, Victor?" the other shouted back. "What is it?"

"What'd they say they saw in there?" the rider asked, referring to the men moving from the house and making their way to another.

"Blood," Kristoph answered. "Drag marks to the door and that's it."

"No bodies?"

"Nope."

"This is the second one for us," Victor informed him. "Both the same."

"Third one for my lot," replied Kristoph. "Do you think they're all like that?"

"Don't know," he answered.

"We're moving on to the next one, horseman," an infantryman said. "You coming?"

"Yeah," Victor answered. He then looked over to Kristoph. "Oy. Where do you think they took all the bodies?"

"I don't know. But that's not what I've been wondering," the other called back. "Who, or what, killed them all and why?"

Kristoph felt a chill move up his spine.

"Horseman?" The infantryman beckoned with his hand. The other three men were already at the next house's door.

"Yeah," he said, urging his steed on.

***

Over the next hour, reports frequently made their way to Brondt and Alice. They were all the same. There were no people and livestock, only empty buildings and evidence of violence by blood and carnage.

"Should we risk going in?" Emily asked her daughter.

"I don't like it, Kayl'sro," Nola'ee said.

"Me either," Alice replied.

Brondt looked to Amicia, about to suggest something, then he remembered who he truly answered to and turned to speak to the girl.

"We need somewhere to rest," he told her. "Either we set up camp before the sun gets too low, or we utilise the structures of the town to our advantage."

"The houses are filled with blood," Ursula reminded him. "No man would want to stay where someone was obviously slaughtered."

"The houses are, yes," Brondt replied. "But the stables and storehouses aren't. They've simply been emptied. We could shelter inside those for the night. There are more than enough to offer shelter for the men and horses."

"Not the dragons, though," Alice put in.

"No," the commander admitted. "Not the dragons."

The girl looked to Gruloch.

"What do you think?"

"I'm uncertain about the safety that the town might provide," he returned. "Considering there isn't anything large enough for our dragons to take refuge in, I would suggest the Haigok establish a camp on the open ground to the west." He pointed to a flat area not too far from the settlement, and a stone's throw away from a thick pine forest.

Alice nodded as she pondered his words.

"If you think it is safe, Commander," she began, putting her attention to Brondt, "have your men stay in Ironfields. I will camp with the Haigok, along with the Agrodien and any others who wish to join me. Present company included."

"You don't believe it to be safe?" he asked.

"I don't know," she answered. "I feel some unease about this. And, for the moment, the only certainty that I have is that Takmel has his hand in whatever occurred here. I'll stay close to Liana tonight."

"I don't want to stay in the town," Amicia whispered to her husband. "I'd rather be near Alice. I don't feel right about this place."

"We could continue on," Brondt said to her quietly. He then turned to the girl seated high upon the dragon. "We could continue on instead. There is still enough daylight to find a suitable place farther north to camp for the night."

"No," she replied. "We would be safer returning to Erimoor and making camp in its ashes. At least we would be out of reach of any forces Takmel may have waiting for us."

"Do you think he has soldiers nearby?" Akasati enquired.

"Who can say?"

"Can't you detect them?" Schoenbach gestured to the members of the Four. "Join together and find them."

"We can't," Catherine replied. "We are reverting."

"What do you mean, *reverting?*" the old seafarer questioned.

"We're returning to what we once were," Ursula clarified. She lowered her hood to her shoulders. "You can see for yourself. My hair is turning dark again."

"It's more than that," Amicia added. "We are still connected, but we no longer sense one another's feelings like we did before, when we first came together."

"It was temporary," Alice put in. "We will always be connected, but the core strength that brought us together is fading. The closer we draw to the Maji and his stronghold, the quicker we seem to change back to our old selves."

"So..." Brondt looked at her curiously. "He is stronger than you?"

"Different would be a more apt way of putting it," the girl answered. "He is strong. But he can be even stronger by absorbing the power of those he has a connection to. Sadly, for him, they have been dying off one by one and his power has been tested as a result.

"He fears us," she continued. "We four have a stronger bond than he does with his queens; one that we have each chosen to keep. He has forced his bond onto the others he calls his wives, but without their prime, they have drifted apart.

"He is desperate," she added. "That makes him dangerous. With so much blood spilt in this town, and his visitation to me the other night, I fear he may have arranged an assault that we may be unprepared for."

Alice looked over Ironfields below their vantage point. She could see soldiers moving about the streets, continuing to search the structures.

"We'll camp here for the night," she said to the commander. "There is no point in pushing on to Wintermarsh, or what lies ahead, without giving the men and horses some decent amount of rest. And I'm not one to consider turning back when we've come this far.

"Set a watch if the men intend to stay in the town," she added. "I want soldiers patrolling the streets throughout the night in shifts. Keep the fires low and tell the men to avoid moving about as much as possible, or making loud noises."

"Of course." Brondt smiled, a reaction to hearing her commands.

"What is it?" she asked, noticing his expression.

"We should find you a rank that supersedes mine," he suggested. "You're good at this. You have a military mind."

"The best trained me," the girl replied, looking over at Akasati.

Seven

Night came quickly.

Takmel walked into the throne room, holding the twins by their hands. The one on his left wore black, while the other on his right dressed in scarlet. He started across the floor to the inglenook, passing a few guards that had gathered by the heat. The fire inside was burning brightly, keeping the marble room warm and comfortable.

Commander Saruun Versel moved into the room behind the Maji and his two little brides. She looked over at the soldiers and, with a quick gesture with her head, instructed them all to leave the room.

The soldiers quickly retreated into the corridor before Versel closed the door behind them, latching it shut. She then turned to face her master, standing with her hands behind her back, ready for his command.

"This will do," Takmel said with a gentle voice, lowering himself to the floor. He crossed his legs. "Sit down here," he instructed the twins.

Each complied, keeping his hands in theirs as they sat down.

"Join hands," he told them. "Complete the circle."

They did so obediently, peering to him in question.

"You're wondering why we are here," he said. They continued to hold their gaze, waiting for him to enlighten them. "Tonight, we are going to play a game. It's a lot like the one we played with the little straw dolls. Only, there are no dolls. Tonight, we are going to play with other toys. I need you to concentrate. I need you to share as much of your power as you can with me. Do you think you can do that for me, my sweet queens?"

Both girls nodded.

"Of course, you can." He smiled. "All I need you to do is focus. Think of your gift as being a river flowing into a lake. Picture me as the lake. Now close your eyes and see it in your heads."

They followed his instruction.

"Concentrate," he whispered, scrutinizing them.

He could see movement beneath their eyelids.

"Concentrate," he repeated, his voice smooth and calming.

A faint flicker of light emitted through the thin membranes of skin over their pupils.

"Are you ready?"

Their eyelids opened, revealing glowing white orbs.

Takmel smiled menacingly. "Then let us begin."

***

A thick cover of clouds had rolled in from the north and spanned the sky above Ironfields. A gentle drift of snow fell just as Alice was finishing wrapping Liana in her canvas sheet.

"Just in time, hey girl?" she said to the dragon, rubbing the beast on the snout. Liana offered a friendly chirp.

The sound of laughter, shouting, and raucous frivolity resonated from the township, from far across the open ground. Alice peered towards a larger structure near the centre of the community; a tavern with an upstairs level.

"So much for keeping things quiet," Gruloch said, stepping to her side.

"I think some soldiers must have found the ale," she replied. "They can probably hear that all the way to Wintermarsh."

Gruloch smiled. "I think if there was anyone watching us, we would have noticed by now," he told her. "We've checked the surroundings. There's no one here. The worst that could happen is that those men will get drunk and wake up with painful heads in the morning."

"Which isn't good," Alice returned. "We make for Wintermarsh at first light. We'll be engaged in battle by nightfall tomorrow."

He looked at her, then to the township. He could read her intentions. The scowl on her face told him everything.

"Do you want me to accompany you?"

"No," she answered. "They wouldn't listen to either of us. They take orders from their superiors. It needs to be Brondt or Thornton."

She clasped a hand onto the Haigok's arm, silently thanking him for the offer, before moving away to the fire where the others had gathered.

Gruloch watched her moving away before turning his attention back to the noise coming from the town. Liana gave a soft chirp, peering after the girl.

"Hello, little one," the Haigok said in a friendly whisper, reaching over to rub her snout.

***

Commander Jonathon Brondt started across the open ground on foot. As he trudged through the snow, he strapped his sword to his waist, almost tripping several times as he tried focusing on his buckle in the dark.

"Bloody thing," he muttered angrily.

"She's right, sir," Thornton said behind him. "Those bastards will be of no use to us tomorrow if we let this continue."

"I know," the commander replied. "It's just that it's only a few men. Look." He gestured to the surrounding buildings. Small fires had been lit inside stables and sheds. Doors were closed, or blankets hung in place, to keep the warmth in. "Most of the men are inside and preparing for rest."

"I don't know how they will get any rest with that lot carrying on like that," the captain put in. The merriment seemed to grow louder with each step they made. Some man inside the tavern kept hitting ear-shattering high notes, shrieking with each outburst of laughter.

"Someone putting his balls in a vice?" Vawdrey asked jokingly.

Jendryng chuckled.

"Shut it," Lieutenant Brook growled. He gestured with his chin to the commander.

Both men looked ahead to see Brondt glaring at them.

"Sorry, sir," Vawdrey said. Jendryng repeated the apology and lowered his head in shame.

"Sorry, sir," Thornton grumbled.

"Not your fault, George," the commander replied softly, so that those following couldn't hear. "Your men weren't doing anything terrible. I'm just frustrated. I mean, I don't know what I'm going to do when I get in there. How would you handle this if it were your men behaving like that?"

"Not sure, sir," he answered, continuing to trudge after Brondt. They reached the end of the street and made their way along the centre of the empty road. "Take their blankets away and make them huddle together by the fire for the night? Smash all the bottles of grog? Break all the barrels before the bastards can drain them dry?"

"I don't know about taking their blankets from them," the commander said as they neared the tavern. "Making them destroy the ale seems like a fitting punishment."

"No," Sparrow protested. "You can't do that, sir. Please. Let us take the ale. We can use it to celebrate when we have taken Wintermarsh."

"Shut it now," Brook barked.

"Come on," the other whined. "Just because one small band of cocks does the wrong thing, the rest of us get punished also? That's not fair."

"I'm setting a decree for all men under my command as of right now," Brondt said, stopping in his tracks and turning to address Sparrow directly. "There will be no more ale. No more rum. No more strong drink until we return home. I want everyone to be at their full capacity at all times."

With that, the commander spun on his heels and continued towards the tavern. Thornton gave the man a reprimanding glare before pursuing the Brondt.

"I told you to shut it," Brook rebuked as he passed the soldier.

"Thank you, Morys," Vawdrey said sarcastically as he moved away.

"Yeah," Jendryng chided, trying not to laugh as he pushed his face within inches of Sparrow's. "Thanks a lot."

"What are you angry about?" the other called after him with a cheeky grin. "You're too young to drink, anyway."

"Fuck off," the younger man replied.

Sparrow couldn't contain himself, emitting a deep chuckle as he started after the crew.

Brondt stormed into the tavern, confronted by a scene of utter chaos.

There were two men, shirtless and wrestling upon the floor, surrounded by several others who were pouring ale over them. Their laughter boomed and echoed so loudly that the commander's ears felt as if they were about to burst.

Some more men sat around at various tables near the edges of the room, watching and laying bets on the sport that was underway. There was one man so drunk, his eyes were closed and he appeared as if asleep with his head resting against the wall. Brondt almost believed the man to be dozing, except he raised his mug to his mouth to sip at the ale without spilling a drop.

"Bugger me," Thornton huffed as he took in the surroundings.

There was a thick, dry bloodstain on the floor that the wrestlers were rolling over. Vomit collated at various points around the room. The smell was unbearable.

Brondt gazed at the captain with the look of someone at a loss.

Thornton moved to a table near the door where three drunk soldiers were viewing the fighting match, cheering and calling out. The captain tipped the table off the floor with one hand and sent it toppling over. Mugs of ale shattered on the floor and frothy drink went splashing about in all directions.

"Oy!" one man shouted angrily, rising from his chair to challenge Thornton.

The captain swung his fist hard and fast, knocking the other off his feet to end up sprawled across the floor, landing in a heap.

Another, upon seeing his drinking companion laid out, rose to his feet and clumsily prepared to fight. Thornton simply grabbed a fistful of the soldier's hair at the back of his head and forced the man's face onto the wall beside the door.

The timber panel split.

The man fell unconscious.

The room fell suddenly silent.

"Shit," one of the drunken soldiers hissed when he saw who stood by the door. "It's the commander."

Brondt glared at them, his rage clearly displayed on his face.

"This joyous occasion is over," he breathed. He moved his angry gaze across the room. "There will be no more drinking for the rest of this mission."

"Aw, come on, sir," one wrestler, a brawny man with long hair, grumbled.

Brondt turned to Lieutenant Brook.

"Take him outside and teach him a lesson," the commander ordered.

Brook looked to Vawdrey and Sparrow, who rushed forward and took the man by the arms. He fought back, struggling against them. Vawdrey hit the man hard, just beneath his sternum, knocking the air out of his lungs. Sparrow grabbed a handful of hair at the top of the soldier's head and pulled hard.

The brawny soldier let out a shrill scream.

"Balls in a vice," Vawdrey smirked. "This is the one we heard from way out there."

They dragged the man outside and into the middle of the street.

As the sound of punches and kicks ensued, Brondt moved to the centre of the room and addressed the remaining men with a calm demeanour.

"I ordered you to keep a low profile tonight," he told them. "Those were my orders. Mine! And you disobeyed me. If it were up to me, I would lock you in here with your grog and burn this establishment to the ground." He looked at a set of stairs and pointed. "Are there any people up there?"

"No, sir," a man replied.

Brondt nodded slowly.

"Pour all barrels, flasks and bottles out right here." The commander pointed to the floor beneath him. "Empty the remaining contents of your mugs here also." The men stared blankly at him, seemingly too afraid to move. The sound of a terrible beating ensued from beyond the doors.

"Do it now," Brondt said a little louder. He gestured to Thornton and the others who had come with him. "Otherwise, these men will do so on your behalf, and the doors will be barred, and torched."

The men reacted instantly, sobering rapidly when they realised the seriousness of the matter.

They emptied mugs first. Barrels and bottles were next. As the soldiers raced to find every vessel containing ale, mead, wine and any other fermented beverage, Thornton drew close to his commander.

"Sir," he whispered. "You're not intending to burn this place down, are you?"

"Why?"

"It's just that Alice commanded no large fires," the captain reminded him.

"You don't think the noise this lot made would be enough to draw attention?"

"A think a fire large enough to burn this place down would be like a beacon and would reach further than the noise this lot made," Thornton replied.

"Point taken." Brondt nodded. "There won't be any fire."

The last of the grog poured out and the barrels and bottles left discarded on the floor by the bar.

"That's all of it, sir," the other wrestler said. "Even all the stuff kept in the larder."

"Good," Brondt said.

"Sir," Sparrow called from outside. "You should come and see this. All of you."

Brondt turned and let out a long sigh.

"What now?" he said, moving out into the street, a small gathering of drunken soldiers following. Sparrow and Vawdrey were standing over the shirtless, brawny wrestler who was groaning from the punishment he had endured and shivering from the cold. "Get that man some clothes," Brondt commanded.

"Sir," one of the drunk men replied as he returned inside the tavern.

"Up there." Sparrow pointed along the street.

Brondt followed the other's signal.

Standing in the middle of the far end of the street was a lone figure. A man.

He wore a dirty tunic over dark armour. Long, matted hair covered his face. A long sword hung precariously from his right hand so that the point touched the ground.

"Who is that?" Vawdrey asked. "He's not one of ours, is he?"

The figure started forward, stepping clumsily as it walked, almost like a drunkard, dragging his sword behind to leave a snaking trail in the snow.

"Could be one of this lot coming back from taking a piss," Jendryng offered. "Looks drunk enough."

"I don't think so," Thornton put in. "That's not our armour he wears."

The figure continued to approach.

"I think we know this fellow," Brook put in.

"What?" Brondt questioned.

"I'm certain of it," the lieutenant said, staring at the man. The figure seemed to stumble over something unseen in the snow before correcting his gate. Still, each step was clumsy, awkward and strange to observe. "Yeah," Brook huffed. "Back at the glade. I think he's the one who took the boy that night."

"Arthur?" Thornton asked.

"Yeah," the lieutenant replied. "You remember?"

"I do," Thornton answered. "He took Arthur and then Arthur lost an arm. We never did get this fucker's name, did we?"

"If we did, I don't remember it," Sparrow said.

"Can't be that important, then," Vawdrey put in.

"I don't think he's in a position to tell us even if we wanted it," Jendryng told them as he scrutinised the figure moving along the street.

"Why's that?" Brondt enquired, watching the figure stumble a little before continuing its advance.

"I think he's dead," the younger soldier offered.

Suddenly, the figure stopped moving when he reached the centre of town.

He seemed to have frozen in place.

Unmoving.

Unflinching.

Silent.

A long moment passed. Eventually, Brondt turned his head towards the gathering of men near the tavern door, all the while not taking his eyes away from the lone figure.

"Where are your weapons?" he asked them.

"We left them with our bedrolls," one man replied.

"You may need them," the commander said. "Get them." He then looked at the unconscious soldier still lying on the tavern floor. "And wake that fellow up, one of you."

The men moved off the boardwalk and into the street. One man, who had retrieved the brawny wrester's shirt, threw the item of clothing to the man who was still sitting in the road.

"Thank you," the wrestler said.

At that moment, scores of people appeared from lanes and alleys, spilling into the street. Their movements were as awkward as the first figure, who was still standing rigidly on the road.

Some wore armour like his. Others dressed in clothing of miners, farmers and merchants.

There were men, women and children amongst them. Some were missing limbs. Some trailed innards. Some bore deep wounds from having necks and stomachs cut open.

Walking.

Crawling.

Scraping.

Creeping along the snow.

Edging their way closer, closer towards the terrified soldiers.

Eight

A shrill cry echoed through the darkness.

Alice stood up, peering towards the township of Ironfields.

The horses twitched their ears, turning away from their straw.

The dragons raised their heads high to see what had made the sudden call in the night.

"What was that?" Warren, the stableboy from Erimoor, asked. His voice was quiet and trembling.

"Stay here," Alice said, reaching for her swords resting in their sheaths by her feet.

Yuri picked up his blade to follow her as she moved around the fire. Emily got to her feet with the full intention of joining her daughter.

"Stay here." Alice pointed to the auburn woman. She then gestured to Nola'ee and Nakrah. "You two as well. Stay and watch over my family."

"And us?" Akasati asked.

"You *are* my family," Alice replied before starting across the open ground with eight Agrodien warriors in tow.

They moved in haste, running almost as fast as any horse could run. Alice could smell fresh blood as they drew near to the edge of town.

Shadows raced from buildings before her, soldiers with chest plates on and swords at the ready. They were running into the centre of town, but she noticed it wasn't towards the battle. It was a retreat from an enemy she could not yet see.

The smell of decay laced her nostrils as she drew closer.

It reminded her of a recent encounter.

The beacon tower of Erimoor.

She pulled to a halt and crouched by a fence at the edge of town, looking over it towards the streets beyond. The Agrodien crouched near to her, Yuri by her side.

"I smell death," he said in his tongue. "A lot of death."

In the shadows, she saw a group of seven young children and three women, perhaps older girls from their build, a little older than herself, moving stiffly, awkwardly along an alley not too far away. One woman was missing an arm. A very young child was toddling about without its head.

The sight made her stomach tie into knots.

"Death is everywhere," she replied in kind. "It walks like the living."

He looked at her confusedly. She gestured with her eyes for him to look for himself.

Carefully, he lifted his head just high enough to see.

"Q'sharh!" he spat when he saw them.

The children and women emerged onto a street where two soldiers had gathered. The men swung their swords and cut into the bodies of the dead. Some limbs were discarded, but it didn't slow the attack.

The young children surrounded the soldiers and closed in quickly, tackling the men to the ground.

Bloodcurdling screams pierced the night air as the living corpses dug fingernails and teeth into the soldiers' flesh. Soon, the three women were down on their hands and knees, burying their faces into the bellies and necks of the men.

The dead children tore strips of wet, blood-soaked skin from their victims. They opened the bellies of the soldiers and pulled their intestines out of them as the men continued to scream.

Alice stared, wide-eyed.

"We can't kill them?" Bein said, spying through a gap in the fence palings.

"No," Yuri replied. "They are already dead."

Within moments, the seven children and three women rose to their feet and started away, moving on into the town.

Alice felt bile rise in her throat as she watched the two soldiers sit up, stand and lift their swords. Both men followed the group that had just attacked them, trailing their guts in the snow behind them.

"Are they alive?" Kavnu questioned. He bore an expression of loss and fear. "What happened?"

"They are in the ranks of the dead," Yuri explained. "We should leave," he suggested. "We should go back and get the dragons. They can burn every one of them to ash."

"I agree," Alice replied. "Except that there are men still alive here. We need to get them out first."

**

Thornton found himself engaged in battle with two armed soldiers dressed in dark armour covered with white tunics that were stained with grit and blood. Their own blood.

The wounds in their torsos, one with a great gash across his chest, informed the captain that these men had suffered an ill fate, possibly during battle.

As he parried blows, blocking their blades with his own, he couldn't help wondering who had bested them and how they came to be in such a predicament as this. Dead men walking.

"Has Ironfields been cursed?" Brook called from a few yards away. He, too, was fighting for his life. One soldier in white was slashing his long sword down over and over, chopping through the air as it stepped towards the lieutenant.

Brook sidestepped and dodged each strike, looking for an ample moment to hit back. Even with the enemy making such awkward movements, the soldier's blows were fast and on target.

"What?" Thornton called back as he lopped the head from one of his foes. The dismembered cranium bounced away before rolling onto the side of the road. The captain felt his stomach turn as the head rolled its eyes to peer directly at him. It opened its mouth and lolled its tongue over its lips slowly.

There wasn't time to stare at the strange oddity, however.

The second soldier raised his sword and attacked. The headless body did the same.

"Do you think Ironfields had been cursed?" Brook asked again as he stabbed his attacker through the face, pushing his sword through the back of the soldier's skull with a loud crunch. "Like the tower in Erimoor?"

Thornton shot him a curious glance before returning his attention to the two dead soldiers.

"What do you think?" he said sarcastically. "I would have thought it obvious."

Brook's foe wrapped his fingers around the sword still sticking through his face. He slid his hands along the blade, towards the lieutenant, slicing the little finger from his left hand before reaching out to Brook.

Dirt-stained fingers stretched and curled inches from the lieutenant's skin.

Raising his leg and planting his boot against the dead man's chest, Brook pushed the soldier away, retrieving his sword from the corpse.

The soldier stumbled backwards a few paces.

Brook leapt towards him, chopping from the side with his blade, slicing all the way through the dead soldier's upper thigh. Like a flash, the lieutenant mirrored the action, swinging his sword back around to take the other leg also.

The dead soldier fell to the ground, hard.

Both legs writhed about, kicking and rolling this way and that over the ground.

The soldier flipped to his belly and, still gripping his sword in one hand, dragged himself back towards the lieutenant.

"Bugger this," Brook muttered, looking about quickly.

There were more men fighting farther along the street in both directions. He witnessed one of Brondt's men get pulled to the ground by five little girls garbed in long, tattered nightgowns. Their faces, hands and feet ripped open to reveal white bone beneath decaying flesh. They tore at the Newholt soldier's clothes with their fingers before digging into his flesh with their teeth.

There were others meeting similar fates. The sounds of men screaming rang out from all over the township. As soon as one died away, another would start.

Brook's gaze landed on a lit lantern hanging from a nail stuck to a post outside the tavern. He moved towards it, stepping past the fallen soldier crawling towards him. The dead man reached for him as Brook brushed by.

"What are you doing?" Thornton called as he sliced through the headless warrior's arm. "I could use some help here."

Brook took the lantern from the post, walked back to the dead man on the ground and dropped it onto the soldier.

The glass chamber broke, spilling burning oil over the corpse.

The soldier twisted and turned as the flames spread over his flesh.

There was no screaming.

No sign of pain.

The soldier continued to reach out for Brook, who had stepped out of reach.

"Can't do that to all of them," Thornton remarked.

"Look at it," Brook said, staring in disbelief. "It still moves. I was certain..."

"Help me," the captain hollered.

The lieutenant snapped back to reality and quickly stepped to Thornton's side. Now the odds were even.

As each man battled against the dead soldiers, Brook turned to see the burning man, fully aflame, still crawling towards them with sword still firmly clasped in hand.

Farther along the road, the five little dead girls were making their way towards their position. Fresh blood covering their nightgowns.

Behind them, the Newholt soldier sat up, staring directly at the lieutenant and his captain. One of his eyes popped from his socket, dangling by a thread of wet tissue, rolling against his cheek.

Thornton, too engrossed to have noticed what was coming their way, slit the headless soldier through the waist, into the abdomen and out the other side. The wound was deep, spilling intestines over the warrior's hips. The top half of the dead man's body tilted back, opening the fresh cut like a wide mouth. The headless soldier reached out to Thornton with grasping hands as his torso slanted farther and farther backwards. Eventually, there was a loud sound of the figure's spine snapping. The headless soldier's upper body swung precariously over the back of his own legs, held in place by twisted sinew and rotting skin.

"Fuck," Thornton gasped, his stare fixed upon the soldier's broken white spine that stuck from glistening muscle and tissue at the figure's waist.

"Language," Brook snapped as he blocked yet another strike from his opponent.

Amazingly, the headless corpse remained on its feet, stumbling to the left before over-correcting and almost falling to the right. It continued to cling to its sword tightly as it jerkily moved towards Thornton again. It swung the blade towards Thornton's ankles. The captain responded by shoving his boot into the dead man's crotch, forcing the soldier to topple onto the ground.

"Come on," they heard a familiar voice calling from the end of the road. "This way."

It was Alice.

She wasn't directing her voice directly to the captain and his lieutenant. Instead, she was shouting for all the men fighting against the dead to follow.

The living soldiers were quick to retreat from the dead. They knew their numbers could never match those of the walking corpses. Even as they cut pieces away from their enemy, the dead would continue to fight on as if unscathed. For every one of Newholt's or Woodmyst's fallen, another added to the ranks of the adversary.

"Back to camp," she shouted to the many infantrymen racing through the street as they dodged the cold, grasping hands and gnashing teeth of the inhabitants of Ironfields. Thornton and Brook ran towards her, leaving their three challengers behind.

The fiery corpse on the ground used one arm to drag himself after them. The headless soldier lifted himself back to his feet, his torso swinging and flopping about recklessly against the back of its legs. The third walked stiffly, dragging its sword behind it as it pursued the two men.

"Where is Commander Brondt?" Alice asked as Thornton drew near to her.

"I saw him over that way," Sparrow answered, running up to them from behind a small house to their side and pointing back towards the way from which he came.

Jendryng and Vawdrey were on his heels.

"There's too many," the younger man reported. "I saw more of them crawling from underneath houses back there."

"We can outrun them pretty easily," Vawdrey put in.

"We stay and fight," Yuri growled.

"No," Alice told him. "William is right. Running is our best option. Help them all get back safely." She walked away.

"Where are you going?" Bein called after her in his tongue.

"To find Commander Brondt," she answered in kind.

"I'll help you," he said, starting after her.

"No," Alice ordered him. "You help Yuri get the men to safety. I'll be right behind you."

He hesitated, watching her sprint away.

"Come," the older reptilian told him as the last of the living men raced by, charging for the open ground between the township and the campsite. "Kayl'sro Alice has given you an order."

Reluctantly, Bein obeyed, following Yuri out of the township and back onto the open ground.

Alice rounded the corner to see a myriad of dead figures crawling from beneath structures, slowly moving through alleys and laneways in the general direction of the camp.

She moved her gaze to the middle of a small fenced-in yard behind the tavern. There, two men faced each other in the shadows.

Swords clashed.

Blows were exchanged.

Only one figure made any sound as the other struck him.

Soft grunts.

Heavy breathing.

Vapour emanating from his mouth.

Brondt.

He returned with an attack, jabbing his sword into the other's belly.

The opponent didn't react except to stare blankly through his long, matted hair with lifeless eyes.

"How does that feel?" the commander asked. His voice sounded weary.

The dead man pushed Brondt hard with the palm of his hand, forcing the commander to stumble and fall onto his back, leaving his sword sticking from the corpse's torso.

Alice then noticed a gash on the old soldier's leg. It was bleeding profusely, spilling from his thigh and over his knee and onto the snow.

The corpse had struck the commander deep before she had arrived.

He was bleeding out, but not willing to give up without a decent fight.

"Bloody pansy," Brondt grunted. "That's the best you can do? Push an old man down?"

The dead soldier pulled the commander's sword from his belly and dropped it on the ground. He then raised his own blade and shoved it through Commander Brondt's chest plate, pushing it through his body, piercing into the ground beyond.

Brondt spluttered drool and blood from his mouth, over his chin. His head lolled to one side as he stared blankly towards the sky.

The vapour rising from his mouth drifted away to nothing.

Alice heard someone cry out loudly. It sounded distant, as if in a dream.

When the dead man turned his head to peer in her direction, she realised the sound was coming from her.

The dead soldier, Brondt's killer, pulled his blade from the commander's body and started towards the girl.

Alice tightened her grip on her swords. She looked to the left and right, noticing that the other corpses nearby had placed their attention onto her as well. They changed direction. Instead of heading west, towards the camp, they were now making their way towards her.

Brondt's killer was closer than the others.

He was dragging his long sword behind him, slowly approaching the girl, making awkward steps.

His sword lifted to the sky as he drew near.

She blocked the strike with one blade, slicing through his throat with the other.

The cut wasn't deep enough to take his head. Instead, it simply flopped backwards to touch against his shoulder blade.

The dead man recoiled and lifted his sword to strike at her again.

She blocked it and quickly finished the cut to his neck, causing his head with all of its matted hair to drop into the snow at his feet.

Alice quickly looked to the left and right again.

The massing dead were gaining ground quicker than she had hoped.

At that moment, Commander Brondt sat up.

A part of her hoped he was all right.

Her common-sense knew better.

The commander crawled across the snow, leaving copious amounts of blood in a thick trail behind him. He retrieved his sword from the ground and stood to his feet, glaring at her all the while with dead eyes.

He started towards her as she blocked another blow from his killer. His sword lifted high as he stepped closer and closer.

"Sorry, Commander," she said, quickly swinging one sword so that it cut diagonally through the killer's torso, bone and muscle, while chopping the other blade through Brondt's shoulder.

The killer's body separated from the right side of his neck to his left hip, sliding to the ground and making him drop his sword.

Brondt's left arm came free and flopped upon the snow like a fish out of water.

With a swift kick, Alice sent the commander flying and into the nearest group of approaching corpses. They fell over each other clumsily, struggling to get back to their feet.

Alice seized the opportunity to turn and run.

Within moments, she was fleeing through the edge of Ironfields and towards the open ground.

She soon caught up to Bein and Yuri, who were keeping to the back of the retreating soldiers.

"They move too slow, Kayl'sro," the older reptilian reported, referring to the men in front of him.

"Faster than those things back there," she replied.

"Where is the commander?" Yuri questioned, looking about.

Alice answered with a shake of her head.

Bein peered back to the town, where he saw countless shadows moving from between buildings and onto the open ground.

"We can't defeat them, can we?" he asked, knowing the answer already.

"We can outrun them," Alice told him. "But we cannot stay and fight. One or two maybe. But soon we will be overwhelmed."

Yuri looked at the men ahead of him.

"We can't run forever," he stated. "The men will tire first and will all be slaughtered. We will follow soon after. The only escape is in the clouds, and I don't think the dragons could carry all of us."

"No," Alice agreed, peering over her shoulder to see the increasing numbers of corpses moving upon the snow. "The dragons cannot carry us all."

She let out a long and loud whistle that pierced the air.

Nola'ee stood to her feet. She looked towards the township.

"Kayl'sro?" she hissed.

Gruloch was on his feet in an instant, looking across the open ground between the camp and Ironfields. He had heard it too.

A great and mighty roar erupted from amongst the dragons.

All gathered about the fire, stood and watched as Liana spread her wings, tossing the canvas sheet from her back. She instantly took to the air and sped towards the township.

Gruloch looked over to the Kazrekh riders. One of them was already lifting his trumpet to his lips.

The call went out.

Eight dragons, all from the Spine Mountains, leapt into the sky and raced after Liana.

She slowed her approach, almost to a hover, as she neared the girl.

"There, girl," Alice pointed back towards Ironfields. "Go."

The dragon flapped its great leathery wings and darted towards the township. She saw the figures moving upon the ground, chasing after her keeper.

With a great jet of flame, she attacked. Skin, muscle and bone instantly turned to ash.

The eight Kazrekh dragons flew to her side, breathing their own barrage upon the dead. They continued to do so until the open ground was clear of movement, except for the living who continued to flee towards the camp.

Liana turned her attention to Ironfields itself.

She swung high into the air and tilted her wings to the left to circle about the structures. There was plenty of movement on the streets below. All the figures she could see were moving towards the edge of town, towards the girl.

The dragon dived steeply and swept over the rooftops, spilling fire over everything beneath her.

Behind her, the eight other dragons lined up and followed her approach. Each of them filled the streets with flames.

Buildings burst into flames.

Bodies instantly burned.

Soon, nothing moved in Ironfields except smoke and fire.

The infantrymen assembled near the wagons. The orange glow emitting from the township illuminated their frightened faces.

Alice turned to watch the dragons circle about and send a barrage of fire over Ironfields again and again. She slid her swords back into their sheaths upon her back.

Emily appeared from nowhere, almost tackling the girl to the ground as she flung her arms about her daughter.

"You're all right," she gasped, squeezing Alice tightly.

"I'm fine, Mama," the girl replied.

Ursula was already holding Thornton about the waist and pressing her head against his chest, sobbing.

"Silly girl." He smiled as he wrapped his arms around her.

Amicia looked about, searching frantically in the crowd. Tears were streaming down her cheeks as she came to realise her husband was not amongst those who had returned.

"Jonathon?" she called with little hope.

Alice felt her stomach tighten and a lump form in her throat.

Amicia called his name again before collapsing to her knees, moaning.

Nine

He cried out in frustration, squeezing the two little girls' hands so tightly they winced, screaming silently. They still joined together, hand in hand, in a circle of sorts upon the marble floor by the inglenook.

The twins tried to pull away from him, but his grasp was strong. His hands clutched more and more forcefully, their pain intensified so incredibly that each of them believed their little fingers would burst and break.

When he finally let go, he flung his wrists, making them slide away from him on their rumps a short distance across the smooth, cold floor. He lifted himself to his feet and looked at them indifferently.

The girl, dressed in scarlet, scurried across the floor like a frightened mouse to her sister, who was closer to the hearth. She quickly wrapped her arms around the girl dressed in black.

"You failed me," he growled at them. "Neither of you is strong enough to be my new black and scarlet queens. Now, she will make her way here with all of her men and dragons." He stepped towards them. They both cowered, sniffling and scared that he might hurt them again. "You have just seen what dragons can do, haven't you? They will come and devour you both. I would be doing you a favour if I crushed the life from you right now."

He balled his hands into tight fists.

The girls writhed on the floor in agony as they felt pressure building against their bodies.

Their mouths opened, unable to breathe.

Tears streamed from their eyes.

He let them go, relaxing his fingers.

They both fell against the floor and took in deep gasps of air.

Abruptly, he turned away from them and hurried for the door.

General Saruun Versel, dressed in her armour with her sword strapped to her side, waited for him there, watching the exchange take place. She turned and unlatched the door before opening it for him.

"Watch over them," the Maji ordered as he strode by. "I'll be in my chambers. I need to be alone."

"Yes, my lord," she replied, standing at attention. When he was gone, she looked at the two girls by the fire. They were back in each other's embrace, crying profusely. "You had better try harder for him," she warned them. "He will only hurt you worse if you don't."

***

Not one soldier, Haigok or Agrodien, felt a desire to get any rest. Nor did they wish to stay in the eyesight of Ironfields any longer than necessary.

A place was cleared in a wagon, occupied by camping supplies and a small boy, for Amicia to travel in. Ursula and Catherine rode with her as the troop marched northward again.

Alice and the Haigok scouted ahead from their dragons' backs. Occasionally, they met up with the army in a clearing, one or two dragon riders at a time, to inform them of what lay ahead and to advise of a better route to take.

It was still dark, but they made good progress through the night with the Agrodien warriors guiding them.

By first light, they had travelled along a well-worn road in a thick pine forest. As the troop came upon the next clearing, a large patch of ground overlooking a deep vale filled with more trees, they found all thirty-three dragons gathered together with their keepers.

"This is it," Alice said to Thornton. "The last safe place for us to gather before we come to Wintermarsh."

"How far?" the captain asked as he rode his steed over to the girl seated on the dragon.

"A few miles or so in that direction." She pointed northward, a little to the west. "There's another stretch of open land just beyond that rise. Haildur of the Traruk Clan reported a large ground force waiting for us there."

"You could use the dragons to burn them all, right?" Jendryng asked.

"We'll try," Alice replied. "But I'm sure Takmel has thought this through. He knows we are coming. He knows we have dragons. He would have a plan."

"How many men does the Maji have out there?" Thornton queried.

"Haildur said a few hundred that he could see," she answered.

"We are less than two hundred now," Sparrow put in.

She saw growing unease on the men's faces. Even Yuri appeared a little anxious, with his eyes darting around.

"We are tired," she stated. "We've been travelling all night. Let's use this time to rest. We can stay here until noon. After that, we will need to go."

"You have a plan of attack?" Brook asked.

"Not really," Alice replied.

"Then we can use this time to come up with one," Thornton told them.

**

Ruttger Harrow had hitched his horse to the wagon and was loading blankets and other supplies from the cabin's storeroom, set back inside the cave behind the structure. Courtney, his wife, emptied cupboards and drawers of their contents. Clothing, cooking implements, a bow and quiver and a wood-axe were among it all.

"The sun has barely touched the sky," said Terix, Kygra's wife, "and you're already leaving?" She accompanied the other three wives of the Northern people, Lilen, Kulumie, and Anabatt. All were rugged up with thick clothing that they held tightly about themselves.

Ruttger looked up to the clouds drifting overhead. Snow was falling gently, steadily in the glade.

"I don't think we'll know if the sun has touched the sky or not," he replied.

"We need to get back to let Arthur know of your decision," Courtney put in as she hoisted an arm full of clothing, mostly Arthur's tunics and trousers and what little items Alice kept for herself, onto the cart.

"And you're emptying the house?" Kulumie questioned.

"Arthur asked us to," Ruttger explained. "I told your husbands this last night."

"My husband!" The woman snorted. "I'm lucky to get a good morning from him on the best of days. He doesn't tell me anything. Partly, because he can't remember anything."

"Porf remembers things," Lilen said sympathetically. "He remembered your birthday that one time. How many years ago was that now?"

The other women giggled. Kulumie smacked Lilen on the arm playfully.

"Where are your husbands?" Ruttger enquired, looking back at their cabins at the western edge of the clearing. "Too cold for them to come out and say goodbye?"

"They're off hunting," Lilen replied. "They've taken some of the young Agrodien lads out for one last romp before we leave."

Ruttger pondered her words for a moment. It was good that such bonds were being formed among these people. He supposed they might need the support of one another in the days to come. At least until Woodmyst grew accustomed to them.

"I hope they catch something large and tasty," the old man said.

"I hope so too," Anabatt agreed. "It's been hard to find decent game for the past few days, what with all the rukyul running about out there."

"Rukyul?" Courtney questioned, giving them a worried look.

"We think Alice's rukyul kept the others at bay," Terix told Courtney and her husband. "No doubt it was marking its territory, as most creatures do. That was probably enough to dissuade them. But now, with it gone, and the winter snow falling, game is becoming scarcer and the rukyul are becoming more adventurous. We saw them in the clearing a few nights back, moving the livestock towards the trees."

"The dogs raised the alarm, and the younglings chased the beasts away," Kulumie put in. "Think I'd run with my tail between my legs too if I saw fifty little snarling Agrodien running towards me."

A smile crept upon Ruttger's face as he pictured the little reptilians with their teeth bared and claws ready to strike.

"We'll send some people to herd the livestock to the Woodmyst pastures as soon as we get back," he told them. "I'll request that they leave a couple of heifers and a few goats, just in case the hunt proves unsuccessful."

"Leave us some horses too," Lilen replied. "We'll need something to hitch these wagons to."

"We can leave enough for you all to ride," Courtney offered.

"Thank you," Terix replied.

Ruttger looked to the snow falling. "This doesn't look to be easing up," he said. "You should all get back inside where it is warm. And we still have a lot of loading to do."

"Of course." Lilen smiled, stepping away and tapping the others with her on the shoulder, prompting them to leave the old soldier and his wife be.

"See you tomorrow," Anabatt said with a wave.

Ruttger and Courtney returned the gesture as they watched the four women start back across the snow to their cabins.

***

Arthur had woken early. He had eaten a quick breakfast of toast, chasing it down with a cup of tea. He had listened to his father's loud snoring during his quick meal. There were moments when he thought the house might shake apart from the noise.

He returned to his room and dressed in his trousers and boots. When he re-emerged, snoring thundered from behind David's bedroom door.

He found Becka sitting at the table with a mug of steaming tea in her hands.

"Good morning," he said, crossing the room to the fireplace.

"Good morning, Arthur," she replied, sounding weary.

He picked up the iron poker leaning against the hearth and began stoking the fire.

"Did he keep you awake with that noise?"

"I can't hear him from my room," she replied. "I have a better chance hearing you, with your room being between ours."

He looked at her questioningly. His face was almost like that of a child being discovered performing an act that they were told not to.

"I can't hear you either," she assured him.

He was silently and internally thankful. Not that he had done anything worth chastisement or reprimanding, but Arthur sobbed most nights of late.

"I'm heading out," he said, moving for the door.

"Where to?"

"To the stables," he answered. "To pay an old friend a visit."

She nodded as she considered his reply.

"You should take him out," she told him. "Just for a stroll. I think he would like that."

***

The chestnut stallion plodded along the street at a slow pace, nodding its head with each stride. Its hooves crunched the snow beneath it, occasionally striking the stone pavers with a soft click.

Arthur had covered the horse with a thick, grey caparison before saddling and harnessing the beast. He believed it was the first time the creature had endured such attire.

The stallion didn't protest or display any sign of discomfort. In fact, it nickered gently as the boy moved about the steed, trying his best to put the garment in place with one hand.

As he rode along a wide, almost empty avenue, he noticed no movement in the saddle. The caparison remained in place. The stallion seemed content.

The sound of another horse approaching from behind gave him some amount of displeasure. He had been enjoying the silence, left alone to his own thoughts as he slowly rode through the falling snow.

"Arthur," Andris called softly from behind.

"Andris," the boy returned, trying to sound as pleased as possible.

"You shouldn't be out here on your own," the other told him. "The stable master informed me of where you were. You could be in danger. There may still be people loyal to the Maji here."

"I don't care," the boy answered. "I shouldn't need an escort when I want to do something on my own. My own father thinks he needs to accompany me each time I need to shit. If there are still any faithful to Takmel here, then weed them out."

"We're looking," Andris assured him.

"I know," Arthur replied, sounding supportive.

They rode a little farther in silence.

"I've set men to clearing out the vacant houses as you requested," the soldier reported. "There's not much in the way of blankets and bedding. It appears the previous occupants took most of what was in there."

"See what you can take from the stores," Arthur instructed him. "Just bedding and basic furniture that may be needed. We'll concern ourselves about firewood and food stocks when we hear from Ruttger and Courtney."

Arthur pulled to a stop. He moved his gaze to a large iron fence. Looking through the bars, he could see a wide space, void of life, covered in a thick blanket of snow.

"Do you know what was here once?" Arthur asked the other, knowing the answer.

"The tree of the Seven," Andris replied. "The Great Hall before that."

"The Seven never had ownership of the tree," said the boy. "But it was a place of power for them. Do you know why?"

Andris shook his head. He had never understood the ways of witches and magic. He had only feared it.

"I've thought about this a great deal," Arthur told him. "I read histories regarding sorcery, but none has ever claimed to really know much about it. I've talked to Alice many times, before and after she came into her full power, and even she is uncertain. I suppose these things will always be a mystery. However, I have a theory about this place," he continued. "And there are some people who agree. Magic is attracted to tragedy."

Andris looked confused. "I don't understand."

"Right there," Arthur said as he pointed to the empty yard, "hundreds of people burned alive. Men and women. All in one instant. A dragon killed them all. I'm sure you have heard this story."

"Yes," the soldier agreed. "Everyone across the land has heard this story."

"I believe that when so many suffer such a tragedy, something opens in the realm of magic," Arthur explained. "At that moment, when all the women and all the men were taken from this world, something inexplicable came to Woodmyst and has never left. Something that has not yet been named. Something like the gods. Or what we perceive to be the gods.

"The tree grew large and strong, so far away from the edge of the woodland," he went on. "How did it get here? The seed, I mean. A bird? A squirrel? How did such an animal, with barely any level of intellect, know to drop an acorn right in the place where hundreds had perished? Why would it even care to do so?"

"It was by chance," Andris opined. "Nothing more."

"I disagree," said Arthur. "Something unseen dwells here. Something in the earth. The Seven drew power from it. I wonder if it drew power from them also. Perhaps growing, becoming stronger as they gave it their attention.

"Takmel gathered his mother's ashes and placed them here, beside those of Alice's father. Do you know who she was? What she was?"

"Yes," Andris answered. "I was once in the service of the Sovereign, remember. But, I think you've put too much time into this theory of yours."

Arthur turned his attention away from the iron fence to look at the soldier. "What do you mean?"

"By your standards," Andris replied, "every battlefield would have such a thing dwelling upon it... within it... whatever. Every town that had been raided, where all inhabitants were slaughtered. Every city that had been overthrown where its people were destroyed.

"So what if something dwells in there?" he continued. "Let it lie. Let it die. Let it live. Who cares? Does any of this help Woodmyst? Does it help Alice?"

"It may be something that encourages evil," Arthur tried to explain.

"And so..." Andris put his elbows on his thigh and leant in his saddle. "How do we defeat it?"

Arthur stared at him blankly. "I... I don't know."

"Neither do I," the soldier replied. "And I don't care. It may be evil. It may be good. It may not give a pile of steaming shit about any of that, or it may be nothing at all. Just in the heads of witches and those who think they can try to understand sorcery.

"Ride your horse, Arthur," Andris continued. "When you're done, unsaddle him and give him a brush down. Feed him some oats and go home where it is warm and think about your wife.

"But, please, don't give mind to this place again. There isn't anything here that will help you or make you feel better. This is a place of sorrow. Ride your horse, then go home."

With that, Andris pulled his steed about and trotted away.

***

"I think he suspects," Sarah said, tightening the cords of her blouse.

"Who?" Braden lay in bed, watching her dress. "The Maji?"

"I think he knows about us," she replied, sitting on the edge of the mattress. Her legs were still bare. He instinctively ran his hand over her smooth skin, slowly from her knee and along her thigh. She writhed a little as he touched her.

"I don't care," Braden told her. "And neither do you. If you did, we wouldn't be here like this right now."

He was right.

She didn't care about Takmel and what he thought. She didn't care if he knew she preferred her personal guard's touch over that of her husband. She didn't care if he learned she was falling in love.

Falling in love only for the second time.

The first time was with her first love, Stephen.

The memories of her first husband, her real husband, came flooding back. Stephen was a good man to her. The best man for her. If not for Takmel, Stephen would still be the only man for her.

And, even though she plunged the knife deep into the chest of the only man she really loved, it was Takmel who had taken him from her.

Takmel would take Braden from her, too. She knew it deep in her heart.

While she didn't care that Takmel knew about what she was doing with Braden, she cared what the Maji would do to him out of spite.

"He was watching you in the throne room," Sarah said, turning onto her stomach to snuggle next to the scarred man.

"So?"

"I think he might hurt you," she replied, a small tear welling in her eye. "I don't want him to."

Braden smiled.

"I'll cut him down with my sword if he tries." He chuckled softly.

Her face was sad, frightened. "No, you won't," said Sarah.

He saw the deep concern on her face.

"All right," he whispered, pulling her closer to him. "If I can't defeat him, then I'd best satisfy my queen at every opportunity given to me. Who knows how long we have together?"

As he spoke, he untied the cords of her top, pulling the knots free with one hand.

"We may not have long at all," she replied, peeling the blouse off her skin.

He pressed his lips to hers, flinging the covers away from himself and pressing his body to her.

"Then, may I suggest we remain in your bed until our time together is ended, my queen?" he whispered into her ear as he pushed into her.

She moaned as a wide smile stretched upon her face.

"Stop talking, Braden," she ordered, taking his face into her hands and pulling his lips to hers.

Ten

"There they are, Colonel." A soldier of the white army pointed across the vale and towards the tree line on a ridge.

"I see them, boy," the old soldier grumbled, seated upon his steed and brushing gathered snow from his white tunic. "You'd think they could have chosen a better time of the year to pay us a visit."

"Yes sir," the other said, watching the horsemen and infantry from the lands of the east move into the clearing. After a while, the advancing army halted and formed ranks. "I think that's it, sir."

The old colonel stirred, as if from slumber.

"What?" he muttered, moving his gaze to the far side of the valley. The small size of the opposing force surprised him. "That's all of them?"

"It would appear so, sir."

The colonel leant forward in his saddle and peered first to the left, then the right, making a mental note of how many men he had at the ready.

"We'll have this over and done before tea," the old man chortled.

"Beg pardon, sir. We are yet to see the dragons," the young soldier interjected.

"Dragons," the old colonel grumbled. "Stories. Nothing more. They sent us on a shit job, boy. Do you know what I mean by that?"

The young soldier shook his head.

"No, sir."

"We are the shit cleaners, just like the stable hands in the stable house," the old man replied. "Only, we use swords and spears instead of shovels."

Why else would Versel be called back to the city?" he continued. "If this was going to be an actual battle, surely the Maji would have his best commander and captains here. There are no bloody dragons. Never were. It's just a shit job."

"Yes, sir," the young soldier replied.

"Ready the archers," the colonel ordered, turning to the rider to his right. "I don't even see the point in getting our horses' legs dirty for this one."

They passed the order down the line, and the archers moved from the security of the ranks, filing between the steeds and foot soldiers and onto the open ground before the assembled forces of Wintermarsh.

"Nocks," the old man called. His voice was too soft for the entire company of archers to hear, so they relayed the command along the line.

The bowmen placed their bolts upon the strings.

"Mark," the old man commanded.

The archers raised their bows and pulled the strings tight, taking aim.

The colonel prepared to give the next command, pressing his tongue to the roof of his mouth.

"L—"

A sound like rolling thunder and painful screams filled his ears. He couldn't see anything ahead to show the source of such a horrific sound, but it intensified and grew louder.

"Oh shit," the young soldier on the ground blurted, turning about and pointing to something behind them. A great orange glow reflected from his face and armour into the colonel's eyes.

The old man turned in his saddle.

A wall of bright flames and thick, black smoke rolled over the ground, devouring his men and stretching as far as he could see to his left and right.

The heat struck him first, his flesh cooking inside his chest plate as if in an oven.

A scream fell from his lips involuntarily as the skin on his face peeled and bubbled.

Thornton watched all thirty-three dragons speed off into the sky. Their attack was tremendous to have witnessed. Smoke and fire lifted into the air like a large billowing ball rolling away into the clouds. There was nothing left of the five-hundred-strong army that was waiting for them.

"That'll do it," the captain remarked.

"Bloody heck," Jendryng gasped.

"Told you." Vawdrey smiled. "They were only expecting a front-on assault. I was right."

"Good for you," Brook said, leaning in his saddle to pat the other on the back. "You almost are as smart as you look."

"And you don't look very smart," Thornton growled.

Yuri watched the dragons circling in the sky. One of them dived again and sent another barrage of flame over the scorched ground.

"We go kill Maji now?" the Agrodien asked the captain.

"We'll try," Thornton replied. "But I dare say they won't fall for that trick again. And, the Maji is bound to have better soldiers who are far better prepared than these in his immediate vicinity."

"Agreed," said Yuri. "We kill them, too."

***

"Sir," the crewman posted on the lookout called. He was pointing to the shore.

Commander Willard Zakhar, standing at the bow, followed the man's gesture and saw a thick, dark cloud on the horizon.

"What in blazes is that?" First Officer Grady blurted.

"Blazes is right." Zakhar smiled. "That's our signal."

"Really?" the other questioned, perplexed.

"It's close enough." He turned and started barking orders, Grady on his heels and repeating them a little louder. "Hoist the sails. Raise the anchor. Prepare the guns. We're going to into battle, lads."

***

A horn trumpeted.

The dragons formed up in a long line behind Alice as she circled the valley once more. Peering over Liana's side, she saw the troop below moving across the valley towards the west, bypassing the newly charred and burning ground.

"Let's go, girl," she said to the dragon, leaning her frame to the north.

Liana corrected her trajectory, flapping her great leathery wings to gain speed and altitude. She led the other dragons over a wide patch of pine forest, keeping as low as she could without touching the tips of the tall trees.

The wind being dragged behind the flying beasts made the woods tremble beneath them, kicking up swirling clouds of white powder about them as they flew. They advanced at tremendous speed, almost skimming the surface of yet another open plain as it rose gently to a smooth ridge.

Suddenly, they were high in the air again as the ground dropped away beneath them. Liana let out a small chirp as the immense city came into view. It was still far in the distance, spreading wide across the land, reaching from the sea to the west almost all the way to the hills far to the east. Even with haze and fog caused by falling snow shrouding the city, she could see the tall, white palace looming menacingly over the far side of the city clearly enough.

He was there.

Alice could tell.

It wasn't a feeling brought on by some mystical power. She didn't have a sense of connection to the Maji.

It was gut instinct.

A hunter's intuition.

They passed over the outer edge of Wintermarsh. A few houses and storage buildings slid by far below.

Alice kept a wary eye out for movement.

There were people scurrying about, racing for shelter upon seeing the giant winged creatures approaching. Most of them were civilians, women and children, but there was the occasional soldier, too.

Suddenly, something caught her attention just to the right. An object flashed through the air, barely missing her and Gruloch trailing just behind her.

The dragon behind him, carrying Jhakarh of the Mohaa Clan, folded its wings and plummeted. It let out a terrible cry, both shrill and guttural as it fell.

Alice felt her stomach fall as she saw what had happened to the beast.

A great shaft stuck from its side.

Alice couldn't take her eyes from the falling dragon.

Down it tumbled, crying out all the way until it hit the ground hard, crushing a few small buildings upon impact.

Jhakarh was flung aside where he tumbled on the snow. He came to a stop a few yards from his dragon, lying in an awkward position. Neither dragon nor rider moved.

Gruloch let out an anguished cry.

Alice saw the next giant bolt approaching fast.

"Climb," she hollered, urging Liana to turn towards the sky.

"Scorpion," Thornton called to his men as he watched the large arrow streak through the sky.

They had just seen one dragon fall, and now they watched as the others flew higher to avoid being struck again.

It was too late.

It struck one of the riderless dragons near the end of the line in the belly. It flapped its wings desperately, trying to stay in the air with the others, but it grew too weak too fast. Thornton could see, even from so far away, copious amounts of blood spilling through the beast's abdomen, falling through the air in great clumps to splash in thick and wide spatters over the ground.

Before long, it also dropped to the earth and beyond the troop's sight. The sound of the impact reached them like a low rumble of thunder. A cloud of white powder flung into the air.

"Poor bugger," Sparrow whispered.

"There must be at least two of those weapons," Brook said. "Perhaps more. It takes longer than that to load a scorpion, even with the best team operating it."

Thornton agreed, nodding.

"That's our mission," he told the others. "Pass the word. We find these weapons and destroy them and the men operating them."

***

Zakhar's galleon moved slowly towards the docks of Wintermarsh, five frigates following in wide formation. The rest of the fleet remained out of range of the guns that waited along the waterfront.

The wind was not in their favour, causing the crew to turn the sails almost at a straight angle parallel to the line from bow to stern. As a result, the ships were almost moving sideways on approach.

While this was slow going, and offered their enemy larger targets, it also gave them more time to load and fire their cannons on their starboard sides to prepare for an attack.

Wintermarsh, however, fired first.

A colossal eruption of black smoke burst from the waterfront. At least forty guns, from Zakhar's estimate, fired all at once.

The water, only a few feet from the galleon's starboard bow, sprayed into a frenzy as cannon mortars splashed harmlessly into the harbour.

"They won't make that error again, boys," First Officer Grady shouted. "And we don't have the luxury of making any of our own. Right now, they're making corrections to their guns. Let's show 'em what we got in the meantime."

He looked to Commander Zakhar.

"Fire when ready," the commander said.

"Fire," Grady hollered.

The blast caused the galleon to shudder and sway.

A cloud of thick smoke appeared on the starboard side of the ship.

The other five vessels accompanying Zakhar's ship fired their guns immediately afterwards.

The smell of black powder wafted over the deck.

Something about it invigorated Zakhar.

"Reload," he commanded the gunner as he climbed the steep steps to the poop deck near the aft of the ship, to get to a better vantage point.

Grady repeated the order, staying in place on the quarterdeck, one level lower than where his commander had relocated.

The smoke drifted away, revealing the waterfront.

Several places were aflame.

The pylons of one pier splintered, making the great platform tilt over slowly. As the crew watched on, a few cannons and their operators fell into the water just before the whole pier came crashing down on top of them.

"Fire again," Zakhar shouted.

"Fire," called Grady.

The guns roared to life.

Zakhar felt the deck vibrate beneath him.

From the higher position, he witnessed the waterfront receive the payload.

Buildings, docks, and structures along the piers splintered and burned.

Zakhar heard the screams of men in the turmoil.

But it wasn't enough.

The docks replied with a barrage of their own.

White spouts of water flared about the vessels as projectiles landed about them. Some found their targets.

The mizzenmast split about two-thirds of the way up. The sails handing upon it swayed oddly to the side before the thick beam cracked.

Several holes appeared in the mainsail, near the middle of the ship, and the foresail towards the stern.

Grady shifted his wide eyes between the two giant pieces of fabric.

"Any closer, and those bastards would have knocked our heads off our shoulders," he growled.

"Reload," the commander shouted.

"Reload," Grady repeated, turning from the sails.

The mizzenmast fell to the port side, taking its two sails with it.

"That'll slow us down," the first officer observed.

"Any slower, and we would stop," Zakhar replied. "Fire when ready."

"Fire," Grady shouted.

The cannons roared.

Smoke filled the air.

Warehouses burned, and two more docks crumbled into the water after receiving a barrage from the six vessels.

Wintermarsh replied with another volley of projectiles flung from catapults and fired from large cannons lining the edge of the water.

They pummeled a frigate with a large rock and a few balls of iron. Splinters and smoke burst from countless points over its hulk. The sails tore, and the mainmast cracked. But it remained afloat.

They hit other vessels with a blow here and there. Some tears formed in sails. Some timber broke. Nothing kept them from their task.

Several cannon blasts struck the galleon, cracking the hull open just above the waterline. Zakhar knew they had limited time on board. Eventually, the ship would sink. For now, she limped on to continue the fight.

"Fire at will," he hollered. His first officer repeated his command.

The cannons roared to life, echoed by those of the surrounding five frigates.

The waterfront erupted in a cloud of flame, dust, and dark smoke.

A great fireball exploded directly ahead of the galleon. Several large cannons thrust into the sky before they tumbled into the sea. A large section of the shipping yard collapsed as fire swept through buildings and beneath the wharves. Men cried out in agony. Others ran about, engulfed in flame. Some dropped into the sea from the high platforms of the dockyards, hoping the icy water would offer relief.

"We hit a powder keg," Grady cheered.

"Good," Zakhar shouted. "Reload the guns. Let's hit another."

The catapults, set far back from the shoreline, sent another barrage of stone.

One large rock struck the excessively damaged frigate near the galleon. It penetrated the decks and disappeared into the ship. Almost instantly, the vessel slipped into the sea.

"Get off her, lads," one of Zakhar's crewmen shouted to the men on board.

"Not yet," Zakhar heard their captain call. The commander turned his head to see what was happening. He intended to give the officer on board the frigate a reprimanding glare. Instead, he heard the man shout another order.

"Fire!"

The frigate's guns erupted. The docks exploded again. They hit another powder keg.

Zakhar shook his head in disbelief.

"Abandon ship," the captain of the frigate commanded.

"Get over here, boys," Zakhar called as the crew jumped from the sinking vessel. "Lower the ladder. Portside."

The crewmen dropped a wide rope net over the side of the galleon.

"Fire," Grady barked. The guns on the starboard side opened up.

The men from the sinking frigate clambered onto the deck. The last was their captain.

"Permission to come aboard, sir?" he said, hanging from the ladder with one hand, just fractionally lower than the deck, holding his other hand out to Zakhar.

"Permission granted, Captain Rashiid." The commander smiled, pulling the other onto the deck.

"The shore cannons have stopped firing, sir," Grady reported.

"Take us to the docks," Zakhar commanded. "Call the other ships in. Prepare for land assault. We need to take out those ballistae."

"Aye, aye, sir," the first officer replied.

Eleven

"We can't stay up here all day," Gruloch called from Alice's side, trying his best to project his voice over the wind.

They had been circling in the clouds for some time.

Alice had considered leading the dragons and their keepers back to the southern plain, where smoke still rose into the air from the welcoming party that the Maji had sent to greet them. They could regroup and discuss tactics instead of remaining above the cloud cover where the ground forces couldn't see them.

Haildur, the oldest of the Haigok and leader of the Traruk, pulled alongside Gruloch. He started shouting with his raspy voice, something that Alice didn't understand. The exchange went on for a short time, accompanied by hand gestures and lots of pointing to the ground below. Eventually, the Lord of the Haigok turned to Alice.

"What did he say to you?" she asked, looking to Haildur, who remained in place.

"He said that we should strike and retreat," Gruloch answered.

"What?" the girl inquired, shaking her head, not understanding his meaning.

"Strike and retreat," he repeated. "We separate. Attack different points on the ground at the same time and quickly retreat back here. We then attack again at new locations and retreat."

"They won't have time to adjust their weapons," Alice said with a grin. "They won't know where we will be striking next. Good idea. Only there is one thing we need to remember."

"What's that?" Gruloch asked.

"We have friends down there," she told him. "We have to be sure that none of them are in our paths. I need you to instruct the riders to turn from their attack if they see any of our people before them."

"I'll pass the word," Gruloch told her, pulling away.

***

Brook peered up into the sky, just for a moment.

The clouds swirled about over the city like a giant maelstrom, round and round. He knew the dragons were up there, causing the spectacle as they circled about, out of view. The trick was trying to make a way for the winged beasts to begin their assault.

"I see seven from here," Thornton announced as they charged for the city. He quickly pointed to several large scorpion weapons tucked neatly in between buildings on the southern edge of Wintermarsh.

"Eight," Brook gestured to another a little further to the east, where a lone farmhouse was situated.

"We take that one," Yuri growled before signalling the other Agrodien warriors to follow. They raced away on horseback before Thornton could protest.

"Be nice if we made a plan first," the captain grumbled.

"They're too busy looking at the clouds to see us," Sparrow said.

"What?" Brook asked, furrowing his brow.

"Look." The other pointed ahead.

Sure enough, the soldiers guarding and operating the enormous weapons were engaged in watching the swirling clouds in the sky.

"All right," Thornton said. He pointed to the weapons closest to their position. "Infantry will take the two in the middle. Cavalry will spread out and take down the rest."

"What about us?" Vawdrey queried.

"Take your pick," the captain replied. "If we separate, we'll meet back up somewhere along the way."

Before long, horses and men were charging towards different points along the city's edge.

***

Yuri led his warriors to the rear of a large barn.

They grouped their horses together, out of sight behind the building, before moving to press their backs against the timber structure, where they formed a line along the wall.

Crouching low, Yuri peered around the edge and saw the weapon in the middle of the ground between the barn and the small farmer's cottage across the way. He counted eight men standing around the contraption, looking to the clouds above. Another soldier was manning the device, tilting it upon its stand and swivelling around to direct the projectile towards the middle of the vortex.

"What's happening?" Nola'ee hissed, nudging his shoulder gently with her elbow.

"One soldier is pointing the weapon at the clouds," Yuri reported.

"Surely, they can't shoot that far," Nakrah asked from beside Nola'ee, looking up to the sky.

"I think they are preparing," Bein suggested. "Kayl'sro Alice won't stay up there forever."

"No, she won't," Yuri agreed. "And we don't know how long it will be until she returns. We need to destroy that thing, and all the others of its kind."

"How many soldiers?" Varssk enquired, leaning forward from the wall to look at his commander.

"I see nine," Yuri answered. "No. There are six more on horses behind the hut. There could be more where I can't see."

Varssk turned to Rabor and whispered something that the older Agrodien couldn't make out. A brief conversation ensued.

"What are you two discussing?" Mralner put in.

"We should take down the horses first," Rabor answered. "Before they can get away to inform others of our presence."

Yuri considered the young warrior's words.

"We'll split up," he told them. "Rabor, Varssk, Kavnu, Draav, Duga. Go around that side of this building and kill the horsemen." He pointed to the far corner of the wall they were pressing their backs on. "try to keep the horses from running away, tie them to something or put them in one of the buildings." The others offered him a strange look.

"A riderless horse running away might cause someone to come looking for the missing rider," he explained.

"And us?" Nola'ee asked. "What do we do?"

"You lot will help me take down these men here and destroy that weapon." He poked his head around the corner again. The soldiers and riders were still in place, all eyes peering into the clouds. "Watch out for any soldiers that may be hidden inside. Ready?"

Stealthily and swiftly, the Agrodien warrior moved around the outside of the barn.

The soldiers near the scorpions were caught off guard. The Agrodien cut most of them down before they realised what happened.

A short skirmish followed, but not before the reptilians tackled five of the riders to the ground. The Agrodien warriors were quick to slaughter them. Only one turned his steed and start charging away from the small farm, back towards the city.

Duga lifted his bow from his back and loaded an arrow. Within a blink of an eye, he fired the shaft and pierced the fleeing steed through the leg, just below its rump. The horse reared up and fell to its side, emitting a loud squeal.

The rider fell down with the horse, his leg crushed beneath the weight of the beast with a loud crunch. He cried out in pain, but was silenced quickly as another arrow stuck through his temple.

As the rider slumped into the thick snow, the steed continued to writhe. Duga shot a third arrow to finish the creature.

The Agrodien warriors were the first to have victory. The men standing about the weapon killed simply with cuts to their throats or stabs through their chests. Yuri disabled the scorpion by putting a blade through the various cords that kept the contraption taut. With a loud snap, the ropes fell apart.

"Find an axe to break the weapon," Yuri commanded the others.

"We could burn it," Kavnu suggested, leading three of the horses across the ground towards the barn.

"No," the older reptilian said, shaking his head. "The fire would draw attention. We try to keep ourselves unseen for as long as we can."

Mralner and Bein soon found wood axes in the barn and went to work hacking the scorpion apart.

"We don't need firewood," Yuri growled. "Just break the pieces at the joints. We need to get moving."

As the two warriors dismantled the weapon, Yuri peered to the western edge of the city, by the sea, where he saw a wide plume of smoke rising into the air.

"I hope our friends on the sea are faring well," Nola'ee commented.

"So do I," he replied.

"I think that's the best we can do for now," Bein suggested, looking at the pile of timber and rope at his feet.

"Good enough," his commander acknowledged.

"Look." Rabor pointed to the north. "There's another one."

Yuri turned, following the younger Agrodien's finger, and saw another scorpion positioned near a house, far across some fields, closer to the city's edge.

"We go on foot this time and do exactly what we just did here," he told the others. "If there are horsemen, you five will take them down. We will take any that are on foot. Understood?"

"Yes," they all hissed before following their leader across the open ground on foot, leaving their horses behind.

***

Takmel watched from the window of the sitting room as thirty dragons burst from the clouds. Their immense forms were both awesome and terrifying to see, especially in such numbers. With their giant wings spread wide and their gaping jaws filled with jagged teeth, he doubted, just for a moment, whether he held any chance against them.

His stomach turned.

His heart leapt from his chest and into his throat.

He felt his body stiffen as the great winged beasts dived swiftly for the ground.

Each of the magnificent beasts let out a long jet of flame.

The flames swept over thirty different places around his city.

One came terribly close to the wall surrounding his palace.

Even through the window, he could feel the heat from the dragon's breath touch his skin.

"Shoot them down," he screamed in frustration at no one in particular, at all of his soldiers manning the weapons out in the streets.

No weapon fired.

No bolts pierced the dragons' hides.

Instead, the beasts turned about and climbed back into the sky, vanishing into the clouds.

Smoke and flames rose from thirty different places about Wintermarsh.

Shops, houses and people turned to ash before his eyes.

It was so quick that he had barely believed it had happened.

He gnashed his teeth and glared at the streets below.

"General Versel," he bellowed.

"My lord," her voice replied calmly from the doorway.

"Find that bitch, Alice's mother, and bring her to me," he commanded. "She will be here somewhere. If those weapons will not bring her down, then I'll use leverage to do so. Find her. Bring her. Hurt her if you have to."

"Yes, my lord." She clicked her heels together, moved the helmet from beneath her arm onto her head before starting away.

Twelve

Emily sat upon her horse, peering from atop of a hill where the cleared ground met the edge of a wood. Behind her stood the wagon that housed Amicia, Ursula, and Catherine. Its horses had been reassigned to cavalry duty, as had the wagon driver who took one steed into battle.

Sitting upon chargers of their own, near to the auburn woman, were Akasaki, Karlena, and Schoenbach. They waited by the vehicle, keeping guard over the three women, watching many tall columns of smoke rise from the city.

The cavalry had moved to the east. Schoenbach followed them with his spyglass as two groups of horsemen reunited near a small hut by the south-eastern edge of Wintermarsh.

"Some of them have regrouped," he told the others beside him. "It looks as if they found two more of those scorpions."

"I see fire down there." Akasati pointed to an area directly ahead of them, far into the distance.

The old man looked to where she was gesturing before aiming his scope.

"The infantry has set another scorpion on fire," he reported. "I suppose it is pointless to try and stay hidden with your daughter starting her attack."

"They need to get all of those things," Emily said. There was deep concern in her voice. "You saw what happened to the two dragons that were hit?"

"We saw," Karlena replied. "The men are doing their best."

103

"What of the Agrodien?" Emily asked Schoenbach.

He trained the spyglass to the west.

"No," he muttered, moving the scope back and forth. "I've lost them."

The dragons emerged from the clouds again.

Her heart almost froze as the dragons fell from the sky to ignite more of Wintermarsh. She wondered if one of those weapons was going to find her daughter this time, hoping that she would see all flying beasts climb into the sky again unscathed.

Large bolts lifted into the air from various points around the city. They arced slowly through the sky.

One lodged into a dragon, just beneath its right-wing, as it dived for the ground to the far side of Wintermarsh.

"No," Emily gasped. Her eyes widened in fear as she presumed the worst.

"It's not her," Schoenbach was quick to reply. He hoped to ease the girl's mother of any stress, knowing that losing one of their allies wasn't to be taken any easier.

Even from so far away, they could hear the dragon scream as it tumbled, tumbled, tumbled to the ground.

The remaining twenty-nine dragons swooped over the city, vomiting flames over the streets before climbing into the sky again.

Alice is still alive, Emily thought.

A noise coming from the wagon made her to turn about in the saddle. Catherine was climbing down to the ground, holding the flap open so that the other two women could also exit the vehicle.

Amicia bore tear streaks over her cheeks. Emily knew that the poor woman had been sobbing this entire time and still was in need to grieve more.

"What's the situation?" the queen asked, wiping her eyes on her sleeves.

"All the men are attacking Wintermarsh," Schoenbach replied. "They have strong resistance. It looks as if we have been wearing down their defences, but they have the numbers where we don't."

Emily stared at the three women in silence. They were different.

"Your hair," she said. "None of you bears the streaks of snow as you did before."

"Mama," Catherine said, peering up at her mother with eyes the same as hers. The piercing blue that the Four had once shared was gone. "It's all right."

"Have you lost your power?" the auburn woman asked.

"No," Amicia answered. "We will always have our power. Where are our people, exactly?"

"Ah!" Schoenbach looked to the coast, still holding his spyglass in his hand. "We assume that Commander Zakhar and his men are storming the docks, possibly moving farther into the city from the west. The Agrodien were moving in that direction also, but I lost track of them some time ago." He pointed to the east. "Captain Thornton and his men led the cavalry in that direction. They have spread out rather wide and are focusing on destroying those weapons. And most of the infantry are moving through this region here." Schoenbach gestured to the quadrant directly in front of them.

The dragons suddenly appeared again. They burst from the clouds and dived steeply towards the surface. Great jets of flame swept over the ground at several locations as giant arrows flung into the air again.

Amicia could immediately see that there was no particular strategy; just sheer hope from both sides that they would hit something of value.

Luckily, for their part, no dragons were hit this time.

"We need to give Alice an advantage," the queen said to Ursula and Catherine. "Let's hope she's a smart enough girl to work this out."

"She is," Catherine assured her as she stepped past the wagon and onto the edge of the open ground, a few paces in front of Emily and the others.

Amicia moved to the girl's right side and crouched to the ground, pressing her bare hand to the snow.

"What are you doing?" Akasati asked, watching curiously.

Catherine placed her right hand on the queen's shoulder as Ursula positioned herself on the girl's left. She then reached to the sky with both hands as Catherine touched her left hand on the back of the witch of Whitekeep.

Without warning, a sudden gust built up around the three as their eyes turned pitch black.

The blackness spread under their skin, like webs growing from their dark orbs, through their cheeks and brows.

The snow swirled around their feet as the vortex in the clouds above Wintermarsh started spinning faster and faster.

***

"What is this?" Gruloch called as he whooshed by Alice and Liana, passing beneath her. A great gust had built up around them, catching in the dragons' wings like sails on a ship. The beasts tossed about roughly.

A bright flash of light burst into life not too far from their position. There was a loud crack before the clouds flashed intermittently around them.

"We need to get above this," Alice shouted over the breeze. "My coven has joined the fight."

"Where do we go?" the other enquired.

"Above the clouds," the girl shouted. "Well above the clouds."

With that, Alice urged Liana into the sky.

The Lord of the Haigok called out to the nearest riders.

A horn blew from somewhere in the turmoil, alerting the others to take to the sky.

***

"Your sister is in there," Emily protested, peering at the clouds worriedly.

Her plea went unheard. The three were as if in a trance.

Tendrils of darkness continued to spread from their dark orbs, over their faces and around their heads like thin streaks of black smoke.

"Tremble," Amicia said with an empty, emotionless voice. It rang out like thunder and rumbled over the ground towards the city.

Buildings shook violently as the tremor rolled like a growing wave into the middle of Wintermarsh.

Several structures collapsed along the way.

It culminated a little to the right of the palace, where it shook everything upon the surface with great ferocity.

There, the ground opened beneath people, soldiers and civilians alike, and swallowed them in a cloud of dust and filth.

Stones and bricks toppled over, causing large structures to flatten as great pieces of stone from beneath the earth churned about, lifting sections of streets and laneways from their places before rolling them into the ground.

"Strike," Ursula muttered. Her voice boomed through the sky like a tremendous roar.

Suddenly, the sky above Wintermarsh opened up.

Several thick bolts of white light rushed from the clouds and smashed into the turbulent destruction occurring on the ground.

A plume of dust and fire erupted from the earth as the lightning branched out and lapped at the ground nearby like forked tongues made of light.

Smoke and flame, dust and grit, rose and fell from the surface as the ground continued to shake and the jagged bolts of light fell from the sky.

Soon, a large, thick cloud covered the middle of Wintermarsh. Orange flares grew inside the haze as fires took hold. Screams resounded as people cried out in agony, even at such a great distance from where they watched from at the edge of the city.

The scene, from Emily's perspective, was horrific and terrifying.

The lightning stopped suddenly. The quake dissipated rapidly. All three women fell to the ground, exhausted.

"Catherine," Emily blurted, dropping from her horse to race to her daughter's aid.

"I'm all right, Mama," the other answered wearily. "I just need a moment."

Amicia and Ursula sat on their haunches, peering into the city before them.

"By the gods," Schoenbach gasped as he took in the view before him.

"Alice?" Emily looked at her elder daughter, hoping there was an active connection between the two. "Is she...?"

"She's fine," Catherine answered, lifting herself to her elbows. She pointed to the sky. "Look."

The dragons emerged from the clouds again. They dived for the ground, sending another barrage of flame over parts of the city.

No Wintermarsh weapons fired in response.

No large bolts arched through the air.

"I think you have been successful," Karlena supposed.

Akasati furrowed her brow. She was watching a cluster of buildings near the edge of the city.

"We've got company," she hissed.

The other six turned their heads to behold a frightening sight. Thirteen riders fanned out before them with bloodstained swords drawn, two with crossbows strapped over their shoulders. Their dark armour glistened, and their white tunics splotched with marks accumulated through battle.

The lead rider, a woman, pointed with her sword at the three witches.

"Take them," a woman's voice commanded from beneath a helmet. She directed the tip of her blade to Emily. "And that one. The Maji has no need of the others."

Akasati was quick to pull the bow from her saddle. She loaded an arrow in the blink of an eye and pulled the string tight.

But not quickly enough.

Her attention was upon the lead rider, not the men at either end of the line.

One of them flung a small dagger that buried itself deep into the Erilian warrior's face, just below her right eye.

She fell to the ground, hard.

"No," Karlena gasped, pulling her sword from its sheath. She kicked her heels into her steed's flanks, causing it to lunge forward.

Two shafts flung from two crossbows smacked into her chest.

Karlena tumbled to the ground, dead.

Akasati groaned from the physical pain from her injury, and the heartache upon seeing her friend fall.

"Sister," she breathed.

Emily drew her sword as Amicia, Ursula, and Catherine rose to their feet, starting for what safety the wagon offered.

"My name is Saruun Versel," the lead rider said, lowering herself from her steed. "First Garrison Commander of the Maji. General of his army."

Captain Jeremy Schoenbach was off his horse and on the ground, kneeling with Karlena in his arms. He bawled profusely, uncontrollably, ignoring the riders nearby.

Within an instant, two more bolts fired from the crossbows, striking him through his back.

"Stop," Emily cried, tears welling in her eyes.

Versel cocked her head.

"Stop?" The commander pointed her blade at the burning city behind her. "Look what your friends have done to my home. And you want me to stop."

One rider dropped from his charger and started towards Akasati, who was crawling across the ground towards Karlena and Schoenbach. The Erilian sobbed profusely as she dragged herself over the cold ground. The old captain was now slumped lifelessly over his wife.

Emily moved to intercept the soldier's advance.

The man raised his sword to hack into Akasati. As he brought his blade down, Emily blocked the blow with her own. With a quick swipe, the auburn woman slit the soldier's neck open before kicking him onto his back with a boot to his stomach.

The two crossbows reloaded and raised at the ready.

"No," Versel barked. "The Maji wants this one alive. Get the three witches there and tie them up."

Emily moved back and thrust her sword towards Versel. The commander dodged the attack and hit the thin Erilian blade away with her thick weapon.

The auburn woman felt a tremendous amount of strength behind the commander's strike, making her believe she may be, in fact, facing a man with a woman's voice.

Versel didn't wait to be attacked again. She moved quickly, striking blow after blow in an attempt to relieve Emily of her blade.

Each strike sent shattering tremors along Emily's arm. A painful twinge built up in her elbows and her fingers filled with the sense of pins and needles.

A sudden realisation filled her thoughts as she blocked each of Versel's blows.

She was getting older.

She was fighting someone in her prime.

She was losing.

Seven riders had caught up to the three witches before they reached the wagon. Three of the riders reached down from atop of their horses, and each grabbed a woman by her hair before dragging her back to where the other riders awaited. The remaining five riders were already upon the ground, rope at the ready to bind the witches' hands together.

One man got a little too close to Catherine as he wound the bindings around her wrists.

She took him by the fingers.

"Absorb," she whispered.

A ghostly wisp of energy flowed from his eyes and mouth and into her own. His cheeks sank and his skin became paler and paler as she felt herself growing stronger and stronger. The orbs in his eye sockets melted away as his flesh turned an ashen shade.

Suddenly, a steel gauntlet smashed against the side of her face, making her fall upon her side.

"No," Emily cried, losing her focus.

Versel didn't hesitate. She leapt forward and hit the auburn woman across the head with her own iron glove.

Emily saw stars spinning around her head.

Darkness seized hold as she saw the ground flying up to meet her.

Both mother and daughter were on the ground, unconscious.

"Tie their hands behind their backs," the commander instructed the men. She pointed to the dead soldier on the ground. "We don't need another incident like that."

It wasn't long before the riders started away, heading back into the city. Four of them had prisoners, gagged and bound, draped over the laps.

The flap of the wagon moved.

A tiny figure climbed out and crept quietly over the snow. His chin quivered and his eyes filled with tears as he peered at the bodies of Akasati, Karlena and Schoenbach.

He was alone.

His gaze moved to the riders moving away towards the city. They hadn't seen him. They didn't even know he was there.

Carefully, quietly, he crawled to Akasati. She was still on her belly, her hand reaching for Karlena and Schoenbach, only a short distance away.

He reached down and moved Akasati's and Karlena's arms closer so that their hands could touch.

"I'm sorry," the boy said to them, as if they could still hear him. But they were gone.

He pulled the blade from Akasati's face and tucked it into his belt.

"I'm so sorry." He looked at each one of them and wished he could do more.

He returned his attention to the riders. They were just beginning to move into the streets and out of view.

He rose to his feet and started after them, keeping low to the ground, close to obstacles and structures, careful to stay out of sight.

Thirteen

Charging just inside the south-eastern edge of the city, Thornton and the cavalrymen steered their steeds through narrow streets and around sharp corners. They had destroyed two of the scorpion weapons before entering Wintermarsh, and another just inside the metropolis, in a yard behind a quaint tavern.

The captain had ordered the contraption, and the establishment that housed it burned to the ground. Considering that many fires were already underway across the city, he didn't think lighting a few more would be a problem.

The dragons breached the clouds above him.

He pulled his horse to a stop. Some other men raced by him to cut down some fleeing soldiers wearing white tunics.

The sight of the dragons brought Thornton's heart to a standstill. He didn't think he could ever get used to such a thing.

He watched as one of the winged beasts dived for an area not too far from where he and the horsemen were located. A great pointed shaft shot into the air towards the dragon. It missed, but only narrowly.

"Did you see that?" one rider called, pointing his bloodied sword to the north. "It came from over there."

"I saw it, Victor," another called before Thornton could respond. He had thought the cavalryman was speaking to him until the other answered. "We should let the captain know."

"I'm right here," he growled. "And I saw it too. What are your names?"

"Lieutenant Victor Castell, sir," a man answered.

"Lieutenant Kristoph Greer, sir," the other replied.

"Who is your commanding officer?"

"You are, sir," Kristoph answered, looking perplexed.

"No," Thornton shook his head frustratingly. He didn't believe he could be speaking to an officer with such a low intellect. "I know I'm your commander. I mean, who do you report to directly?"

"Lieutenant Beresfield, sir," Kristoph replied.

"Beresfield?" the captain repeated, looking at the rest of the cavalry forming up behind him. "And where is Lieutenant Beresfield?"

"Dead, sir," Victor explained. "Kristoph here cut his head off."

Thornton furrowed his brow and looked at the two men oddly.

"He was already dead," Kristoph explained. "In Ironfields, sir. One of the women there bit him in the neck during the battle. The next thing we knew, the lieutenant was coming at us with his sword. What else was I to do?"

"Join the ranks," Thornton commanded the two men, gesturing with his chin at the rest of the horsemen. The two men complied as the captain led the charge through the streets again, heading towards the next scorpion weapon.

It was a quick run.

The captain was first to come upon a small market area. A weapon stood upon the tiny plaza and was being reloaded by six men in white.

"Hurry it up," one of them hollered. Thornton gauged he was an officer of some rank, barking orders the way he did. "They could be back any moment. And make sure you aim better, Thurly."

"It's heavy, sir," a young man replied. "I need more practice."

"No time for bloody practice, is there?" the officer replied.

"Oh shit," another bellowed, seeing Thornton right near to them.

How they had not seen the captain and the horsemen he led was beyond Thornton's comprehension. The only feasible explanation was that they were nervous, untrained and too focused upon the threat from above to be concerned about what may come for them from the surface.

"Oh shit," the officer repeated, reaching for his sword still tucked away in its sheath.

It was useless. Thornton's blade was already slicing through his neck before his hand touched the hilt.

The captain charged by the weapon as the officer's head fell to the ground.

The others manning the scorpion pulled their weapons free as the rest of the cavalry came into their view.

"Bugger me," Thurly, the weapon's operator, huffed as he saw the number of horses charging towards them.

Thornton pulled his steed to a stop. He sheathed his blade and waited for his men to finish the job.

The skirmish was brief.

Some ringing from clashing blades filled the marketplace for a slight moment.

Before long, six men wearing bloodstained white tunics over their armour lay lifelessly upon the snow.

"Burn the weapon," Captain Thornton instructed one rider.

"Yessir," the other replied.

Thornton looked about and saw the two lieutenants he had spoken to a little earlier.

"Greer," he called. "Castell."

"Sir?" they both replied, riding over to the captain.

"Scout ahead," he commanded them. "Keep out of sight and find our next target."

"Yes sir," they both answered, riding away at a trot.

Turning back to the weapon, Thornton watched as a rider sliced through the taut cords with his sword. The scorpion emitted a strange sound as the thick timber bow straightened slightly when he cut the ropes away.

***

Crouching low, keeping behind crates and debris, the commander of the Dendadian fleet, and a massive contingency of the navy men with him, moved through the dockyards, gripping their swords tightly. Arrows flung in their direction, usually overshooting their targets by mere inches. Several of the bolts found a man or two during the advance.

All in all, Commander Willard Zakhar, wearing his bicorn hat, considered himself and his comrades to be extremely lucky. None had perished since landing.

A few men had pulled the injured sailors to shelter nearer to the longboats, resting by the shore of the bay by the farthest edge of the waterfront from the city. The land curved from the south in a wide arc to jut towards the sea there. Several structures, flattened during the battle on the water, burned along the piers.

It was there that Zakhar and his men were attempting to gain ground. After each barrage of arrows fired from farther around the bend of the shoreline to the south, the commander would make a quick dash for the next piece of visible cover.

"Come on," he would shout each time.

It became the highlight of the expedition, bringing a heightened level of excitement and bravado to the men of the fleet. Each time their commander gave the call, they, too, would cry it out with him.

"Come on," they roared, racing to the next barrel, wooden box or heaped hessian sacks full of who knew what.

First Officer Grady laughed with each development, pausing long enough once he was behind cover to shout out to the enemy.

"We're getting closer, boys."

It was enough to invigorate those in the navy who were experiencing anxiety and fear, giving them the boost they needed.

The bowmen's fears, however, increased with each roar that the fleet men made.

Louder and louder it grew.

Closer and closer they came.

Each and every shot they made at the Dendadian navy meant one fewer shaft for them to fire.

Soon, they would be out of ammunition.

Soon, the enemy would be upon them.

Soon, they would have to flee or die.

"Come on," the roar went up again.

It was so loud that it shook the boards beneath the archers' boots.

Then came the rumble as the mass of nearly four hundred men raced to the next piece of cover.

The archers fired again.

Thin wooden bolts stuck fast into discarded cargo and stores lying upon the pier.

Not one of the Dendadian men suffered a wound during that barrage.

"Come on," Zakhar shouted again, rising to his feet and charging for a tiny overturned fishing boat. It already had several arrows sticking from its hull, signalling what terrible shots some archers were.

The commander took a quick note of how far they had come and how far they had yet to go.

Beyond the little vessel, lying on its side, was a long patch of open boardwalk. There were small fires along its length, but nothing of substance to offer cover for the men.

Ducking behind the boat and into its hull, Grady by his side, he dropped low as dozens of projectiles thwacked harmlessly into the hull.

"Almost there, lads," the first officer called out.

"Stay where you are," Zakhar shouted to his men, holding his hand up to signal the sailors behind his position to freeze in place.

"Hold," one of them called down the line. The word repeated again and again.

"What is it?" Grady asked his commander.

"No more cover," Zakhar informed him.

More arrows hit the belly of the boat.

When the barrage was over, Grady took a quick look over the vessel before ducking back inside.

"We'll just have to run at them," he stated, gesturing to the men behind them. "All of us at once."

Zakhar pulled a face as if he was in pain. "Some of us might get hit," he said.

Grady shrugged.

"It's battle," the first officer reminded his commander. "Some of us have already been hit. Besides," he added, "how am I meant to impress the ladies if I don't have a war wound or two to show for the stories I intend to tell them?"

Zakhar nodded just as another barrage of arrows thudded into their cover.

"Let them know," he ordered his first officer.

Grady looked back along the line of men ducking behind piles of cargo.

"Get ready to attack," he hollered.

The word passed along in a series of shouts.

The commander waited for just the right moment.

He felt a tight knot form in his stomach.

The shafts pounded the little boat's hull and stuck into the surrounding boardwalk.

"Come on!" he shouted, rising to his feet and charging forward.

All the men chorused the call, roaring with great ferocity as they sprinted along the waterfront towards the awaiting enemy.

The archers loaded their bows as quickly as they could. Many nervously, fearfully tried to place the shafts onto the lines, fumbling and dropping their arrows to their feet.

Some bent to retrieve the shafts. Others noticed how close to them the navy had advanced, choosing to drop their weapons and hightail it out of the dockyards instead.

A larger number fired their bows.

At least twenty of Zakhar's men dropped to the pier, some still alive and holding their wounds, a larger portion of them died in an instant.

Most of the arrows, however, were cast high into the air or wide, either into burning structures or the water to their sides.

"Cut them down," Zakhar cried, leaping towards the first archer in the defensive line.

Several of them dropped their bows, knowing they had no chance at all of reloading their weapons. Some pulled daggers from their belts. Others fled as fast as they could.

Commander Zakhar and First Officer Grady were already chopping through several enemy bowmen by the time their men caught up with them.

It was a bloodbath.

Men in white tunics sliced apart, thrown into the swell below the dock or left to bleed out on the boardwalk.

When the Dendadian navy was done with the three hundred archers, or thereabouts, who stayed to fight, they gave chase to the ones who had fled the scene.

With a mighty roar, the navy raced from the waterfront and into a large area lined with warehouses. Two catapults and a scorpion weapon rested on the ground at the far end of the yard.

There, the white archers found reinforcements.

Infantry.

Zakhar and his men froze in place.

The archers combined with the foot soldiers outnumbered their four hundred by almost two to one.

The white soldiers brandished their blades, appearing to know how to use them.

Zakhar remembered the talk around the campfire as they journeyed with the troop.

Most of these men were nothing more than sellswords. Some might have military experience and training, but not all of them.

And the archers had only little knives.

He gave them a salute, touching the tip of his bicorn hat.

With a deep breath, he prepared himself to engage. "Come on," he shouted.

The navy let out an eruptive roar.

Two sides ran at each other, across the wide ground by the warehouses, shouting all the way.

Swords clashed, and flesh fell.

Blocking, parrying and hacking ensued.

Blood sprayed over the snow-covered ground, turning the clean frost into a dirty, red slush.

White tunics dropped into the muck unceasingly as the navy sliced their way through the enemy.

Several more men in blue uniforms fell during the fray, but eventually, they were the victors of the battle.

Covered in blood and grit, the navy got busy with collecting their dead and wounded, as well as finishing any survivors of the enemy's forces.

"Make sure they're all dead," Grady hollered as he closed upon a white soldier crawling over the ground with one leg missing. The first officer plunged his blade through the man's back and into his chest. "No prisoners. No parley. I guarantee, these men wouldn't do so for you."

"Captain Rashiid," Zakhar called.

"Sir?" came a reply. An officer approached, almost unrecognisable from the caking of blood and filth he had obtained during the skirmish.

"Count our numbers," the commander ordered as he wiped his blade clean on a kerchief from his coat pocket. He then pointed the blade at the ballistae and scorpion. "And set some men to destroying those weapons."

"Aye aye, Commander," the captain replied with a salute.

***

"It's your fault, you know," Victor said to the other. They were plodding slowly along a darkening street.

Deep shadows formed as thick smoke rose rising from the city, added to the existing gloom cast by the swirling clouds above. The sun, just barely observable as a faint white orb behind the mess, was slowly moving towards the western horizon.

Real darkness would be upon them soon enough.

"What?" Kristoph asked stupidly, wondering what his comrade was going on about, wishing he had just kept his mouth shut.

"Being out here, scouting the enemy's territory. It's your fault."

"Oh yeah," said Kristoph. "How do you figure that?"

Victor leant towards him.

"You had to mention Beresfield."

"The captain asked who our commanding officer was," Kristoph said, defending himself. "What was I meant to say? Besides, you're the one who told him I cut the lieutenant's head off. Not me."

"Well." Victor shrugged. "I was nervous. Captain Thornton scares me."

"Scares me, too," the other replied. "But, you know what?"

"What?"

"I think this is a golden opportunity." Kristoph smiled.

"What?" Victor gave him a puzzled look.

"Yeah." The other nodded. "See. The captain has entrusted us with this mission. Maybe he's thinking of adding us to his squad. And you know what else?"

"What?" Victor sighed and looked away as he got a little annoyed.

"I think Captain Thornton will become the new commander of Newholt."

"You what?"

"Yeah." Kristoph nodded. "Who else has had as much experience of commanding in battle as Captain Thornton? He's got to be next in line for the job."

"Shut it," Victor hissed. He pulled his horse to the side of the street and peered ahead as he slowed down.

"I'm only saying that, if there were any others worth consider—" Kristoph continued.

"No," rebuked Victor in a soft whisper. "Shut it and get up against the wall."

Kristoph peered ahead.

A large building was blazing away at the far end of the road, where it met at a T-intersection. To the left, the road bent to the north, where they could see several men standing inside a large fenced-in yard. The men were talking to others, hidden from view by a row of houses that lined the street. In the midst of them, another scorpion weapon pointed to the sky.

"I think we just found our next target." Victor turned his horse about. "Quiet," he said as the steed's hoof struck stone just below the snow cover.

"Slow going," Kristoph whispered, peering over his shoulder as he urged his steed back along the way they had come from.

The men by the weapon hadn't seen them. They didn't respond to the sound of the hoof striking the cobblestone.

"Too far to have been noticed, I guess," Victor surmised.

Kristoph smiled, "Thank the go—oahghdssss..."

An arrow stuck through his face, piercing the bridge of his nose.

Victor didn't wait to see his friend fall.

He didn't stay to see Kristoph jerk and shake all over the ground as blood spurted from his eyes and nose.

He couldn't remain in place to receive the next shaft from the marksmen that were well hidden nearby.

He just fled.

He fled as fast as he could with Kristoph's horse in tow.

Fourteen

The stableboy pressed himself against a storefront door. He saw candles burning through the window, near to the back of the quaint shop. The fabric of different colours, dresses upon hangers, things he had no interest in was on display inside. The candles informed him that there must be people in there too. He couldn't see them as the flare from many fires nearby reflected off the window panes. Just because he couldn't see whoever was inside the store didn't mean that they couldn't see him.

It didn't concern him all that much if they could.

After all, who was he except a small boy with dirty clothes and messy hair?

If they were decent people inside, they would have offered him a place to shelter.

They didn't.

So, either they didn't care, or they hadn't seen him.

Besides, his interest didn't lie inside a store where he could try to stay safe from the dragons in the sky or the fighting in the streets. He was engaged in a chase of sorts.

He had caught up to the white riders with no trouble, hiding in dark shadows and keeping himself behind obstacles where they couldn't see him.

There were times, keeping close to the walls as he crept along the streets, where he wondered if he needed to take such precautions at all. Not once had any of the riders turned to see if they were being followed.

They focused upon the sky, the way ahead, the intersections to their left and right, and their four prisoners.

Warren, the stableboy of Erimoor, had seen the riders shove and hit the women a few times during the journey. It didn't dissuade any of the four captives from continuing to struggle against their captors.

The boy admired that fighting spirit.

However, if their destination was the tall palace far across the city from where they were, the women would need to endure a lot more punishment. Warren didn't like that idea at all.

Seeing his opportunity to advance, as the riders moved to the left of the road as they rounded a corner, Warren sprinted into the street and raced as fast as he could to a small alley to the right. It put him very close to the last rider in the mob, but the shadows were deep and he was small.

No one noticed him.

He considered trying to free the four prisoners. He did not know how to go about it.

He was no fighter.

He had no weapon, save for the blade he took from the Erilian woman.

There were too many riders for him to fight, and they were big men with big swords and crossbows.

The woman leading them frightened him the most.

He had seen her fight against Alice's mother. She was fast and strong.

No, Warren thought. *I won't be attempting to free anybody. Not yet.*

As the riders moved into the next street, passing the corner, the stableboy ducked from his hiding place to the building across the way.

He pressed his front against the wall and peered carefully around the corner. The riders were moving on, scanning the sky and watching the road ahead of them.

Great plumes of smoke rose about them to the north and the south, but the greatest was directly ahead, to the west.

Even from so far away, he could see the orange glow of flames flaring against the underside of the dark, rising cloud billowing from the area.

"The docks burn," Warren heard one rider announce.

"That problem rests with Reilly and Norris," the leader replied. "If they require reinforcements, they will send word. Our place is the palace."

The palace, thought the stableboy. *She is taking them to the Maji after all.*

Continuing towards the west, the riders moved on, veering to the right side of the road.

Warren scanned the way ahead and noticed a small lane between two stone houses across the way.

The riders were busy looking at the smoke rising around them, so he seized the opportunity to move a little closer.

With haste, he dashed over the street.

One rider turned his head, just at that moment when Warren reached the laneway.

"Hey!" the riders called.

"What is it?" another asked as the stableboy frantically ran deeper and deeper into the narrow passage. He ducked behind a barrel that smelled putrid and full of rot. Warren covered his mouth and nose by pulling the collar of his tunic over them.

"Go and see," he heard the leader instruct them.

As the hoofbeats grew louder, drawing nearer to the entrance of the lane, the boy tried desperately to slow his breathing.

His heart raced in his ears and pounded heavily in his chest.

He winced, not from pain, but from the terrible stench wafting from the barrel that he pressed against. Slops and discarded offcuts, he supposed. He hoped it was just potato peelings and the pieces no one ate from their garden crops, but it smelt much worse, making him think of brown slosh with chunks of floating blocks swimming about inside.

He wanted to get out of there as quickly as he could.

But he was trapped.

The riders were peering into the lane, and as far as Warren could see, that was the only way out.

"What did you see?" asked one of them.

"Something ran into there," the other answered.

"Too bloody dark to see anything," the first said. "Was it big or small?"

"Small," the second rider replied.

"A 'man-size' small?"

"No." The other shook his head. "Too small to be a man."

"A child?" the first queried. "No one would let their child out in this. You're seeing things."

"I saw something," the second rider said adamantly.

"Then you probably just saw a fucking dog," the first argued. "There's only rubbish and shit barrels down there."

Shit barrels.

Warren felt the sting of bile in his throat as he pictured the contents of the barrel he was hiding next to.

"Yeah, all right," the second rider conceded. "Probably just a dog."

The riders turned and started away.

"Nothing here, commander," the first called to the woman leading them.

Warren heard all the horses moving off.

He rose from his hiding place and hurried to the end of the lane, shuddering and brushing his clothing off, as if to remove the filth he may have contracted from the shit barrel.

He peeked around the corner, just in time to see the last rider disappear into another street to the right.

Silently, he raced along the street, keeping close to the buildings lining the road. Upon reaching the intersection, he took a quick look around the edge of the house there and saw the riders moving towards the north.

The palace was still a long way off.

Pillars of smoke rose from the surrounding city.

"Look," the rider with the auburn woman draped over his lap called. He was pointing a little to the east of north.

Warren couldn't see what he was gesturing at.

A quick dash across the street, to hide against the building on the adjacent corner of the intersection, revealed the spectacle.

The auburn woman twisted and looked to the sky in that direction, calling out a single word over and over. The gag muffled her cries in her mouth, but the stableboy knew to whom she called.

Alice.

It was in vain.

The girl was too far away.

To the boy's amazement, he watched as several dragons emerged from the clouds far to the north, beyond the edge of the city.

"Nothing we can do about it," the leader said. She turned and pointed to the auburn woman. "And get your prisoner under control."

The rider landed a swift fist into the woman's face.

She went limp; the blow knocking her out.

Another prisoner, also with auburn hair, but younger, called out. Again, the gag she wore hindered her cries.

"You'd better not have damaged her," the leader reprimanded.

"Sorry, Commander," the other replied.

The leader glared at the rider through her visor for a moment longer before turning away and urging her steed onwards.

Warren had watched it all.

Even her own men fear her.

His gaze moved to the north, where he saw many dragons in the sky. They were moving too fast, crossing over one another and twisting through the air as a great number of shafts were flung towards them.

***

Alice held on for dear life, thankful that she strapped herself into the saddle, as Liana dipped to the left sharply. A great shaft of timber with a sharpened tip whooshed by, travelling along the same trajectory line that they just left.

Liana straightened her approach and glided directly towards the weapon that had fired the projectile while the girl peered about to see how the other dragons were faring.

They had lost three more during the skirmish. Two of them lay on the ground below, dead. The third, having just crashed into a farm-house near one scorpion, was still moving about. A long shaft was sticking from its side, hindering its movement. There was no way that the poor creature could return to the sky in its condition.

As twenty men in white approached with swords drawn, the dragon blew a long trail of fire towards them. The Haigok rider dropped to the ground with his own blade held high, ready to defend the beast.

Men burned and fell, but not all of them.

Five soldiers were quick to move in and take the Haigok rider down, hacking into him with their swords and axes.

The fallen dragon arched its neck, crying out as the rest of the remaining infantry dug their blades into its body.

She couldn't watch.

Alice turned her head to focus on the weapon before them. Liana was still gliding towards it.

The soldiers manning it were loading another long shaft of timber into the cradle. Another started winding the crank that tightened the cords.

Liana snarled, puffing a dark cloud of smoke from between her teeth as she drew nearer.

The soldier working the crank stepped away from the contraption. His eyes widened in terror as he saw how close the dragon was to them.

"Run," he called out, fleeing.

The rest of the men turned to see for themselves that it was too late.

Fire erupted around them like a torrent in flood.

Their armour glowed an intense red as their skin bubbled and blistered, their flesh peeled from their bones.

The dragon swept back into the air, shooting straight up towards the clouds. Peering around again, Alice saw the fallen dragon dropping its head to the ground.

The twelve men about it continued to hack into its flesh, ensuring that they extinguished any life left in it.

"Over there," Alice called out, twisting her legs and leaning towards the scene.

Liana responded immediately, turning from vertical to upside-down in the air in order to begin her approach. She then twisted right side up and levelled out again.

The men on the ground hadn't noticed. They were engaged in slicing and chopping into the dead dragon's flesh.

They had left the scorpion unguarded.

Alice steered Liana towards the contraption.

As the twelve men hacked, chopped, stabbed and sliced through the dead beast's rough, thick skin, the scorpion weapon behind them burst into a ball of flame.

It caught them by surprise and brought them back to reality.

They watched as Liana sped by, moving over the ground and a short distance to the north. There, she lifted slightly in the air to turn about.

"Go get them, girl," Alice said, a scowl set upon her face.

Liana flapped her great, leathery wings and increased speed, diving towards the men surrounding the dead dragon.

A couple of them fled onto the open ground. They weren't quick enough.

A jet of flame swept over the fallen dragon and its rider, engulfing the white soldiers nearby.

Liana shot back into the sky with a great and terrible roar.

The flaming men fell into the snow.

"The area is clear," Gruloch called, approaching her left.

Alice looked about her and saw the other scorpion weapons in the area blazing in flames as well. She counted seven new fires, but they had lost three more dragons.

She wasn't willing to call this skirmish a victory. The odds were still against them.

"We number twenty-three," she told him.

"It was an excellent strategy, Alice," he assured her. "I don't like the losses either, but it was inevitable. And I think this tactic gives us the best chance. Look," he said, pointing to the south and then to the west. "Our friends are fighting on the ground over there. I see more smoke rising, and not from our dragons."

Alice had seen the damage on the docks from high in the sky, as well as pockets of smoke rising at new locations to the south.

What she didn't tell her ally was that she had a deep, unsettling feeling in the pit of her stomach, telling her that something was wrong. She wanted so much to go back to the southern hill that overlooked Wintermarsh. She wanted to check the wagon with Catherine, Amicia and Ursula. She wanted to see her mother again.

"We should continue to work our way into the city," she said instead, pointing to the large damaged area the sorcery of the three witches had caused. "We should work our way to that location."

"We could simply burn down that palace with the Maji inside," Gruloch suggested, gesturing with his hand to the enormous structure to the north-western side of the city.

Alice shook her head. "He might flee," she explained. "He can turn into a cloud of smoke. I have seen it. I need to be sure he is dead. I need to be there and see it with my own eyes."

Gruloch looked to Wintermarsh below. "Then I suggest we make a path for ourselves from here to the palace," he suggested. "Then we turn south and clear the way for our friends."

Alice moved her gaze to the south, a short distance farther than the burning docks, and saw another fire ignite. Another victory for her allies, she hoped.

"All right," she replied to the Lord of the Haigok. "I like your plan better."

"Then we'd best get started," he said, turning his dragon away from hers.

Fifteen

A scorpion weapon and two catapults burned in the middle of a plaza, near the southwestern district of the city. The Agrodien were finishing any survivors of the white infantry that still squirmed and crawled across the ground.

Nearby, crouching in the ruin of a small house, was a young woman. Her face was wet from tears and her eyes wide with fear as the Agrodien warriors moved about the area surrounding her.

Yuri looked over at her now and then as he inspected the region. She watched him cautiously, turning her gaze to a pile of rubble on the far side of the plaza. Her expression was one of concern, not for the reptilian monsters, but for something else unseen.

Bein had climbed onto the roof of an inn to scan the way ahead and see what else lie around them. He was high above the plaza, the two-storey building giving him a reasonably good view.

"I can see the waterfront," he called down to Yuri.

The large reptilian standing on the ground kept his eyes upon Bein as the sound of Agrodien blades cutting throats ensued behind him.

"What do you see there?" the older Agrodien queried. He looked to the woman who was staring across the way, to the rubble on the other side of the court.

"The boats," Bein replied. "Lots of fire. If there are men over there, I can't see them. The structures are tall and may hinder my view."

"What about more of those weapons?" Yuri asked. He started towards the rubble that had the woman's attention. With a few flicks of his tongue, he could find what had her interest.

"No," the woman called urgently, rising to her feet and stepping from what remained of the house.

Bein turned his head back to the south and around to the west of their position. "There are three small campfires beyond the city," he reported. "There could be weapons, I suppose."

"No," Yuri said, shaking his head. "We're not going back out there. Tell me what you can see in the streets."

The woman moved into the midst of the plaza, stepping over the bodies of white soldiers, past the other Agrodien as she followed Yuri to the rubble.

Bein swivelled on the roof, crouching as he held onto the apex with his hand.

"There is one over there," he answered, pointing towards the docks. "Not too far away."

"Not on the waterfront?" asked the older warrior. He cocked his head as the sound of soft gurgling and rustling reached his ears.

"No," the younger reptilian replied. "About half the distance."

Yuri nodded as he turned to see how the rest of his group were faring. They were all watching the woman, standing a few yards from the large warrior. Her eyes pleaded as they shed tears.

He crouched in the rubble and lifted a plank of timber to the side. Beneath it, in a hollow, was a small infant, wrapped tightly in a white blanket.

"Please," the woman said. She dropped to her knees and clasped her hands.

Yuri lifted the baby gently with one hand. The child cried.

The young woman began bawling uncontrollably, stretching her hands out to the infant.

"She thinks you plan to eat the youngling," Nakrah remarked.

"She must have hidden the little thing before we arrived," Mralner said. "She thinks we are mere beasts."

"She's protecting her young," Nola'ee interjected as she thrust her sword into a white soldier writhing on the ground. The fighter ceased his moving and went flaccid. "We would do the same if we were threatened."

Yuri stepped over the debris and back to the plaza. He lowered the baby into the woman's arms. She instantly brought the child to her breast and continued to weep.

"Go that way," Yuri told her in as soft a voice as he could muster, using the common language, pointing towards the south. "Find a safe place to hide."

She looked at him, surprised. After a moment, she wiped the tears from her face on the back of her sleeve and nodded.

"Thank you," she whispered. She rose to her feet and started away.

"Come back down," the older warrior called to Bein as he continued moving to the centre of the court.

Nola'ee pulled her blade from the chest of a soldier lying on the ground.

"That's all of them," she said as Yuri drew near. The others gathered about.

"We're moving on," he told them. "Bein says there is another weapon in that direction." He pointed towards the northwest. "When we are done with it, we will go to the docks and see if the boatmen need our help. If they don't, we will join up with them and continue to the Maji's palace."

"Will we try for the Maji?" Varssk asked.

"I think the Kayl'sro should have that honour," Yuri replied. "But if she isn't able to, for whatever the reason, then yes. It is our duty to see the Kayl'sro's mission fulfilled. We will try for the Maji."

Bein moved into the group, placing himself beside Yuri.

"You need to lead the way," the older Agrodien said to him. "Are you ready?"

"Yes," hissed Bein, holding his blade tightly in his hand.

"Then, let's go," Yuri said, waving his hand as though he were shooing a bug away from a plate of food.

Bein smiled and quickly glanced around at his comrades before jogging across the plaza to the north. He pressed himself against the corner of a building there as the others followed, peered around the corner to make sure the way was clear, and proceeded into the dark street beyond.

The way was clear, mostly, and it was some time before they came upon any sign of trouble.

The Agrodien warriors had kept to the shadows, using stealth and caution as they wound through twisting streets and back alleys. They leapt over fences and ran along rooftops, surreptitiously keeping a low profile. Not even the cats poking about in barrels for scraps noticed the giant lizards until they were almost upon them, frightening the felines half to death.

Soon enough, they came upon a group of eight men, still a block away from where Bein believed the weapons to be.

The men, lined up along a wall in a laneway to relieve themselves, hadn't seen the Agrodien, or heard them approach. The reptilians had sneaked up on the soldiers by clambering over the tops of huts that lined the street from which the thin lane debouched.

Yuri gestured with his eyes and claws, pointing to the eight male warriors with him to align themselves to an enemy soldier directly below them.

Silently, each of them did so in haste.

Nola'ee pointed to herself, showing to Yuri that she wasn't sure of her part.

He responded by pointing to her, then to the rooftop she waited upon.

She appeared disappointed.

The eight warriors looked to Yuri for their next command.

The Agrodien leader observed the men.

One of them had finished his business with the wall and had tied the cords of his trousers.

The others, he knew, wouldn't be there for too much longer either.

The finished soldier turned to start away.

It was now or never.

Yuri nodded to the eight Agrodien warriors, signalling for the assault to begin.

In silence, the eight males leapt from the rooftop.

They landed directly on each of their assigned targets.

Using blade and claw, they made quick work of the soldiers.

There was no time for an alarm to be sent, no time for help to be called for. Throats were torn out, heads cracked open and necks broken.

Quick.

Efficient.

Silent.

Unfortunately, another soldier rounded the corner and entered the lane just as the Agrodien warriors were finishing up.

"You lads must have drunk a lot of that ale," the newcomer said as he approached. "You've been in here for a long time. Some others think you're all in here playing with each other's co—"

The soldier froze as all eight Agrodien warriors glared at him.

"Fuh… Fuhhh," the soldier called as he backpedalled out of the laneway, keeping his wide-eyed stare on the reptilians. "Fucking devils. Fucking devils."

The soldier was back in the street and bolting towards the north, to where Yuri could only presume more soldiers awaited.

"Q'Sharh," he spat, standing to full height and dropping into the laneway.

"So much for being quiet," Nakrah said as Nola'ee leapt from the rooftop.

"Let's just hope there aren't too many," she added, moving towards the street.

Yuri followed her out of the lane and into the open.

From the middle of the street, they could see the scorpion weapon sitting in the centre of a cross-intersection farther down the way. A small campfire was lit to its side and at least twenty men wearing white tunics sat around it.

The soldier who had discovered the Agrodien in the laneway was still running towards his comrades.

"Devils," he hollered, pointing back along the street. "Fucking devils killed them."

His alarm brought the attention he desired.

The men seated about the fire looked past the soldier and saw the ten reptilians standing in the street.

They pulled swords from sheaths and lifted axes from the ground.

The men moved into position, standing at the edge of the intersection between the Agrodien and the scorpion weapon.

Yuri took a deep breath. "Ready?"

"Ready," Nola'ee replied, her grip tightening on the hilt of her sword.

Yuri snarled as he ran towards the white soldiers.

The Agrodien warriors kept pace with him, charging swiftly, teeth bared, swords at the ready.

The twenty men tensed, correcting their stances and preparing for battle.

Closer and closer, the Agrodien drew.

One man cried out, a poor act of bravado that was meant to be a roar. The others joined in a sad attempt to display solidarity amongst the soldiers.

Yuri could sense their fear, hearing it in their voices.

The white soldiers started forward, running towards the speeding Agrodien.

Both sides were closing upon each other rapidly.

Suddenly, Yuri leapt high into the air. The other nine Agrodien followed.

It caught the white soldiers off guard. They suddenly skidded to a halt in the middle of the street. Their heads bent back as they followed the trajectory of the reptilians.

Before they realised what had happened, all ten warriors crashed down upon the soldiers, digging their blades into the men and slicing into their flesh.

It was quick.

Six men remained, peering about dumbly as the other fourteen of their comrades lay on the ground. Some were killed instantly. Others held their hands against wounds in their necks or bellies that sprayed dark blood over the snow.

Yuri lopped the head off another with a quick swipe of his blade.

"Nola'ee, Nakrah, Bein," he growled. "Destroy that weapon."

The three warriors raced away to fulfil the command. Yuri sheathed his blade as the other five reptilian warriors skirmished with the remaining white soldiers.

It wasn't long before all men were on the ground and the scorpion weapon was ablaze.

"Bein," Yuri called after he had scanned the scene, checking that they had cleared the area.

"Let me guess," the other Agrodien growled. "You would like me to climb to the rooftop and see what lies ahead."

"Just what lies between here and the docks," the other replied. "And make sure you count any men you can see. Let's try to avoid any sudden surprises."

***

Captain George Thornton peered cautiously around the edge of a building, into the street where Kristoph Greer lay dead on the ground. A wooden shaft still stuck from the dead man's face as he stared lifelessly into the sky above.

"Do you see him?" Victor asked from his side, a little too loudly for the captain's liking.

"Yes, I see him," Thornton hissed. "Keep those horses steady."

Victor tightened his grip on the reins of both his and the captain's steeds.

Thornton moved his gaze to the rooftops of the buildings a little farther along the street. If the marksman, or team of marksmen, were on top of the structures, they were buried in the snow and could tolerate the freezing conditions, or they were out of view behind the peaks of the roofs or hidden in the darkness of alleys and behind the fences below.

Or maybe they had left the area entirely.

The captain didn't think the region was clear of any enemy soldiers. He figured that the marksmen, if there were more than one, still occupied the street.

He looked back at the men gathered behind him.

They had all dismounted and held their mounts by the straps.

"Tether the horses to something," he whispered, loud enough for the men to hear. "We go on foot until we clear this area."

The men complied, tying their chargers to fences, pylons, and posts. Thornton then split the soldiers into groups, commanding some to take back lanes, hop over small walls into yards, and move around and behind the buildings that lined the street.

"Locate and dispose of anyone that isn't friendly," he commanded them.

He, on the other hand, took a team of five men, including Victor, into the street where Kristoph rested.

Slowly, guardedly, they kept to the walls as they crept along, watching the rooftops, eyeing the dark passages to the sides of the road, spying the windows and doors for any sudden movement.

Thornton peered at the body in the street. The gentle snow drifting down had started to cover Kristoph, filling the depressions in his face to cover his eyes and building up against the side of his nose.

The dark blood that had spilled over his skin and onto the street had frozen in place. His flesh had turned a pasty grey and almost appeared as porcelain.

Victor uttered his friend's name.

"Shhh," Thornton hissed in response, turning his gaze to the roofs again.

The captain felt eyes upon them. Someone, or something, was watching.

He continued to move along the front of a store, glancing into the window only to see darkness inside.

A sudden shuffling sound prompted him to freeze in place.

The men beside him followed suit. All five of them looked around. They had all heard the sound.

"Could be one of ours," one man whispered.

Thornton nodded. He had considered that.

The sound recurred, and this time a small portion of frost fell from an awning sticking from a structure beside the shop, only a few paces from where they stood.

The captain tilted his head warily, trying to find the source of the sound and see what had caused the clump of snow to fall to the ground.

There was nothing, at least from what he could tell.

He looked back along the line and pointed to two of the men following him. He then gestured to a lane across the way.

The two men raced into the street, leaping over Kristoph's body.

A loud thwack, followed instantly by a quick click, emitted from above Thornton's position.

A timber shaft stuck firmly into the neck of one man crossing the road. The other turned about instinctively and looked at the rooftop above the captain.

"One man," he called out. "Crossbow. Directly above you."

Thornton heard the cords of the weapon being cranked taut. The marksman was reloading.

No other bolts appeared to take down the second man, leaving the captain to believe there was only one person on the roof.

There was only one marksman in the region.

"My position," Thornton hollered. "My position."

TWACK!

CLICK!

I hit the second man on the road square in the chest.

Now there were three bodies in the street.

A loud clatter arose as the cavalrymen, all on foot, hastily made their way to the captain.

Victor and one of the other men were already looking for a place to climb onto the roof.

"There." Thornton pointed to a series of crates piled against the wall in a thin alley between the store and the building with the awning.

Victor was first to climb.

Thornton ran into the street and looked up at the top of the shop.

A white soldier crouched upon the roof, cranking the crossbow's cord back into place. He peered down to Thornton before glancing over his shoulder to see Victor pushing himself onto the roof.

The soldier dropped the crossbow and pulled his sword free, preparing to fight Victor. When the other cavalryman clambered up after the first, the white soldier reconsidered and placed his attention back upon Thornton down below.

The rest of the men hadn't yet reached the street, but the increasing noise signalled their imminent arrival.

Considering his odds, and making a quick calculation, the white soldier jumped from the rooftop towards the captain waiting in the street.

Thornton was ready, blocking the white soldier's blade with his own before lifting his boot into the enemy's crotch.

The marksman crumpled to his knees, holding his manhood with one hand while swinging his blade wildly at the captain with the other.

With a simple block and parry, Thornton kept the marksman's desperate blows at bay. A swift heel to the white soldier's face sent him sprawling onto his back. His sword went skidding across the street.

Thornton pushed the tip of his blade into the marksman's throat.

The soldier gagged and coughed, spraying blood into his own face and over his white tunic.

A few of the cavalrymen appeared on the scene. Victor and the other man with Thornton moved back into the street.

The captain sheathed his sword as he watched the white soldier choke.

"A fitting death for a coward who hides in the shadows to do his killing rather than face his enemies head-on," said a cavalryman.

"He served his purpose," Thornton said, looking at the three men that had fallen victim to the marksman.

Sixteen

"How many does that make?" Vawdrey asked the lieutenant as he watched Jendryng climb onto the roof of a house.

"Five," Brook replied.

"No." The other shook his head, pointing to the scorpion weapon they had destroyed. "Not those bloody things. How many men do you think we have killed?"

"Was I meant to be keeping count?" the lieutenant queried as he looked up to the younger soldier, who was standing near the peak of the house's roof and peering to the north.

"I don't know." Vawdrey shrugged. "It just seems that the farther we go in towards the middle of this city, the more we come across."

"So?"

"So, don't you think that's a little strange? I mean, wouldn't you put most of your defences on the edge of the city to stop bastards like us from getting anywhere near it in the first place?"

"If I were in charge of the defences, yes." Brook frowned. "I would do anything to stop a bastard like you from getting into my city. But I would consider the people of the city. This Maji is probably hiding up in that palace, and I would bet that he has placed most of his swords nearer to the wall surrounding it because he couldn't give two slices of shit about the people down here."

"Tents," Jendryng called down to them. He was gesturing towards the northeast of their position, away from the direction of the towering structure that overlooked the city. "Looks like a command centre. Lots of soldiers."

"About time," Sparrow growled. He looked around to the rest of the infantry that moved through the city with them. "Now, these lads can finally get their hands dirty instead of it just being us leading the attack."

"We still lead the attack," Brook informed him. "You lot are the most experienced men I have with me."

"That's because we're the only men you know here, sir," Vawdrey told him with a wry smile. "You should really get out more often. Meet some new people. Make more friends."

"Shut up," Brook grunted as Jendryng lowered himself from the house to return to the group.

"Couldn't see any of those weapons over there," the younger man reported.

"That doesn't mean there aren't any," Sparrow countered.

"Doesn't matter," Brook told them. He turned to Jendryng. "How far?"

"Not very. Maybe a hundred yards over there. Looks as though it's in a bit of a clearing. A yard or something."

"Another plaza," said Vawdrey. "What's the bet? Plaza or market square. What I've seen of this city so far has been only plazas and market squares with some houses in between. Should have called it Plaza-Marketsquareland, or something."

"What's the difference?" Jendryng enquired. "A market square is a plaza, isn't it?"

"No, you idiot." Sparrow winced. "Market squares are for markets and a plaza is an open area with seats for sitting in."

"Which sometimes have markets in them." Vawdrey smiled.

"Who'd want to sit about in this?" the younger man asked, holding his hands up to the falling snow.

Vawdrey gave him a puzzled look. "It doesn't snow all fucking year around, does it?"

Jendryng looked at each of them dumbly.

"Well," he said, shrugging. "I don't know. I haven't been here before. Have I? Could snow right through summer for all I know."

"Well, it doesn't," Sparrow said, glaring at the younger soldier. "Take a look around. There are bloody gardens and trees that do better in warmer weather. So, it doesn't snow in summer."

Brook shook his head. "Can we simply focus, gentlemen? You can talk about all the snow and trees and gardens you like after this is over. Right now, I would like to discuss whether we should take down that command post or not."

"Sorry sir," Vawdrey said.

"Yeah, sorry sir," Sparrow put in.

"Sorry," Jendryng said, sounding like a child being discovered doing the wrong thing.

"How many men?" Brook questioned the younger soldier, bringing them back into focus.

"I couldn't say," the other answered. "A lot more than a hundred."

"What do we have?" Sparrow asked. "Numbers-wise, I mean."

"A little over eighty," the lieutenant replied. He looked doubtful as he scanned the men in the street they were standing in. Most of the infantry had gathered about the fire that engulfed the disabled scorpion weapon. Others were checking the bodies of fallen white soldiers for new weapons and supplies worth appropriating.

"We can do it," Sparrow assured him, seeing the uncertainty in his lieutenant's eyes. "Come on, Hugh. We can do this. You know it."

It was rare for the Sparrow to refer to his superiors by first names. The only times he recalled it being done before was once during a drinking game when they visited a tavern in Newholt many years before, and once when the odds were against them during a conflict with marauders that had been raiding villages in the mountains near their city. The words Sparrow spoke then were not dissimilar to the ones he spoke now.

Brook nodded. He didn't need any convincing. They had to take the command centre, if that was what it was. "All right," he called out, gaining the attention of the rest of the infantrymen. He beckoned the men over to him with a wave of his hand. "We have a command post that needs our assistance with its dismantling."

"Yes," said Sparrow, smiling as he peered at the other two men beside him.

***

Freed and Grosset, dressed in dark armour with white tunics draped over the top, stood side by side near to a small fire to the northern edge of the market square. They sheltered beneath a large tarpaulin hoisted upon poles and held taut by thin ropes.

There was some hustle and bustle as a large number of soldiers moved about, using axes, hammers, and ropes to prepare large timber blockades with wooden spikes. Other uniformed men moved the newly constructed barriers into the streets along the southern edge of the square, hoping to slow the advancing combined forces from Newholt and Woodmyst heading their way. Still more white soldiers ran to and fro, passing reports and updated messages to the two superior officers, regarding the progress of certain stations throughout their quadrant of the city.

Sadly for them, the reports had been coming in less and less frequently as the evening drew on, signalling that they were losing ground.

"We should have brought a tent," Grosset said, rubbing his hands together over the flames.

"Put your gloves on, then," Freed told him, stamping his feet to keep warm.

"Yeah," the other replied sarcastically. "Because yours made you so warm and toasty, didn't they?"

"My hands, yes," said Freed. "It's the rest of me that feels this bitter frost."

"Bitter," Grosset huffed. His breath floated before him in a white cloud before dissipating into the frigid air. "Why are we out here? What good can we do here that we can't do up there in the palace, or the barracks?"

"Don't know," answered Freed, shrugging his shoulders as if trying to touch his ears. He shivered.

"I bet the Commander is up there," Grosset muttered. "Standing by that nice big fire in the throne room."

"She wouldn't be in the throne room," Freed said, shaking his head. "If anything, she'd be in the barracks barking orders at everyone, or riding Willis like a wild pony."

"Wild pony." The other smiled.

Both men erupted in laughter.

A soldier came running over, forcing the two officers to straighten up and curb their blitheness.

"Colonels," the man called as he stopped before them to salute.

"Colonels?" Freed questioned. "I don't remember getting a promotion, yet these lads have been calling us that all day."

"Who told you to call us colonels, soldier?" Grosset asked.

"Nobody, sir," the man replied, offering a puzzled look. "I just heard others say it, so I presumed…"

"All right." Grosset held his hand up to silence the soldier. "What have you got for us?"

"Reports that two more of our ballistae burn just to our south," the soldier told them. "The enemy is approaching from two sides."

"Thank you," Grosset replied, dismissing the soldier with a quick nod.

As the man moved away in haste, Grosset turned to Freed and said, "We're not ready for them. We haven't completed building the blockades and putting them in place yet."

"No time," Freed offered, moving his gaze across the square. "We'd best gather the men and place them into defensive positions instead."

"Agreed," the other replied, moving away from the fire and out into the open. "I'll call them together. At least we might get a little warm during a fight. What do you think?"

"I still think I'd rather be in the barracks with Versel shouting down my neck," replied Freed, smiling.

The smile faded fast as the sound of screams and swords clashing erupted on the western edge of the market square.

"Shit," Grosset hissed. "They're already here."

The two men raced across the market square, all other white soldiers nearby joining them as they sprinted to the east. They saw their men massing near the entrances of three separate narrow streets. The throng was building, pushing the men together tighter and tighter.

The white soldiers piled into the thin roads bordered by lofty buildings on either side, forcing them to funnel from the market square and into a small confined and restricted area.

The only advantage they had was their numbers.

Screams and blood spraying above the heads of the men inside the three channels to the front of the swarm informed the two officers that their numbers were slowly dwindling.

The enemy forces wanted them to move into the streets. They wanted to draw the white soldiers away from the market square.

They wanted the fight to be on their terms.

***

"Who came up with this brilliant plan?" Jendryng asked sarcastically, slicing one of the white soldier's faces open as he hacked his blade into the throng carelessly.

"Bloody Sparrow," Vawdrey replied, stabbing his blade over and over at no one in particular, hitting something every time. One of his own men nudged his shoulder. "Hey."

"Sorry, sir," the other replied, also digging his sword into the crowd of white soldiers.

They were all packed in tightly, both sides facing each other in very close combat.

"Sparrow," Jendryng spat. "I hope he's having as much fun as we are."

"I don't," snarled Vawdrey. "I hope someone does this to him." He chopped his sword through the helmet of an enemy soldier, sending a thick spray of blood into the face of another behind him. "And this,"

Vawdrey yelled as he pulled his dagger from his belt to slit the throat of another. "And maybe this," he hollered, sticking a third white soldier in the eye with the dagger before plunging his sword into the belly of a fourth.

"I think that's a bit harsh," Jendryng said, frowning, as he lopped the head from his opponent.

***

"I met a girl from Byview," Sparrow sang, as he hacked and thrust and chopped with his blade, almost in cadence. He sang loudly and un-apologetically, hitting sour notes and grunting noisily with each attack of the blade. "Who gave herself to me. She had no teeth and had no hair, and her eyes could barely see."

Within moments of him starting the song, the men with him, fighting by his side in the narrow street, pressed against his shoulders, joined in together.

"I gave her bronze for bedding," they chorused. "She wrapped her legs 'round me. There's no other girl like the Byview girl, who made my balls itchee."

The sound echoed and shook through the air.

The sudden frivolity exhibited by the men of Newholt and Wood-myst took the white soldiers aback.

"I met a girl from Freymoor, who gave herself to me. She had no arms and had no hair, And her tits were all saggy."

***

"Bloody heck," Brook growled, hearing the commotion rising from the next street over. It was so loud, not even the clash of swords could dull it.

"I gave her gold for bedding," a few of his men beside him started. "She wrapped her legs 'round me."

As he pulled his sword from the neck of a white soldier, a fine spray of red lifting into the air, he simply shook his head and joined in.

"There's no other girl like a Freymoor girl, who made my balls itchee."

***

"Singing?" Grosset stared at the spraying blood that spattered against the stone walls of the houses lining the streets. "They're singing a fucking song?"

"High spirits?" Freed shrugged.

"Or a bunch of madmen," the other suggested. "We outnumber them and they are singing a song while they slaughter us? How many of their men have we cut down?"

Freed shook his head, peering into the three streets along the western edge of the marketplace.

"I can't tell," he answered. "All of our men are in the way."

Grosset looked into a road leading to the south and saw a blockade with its spikes facing away from them. There were no men on the road there. No enemy approaching.

It suddenly dawned on him.

They had only placed the obstacles in the streets to the immediate south of the market square. None of the ways into their position, to the west or east, had blockades in place yet.

He turned about, moving his attention to the eastern streets, and felt a sudden movement in his trousers as he lost control of his bowels.

Fifty horsemen were charging into the market square, blades held high and the glare of wrath upon each of their faces.

Grosset tapped Freed on the shoulder.

The other turned, offering Grosset a confused look.

Grosset dropped his sword and vomited over himself. His skin turned pasty as he dropped to his knees.

Freed followed the other's gaze and saw what had caused the reaction in his comrade.

It was too late to do anything about it.

***

Thornton ran his steed directly over the kneeling man as he slid his blade through the neck of the other.

"Kill them all," he roared, directing his charger to the centre of the throng.

It took the white soldiers a little time to realise what was happening.

Men started dropping around them suddenly.

Blood sprayed upon them from both the front and from behind.

One of them turned to see Thornton bearing down on him. He let out a loud cry, signalling an alarm for the others to hear.

"Horsehhhs—" was all he managed before his head came free.

Screams and clashing swords ensued as the cavalry made quick work of any men racing back into the market square, desperately trying to escape.

The eastern infantry continued to hack their way through the white soldiers of the west in the three thin streets.

The song suddenly silenced shortly after the cavalry attacked, when the Wintermarsh men started back into the market square.

The streets opened a little, allowing the infantry to stretch their arms and move their legs as they pursued the white soldiers.

Swords clashed.

Axes hacked and chopped.

Daggers stabbed and sliced.

Before long, blood-soaked white tunics and bodies lay strewn across the ground throughout the three narrow streets and across the square.

Thornton sat on his steed in the centre of it all, taking in the scene of carnage about him. The cavalrymen formed up behind him.

Brook moved into the area from the western street on the far right, caked in blood and wearing a broad smile as he looked over at the captain.

Vawdrey and Jendryng appeared from the far left, in a similar state to the lieutenant.

"Glad you came, Captain," the younger soldier remarked.

"Where's Sparrow?" Thornton asked.

"There's no other girl like a Linport girl," came a voice from the centre road, singing loudly and terribly out of tune. He and the men walking behind him covered in glistening red streaks that dripped from their skin, armour and swords. "Who made my balls itcheeeeee."

Seventeen

"It will be all right," Isabel told the two little girls.

They had both climbed onto the laps of the Gold and Lilac Queens. All four were blubbering, moving their eyes to the many cracks that had formed in the walls of the marble throne room.

The great calamity that had seen the earth near the centre of the city, tossed about like leaves on the wind and struck with bolts of light from the sky, which had also set the region aflame, had spread its tendrils into the grounds of the palace and deep into the monolithic structure itself.

Across the room from the queens, near the enormous fireplace, a few guards had gathered to watch over the women, and to keep warm.

Isabel had moved her chair so she could hold their hands and console the girls face to face. She too was frightened, but a secret part of her wanted victory for the enemy.

Anything to bring her husband a nasty defeat.

Her tongue kept touching the cut in her lip, given to her by Takmel.

"We will be free of him soon," the White Queen continued. She moved her gaze over the four seated before her. "All of us."

"But, at such a significant cost, Isabel," Sarah sniffled. "Is there no other way?"

She shook her head.

"I don't believe—"

"There you are," his voice thundered as he stormed into the room. "I've looked everywhere."

His damson cloak spread out behind him as he strode quickly across the floor. He reached over the women's laps and took the girls' arms forcefully.

"What are you doing?" Christina protested, instantly placing her hand over the bandaged wound on her head.

Takmel glared at her angrily as he pulled the twins away, cruelly dragging them across the floor.

"Come," he shouted. "You are both required."

The two little girls looked at the three women with wide, frightened eyes in a silent plea for help.

"Braden," Sarah called to a scarred man standing by the inglenook. He understood the command, pulling his sword free and stepping towards the Maji.

As he did so, the Lilac Queen repented of her decision to call for his aid.

"Just a boy," Braden mumbled, attempting to calm his nerves. "Nothing more."

Takmel saw the other's shadow approaching.

He thrust the girls to the floor roughly, and turned on his heels, reaching a hand towards the twins as he stretched the other out to the scarred guard.

Braden lifted his sword.

The two girls moved, as if being pulled involuntarily, slightly towards Takmel.

"Very brave," said the Maji. "Very foolish."

The four scars across Braden's face opened wide. He let out a shrill scream as his skin split open, spilling bright blood over his uniform. A loud clang resonated through the throne room as Braden dropped his sword to the stone floor. His flesh peeled from his face with a grotesque ripping sound.

"It takes a courageous man to face me, and you must be the most courageous of all," Takmel sneered. "Not because you came at me with your sword. No." He shook his head. "Because you thought you could take what is mine," the Maji continued, tightening his hold on Braden.

The guard screamed a shrill cry as his right eye popped from its socket, only to dangle lethargically against his blood-smeared cheek from a thin tendril. "I don't much care what my brides get up to in their own homes, the homes that I have given them. The homes they abandoned. But here, under my roof, in my home, Braden, no one but I get to lie with my queens."

Smattering crimson puddles spread across the clean, white marble floor.

The screaming ceased.

The sickly wet sound of tissue tearing away from the bone reverberated around the room, making the others witnessing the event feel their stomachs churn and their fear growing.

Takmel released the man from his grasp by lowering his hands slowly to his sides.

Braden slumped. His freshly skinned skull clunked noisily as it hit the stone floor.

The twins breathed rapidly, as if they had just exerted themselves.

Sarah screamed, her cry echoing from the walls and ringing throughout the room.

"Anyone else?" the Maji enquired, peering angrily at the other guards standing by the inglenook.

None responded except to look at what remained of the scarred man.

Takmel reached down, took both of the girls by their arms again and dragged them away, out of the room, unchallenged.

"Where is he taking them?" Christina gasped.

Sarah stared at the faceless body of her personal guard. She wasn't able to look away. The whiteness of the bone was almost comparable to the brightness of the marble room itself. The blood surrounding the fleshless skull, dripping from it, spreading from the cavities, was almost beautiful to observe.

She felt immense guilt for this poor soul.

For ordering him to intervene on her behalf.

For commanding him to lie with her.

For falling in love again.

"We need to act now," Isabel told them. She moved her gaze to the Lilac Queen.

"Braden," the other whispered, tears streaming down her cheeks.

"Sarah? Did you hear me?"

"Braden," she said again.

"Sarah?" Isabel called louder, putting her hand on the other's arm.

"Huh?" she snapped out of her trance. "Yes. I heard. We need to act now."

"Good." The White Queen looked over at the men by the fireplace. They were all gawking at the fresh corpse on the floor. "Guards?"

"Yes, my queen?" one of them replied.

"Escort us to the kitchen," she commanded.

"The kitchen?" he repeated, confused. After what had happened, he couldn't believe that someone would want to visit the cook or raid the larder.

"The kitchen," Isabel said again, rising to her feet. She took Sarah by the hand and pulled the stunned woman to her side.

"Yes, my queen." He bowed slightly and started to the door. The other men positioned themselves around the three women as they moved out of the throne room. Sarah looked to the remains on the floor as Isabel towed her away, holding her stare until she could see Braden no more.

***

Takmel pulled the twin girls out through the main doors of the palace. Soldiers were running about this way and that. The smell of smoke and death was abundant in their nostrils.

Both girls would have given anything to be back in their little farmhouse, alone with only one another to keep company. Anything but this.

"Look." Takmel let them go and pointed to the sky. They would have run, but they were too afraid of him. "Take a look."

They followed his gesture to see swirling clouds above the city. Nothing more.

"Wait for it," he told them. "Keep looking."

A moment later, twenty-three dragons appeared. The girls felt their hearts leap in their chests. Their breathing became erratic and their fears intensified.

Never had they seen such a terrible sight.

The beasts fell rapidly and breathed long jets of fire over the ground in places yet to be damaged by their touch. Soon after, they swooped back into the sky, leaving a great sound like fabric being torn as they cut through the air and vanished back into the clouds.

"When they come back," he sneered, taking each of the girls by a shoulder and glaring into their faces, "I want you to bring them down."

They looked at him, perplexed.

"Maji," a woman's voice called. He looked past the two little girls to see Commander Versel returning. "I have the mother, and a gift."

"A gift?" He moved his gaze to the other riders. There, he saw the four prisoners draped over the horsemen's laps. They rode a little farther into the courtyard before tipping their cargo onto the ground.

Each of the women landed with a hard thud.

"Three witches," the commander replied.

"Oh, my!" Takmel clasped his hands together joyously. His eyes fell directly upon one of the three in particular. "Hello, dear wife."

Catherine, gagged and bound with her hands behind her back, spat a barrage of unintelligible muffles and angry groans.

"I missed you, too," he said, smiling, moving closer and closer. "Don't worry. I won't hurt you. Not until I am done with these two first." He crouched inches away from her face as he looked at Amicia and Ursula. "After that, I'll take you into my bed chamber. After that, I'll give you to my men to play with. After that, I'll kill you.

"But first, your mother," he said, standing to full height. "I'm afraid she won't get to enjoy my company as much as you. She will be leveraged.

"Alice will surrender," Takmel continued. "Or I will kill your mother right here. If she surrenders, she is to become my wife by force, if necessary. Your mother will become my property to do as I wish." The Maji smiled.

Catherine emitted a throng of garbles and muffled screams.

"If your sister doesn't surrender, then I suppose I'll just have to..." As he spoke, the dragons appeared again. He rushed back to the twins and turned them about on the spot with his hands before pointing to the sky. "There they are. Do it."

They looked at him, confounded.

"As you did to the soldiers when they killed your father and raped your mother," he said coldly. "Focus on the dragons and rip them to shreds."

Their breathing became quick. Tears streamed down their cheeks.

"No, you little bitches," he growled before slapping each of them over the head. The strikes were hard, emitting sharp sounds that clicked loudly. "Not cry. Kill. Do it!"

They bawled.

He slapped the crowns of their heads.

"Do it!" he repeated over and over, slapping their faces, their backs and their ears.

Suddenly, their eyes emitted a white glow.

"Yes," he hissed. He pointed to a dragon swooping nearer to the palace than the others. "Do it. There."

They were angry. They were focused. They wanted so much to tear the flesh from their husband, but they were too fearful of him.

Instead, they did his bidding. They joined hands and concentrated on the dragon.

The giant beast faltered as it fell. It let out a loud chirp.

Ribbons of flesh tore away from its wings. Its throat opened as its skin and tissue transformed and broke into strips.

The dragon fell, trailing a line of blood behind it.

The Haigok rider desperately pulled the reins this way and that in desperation to level the beast's trajectory, but to no avail.

A loud crash and deep rumble ensued as the beast rolled clumsily over buildings, demolishing anything standing in its way.

"Yes," Takmel cheered, pumping a fist into the air. He turned to the girls and smiled proudly. "Now do it again."

Eighteen

The boy peered up the steep, almost sheer, rocky wall of the immense mound upon which the palace grounds were located. He could see the winding road that snaked up its side, partially wrapping around from the south to the east, where the giant gateway sat far above him.

The woman in armour had led her soldiers, laden with their four prisoners, along the road and into the grounds. He could not follow them.

They had posted guards along the path at intervals of fifty yards, from the base of the rise, all the way to the guardhouse by the gate.

The only way, he surmised, was to climb the rock face and keep to the shadows of the clefts and crevices as much as he could.

Hand over hand, stretching his legs to find secure footing, he started the ascent. The way was slippery. The heaped snow offered false places to grasp and apply his weight, causing him to stumble.

He hadn't traversed very far before his worn boots slipped. His chin struck against stone and his teeth dug into his tongue.

The unmistakable taste of blood filled his mouth.

The pain was immense, and he cried.

Part of him wanted to give up. A little voice told him he was only a boy and that he shouldn't try to undergo such an impossible task. The same voice explained that he didn't owe these people anything. He didn't really know them.

Another voice, a sterner voice, told him to look upwards and press on.

He spat the blood from his mouth, wiped the tears from his eyes and pressed on, carefully checking each finger and foothold before firmly placing his weight on the rocky, slippery surface.

***

The White Queen moved through the corridor with a purpose in mind. Her face was like flint as she gripped a meat cleaver in her hand. Christina and Sarah were on her heels, one with a carving knife, the other with a serrated-edged bread knife they had collected from the kitchen. The accompanying guards filed into the passageway behind them, keeping close to the three women.

They rounded corners swiftly, burst through closed doors, and finally reached the entry hall of the palace.

The large doors were wide open, giving a grand view of the activity in the courtyard.

Isabel stopped in her tracks.

She saw Takmel standing by the twins, smiling as he watched a dragon tumble from the sky, trailing flames from its mouth and copious amounts of blood from its belly, like a macabre falling star.

She saw the horses with their armoured riders and the infamous Saruun Versel seated high upon her steed.

Her stomach tightened, and a fine trickle of sweat dribbled down her spine.

None of these was what caused her to freeze in place.

Her stare fixed upon the auburn woman lying on the ground by the commander's charger.

Emily, bound and gagged.

The White Queen almost dropped the cleaver.

Something of home gripped her heart and brought tears to her eyes.

Woodmyst was here.

Watching, Isabel saw two guards lift the auburn woman from the ground and drag her away from view. Six more guards passed by the door with three more prisoners. She believed one of them was Catherine, but the guards took them away too fast for her to be certain.

"Was that Emily?" Christina enquired. Her voice sounded nervous.

At that moment, a soldier stepped in through the door. All three women instantly hid the kitchen knives behind their backs before the uniformed man could see them.

"Begging pardon, my queens. The commander has ordered the acquisition of your guards into the city's defences. They are to accompany me to the barracks immediately."

"Immediately?" Isabel queried.

"Yes, my queen," the other replied before turning away and retreating through the door.

"Sorry, Your Majesty," one of the white guards said with a bow before following the soldier through the door.

The three women stood alone in the entrance hall of the palace, peering out to the cold, cruel scene beyond the open doorway.

The White Queen felt her cheeks turning hot.

Abruptly, she turned from the door to retrace her steps back into the depths of the palace.

Versel had returned. No doubt, Takmel would keep her close by to assure his safety.

That would make it difficult for the three brides of the Maji to fulfil their secret plot.

Emily was his prisoner, and it appeared the three witches of Alice's coven as well.

"Where are we going?" Sarah asked, attempting to keep up with the others.

"I need to think," the White Queen replied. "Circumstances have changed. Takmel has the upper hand."

"What do you mean, he has the upper hand?" Christina questioned as they entered the sitting room.

Isabel moved to the fireplace, where bright orange flames licked at a few chocks of wood.

"I mean," she began, "he has three of the Four bound and gagged. He has Emily under guard and will plan to use them in order to draw Alice into the open. He may even convince her to turn to him and be with him."

"All the more reason to strike now," said the Gold Queen.

"His favourite soldier has returned," Isabel replied. "He'll keep her close."

Sarah, the Lilac Queen, furrowed her brow as she listened to the other's words. She peered into the flames and saw Braden. Her thoughts revisited the scene in the throne room where her guard's face tore open under the control of Takmel's magic. She remembered Braden's touch, his lips pressed to hers, and how she hadn't felt the way she did with him since Stephen.

Stephen's touch had been soft, delicate and had seemed to move through her, sending tingles of ecstasy from the tips of her toes to the top of her head. How he held her every night by their fireplace in the colder times, on their porch when the summer came, in their bed before they slept. How she had wanted so much to give that man a child, and how they had tried.

She missed him deeply, and she shed tears for him as the flames danced in the fireplace before her. She mourned for him, right there in the sitting room of the White Palace of Wintermarsh; something that she hadn't the opportunity to do until that moment.

A great lump formed in her throat as she remembered holding a knife in her hand, similar to the one she held now, taken from the kitchen in her little house in Woodmyst. She recalled how she had plunged it into Stephen's throat, her dear husband's throat, and used the serrated edge to tear the skin and tissue wide open.

He had looked at her, his eyes wide with fear, confusion, a silent question asking her *why?* But, beneath it all, she saw love. Even then, when she was killing him, he still loved her.

She had not experienced such pleasure, such devotion, from Takmel. He had simply taken her when it suited him; the first time to gain total control of her. Other times were for his pleasure only, not hers.

There were no considerations taken for her desires. He'd come to her, then leave satisfied. She had merely become an empty vessel for him to use as he pleased. They all had.

But he was already in her before then.

Long before.

His influence, careful whispers and manipulative ways had crept deep into most people's hearts in Woodmyst, including hers, a long time before he showed his true self. Dropping to her knees and sobbing profusely, Sarah suddenly recollected how she had carved her husband, Stephen, into small pieces and boiled him in a pot over the stove. The memory almost made her violently ill.

Takmel had done that to her. He had done that to all of them. He had driven them to madness, shaping them, steering them into a hell from which there was no escape.

She could never escape.

Never.

"What's the matter?" Isabel asked, crouching beside her.

"He took them both from me," she sobbed. "First Stephen, then Braden. He took everything I love."

"He did that to all of us," Christina told her. "But what can we do? Our powers are lacking compared to his. We have no prime to guide us, and he has the girls."

"And Versel's guards surround him now," Isabel added. "We can't get to him. There's no way."

Sarah wiped her eyes and looked to each of them.

"I think I know a way," she told them. "But I don't think either of you will like it."

***

Commander Zakhar crept along thin streets and alleyways near the dockyards.

The men fanned out into side streets and slowly spilled into the western quadrant of Wintermarsh. They had found some white soldiers here and there, congregating in small groups of four or five at a time. The navy men disposed of the soldiers quickly and quietly, in an attempt to not draw unnecessary attention to them as they moved to the east, deeper into the city.

Zakhar was attempting to put a decent amount of ground between his men and the waterfront, knowing that the large fire still burning along the piers would be enough of a draw for the soldiers of Wintermarsh. He surmised that the soldiers who would reinforce those stationed at the docks would come from the palace, not from the city. So, he led his men to the east first, intending to turn north once they had moved inside the city far enough to evade a mass of well-trained enemy combatants.

Zakhar, accompanied by almost four hundred men, came upon an open market area that had undergone some considerable damage. The immediate area appeared dishevelled and burning in places, mostly deserted. Only a few bodies of women and children lay scattered about, scarred with dark scorch marks. Some buildings had toppled, leaving only a wall or two standing in place. Three of the enormous shafts flung from the scorpion weapons protruded from the rubble.

The fleet commander quickly moved into the clearing, keeping low before ducking behind an overturned wagon near the centre of the square. Grady pulled to his side as the rest of the men silently moved into position behind toppled crates and debris that had fallen at some point during the day.

Zakhar quickly glanced at the bodies strewn about. A deep sorrow filled him as he took in the scene of silent faces holding silent screams as they stared lifelessly at the sky above, from where their terror had approached.

Casualties of war, the commander thought, trying to justify the carnage, as he looked about for white soldiers in waiting.

"Boatman," he heard a familiar growl hiss. "Over here."

He scanned the area before him carefully and saw nothing.

From behind some stacked barrels, pressed neatly against one of the few walls still intact, a large leathery hand stuck out and started waving.

"Boatman," the voice called again.

"Over there, sir." Grady pointed.

"I see," the other remarked. He stood to his full height and crossed the market area quickly.

The reptilian's hand gestured for him to move faster, but to keep low.

Some of the navy men rose to follow their commander. He turned and signalled for them to stay in place, summoning Grady to accompany him with hand gestures, as he continued to the Agrodien.

"Yuri." Zakhar smiled. "Good to see you."

"Shhh," the other hissed. He pointed along the road before them.

The street bent sharply to the left, obstructing any view of what lay ahead, but they could hear the mumbles of voices coming from that direction. "Twenty men," Yuri said. "We all go."

"Sounds like a plan," Zakhar said.

"Sir," Grady whispered. "The street looks narrow. Perhaps we should split the men and attack from two sides."

"No two sides," Nola'ee interjected. She pointed to the streets behind them. "Road is gone. This only way."

Zakhar looked to his first officer.

"We'll take ten men and follow Yuri's lead," the commander told Grady. "He is in charge from here on out."

"You command your men," Yuri said quickly. It wasn't an order, but more of a statement. "I command mine."

"You command all of us," Zakhar replied. "We fight from ships on the sea. You fight on land. We will follow your lead here. If you are ever on one of my ships, you will follow me instead."

The Agrodien pondered the other's words for a brief moment. He then offered a nod and a grunt, agreeing with Zakhar.

A great guttural cry thundered from the sky above.

They all peered up to see a dragon plummeting fast on a course towards the middle of the city. With its wings torn, it rolled uncontrollably as it fell. A long trail of blood, almost looking like a thick, crimson cloud, gushed out from its neck.

"No weapon attack," Bein uttered. "But dragon fall."

"They've been falling steadily," Grady put in. "There can't be all that many left now."

It vanished from their sight. The ground trembled slightly a moment afterwards.

Thornton felt a deep despondency. He hadn't had the chance to spend time with the Haigok and their beasts, but he had learnt enough to know they weren't the monsters they appeared to be. He had also come to know that the dragons were very few in numbers.

After today, who knew what their fate could be?

Without speaking, Yuri started along the street, crouching low and keeping his sword close to his body. He stepped quietly and quickly, moving as close to the wall on the left side of the road as he could.

The others followed in single file.

Grady pointed to a group of men and summoned them over, counting them off as they arrived and directing them after the Agrodien warriors.

Yuri paused at the edge of the structure to peer around the bend. He then beckoned the others to join him at his side. Soon everyone was in place.

"We attack as one," he growled. "Ready?"

The other reptilians nodded in response.

Zakhar wanted a little more time to assess the situation and to prepare his men, but before he could protest, the Agrodien warriors were racing around the bend in the street. They were silent and swift.

"Come on," Zakhar said to his men, racing after the twelve Agrodien, struggling to catch up.

As he ran, he saw the reptilians leap high. Their tails streaked out behind them. Their blades raised and pointed towards their prey.

They each landed on top of a soldier wearing a white tunic, crumpling the men to the ground. Their swords flashed skilfully about them, cutting down several others before any chance of retaliation.

Swords then clashed, sending ringing sounds into the street that grew louder and louder as Zakhar and his men raced as quickly as their legs could carry them to the scene.

During the skirmish, the reptilians' blades cut deep into the men beneath the Agrodien warriors' boots, removing limbs from bodies and dislodging a head or two from necks.

Zakhar arrived in time to plunge his sword deep into one Winter-marsh soldier, the only one left standing, who was also attempting to flee down the street at the seafarers' approach.

"Good work," Bein called to the commander as he pulled his sword from a fallen soldier.

"Glad to be of service," Zakhar replied, as his men finally caught up to him. All were puffing, out of breath.

"I have her scent." Yuri directed his blood-soaked sword to a street veering away to the north. "We go this way."

"Scent?" Grady huffed. "Whose scent?"

"The mother of Kayl'sro Alice," the Agrodien answered. "They take her."

"Sister of Kayl'sro, too," Nola'ee put in as she wiped the blood from her sword onto the tunic of a dead man. "And other witches."

Zakhar looked at the younger female reptilian, soaking her words in.

"Our main objective has changed, gentlemen," he said to the crew-men with him. "Our priority is to rescue Alice's mother and the others being held prisoner with her. Grady."

"Sir?" the first officer answered, still breathing hard.

"Send for the men," the commander ordered. "We go together."

"Aye, sir," the other replied, turning to a sailor to relay the order. Within a moment, the sailor was running back along the street towards the market square.

Bein had climbed a two-levelled building where he clung to the edge of the roof and peered to the north.

"What do you see?" Yuri asked him, speaking in their tongue.

"Men," the other replied. "Lots of them. Small fires and another weapon. One that flings boulders."

"Catapult," Nola'ee corrected him, using the word of the common tongue.

Grady moved his gaze to her.

"Did you just say catapult?"

"Yes," she answered. "Bein say he see one."

Zakhar looked to Yuri.

"Do you think we should disable it?"

"The weapon is no threat," he replied. "Catapult will damage city before it damage us. They won't use it." He sheathed his sword and looked about the street to the fallen white soldiers. "It's men we need to disable. They are in our way."

Nineteen

Willis peered through the iron bars of the cage, staring at the four women still bound and gagged in the tiny cell. He could see the resemblance in two of them, guessing they were related.

But mother and daughter?

They had informed him that this was the case, but the girl looked too old to be the daughter of the woman, who appeared much too young.

The other two bore no likeness to any either of those with auburn hair. Nor did they appear to have any similarity to each other.

"Not a bad one amongst them," said a guard standing nearby.

Willis shot him a reproving look. "Mind your manners."

"Sorry, sir."

"I don't need your apology," Willis corrected the guard.

The man peered at the officer, perplexedly.

"What?" the guard asked. "To them? They're the enemy."

"Yes, they are," Willis said coldly. "And they deserve to receive better manners from their hosts than what you have demonstrated."

"Piss on that," the guard spat. "Have you seen what has become of our home thanks to this lot? Fuck them and fuck your apology."

The others in the room stepped away from the bars, slowly moving back to an area with a trestle table and stove.

Willis reacted quickly.

The dagger slit the guard's throat open so swiftly; it was back in its place on Willis' belt before the first dribbles of blood appeared from the wound.

171

The guard crashed to the floor in a heap.

"Get that out of here," Versel said as she entered the room through a door across the way. She gestured to two guards before pointing to the fresh kill.

"Yes, General," they both replied before moving over to the body to drag it through the door she had just come through. A thick trail of blood snaked behind the dead guard.

"He was disrespectful, General," Willis reported.

"I heard," she replied, moving to the bars of the cell. She moved her gaze over the prisoners.

All four kept their eyes on the floor as they huddled against the wall as far away from the guards as they could get.

There were no cots to rest upon. No cushions to soften the stone floor upon which they sat. Not even a pile of straw.

The tiny prison cell was cold, hard, and deep with shadows. The only light came from a flickering torch posted on the wall outside the cell.

She sighed and leant against the cage, putting her hand to the bars.

"Fetch our guests blankets and water," the general commanded those within earshot. "Offer them some of whatever that stuff bubbling in the pot is."

"We were told not to take their gags out, General," one guard interjected. "On account that they might speak words and make things happen."

"Who gave you such instructions?" she asked. "The Maji?"

"No, General," the other answered, his voice shaking slightly.

"He didn't give me such instructions either," she said, turning to face the young man. "However, I gave orders for blankets and water. I also asked for food to be offered to the prisoners. They can't pull the blankets over themselves with bindings keeping their hands behind their backs, can they?"

"No, General," the guard replied. "But..."

"They can't drink or eat with gags in their mouths, can they?"

"No, General."

"Then," she said, moving away from the prison cell a short distance. "I command you to release these women of their bonds and remove their gags."

He stood motionless for a moment, hesitating as Willis opened the cell door.

Slowly, the guard stepped across the room, careful not to tread on the trail of blood left by the last man who disobeyed an order.

He pulled his dagger from his belt and moved into the cell, approaching Emily first. Carefully, he loosened her gag so that it fell over her chin to hang about her neck.

"Thank you," the auburn woman said, looking at Versel.

"Don't thank me," the general replied. "I am your captor and you are my prisoner. I offer you the only clemency I am permitted to by my master. Nothing more."

"Takmel allows you to feed us?" Emily asked, as her bindings were cut. She rubbed her wrists where the cords had dug into her skin. "I find that hard to believe."

"The Maji has not given specific instructions regarding how I am to treat you," Versel replied. She turned to the guards standing about behind her. "Food. Now."

The soldiers grabbed bowls from the table and crossed the room to the stove, where they dished out stew for the prisoners.

The guard in the cell moved to Catherine next.

"This one is your daughter?" the general asked, jutting her chin to the girl.

"My elder daughter, Catherine," Emily answered.

"You must have conceived her when you were very young," the uniformed woman supposed. "You don't appear that much older than her. But then, I have seen the White Witch of the Mirikin, and the brides of the Maji. All of them have held onto their beauty for many years longer than average women do. Would I be correct in assuming that you have some power inside of you also? Some quality of magic?"

Emily was uncertain how to answer, offering the general a puzzled look.

"You were the Maji's first bride," Versel said to Catherine.

Catherine spat the gag from her mouth as soon as it was loose enough.

"I hate him," she growled. Versel saw the ferocity in the girl's eyes.

"Most wives hate their husbands from time to time," the general supposed. "Especially if their husbands are cruel."

"You believe him to be cruel?" Emily asked as a soldier handed her a steaming bowl. "Why serve him if you think this?"

"It's not my place to question the traits of my master," Versel told her. "I am his servant. He commands me and I obey."

"Of your own free will?" Amicia questioned as her gag was lowered.

"Who of us is truly free?" asked the general.

Emily lowered the bowl from her lips. The concoction tasted salty and bitter. There was evidence of some kind of stringy meat amongst a variety of tiny portions of root vegetables.

"What do you plan to do with us?" the auburn woman asked.

"Keep you here," the general replied as two soldiers approached, carrying blankets. "Have these men watch you until the Maji requires you again. Bind and gag you before I take you to him."

"And, if he commands you to kill us?" Ursula asked, finally free of her bonds.

"I will comply with the Maji's commands," Versel answered, turning away.

"The two little girls with him," Emily said abruptly. The general stopped and twisted her head. "Who are they?"

Versel frowned, exposing just enough of her feelings to let Emily see the concern and worry that the blonde woman carried.

"They are his new brides," she replied. "His black and scarlet queens."

Emily felt a lump form in her throat as tears welled in her eyes.

"He has *taken* them?" the auburn woman enquired. Her voice was soft and caring.

The general gritted her teeth and let a tear fall over her cheek. She answered with a simple nod before starting away.

Emily shed tears of her own. She felt deep sorrow for the sake of the little girls, and immense anger towards Takmel. He was not the boy she knew and love. The boy she had fed and sheltered in her own home. That she had allowed near her own daughters.

"Monster," she whispered.

"Keep them warm and safe," Versel said to Willis. "Fetch more stew and blankets if they request them, and get some water for them immediately."

"And you?" Willis asked as she started for the door.

"I'll be with the Maji," she replied as she vanished from view.

***

The Agrodien led the charge.

They attacked the base camp from the south, sprinting into a plaza with large, paved areas that were tiered at slightly different levels. It appeared to be a place where one could speak and be seen by a large audience, similar to the design of the Assembly Hall in Woodmyst.

Or, at least as close to looking so as it could be, Yuri thought.

The Agrodien warrior skidded to a sudden hold, forcing the others behind him to follow suit before running into each other.

He scanned the area carefully. His ears could hear the boatmen approaching. He could taste the scent of man on his tongue. His eyes saw no soldiers in white.

The plaza was empty.

Tents and canvas shelters flapped quietly in the chilly breeze that filled the area. Small fires dotted the expanse. Snow continued to fall about them.

The sight was tranquil, almost peaceful if not for the glow of fire against the clouds of smoke rising into the sky throughout the city surrounding their position.

"What's this?" Grady queried, looking about in confusion. He turned to Bein. "I thought you said there were men in here."

"I see men everywhere," the reptilian replied, gesturing to the tents and fires. "They were here." He looked at Yuri and spoke in their tongue. "I'm no liar. I saw them. They were all over here."

"I believe you," the other growled, clasping a hand on the younger Agrodien's shoulder.

Nola'ee moved to a higher level to their left, where a large tent was erected. Nakrah was quick to follow, his sword clutched in his hand as he kept darting his eyes about.

"It's empty," she hissed, pulling the flaps back to peer inside. "But, I can..."

She moved her gaze to the plaza, peering to the four hundred men from the ships. She shook her head, as if disagreeing with herself, before turning her face to the empty region before them.

"It's not them," Nakrah assured her. "I thought so too, at first."

She slid her sword back into its sheath and pulled the bow from her shoulders, loading an arrow onto the string.

The two Agrodien crept quietly along the higher level, looking this way and that, sniffing the air and flicking their tongues past their lips.

Nola'ee saw something sparkle near the edge of a storefront wall. At first, she dismissed it to be nothing more than the firelight striking the frost at a strange angle.

But then she saw it again.

And again.

Moving closer to the wall, all the while keeping aware of the area ahead, she inspected the source of the strange reflection.

Glass.

Broken shards of glass lay scattered in the snow by the walls of the surrounding buildings.

She assumed it was damage caused by Ursula's quake, or perhaps it occurred during an attack from the dragons above.

In any case, the scent of man still wafted about her, and yet she could not see a soul.

Yuri held his hand up to the others, signalling for them to fall silent.

The navy men obliged, not because they were paying attention to the Agrodien commander, but because they could see the two on the higher ground stalking farther into the plaza, as if with purpose.

Zakhar, pressed against a wall where the building recessed into a small garden area, poked his head around the corner, peering to the upper level across the plaza from the two Agrodien warriors. There, he saw an extensive area where the upper rooms of the buildings protruded out, offering shelter to the storefronts and houses along its edge.

Peering back to Nola'ee and Nakrah, he noticed that no such cover was on offer for the entire length of the region. They had erected most of the tents and shelters along that side. Most of the small fires had been lit there, too.

He found it strange that the white soldiers had placed themselves on only one side of the plaza; the side that didn't offer any cover from the elements.

If he was commanding the men stationed here, he would have set up his command centre beneath the protruding upper rooms to the right. Even better, he thought, he would have used the little shops themselves and saved time pitching tents and makeshift shelters.

Little shops, he thought suddenly.

"Oh dear," he whispered, turning to Grady.

Continuing their progress, slowly and carefully stepping along the higher level, the two Agrodien warriors absorbed the aromas emitting from the region.

The smell of smoke filled the air about them, masking most things that filled the plaza. The cold drift of snow further suppressed the odours that they were attempting to focus upon.

As they passed tents and small shelters, they checked inside. The scent of man was thickest there, but it was always looming about them. Encompassing them.

She looked back at the men of the fleet. Nakrah grunted disapprovingly.

"It's not them," he told her.

He was right. They had moved too far away from the boatmen for their scent to linger as it did.

Her eyes moved back to the way before them.

There were more tents, more small fires and plenty of empty space.

The walls of the building surrounding the plaza were high and steep. The windows were dark and seemingly empty.

Then she noticed something.

The windows.

There was no glass in any of the windows.

They had all been smashed.

The glass in all the windows of the upper levels had been cleared.

Nola'ee spun on her heels, glancing about the edges of the plaza. She looked to the walls, the rooftops, the windows.

So many windows.

None with any glass.

Then, high above the congregated Agrodien and boatmen gathered near the plaza's southern entry point, she saw movement.

Inside of an uppermost level window of a building behind their position, a figure appeared.

The glint of an arrow tip gripped her attention.

The hand holding the bow protruded from the dark portal, directing the shaft towards the gathering on the ground.

Nola'ee was quick.

She lifted her bow, took aim, and shot her arrow.

It streaked through the air with a high-pitched whistle that resonated loudly through the empty plaza.

It struck the bowman in the chest. He dropped his weapon through the window, where it fell to the ground harmlessly. The archer slumped against the windowsill, his arms dangling.

"Take cover," Yuri roared for all to hear.

As the Agrodien and boatmen fled to the sides of the plaza, in a desperate attempt the find shelter and protection, hundreds of arrows jutted from the empty windows surrounding them.

The enemy had not abandoned their post.

They had been waiting all this time.

And now, the trap had been sprung.

"Loose," came a cry from a rooftop, far across to the northern edge of the plaza.

Countless arrows flung into the air.

Twenty

Hand over hand, Warren crept higher and higher up on the craggy surface of the immense mound. The palace towered far above him and the ground was a decent drop below. Still, he hadn't travelled very far. He was finding the process exhausting and slow.

The wind howled about him as snow struck his face, stinging his exposed skin. He shivered and clenched his fists, making tight balls, hoping to warm his frozen fingers. Now and then, he would touch the blade in his pocket by padding his hand against his coat.

Frequently, Warren needed to pause as soldiers marched along the road. He was a decent enough distance from the path that they took, but he still feared they might see him.

At first, he found it easy to evade their sight. The soldiers would stop to watch the dragons swooping over the city to the north whenever the creatures appeared through the clouds. The attacks from the air were short and the gawking white soldiers continued on their way when the dragons retreated from view.

During the attacks, Warren seized his moment and scrambled as quickly as the slippery rock surface would allow him. He never could make it as far as he intended, wishing the dragons would linger a little longer so he could climb higher more rapidly.

Alas, that strategy came to a close when the dragons engaged in a continuous onslaught of the northern sector of Wintermarsh. The soldiers dawdled as they moved along, commenting about the onslaught and cheering when a dragon fell.

Each time a beast tumbled to the ground, Warren felt his heart sink a little. He had found a thin crevasse to conceal himself as some men in white watched the sky from the road. They were peering in his direction, but they aimed their gaze much higher than his position.

It was during this time, after hearing the men getting a little rowdy, that he turned his head to see what had their attention.

A dragon spiralled to the ground. A great twisting ribbon of blood trailed behind it. The beast screamed so loudly that the air shook.

Warren sensed by its cry the pain and fear that the beast felt.

As the creature crashed into several structures on the ground, the men on the road cheered.

The stableboy couldn't comprehend why they were so extremely happy. He understood that one of their enemies had been vanquished, and that was probably good enough reason to rejoice, but several buildings lay flattened as well. There was a high possibility that people had perished inside.

Their people.

People of Wintermarsh.

Warren shuddered as he took a deep breath. The cold was biting through to the bone.

He waited patiently for the men to move on. It took some time for them to do so. They continued to watch the sky for some time, hoping to see another flying beast tumble through the air.

After a while, when they had waited far too long, they marched away.

Warren stretched his fingers, then made fists with his hands. He shook them rigorously, trying to get some feeling back into them.

He looked up to the tower of the palace, far away.

A quick pat with his hand against his coat pocket told him the blade was still there.

Hand over hand, he climbed again.

***

"Where are they going?" Larson shouted, glaring at twenty white soldiers running southward along a narrow street. He raised his voice so they could hear over the roar of fire erupting from the dragons not too far away. "Cowards."

The command centre they occupied was ablaze.

Everything burned.

"We should go after them," Walters suggested.

"And kill them all for their treachery," the other said, his face pent with rage.

"No," Walters replied, looking about the large yard area that had all of their equipment. Flames rolled over and lapped at the scorpion weapon. The catapult was in pieces, charred and smoking. The tents were gone and the surrounding buildings had all but crumbled. "We should move to the palace. The walls are thick. Perhaps too thick for these devils to break."

Another dragon swooped by, igniting the street where the fleeing soldiers were last seen.

"Serves them right," Larson huffed as flames and smoke filled his view.

"We can't stay here," Walters said, sounding more desperate as he peered into the sky.

Larson glared at him, the same way he had looked at the retreating soldiers.

"If you want to risk making your way to the palace, Walters, go right ahead," he returned.

"Risk?"

"You saw what that dragon just did." Larson gestured to the burning street. "Good luck with that. If you make it, you will have General Versel to deal with. Or worse, the Maji himself."

Walters looked at him, perplexed. His fears were intensifying each time a dragon appeared.

"I can't stay."

"Then go," Larson replied.

"Where will you be?" Walters asked, concerned for his friend.

Larson looked around at their surroundings. Most of the buildings were gone. There was no proper place to hold an advantageous stand against their enemy.

That was, until he spied a tower of sorts.

The corner of an inn's façade was still standing by the eastern edge of the clearing. The rest of the structure surrounding it had crumbled, but the bricks and mortar held in place there.

The inn was a building of two levels. What Larson could see was a thick supporting column built into the structure, with small portions of the upper floor and ceiling protruding from it. At the very top, a crooked section of the shingled roof stood in place.

"I'm going onto that," Larson stated.

Walters eyed the ruin. It was exposed, jutting out high from all the surrounding rubble. He furrowed his brow and turned back to the other. "Are you mad? They'll see you."

"I was assigned this post," said Larson, checking that he sheathed his sword securely. He started across the yard towards the projecting pinnacle. "I'll die defending it. You run along to the palace."

"You're a fool," Walters shouted after him. "You're an absolute fool, Larson."

He didn't stay to watch his friend begin the climb. Instead, he found another street to enter, beginning his retreat south, away from the dragons.

The rubble inside the toppled inn was a tangled mess. Bricks, stones, and broken furniture intermingled with pieces of the roof and upper flooring. Some were burnt and black, but other sections jutted from the wreckage and snow like long, pointed timber shards.

Larson placed his hands and boots carefully upon the broken bricks, locating points to grasp as he pulled himself from the ground. Inch by inch, he climbed the remains of the inn.

He was cautious when he reached the damaged section of the upper floor. There wasn't much to put his hands on. He checked to see how fixed to the wall it was by tugging on a thick beam extended from the bricks. When it appeared to be safe to use, he hoisted himself up to the level.

There was barely enough of a ledge to place his feet.

He used his time on the ledge to surmise his next move. His intention was to get to the tiny section of the rooftop.

Another dragon swooped by, this time directly over where he and Walters had been conversing. It drew low to the ground and let out a long jet of flame a little farther to the south.

Larson reached up and gripped a supporting beam that held what little of the roof there was in place. With all his might, he pulled himself up, lifting himself, his armour, and his sword onto the rooftop.

He felt exhausted.

He had to sit down to catch his breath and allow his muscles to relax.

His heart raced, and he felt his temples throbbing.

With a look about, he slowly took in the scenery below.

The devastation extended far beyond the yard where he had been. More toppled buildings lay in ruin in the streets to the east, west and north. Fires blazed to the northeast, past the edge of the city, where farms and plantations dotted the countryside.

My city is a wreck, he thought. He looked up as he heard a flying beast roar. It circled about, as if preparing to make an attack run.

He felt his temper rising again.

"My city is a wreck, and you bastards are the cause," he growled, rising to his feet and lifting his sword high.

The dragon turned, tilting slightly as it banked around. Larson saw it had no rider on its back.

It didn't matter.

The monster was destroying his city.

"Come on," he shouted, hoping the beast could hear him over the roaring wind.

The dragon turned sharper, faster, bending its neck so it faced the soldier standing atop of the little roof.

Larson's heart raced so hard, so fast, that he could feel it throughout his entire body. His breathing became rapid and sweat trickled down his back.

"Come on," he cried again as the dragon directed its approach towards him.

It lowered itself to skim over the rooftops, opening its jaws wide.

The soldier knew what would come next. He expected it. He wanted it.

"Come on," he whispered, gritting his teeth, ready for the flames to turn him to ash.

A loud creak and crack forced his attention to his boots.

The roof suddenly broke away from the remaining bricks of the corner portion of the inn.

Larson felt light, weightless, as he fell.

The back of his lower legs smashed into the tiny section of upper flooring. His knees snapped, bending both of his legs at an odd angle.

He cried out in pain, but not for long.

With a great wallop, he landed on the wreckage below.

It knocked out all the air in his lungs, his scream with it.

Shards of timber stuck in his back and out through his front; two in his belly, the last just below his chest plate, near the sternum.

His sword rested a few yards away, point in the ground and hilt high.

He tried to suck in some air, but couldn't.

His lungs burned.

Tears filled his eyes.

He was in so much pain.

Looking to the sky, he watched the dragon swoop overhead.

A great gust of wind trailed behind it, so great it caused the corner section of wall to rock and sway.

Oh no, Larson thought as a handful of shingles flittered from the rooftop, making their way towards him.

A loud groan ensued before the roof snapped from its hold and started toppling towards him.

It crashed upon his legs, causing him more agony, but he could not cry out, even though his face winced and opened its mouth to do so.

Another loud groan caused him to open his eyes wide.

One brick fell.

It toppled through the air.

Closer.

Closer.

Thud.

He looked at the brick, lying upon the rubble within reach of his head.

Another landed beside it.

Then another.

His wide-eyed gaze returned to the wall.

The groan had transformed into a series of breaking sounds; clinks and snaps.

The last standing piece of the inn was leaning towards him, tilting more and more as brick after brick broke away.

One of them hit him in the belly.

Another in the shoulder.

Tilting.

Tilting.

A brick struck his forehead, making his helmet ring in his ears and dig into his skin.

Leaning.

Leaning.

The sight of the entire wall breaking apart above him brought an inescapable sense of sheer terror.

He couldn't run.

He couldn't retreat.

The wall fell, blotting out his view of the sky above.

As blackness enveloped him, he heard a dragon cry out in the distance and one thought filled his mind.

Perhaps Walters is right. Perhaps you are a fool, Larson.

***

Walters sprinted towards the south. He kept peering to the palace on his right, believing that it was the most secure site in the city.

He also believed that at the rate the dragons were inflicting damage, there wouldn't be much of a city left soon enough.

Larson's words haunted him as he ducked for cover when a dragon flew above, or when he ran to the next shelter. They constantly swam about in his thoughts every time he saw the palace come back into view when he rounded a corner.

You will have General Versel to deal with. Or worse, the Maji himself.

The closer he got to the towering structure, the louder the voice would repeat the words, over and over.

Eventually, he made his way to the edge of the large destruction caused by the earth tremor and bolts of light from the sky. He had never seen such calamity in his life.

The ground was clear, with only a dusting of frost upon it from the falling snow.

What once was filled with houses, shops and many gardens was now dead.

There wasn't even a sign of remains. No structures. No people. Nothing.

The city surrounding the wide expanse seemed to burn all around.

Wintermarsh, from his point of view, was lost.

He looked at the palace again.

Tall, white and menacing, it appeared the only object in all the city still untouched.

It's not right, he considered. *Everyone is suffering except those up there, above it all.*

He felt a deep ache as he looked into the void in front of him again.

Why should we all suffer for the sake of one man? Not even a man. A boy.

He wept, knowing they would brand him a traitor.

What would it matter? He had already abandoned his post.

Larson was right.

You will have General Versel to deal with. Or worse, the Maji himself.

The palace wasn't the place to run to.

Wintermarsh was not the place to be any longer.

He tore off his white tunic and threw it to the ground.

Piece by piece, he cast his armour as far as he could into the dead region before him.

His days fighting for General Versel, fighting for the Maji, were over.

He didn't wish to fight against them, either.

Readjusting his belt and fixing his sword into place, he started towards the east.

He needed to get out of the city.

He needed to get out unseen.

Twenty-One

The cavalry rode to the rear of the troop, allowing the infantry to take point as they moved towards the northwest. The path that they chose caused them to zig-zag through the city, taking a left turn to the east and a right turn to the north.

The advancement was slow. Thornton, now on foot, took the lead but used caution at every turn. He would stop and check each bend in the road, peer around every corner, before signalling the men to follow.

Billowing clouds of smoke emitted from several places around their position. Obviously, the region had been attacked from the sky earlier, but there were still remnants of abandoned posts along the way, as well as one or two white soldiers that had remained behind here and there.

Thornton made it a point to check alleys and lanes, sending men into perfect hiding places to flush cowering men from the darkness. Occasionally, a quick skirmish ensued. Mostly, the enemy soldiers were simply cut down in place.

"Why don't we take some prisoners?" Jendryng asked, sounding like a naïve boy. He was wiping the blood from his sword onto a white tunic that he had torn from the body of a white soldier along the way. "This is starting to become a little troubling. Almost as if we're killing just for the sake of it."

"No prisoners," Thornton growled as he peered around the corner of a small house, into a street that led to the west.

"Where would we keep them, anyway?" Sparrow asked. "We haven't got any gaol cells."

"And, we can't spare any men to guard them, either," Brook put in.

"We could disarm them and let them..." the young soldier began.

"Don't you dare say we should let them go, boy," Vawdrey interrupted him. "Those bastards will find their way to the next post and get new weapons. Then, they'll backtrack with some friends and cut us all down."

"You don't know that," Jendryng told him. "They might just leave. Not everyone wants to fight."

"I *do* know," the other argued. "Because it is exactly what I would do. Look around you. Look at what we've done to this city already. This is their home. They're not just going to leave after what we've done here."

The young soldier closed his mouth and peered about. He hadn't considered the battle from the enemy's perspective.

Homes were burning. People, soldiers and members of their families, were lying in the street or crushed beneath burning rubble. Some had simply turned to ash.

Jendryng considered Newholt, and how she once had suffered a similar fate. It filled him with rage then. A deep desire to murder all the Black Queen's soldiers had found lodging inside of his soul, at the time.

The tables had turned now.

It was his army, his friends, that brought the devastation.

The inhabitants of Wintermarsh had just as much right to feel as much rage now as he did when his city suffered a similar fate.

"Let's move," Thornton hissed, signalling the army in tow to tail him.

The street was empty, devoid of life or any sign of it.

"Keep to the edges," the captain commanded, standing in the middle of the road and pointing to the houses and storefronts lining its sides. "We're going to be on this path for a good part of the way."

"For how far?" Brook enquired, moving to his side as the rest of the infantry moved into position. The cavalry kept close to their backs.

"Did you feel the earthquake earlier?" Thornton asked.

"Yes," the other replied, with a curious glance.

"And did you see the lightning?"

"And the big dust cloud over there to the north," Brook added, pointing his finger.

"I think that was Ursula and Queen Amicia," the captain told him.

"So?" Brook asked. "What has that got to do with how long we're staying on this street for?"

"I want to keep south of that mess," Thornton replied. "If I were up near that palace, I would have a good view of that area. The dust has settled and the snow would be falling upon it. If I were in charge up there, I'd have eyes on it all the time.

"This road brings us pretty close to it," Thornton continued. "I want to get closer to that palace, directly south of it would be best, before we veer towards it again."

"Fair call," Brook acknowledged. He turned to peer along the lengthy road before them. "We'll need to be careful. Lots of intersections. Lots of dark alleys and laneways."

"And we need to clear all of them as we go," the captain replied.

***

Arrows had hit at least fifty men, by Commander Willard Zakhar's count. They struck some during the rush for cover and hit others in the legs as they sheltered beneath the protruding upper levels of the buildings that they pressed themselves against.

It wasn't long before the navy men and Agrodien broke their way into the buildings, desperately seeking shelter from the constant barrage of arrows being flung at them.

One captain instructed his men to race to the entrance into the plaza, back to where they had entered, hoping to escape. Twelve men had charged for the street to their south.

They were instantly shot down with arrows flung from all sides of the court.

There was no escape.

Zakhar noticed that even the Agrodien hadn't moved fast enough to avoid the sting of a bolt. One warrior nursed a wound gained during the initial attack. The arrow still stuck from his thigh, just above the knee.

He hissed menacingly each time the female warrior tried to touch it in an effort to tend to the wound. The wounded warrior lay upon a kitchen table inside a dark, abandoned house. The other warriors stood around him.

Yuri spoke to them in his tongue. A brief conversation between the ten reptilians ensued before their leader turned to the fleet commander, who was standing with his first officer by the door. Five other fleet men stood near a window, ready to report any movement they could see.

"We cannot stay here," the Agrodien said.

"We're pinned down," Zakhar replied. "We exposed our legs to the archers on the other side. Our wounded, lying on the ground, are vulnerable to every arrow flung at us. And if we try to run..." he gestured to the twelve dead men lying in the snow.

"We no run," Yuri told him. "Rabor is injured. Nola'ee try to help, but he cry like a—" The reptilian said something in his own language, giving Rabor a sideways glance. "...Tuk'hi."

The word must have been an insult to the injured warrior as he glared up at Yuri and hissed.

"I need Nola'ee with me," Yuri continued, turning his attention back to Zakhar. "I need all my warriors. You have man who can help?"

The commander looked at the wound on Rabor's leg. The shaft was in deep. The blood flow was slow, only a trickle.

"My men can dress the wound," Zakhar answered. "But they won't be able to heal him. Rabor will be out of the game, I'm afraid," the commander explained. "I think only Alice holds the power to heal that wound fast enough for your warrior to re-join the fight. And she looks to be a little busy as of this moment." Zakhar crouched slightly to look to the north, where he saw dragons circling in the sky.

"I'm wondering what you might have planned for you to be asking me to watch your warrior," the commander probed. "Where are you off to, Yuri?"

"Up," replied the other, gesturing to the ceiling. "We kill all bow-men."

Arrows suddenly filled the air in the plaza, whistling loudly as they streaked towards their position.

"Cover," a man hollered from farther down the line of buildings. Zakhar and his men pressed themselves against the walls, away from the open windows and broken door.

The shafts stuck fast into timber pylons and the façade of the upper levels.

"Nine of you?" First Officer Grady huffed, looking at Yuri. "The nine of you will take out this lot?"

"We kill as many as we can," the Agrodien replied. "We drive the rest to the ground where you kill them. Or, we die."

"Suitable alternative," Grady said cynically.

"He has a point," Zakhar told him. "If we stay here, we're dead. If we go out there, where they have the advantage, we're dead. Either we force them to the ground where we even the odds, or we're dead.

"What Yuri proposes is that we try something rather than nothing. I'm inclined to agree," the commander continued. He turned to face the Agrodien. "How do you plan to take the upper level? The stairs are outside." Zakhar gestured to the back of the building. There were no doors, or any passages of access, save for a small window.

Yuri pointed to the tiny portal.

"Through that?" Grady chuckled. "You'd be lucky to fit that little dragon girl through that thing."

"I make it bigger," Yuri told him, crossing the room to the window. He started pounding upon the wall surrounding the window frame, using his fists.

Over and over, he struck the wall, hoping to weaken the brickwork.

The glass cracked, and part of the frame broke a little.

Again, and again, he punched and struck the bricks by the edges.

"Yuri," Zakhar sighed. "You'll just cause yourself an injury. Let's find something with a bit of weight to help…"

The unmistakable sound of clinking and snapping emitted from the wall by the window. Zakhar's jaw dropped. He didn't expect to ever see something of the sort.

The Agrodien were a big, robust race. They were strong and agile. Commander Zakhar believed they were capable of many things that a man could not do... but to break a brick wall?

Four of the other Agrodien warriors moved to the window and assisted Yuri in his efforts. It didn't take long before the whole window pane fell from the wall and into the area behind the house.

The five reptilians continued to chip away at the wall, breaking bricks away, until the gap was large enough for them to fit through.

"You need to watch this," Yuri growled, gesturing to the hole in the wall with his chin as he rubbed his knuckles. "The way is open. Enemy could come."

Zakhar nodded, turning to one of his men.

"You watch that opening," the commander ordered. As one man moved in place, Zakhar looked to another and pointed to Rabor, who was still lying on the table, hissing at Nola'ee. "Tend to the Agrodien's wound."

The sailor looked afraid.

"He might bite me, sir," the man protested.

"He no bite," Nola'ee informed him. "He just hiss and cry like a tuk'hi."

"There it is again," Zakhar said, as his man moved to the side of the table. "What is that? A tuk'hi?"

"Tuk'hi is Rabor," Bein chuckled.

Rabor spat a list of angry words at the other reptilian.

"Tuk'hi is crying, baby," Yuri explained. "One that suck from teat and cannot clean own filth. Weak. Need mother."

"Oh," Zakhar replied, peering to Rabor who wore a furious scowl. "I can see how that might be rude."

The man tending to the wound touched around the protruding shaft gingerly. Rabor hissed, baring his teeth to the sailor.

Zakhar shook his head and approached the table tenaciously. He shoved the sailor aside with a soft shoulder barge, tightened his fingers around the shaft and snapped the tail end away to remove the fletching feathers.

Rabor let out a tremendous roar before turning a sour glare to the fleet commander.

"Tuk'hi," said Nola'ee with a soft laugh as she followed Yuri through the hole in the rear wall.

"Help me roll him onto his side," Zakhar commanded the sailor.

Even with all of his hissing and words that none of the men could understand, Rabor complied by rolling with the commander's prompts. When he turned, placing his wounded leg higher than the other, Zakhar moved to look the Agrodien in the eye.

"Now, this is going to really hurt," he said.

Rabor offered a confused look which quickly turned into a wince and a roar as Zakhar pushed the arrow through the Agrodien's leg so that the tip stuck through the other side.

"Pull it," Zakhar commanded the sailor.

Gripping the arrow tip in his fingers, the navy man pulled the shaft clear of the reptilian's leg.

Blood flowed freely.

Zakhar put his hands to the holes in the Agrodien's leg, pressing hard against the wounds.

"Find linen," the commander instructed. "Tear some strips of cloth. Quickly."

Reilly stuck his head out of the window. He peered over the plaza below, moving his gaze to the overhanging buildings to the eastern side of the region.

From his point of view, he could see a long line of houses joined together from one end of the clearing, connecting to the string of dwellings he was currently occupying along the northern edge. Together, the structures formed a long 'L' shape.

The level below was constructed with peat brick walls, while everything above was timber. The only access to any of the upper levels was via the many sets of stairs to the rear of the buildings.

This gave the officer of the white army some confidence and comfort as he had seen all the enemy soldiers, and their reptilian pets, scurry away to hide in the lower levels to his left.

"Nocks," he shouted into the plaza. A hundred arrows pointed from the windows surrounding the area. "Loose."

Shafts of timber with points of iron showered down to the ground below, tinging and pinging loudly as they bounced and ricocheted harmlessly upon the brickwork.

"It's pointless," Norris, the other officer in the company, told him. He was sitting in a nice, cushioned chair by a stove to keep warm. "They're well inside the homes. The only way out is through those doors, and they're not about to come out anytime soon. You're just wasting arrows."

"What do you suggest, then?"

"Draw them out," said Norris, as if it were the obvious thing to say.

"Well!" Reilly nodded. "Thank you for such insight. I'll take it into consideration while you drink tea and do your knitting by the fire, shall I?"

"Look," the other said, rising to his feet and appearing regretful that he'd opened his mouth. He moved to his friend's side. "I didn't mean to question your tactic. It worked. The bastards are cowering over there. But what now?"

Reilly peered to the buildings to his left. He didn't have an answer.

"Let me take a squad or two," Norris urged him. "We'll go down and entice them out."

"Entice them out?"

"I don't know…" The other shrugged. "Call them names. Bare our arses to them. We'll cut them down while you and the lads up here get some target practice."

"Target practice!" Reilly laughed. "The way some of these fuckers shoot, you will be the first man downed by arrows."

"I think it's your best chance at defea—"

A shrill scream echoed from across the plaza, interrupting the conversation.

Both men looked out to the plaza to see the upper torso of a white soldier flung through an eastern window, nearer to the southern end of the clearing, and onto the ground below. They stared, wide-eyed and in awe, as they saw the man, or what was left of him, try to drag himself across the ground.

The figure's mouth was agape, spilling blood over his cheeks and chin. His left arm, his only limb still intact, reached and clawed at the snow. Entrails and spine jutted from the mess of meat, torn flesh and blood just below his ribs. After that, there was nothing else of him.

"Fuck!" Norris blurted.

The lower half of the man followed. The legs flopped into the snow where they twitched slightly before falling still. By then, the upper half of the man had stopped moving also.

"What could do such a—" Reilly began, but suddenly silenced himself as a dozen more bodies were thrown from some upper windows with brute force. All of the men tumbling over the ground had great gashes and wounds, limbs missing and portions torn from their bodies.

A crash echoed through the air, emitting from the upper rooms across the way. Within moments, more bodies came plummeting through other windows a little closer to the two officers' position.

Another crash and more men were ejected from another upper room.

Whatever was causing the carnage was getting closer and closer.

"Fuck!" Norris exclaimed again.

"What is it?" Reilly asked, totally perplexed and in a state of wonder.

"It's the bloody lizards," Norris replied. "They've found a way up to us."

"What do we do sir?" one of the archers asked, frightened.

Norris knew that none of them stood a chance against the reptilian warriors. At least, not in such circumstances as this. With an angry scowl, he stuck his head through the window and did the only thing left for him to do.

"Retreat," he called in a loud, long voice. "Retreat."

Another crash emitted from the eastern upper rooms.

More screams ensued.

Several bodies and pieces of flesh were thrust from the open windows again.

The reptiles were slaughtering everyone in their path.

"Come on," Norris called to Reilly as he made his way to the door that led out of the room.

"That's your plan now?" the other asked as the archers in the room with them bolted out the door. "Abandon our post?"

"Would you rather stay and face the things that will come smashing through that wall?" Norris countered.

Another crash, closer and louder.

They were drawing nearer and nearer.

The screams were so loud, they could have been inside the room with the officers.

"No," Reilly answered, hastily making his way to the door.

Twenty-Two

Liana swooped low to the ground, passing over the northern edge of the city to skim near the rooftops that stretched away from her. The girl urged the dragon to turn slightly eastward, away from the palace.

It seemed that every time one of them flew near to the towering structure, they would fall. The new strategy was to revert to the first one they had tried. Attack and retreat.

The dragon riders would flee to the clouds for cover. Each time they attacked, it would be from a different place. The goal was to get as close to the palace as they could, to clear a way in for their friends on the ground, then dash away before they could be brought down.

Alice had passed high above the grounds of the white fortress in an effort to find the cause of the dragons' demise. She thought she saw Takmel there in his damson cloak, moving about in the yard before the palace entrance. She was too far away to be certain.

Others were there.

Many soldiers were moving about around him.

There was also the feeling of forbidding dread. Something dark, almost like the sense she got when blood magic was near.

Almost.

Alice could not gauge if Takmel was the direct reason for the dragons falling to the ground. She didn't think so. She thought it had to be something else, something he had manipulated and gained control over. Something that feared him, but was bound to him.

Alice believed this was more to the Maji's character.

He was a user, taking power from others around him, compelling them to do his deeds. He was never really one to get his hands dirty, unless it suited his purpose.

Skimming over the buildings, her scarf over her ears, nose and mouth, her hood flapping against her back and her long, dark braid trailing behind, she scanned the streets below.

Men were fleeing, but not towards the palace.

Their splendid weapons of destruction now ruined by fire.

Their hopes of victory had been crushed.

She saw some drop swords in the snow and fall to their knees as she whooshed by.

Sadly, she was in no position to take prisoners.

Alice thought of Erimoor. She thought of how she had led an attack to flood the township with fire. She remembered the sound of screams of pain calling out from the burning houses below.

Looking at the white soldiers on the ground below her, she couldn't bring herself to hurt them. Not without giving them a fighting chance.

Urging Liana back into the sky, she left the white soldiers to flee, hoping they would be wise enough to leave Wintermarsh of their own accord and take as many with them as they could.

We're fishermen and farmers. Nothing more, she heard the voice of Cedric Bauer say from a far-off memory. She had almost forgotten about the kind farmer and the people of Greyrose. *If you move farther along the coast to Pryholt, you'll see more who are loyal to the Maji. Then, if you keep going, the loyalists grow in numbers. It won't be long before you find everyone calling themselves loyal, even if they aren't.*

Alice hoped the soldiers she had seen below, fleeing away from the palace, away from Takmel, were those whose loyalty feigned towards their master.

Liana swam through the swirling clouds, enveloping both her and the girl upon her back into the misty darkness. They burst through, into the clear sky above, to be drenched in the silver light of the moon.

The appearance of the great orb was cold, a bluish tinge spreading from it into the night sky, a stark contrast to the many fires burning throughout the city far below.

Alice thought it was the most beautiful thing she had seen in a long time.

Looking at it made her feel suddenly sad as she wished she could be with Arthur, hand in hand, gazing upon it together.

She felt increasingly tired.

She felt intolerably lonely.

She so much wanted to be back home.

Twenty-Three

Snow covered the parapet, thick enough for the wall guards to consider taking shovels to the built-up frost, discarding it over the battlements to land on the ground outside the city. They would stop long enough to stand to attention, offering a small nod as he walked by.

"My lord," they would say. Again, and again he had heard it. A few times, he had told them to ignore him, but each fresh face he passed by on the wall walk would treat him in such a way.

"My lord," he heard from old men, too far along in age to have accompanied the men that ventured to the west.

"My lord," said by those too young to have joined the ranks of the city's military.

Instead of asking them to stop, preferring them to call him by name, he simply replied with, "Good evening."

His phantom arm twitched slightly. He felt pins and needles in his thumb and fingers that were no longer there.

It was an odd sensation, one that made him want to scratch or rub at the source of the stirring. But what source was there?

He leant against the battlement, not too far from the eastern gate, and peered back to the barracks. There, just behind the building that housed the soldiers, was the prison where he had lost his arm.

Each time he saw the structure, he remembered Takmel's smoke ripping through his flesh. An arcane fear and hatred had developed towards the prison.

It is just a building;; he told himself. *Bricks, stone and iron. Nothing more.*

Dread and doom.

Not nothing.

Since his return to Woodmyst, he had felt its presence throughout the city, snaking through the streets.

He hoped it was something that lived only inside of himself and not in the others. He hoped it was just his mind that was finding it difficult to settle back in again.

His father had tried to talk with him about such things. Becka too. He wasn't able to find solace in their words.

He took a walk along the wall to clear his head. Instead, his thoughts only spoke louder, bringing him more uneasiness.

It was strange to admit, considering his young age, but the only genuine comfort he had ever experienced was with his wife.

He remembered their little home she had built in the cave. For a small moment, they were almost completely alone there. They were truly happy there.

He missed the glade.

He missed the little stream that ran through its middle.

He missed the forest surrounding the clearing. The mountains that stood tall and proud in every direction. The cool, gentle breeze that swept down from them.

He missed her.

Her soft lips pressed against his. Her soothing voice would send tingles over his skin and almost lure him to sleep. Her warm hands, even when it was cold out, softly touching his face. Her fingers running through his hair. The way she would touch his wound and make him feel at ease.

Arthur looked up at the moon. It appeared to have a blueish glow about it, shielded by a thin mist that covered the sky.

He missed Alice profoundly.

***

The *Petty Beggar* packed to the brim with people.

With the construction of the piers complete, all workers had visited the finest establishment in all of Newholt so they could celebrate their achievement.

"Welcome to the *Petty Beggar*," Sheriff Nathaniel Monteacute hollered from behind the bar each time a new patron entered through the doors. "The best pub in all of Newholt."

"The only pub with any grog in all of Newholt, Monty," the men gathered by the fireplace yelled back.

The room would always erupt with laughter. A good joke never got old when the ale was flowing, no matter how bad it really was.

The Whores of Whitekeep kept busy during the night, serving drinks, fetching pitchers and cleaning mugs. Only a few, either brave or foolish, propositioned the girls for an encounter in an upper room. Sometimes, when the requests included a slap on the rump, the men received a hearty fist in the face, sending the patron to the floor with a bloodied nose.

In response, the room would explode into more cheering and laughter.

Seated upon stools by the bar were Sub-Commander Landon Wake and Captain Davine Staiger. They shared a pitcher of ale between them as they talked with Monteacute.

"Any news about the trade routes?" the sheriff asked.

"No," Wake replied. "The blockade is still in place. We need assurance that the Maji is defeated."

"And I suppose that means they await the return of Queen Amicia and Commander Brondt," Monteacute assumed as he looked over to the middle of the room, where some others lifted a man from the floor, blood trickling from his nostrils. "That's twice for that bastard, I think."

Both Wake and Staiger turned to look at the injured, and quite embarrassed, individual. The patrons sharing his table helped him to his seat and continued drinking.

Rose Heron walked behind the bar, carrying an empty pitcher.

"Did you just knock that fellow off his seat?" Monteacute asked her.

"Yes," she replied, looking both angry and proud.

Monteacute put his arm around her and pulled her close, giving her a kiss on the forehead.

"That's my girl," he said happily. "I think that's twice for him."

"Not from me, it isn't," she told him as he released his hold. She gestured to a table by the door and another by a window on the far side of the room. "I've hit that one over there and that one over there. That was his first time."

"Audrey struck him earlier," Staiger informed the sheriff. "I'd like to see if he'll try his luck with Kateryn, as well. Redheads are fiery. Maybe she'll loosen a few of his teeth."

"Can't blame a man for trying," Monteacute put in. "I mean, you do still call yourselves the Whores of—"

"We don't do that anymore, Monty," Rose interjected, pointing a scowling finger at the sheriff.

"I know," he replied, holding his hands up in mock surrender. He looked to the door and saw five new customers entering the tavern. "Welcome to the *Petty Beggar*. The best pub in all of Newholt," he called out.

"The only pub with any grog in all of Newholt, Monty," came the reply.

Laughter filled the room again.

The sheriff turned to Rose.

"Go and see to those gentlemen," he told her. "I can see an empty table by the window."

"Might be standing room soon," she said, placing the empty pitcher on the bar before retreating.

"You ever seen a tavern so busy in yer life?" Staiger asked before swigging from the mug in her hand.

"No," Monteacute answered with a smile. "But, we are the only tavern in operation in all the city."

"Minus the whores," she added.

"No." He shook his head. "We got those. They just don't work like that anymore, as you just heard."

"Why the change of heart?" Wake asked, swirling the ale in his cup.

"What do you mean?" Monteacute queried.

"I mean, why did they stop whoring if you still call them whores?"

"Ursula," the sheriff answered. "Since she left to travel with the queen, these three have never been the same. Maud was always a mother to all of them. She practically raised Ursula as her own, but Ursula was always a carer for those three."

"They all appear to be…" Staiger started, looking at the girls quizzically.

"The same age as Ursula?" Monteacute finished for her. "I think Ursula may be a little younger. I can't be certain. But she was shrewd and knew how to handle their business."

"She was their madam?" Wake asked.

Monteacute nodded.

"Who are her parents?" the sub-commander asked.

"Sorry?" the sheriff furrowed his brow.

"You said that Maud practically raised her," Wake said. "I was just wondering who her parents are."

Monteacute shrugged his shoulders and shook his head.

"Don't know," he answered. "Same with the girls there. They showed up in Whitekeep at different times. I suspect they were running from someone or something. I never asked. I never will. Sometimes a person's history doesn't need to be stirred up, if you know what I mean."

Wake nodded.

"I promised I would look after them as best I can," Monteacute continued. "With Maud gone, I'm all they've got until Ursula returns. I suppose I'm obligated to. I was their best customer in Whitekeep, and I still owe them some coin for that."

Staiger giggled upon hearing the sheriff's report.

"You still humping them now?" she asked.

Monteacute gave her a smile that told her everything she needed to know.

"You dirty boy," the captain chuckled. "All three of them? Maybe that's why they don't whore themselves anymore. Maybe yer all they need, Monty."

"Maybe." He grinned.

A loud smack resonated through the room as the man, seated at a table in the middle of the room, fell from his chair for a third time. His mouth filled with blood.

Kateryn stood over him, shaking her hand that she had used to knock him down.

The patrons cheered and applauded.

"Next time any of you try to touch me or my friends on the arse," she said irately, "I'll kick you in your ball sack."

Monteacute smiled proudly. "That's my girl."

Twenty-Four

Ursula looked over at a group of soldiers seated about the table. They were scoffing down bowls of stew and tearing off chunks from a loaf of bread being passed around.

Each of the men appeared dirty and tired. Their white tunics covered in mud, grey ash and stains that appeared to be blood.

"What are you looking at?" one of them called to her, catching her glancing at them. He stood up and started around the table.

"Leave it, Damon," one of the other men said. "Sit down and eat your food."

"Nah," Damon replied. "She's eyeing me like she's better than me."

"She probably is," another grunted as he put a portion of bread into his mouth, facing away from the prison cell. He swivelled to see the young woman. "What is it, love? You better than him? I bet you are. I bet you are better than him in more ways than I can count."

Ursula dropped her gaze to the floor.

"What?" Damon said angrily. "Too good to even have you look at me now? Fucking bitch."

"Watch it," Willis growled from near the door. "Show some respect."

"Sorry sir," Damon replied. "But I need to ask her something. I need to know if she knows what's really going on out there."

"No, you don't," the officer told him.

"You know what this is?" Damon asked, turning to Ursula. "Oy."

Ursula kept her eyes on the floor. She felt her body shake as her nerves built up inside.

"She knows," Amicia snapped, moving to Ursula and putting her arms around the young woman. "Leave her alone. She isn't hurting you."

"Isn't hurting?" Damon responded. "Did you hear that, lads? She isn't hurting me." The soldier came close to the bars and glared at the women in the cell. "You filthy bitches destroyed a big part of my city out there. People I know. People I love are all dead because of you." He grabbed the hem of his tunic and thrust it towards the cage. "Do you see that? Do you know what it is? It's blood. Do you see?"

"Soldier," Willis warned the man.

"Do you see?"

"I see," Ursula replied. "Probably from one of our friends that you cut open with your sword."

"Wrong," Damon told her. "None of us has seen hide nor hair from any of your soldiers. What we have seen is your fucking dragons throwing fire over everything. Buildings burning and toppling over. People crushed beneath the rubble.

"This," he said, as he held the stain towards Ursula, "this was a little boy I pulled from a toppled house. He must have been all of four fucking years old. Poor little thing died in my arms.

"You want to know the last thing he said to me?" Damon asked them. Tears had welled in his eyes. His face had reddened. "He said, *look*. That's all he said. He was smiling. Smiling and pointing, right at one of your dragons flying over us."

Damon moved away from the prison cell. He slowed his breathing and wiped his eyes.

The four women in the cell wept after hearing the soldier's words.

"Then he died. That's what is really going on out there," he said.

"Come on, lad," one of the other men seated at the table muttered, reaching over to pat Damon on the arm. "Get some of this slop into you. You need to keep your strength up."

Damon moved to his seat. He stared at the table for a long time before lifting his spoon again.

***

Thornton crouched slightly as he edged along the right side of the street, keeping as close to the walls as he could. Two long lines of men followed him, one behind him on the right side of the road, another keeping parallel to the left. Behind them, the cavalry had split into two, closely following the infantry.

He shivered slightly as a strong, cold draught flowed along the road, channelled through the city to hit them head-on. It felt immensely colder when he crossed an intersection where the avenues and lanes moving from north to south funnelled the northern wind directly into him.

One such juncture was coming up. It was a wide street that appeared to be lined with storefronts. Each had large windows that would have normally displayed merchandises. Instead, most contained broken shards of glass or large cracks that stretched over the windowpanes. Others appeared empty, possibly because of the shopkeepers emptying stock when the battle began, or to looters who seemed to always find their way into a war zone to profit from the misfortune of others.

The captain gestured with two fingers to the south, then again to the north. Four soldiers rushed forward, keeping as quiet as they could. Two went left. Two went right.

Pausing at the edge of the intersection, Thornton signalled for the others in tow to halt in place.

A moment later, after shivering some more and wishing he was by a fire instead of in the middle of Wintermarsh, he saw the four soldiers return to him.

"Looks empty, sir," one man who had gone north reported. "We only went to the next corner."

"We did the same," a man who had gone in the opposite direction put in. "We saw a few soldiers farther to the west in the next street over. Should we go and inspect it more closely?"

Thornton shook his head.

"We'll split the team," he replied, turning to Lieutenant Brook behind him. "I'll take half the men and go to the next street over. You continue along here. Take the cavalry with you."

"And if one of us needs support?" Brook asked.

"Call out, give a whistle, something like that," Thornton answered. He darted across the street to meet up with Morys Sparrow, leading the troops on the other side of the road.

"Captain," Sparrow said, almost in a whisper.

"We're going south to the next street," Thornton informed him, loud enough for the men directly behind to have heard. "Pass it along. We'll turn west again and keep on that heading."

"Away from the palace?" Sparrow questioned.

"The scouts reported they saw enemy soldiers down there," the captain replied. "We didn't come all this way to simply see the sights."

"What sights?" The other grinned. "This place is an absolute shithole."

"Well, it is now," Thornton agreed. "Didn't look too bad before. A coat of paint, some minor repairs, and it might look nice again."

Sparrow chuckled. "All right. Lead on, Captain."

"Stay close," Thornton grunted as he turned, darting around the corner and into the street heading south.

Lieutenant Brook waved to the men behind him, on his side of the street. He tapped the top of his head, signalling the soldiers to follow his lead. He then moved diagonally through the intersection to the left side of the road. His intention was to keep as close to his captain as he possibly could.

Two lines of men snaked their way through the crossing, one south, one west.

Pressing his back to the corner wall of a shopfront, Thornton peered around the corner towards the west.

Sure enough, he could see five white soldiers quite some distance away. They were standing in the open, seemingly in discussion, acting oddly. He guessed they were nervous about something, but couldn't tell what.

"Keep tight," Thornton whispered to Brook. "Keep to the walls. Keep low. Keep quiet."

With that, he moved onto the next street.

The troop moved stealthily, trying to keep to the dark shadows cast by the light of the moon, thankful when they passed beneath awnings jutting from houses along the way.

The white soldiers remained in place, continuing their discussion, constantly looking to the south and the west, but never to Thornton's troop approaching from the east.

Eventually, Thornton came to another cross-street. He glanced to the south and saw nothing but fires and structures. Turning his head to the north, he saw Brook waving to him.

The captain signalled for the lieutenant to continue on his bearing. With a nod, Brook moved on.

Thornton kept his eyes on the white soldiers as he tiptoed into the light of the moon, crossing the new intersection before returning to shadows on the other side.

The soldiers hadn't seen him.

Without taking his gaze from them, without even blinking, he signalled Sparrow to come to him.

"Signal the next man," Thornton growled in a low voice before moving a little farther to the west.

One by one, the troop crossed the street unseen, reforming on the other side, edging closer and closer to the five white soldiers.

"We should get to the palace, I'm telling you," one of them said nice and loud. "That's where the colonels will go. We should go there too."

"The colonels won't abandon their post," another argued. "We should go back."

"Will you two keep your voices down?" a third snarled at them. "I am not going back. Those things back there tore our mates up, and I don't want them to find us out here. So, shut up."

Thornton crept slowly, carefully, keeping himself well concealed in the darkness. With his dark cloak around him, his hood pulled over his head, he and his troop had become shadows.

"Staying here isn't going to work in our favour, either," said the first. "We'll get seen, or worse, freeze to death. We should go to the palace."

"Go to the palace," the second mocked. "Go to the palace. That's all you say."

Slowly, silently, the troop drew closer and closer to the unsuspecting white soldiers.

"He's right," a fourth put in. "We should go to the palace and offer our services to the commander."

"She'll tear our skin from our bones if we show up there," replied the third.

"The worst she'll do is make us dig shit trenches," the fourth contended. "She needs us alive."

Closer.

Closer.

Closer, the troop skulked.

The fifth man, who had been looking around the corner to the south, then to the west, turned to speak to them.

"We were commanded to leave our station," he said calmly. "If anyone is going to be skinned, it'll be Reilly and Norris. Sam's right. We should go to the palace and offer our services. We can't stay here, and we can't go back. We might have stayed too long already."

"You're right about that," came a low, soft growl from the shadows.

The five men turned to face the darkness lining the northern side of the road.

The shadows came alive and lunged at them.

Glints of steel slashed before their eyes.

Before they knew what had happened, they were on the ground, bleeding from fresh wounds in their necks and stomachs.

Thornton peered down at the five bodies in the street.

"Keep alert," he said to the men beside him. "There will be others."

As if to prove his point, over a hundred men suddenly appeared in the distance, approaching from the south.

"Here we go," Sparrow sighed.

***

Commander Willard Zakhar parried and blocked every strike of his opponent. His training and focus gave him the upper hand over the young white soldier, who was desperately trying to overcome the fleet commander in order to continue his escape.

It seemed only moments before, the enemy trapped them in the plaza, pinned by showers of arrows that kept them at bay. After the success of Yuri's strategy of breaking through to the upper rooms and clearing them of enemy soldiers, the command call to retreat by one of the Wintermarsh officers rang across the court. Zakhar shouted a command of his own.

To attack.

The wounded men, and one reptilian, remained inside the homes where they were sheltering, with a few men to care for them, as the rest of the fleet men, nearly three-hundred-and-fifty strong, raced through the plaza and through its access to the north.

There, in the street bordering the northern edge of the buildings surrounding the plaza, they saw hundreds of soldiers wearing white tunics fleeing in all directions.

The sound of a crash made Zakhar turn and look up a flight of stairs.

Yuri appeared through a door, caked in blood, and appearing as menacing as he ever could.

The reptilian pointed his finger towards the crowd of white soldiers as he flicked his tongue from his lips.

Zakhar followed the reptilian's finger to the throng of men running into side streets and lanes that weaved through the city in the palace's direction.

Nola'ee pulled to his side. She appeared just as he did. Blood smeared over her clothing and skin. She leapt from the top of the staircase and onto the ground, where she immediately gave chase.

Nakrah and Bein were fast on her tail, cutting and hacking their way through the crowd, appearing to have a certain target in mind.

"Where are they going?" the commander asked, turning to the Agrodien as he descended the steps.

"The ones who give orders have gone that way," he replied. "They were in that room when retreat was called. I smell them. They go that way."

Zakhar led his men into the throng.

They started after the three Agrodien who had raced ahead, chasing the officers of the Wintermarsh army.

Soon, Yuri and his five other able warriors were in the fight alongside the naval men.

Zakhar stepped and turned, avoiding the enemy's blades, stabbing and slicing precisely with his own. The preparation and education he had received during his time in the Dendadian academy were proving to be a success, even with the odds stacked so highly against him and his men.

Truthfully, he reflected, most of the Wintermarsh soldiers just wanted to run away. There were few who wanted to stay and fight.

And who can blame them?

Zakhar glanced over to his reptilian friends, who fought with sheer brutality. Their intimidating forms, taller and broader than the surrounding men, lumbered fearlessly and cut through the men like one hacking through the undergrowth to make a path through a thick forest of trees.

There was no training there, the commander observed. There was instinct and experience, something neither he nor any of his men truly had. At least, not when it came to fighting on land.

The throng of enemy soldiers continued to race away to the north with the Agrodien and Dendadians in close pursuit. The white soldiers turned to face the swords of the navy and reptilians only when they had no other chance of escape.

Soon, the ground in the streets and lanes was patches of snow mixed with pools of blood, adorned with bodies and discarded limbs, a macabre trail of carnage left behind by the fleet men and the Agrodien.

Still, hundreds of white soldiers ran for their lives, swords clasped in their hands and bows slung upon their backs. Their quivers emptied quickly as their arrows jostled out of the casings and onto the ground.

Some stupidly turned to pick up their discarded property, only to be met with the steel of Zakhar's men, or Yuri's warriors.

As they progressed, the pursuing troop came upon the bodies of white soldiers already slaughtered, constantly reminding them that three Agrodien warriors were in hot pursuit of the Wintermarsh officers.

Twenty-Five

"This way," Norris called, urging Reilly to follow him into a thin alley to the right. The bulk of the men raced through a wider street, attracting the attention of the three reptilians in pursuit.

"They might not even be after us," the other officer suggested as he brushed past some rancid barrels near the passageway's opening. "They could be simply after everyone."

"All the more reason to evade them," Norris replied. "Let them chase the others. We can find a place to hold up until this is all over."

He reached a tight intersection that broke into four directions. Turning left, he started north again. The walls of the surrounding buildings were tall and narrow, so close that he could reach out and touch both sides of the laneway if he desired.

He had no craving to do so.

The bricks and stone were dirty, covered with dust, ash and soot that had fallen about during the day's attack. Whether it had come from dragon fire or the churning of the earth some distance to the north, he could not tell.

The ground had turned to slush and formed a muck that rose almost ankle deep.

"Come on," Norris called in a whisper.

"Coming," Reilly answered, moving around the corner to see his friend a few paces ahead. "What do we tell the general?"

"What about?"

"About how we got separated from our men." Reilly looked over his shoulder to the street. A small, thin view of the road beyond the alley displayed Wintermarsh soldiers speeding by as they fled the terror approaching from the south. "How do we explain to her how we survived?"

"We just tell her we found a place to hole up," Norris answered, moving forward slowly, peering up at the narrow line of the sky that he could see above him.

"I somehow don't believe she will be as lenient with us as you thi..." Reilly paused mid-sentence. He dashed through the small intersections of laneways and into the passage Norris had taken. Pressing himself to the wall, he peered around the corner.

A tall, cloaked figure stood at the mouth of the alley with a sword gripped in its hand and a long tail coiled behind them.

It sniffed the air before making a horrid grunt. Its head swivelled to the barrels lining the wall. Some words spat from the creature's mouth, sounding as if the odour the barrels gave off offended it.

Stepping backwards, the cloaked creature started for the street.

Reilly breathed a sigh of relief.

"You coming or not," Norris called in a harsh, hoarse voice.

The creature froze.

Reilly's heart raced.

The hood upon the figure's head tilted, as if listening.

The soldier watched, frozen in place with fear, as the creature crept back into the alley.

It moved by the barrels, keeping its head high, as if paying attention to the air beyond the stench.

The officer knew he couldn't linger. He forced himself to move.

"There's one coming," he said, rushing towards the other officer. "Run."

Norris didn't hesitate. He raced through the lane, noisily splashing mud all about. His boots flung it against the walls, over his clothes and into Reilly's face.

The cloaked figure sprang through the tiny intersection and bounded after them, moving much faster.

Reilly swore as a large ball of slime splatted in his eyes.

He wiped the muck away as he continued to run blindly through the tiny passage.

The sound of Norris' footfalls drew him on.

He opened his eyes, but the view was too blurry and the uncomfortable feeling of something swimming beneath his eyelids suddenly became unbearable.

Still running, he lifted his tunic with one hand and tried to remove the filth from his eyes.

The splashing from Norris' boots was drawing away.

The sound of the creature behind him was growing louder.

"Wait for me," Reilly called to his friend.

The other moved farther away.

Reilly couldn't see anything except for a dark blur. The alley was too full of shadows for him to discern one thing from another.

It was just one big mess.

He tried wiping again with his tunic, but it only became worse. Splotches of filth caked the garment. Reilly was simply adding to the muck he was trying to be rid of.

Closer and closer, the splashes behind him became.

He had no chance of escape.

The reptilian was too fast.

He stopped running.

He knew he was about to meet his death.

Turning, he brandished his sword towards the pursuer and swung wildly in all directions.

"Come on," he hollered, striking wall and drawing sparks as steel kissed the stone.

Sharp pain bit into his ribs just above his belly. He heard the crack of bone as another sting ensued from his back.

He had been pierced through.

His sword fell to the muck, where it sank quickly beneath the surface.

A warm sensation filled his trousers as coldness spread along his spine.

It wasn't the way he wanted to go out of the world. Pissing himself before he breathed his last.

At least you faced them head-on, he told himself as the sword was pulled from his body.

He dropped to his knees.

"I can't see," he said, not completely knowing why. "Who are you?"

"I Nola'ee," the other replied. The voice was gravelly, but distinctly that of a female. "You brave to face me. You will die slow, in pain. I make it quick."

Reilly frowned, straightening his back as much as he could.

He peered up at her, still not being able to see much more than a foggy image standing before him, and nodded.

"Please," he whispered.

She lifted her sword and swiped it through his neck.

***

Norris ran hard and fast.

He didn't care how much mud he kicked and splashed about. He was no longer concerned for the noise that he made in his desperate effort to flee.

The beast had come for them. It had taken his friend.

There was nothing he could do to help, or at least he argued with himself that the case was so. He didn't even look back when his comrade had called after him, pleaded with him to wait, because he knew it was futile.

The creature bore down on them, relentlessly pursuing them like prey. A hunter and its game.

With his heart throbbing so loudly that it rang in his ears, sweat soaking into his clothes, he ran and ran.

He wasn't even sure if the creature was behind him any longer, but he knew there were others.

There were more beasts, just like the one that came for them.

Beasts with long claws and sharp teeth, coarse skin like leather and stronger than two men combined.

He would not wait for them, or try to hide from them.

One had found them easily enough amongst a crowd of men. Surely, the others could do the same.

Norris knew he needed to make as much ground between the lizard people and himself as he could.

So, he ran.

And ran.

Before him, the lane opened into a street that ran from east to west.

He knew now that entering the alley was an error that had cost him his friend's life. His intention, his new plan, was to get back to the wider streets and run to the palace with the rest of the fleeing men.

A loud splash behind him brought a sudden knot to his stomach.

The beast had caught up to him, or another like it.

He didn't turn; he didn't want to see.

Instead, he kept his eyes on the road ahead. He was closing upon it rapidly.

The splashes behind him intensified. There were more of them. They were gaining upon him.

He moved to the right side of the lane, passing some stacked barrels and boxes that were packed against the wall to the left. The stench struck him hard in the face as he sped by.

Running.

Running.

The road was only a few paces away.

The sound of a barrel or two crashing to the slush almost made his head turn.

He fought the urge, keeping his face forward.

The view opened up. He looked left, knowing there was a street in that direction not too far away.

As he spilled into the street, he turned right.

A sword plunged straight into his chest.

There were men fighting in the street; his men and others he didn't recognise.

Swords were clashing and blood was spraying about.

He had completely focused on what was behind him, so much so that he didn't hear the skirmish.

He looked into the eyes of the man who had stuck the blade into him.

It was an older face, scruffy and weathered.

The sword twisted in him before it retracted.

Norris dropped onto his back.

He felt little pain. Just the overbearing sense of weakness.

The beasts, three of them, appeared at the mouth of the lane.

"Looking for this?" said the man in a harsh voice. "We could use your help."

The man and the three reptilians moved into the fray, leaving Norris to lie upon the cold snow.

He felt numb as the air around him seemed to grow intensely colder and the night immensely darker.

Closing his eyes, he heard the sound of blades ringing and others crying in pain.

Slowly, gradually, the sound grew quieter and quieter, until there was silence.

Twenty-Six

Walters continued to make slow progress, moving eastward along one of the long streets through the northeastern sector of Wintermarsh. He had found a thick blanket amongst the debris of a toppled house and wrapped it about him like a cloak.

Occasionally, he ducked for the nearest shadows or shelter still standing in place as a dragon or two swooped by overhead, or a squad of men wearing white tunics marched by. He remained undetected and was considering himself lucky as he looked to the hills at the edge of the city limits, and the mountains beyond.

That was his intended destination.

Far away from Wintermarsh.

Far away from General Versel and the Maji.

Far away from the commands they gave.

Far away from the insanity that was unfolding around him.

Far away.

He trudged on, moving along the lengthy road that seemed to stretch on forever and ever.

The houses and buildings flanking his path seemed to be less and less damaged the farther he proceeded.

Fires still burned about his vicinity where dragons had attacked the ballistae. The region appeared untouched otherwise.

The flying beasts seemed to evade the area altogether. Their interest was in the district to the west, closer to the palace.

Gradually, Walters came upon a wide boulevard that moved from north to south, crossing his path. He approached it with caution, keeping close to the darkness and well out of sight.

The sound of men talking and moving about stimulated his fear and anxiety. He needed to cross the region without being seen.

The sight of him would encourage questions to be asked. Questions that he didn't want to answer. Answers that would resolve in conflict because he was far away from his post.

The difficulty in crossing the road was that the road was extremely wide, with gardens and small courts stretching through the centre of the access through quite a few crossroads.

At least five long blocks, Walters recalled. The area was open, and there would be no way to avoid being seen.

He thought about going south to detour around the area, but there were fires that appeared to be burning in a long line all the way to the edge of the city. He couldn't be sure there was a safe way through.

The north was the soundest way.

There were fires there too, but they were more to the west of his position now. A few spots of flame dotted the landscape in the distance. Nothing that could prevent him from being able to move around the boulevard. Nothing that would prove an obstacle.

He started into a street to the left of the road he had been travelling. Slowly, carefully, trying to keep the sound of his footfalls as silent as he could, he pressed on.

His plan changed as he felt a slight reinvigoration fill his spirit. He would continue to the northern edge of the city before turning east. It made more sense for him to do so. The open land was closer to the north than it was to the west.

He would have less Wintermarsh to journey through. Less chance of encountering one of the soldiers marching about.

It wasn't long before he reached the first intersection.

Fires burned to his left. Large, catastrophic blazes had engulfed entire blocks.

The boulevard was to his right. He saw men milling about in the centre of the road. A large scorpion weapon, possibly one of only a few left in all the city still intact, loaded and ready to fire a large, pointed shaft directed towards the west where the dragons now circled and swooped.

The beasts were too far out of range. Walters believed their riders, and the dragons themselves, were too smart to come closer to the weapon. Still, the men standing nearby were in position, ready to release the projectile at a moment's notice.

The street Walters needed to cross was narrow. However, the soldiers manning the scorpion were all facing in his direction.

The way was dark. Deeply dark.

There was more than a good chance that they wouldn't see him.

Feeling a great surge of energy, Walters took the plunge.

He dashed over the road and into the street on the other side of the intersection.

Pausing, pressing himself against the wall, he listened.

His heart raced and his breathing was rapid, both sounds filling his ears.

Focusing, using all of his effort and control, he slowed his breath to bring his heart rate down.

It was difficult.

His heightened fears and anxiety were at their peaks.

Still, he listened.

And listened.

No one called after him.

No one came running to investigate anything that they may have seen rush across from one side of the road to the other.

No one.

He had made it.

He was safe.

At least, for now.

At least, until the next cross-road.

Turning back to face the north, Walters continued on.

Slowly, steadily, he made his way through the narrow street, keeping to the shadows.

Now and then, he would find a dark place to hole up and listen, making sure his way was clear and that he wasn't being followed. Then, he would move on, hugging the blanket tightly about him.

The next crossing was clear.

Fires still burned to his left, but there were no eyes watching from the right.

He crossed with no interference.

Onward he moved, edging slowly to the next crossing, his confidence building with each step.

It wouldn't be too long before he would reach the edge of the city. It wouldn't be long before he was out of Wintermarsh.

When you reach the last building, he told himself, *run for it. Run to the nearest farmhouse, snow mound, rocky crag, anything. Then wait. Wait and see if anyone follows. Wait a while. Don't rush. You don't want to make any silly mistakes.*

He shook his head. *No, I do not.*

Following his routine, he continued to pause every now and then. He listened and looked back to see if anyone was tailing him. When he saw it was safe, he continued forward.

Almost there.

The next intersection was coming up.

Not too many more streets to cross now.

He moved close to the walls of the structures lining the right side of the road.

The glare of fire illuminated the facades of the buildings to the right, and into the street he needed to pass through.

Edging along the wall, intending to poke his head around the corner to see if anyone kept watch to the west, Walters crept.

He was only a few inches from the corner when a white soldier appeared in his view.

The soldier was rifling at the cords on his trousers.

"Come on," the man hissed, obviously in desperate need to relieve himself. He undid his ropes and expose himself as he rounded the corner. He was about to face the wall and release when his eyes met those of Walters.

The look of horror on the soldier's face mirrored the sensation Walters felt.

The soldier's brow creased as a tiny groan escaped his lips.

He coughed, splashing piss over Walters' trousers in the process.

A small trickle of blood spilled from his mouth.

It was then that Walters realised that, by mere instinct driven by panic, he had stuck his blade deep into the poor soldier's belly.

The white soldier fell sideways, back into the cross-street.

Staring down at the body, bloodied sword clenched in his hand, Walters was dumbfounded and frozen in place.

A large red puddle expanded from the soldier's belly. His manhood shrunk in the cold air as his life fell away.

"Bloody heck," a voice hollered from around the corner.

His awareness became alert.

His mind returned to the here and now.

Run, you fool.

His legs pounded against the road. He cut across the intersection and into the street across the way.

His heart was racing again.

His breath was rapid.

"Who was that?" someone shouted.

"Who cares?" another called back. "Get after him."

Walters bolted as fast as he could.

Almost there, he thought. *Only a few more streets to cross. Get out of the city. Find somewhere to hide. You can do it.*

Running.

Running.

Footsteps filled the street behind him. There were many on his tail, but he didn't dare turn his head to see how many.

Into another intersection.

More men to his right. At least five.

He sprinted through the crossing as the pursuers combined with the newcomers.

Too many to fight, he considered. *If they catch me, they will cut me up for sure.*

His heart raced loudly, pounding hard inside of his chest. His breath was short and hurried.

He just hoped that he had enough in him to outrun those giving chase.

He just hoped.

Running.

Running.

The next cross-street was drawing nearer and nearer.

He saw the open ground far to the end of the road.

A quick estimate, and he believed there to be only three more intersections after this one.

Increasing his pace, pushing himself harder, he pulled away from the soldiers until their loud steps fell away.

He could outrun them. He knew he would make it now.

Suddenly, ten men appeared on the cross-road before him, blocking his way through.

He skidded to a halt.

Now he was caught between two groups of men.

The pursuers slowed their pace. There was nowhere for Walters to go.

They had him.

Their swords brandished, and with smiles upon their faces, they made their way towards him. Twelve men puffed and huffed, knowing they had caught their prey. The ten from the street pulled their blades free and approached from the other side.

Breathing hard, heart racing, Walters lifted his sword for them to see before dropping it to the ground. He placed his hands behind his head, signalling his surrender.

"What do we do with him?" one man from the street asked.

"We take him to Colonel Owen," another replied.

Walters almost swore.

He had almost forgotten Owen had been placed out here. He and Coogan were posted at the north-eastern sector's command station together.

Wishing he had kept hold of his sword, Walters would rather have the soldiers cut to pieces than have to explain his desertion to his two friends.

It was likely they would kill him, anyway. It was more than likely they would send him to General Versel to be punished.

So close, he thought, peering along the road to the open land beyond the city's limits.

So, so close.

Twenty-Seven

Haildur, leader of the Traruk Clan, pulled his dragon alongside Gruloch. A heated discussion ensued, whereby the Lord of the Haigok seemed to disagree with the older rider's arguments.

Alice watched on with interest and concern. It was rare, from her observations, for the two Haigok to ever be in debate with one another. Usually, the two leaders were a solid force, siding with each other and joining together to put their opinion across.

Not now.

She wasn't able to hear the discussion between the two. With plenty of gesturing to the city below by both parties, particularly towards the white palace, Alice could determine that they were arguing over strategy.

Haildur gave the other a shake of his head before turning his dragon away from the gathering of flying beasts circling above the clouds. He and the only other surviving rider from the northern tablelands descended back to the city below.

"Where are they going?" Alice called over to Gruloch as she veered Liana closer to his dragon.

"To attack," the other answered, sounding alarmed. "He said that it was time to attack head-on. I tried to sway him to stay here, but he wouldn't have it."

Tarnas of the Eranak turned to follow Haildur through the clouds. The other three of his kin were close behind.

"Call them back," Alice shouted in alarm.

Gruloch was already yelling something to the riders of the Kazrekh Clan. One of the cloaked figures raised a horn to his lips to blow a long note. Other dragons that had spread out, distancing themselves from one another, suddenly regrouped.

Not those who followed Haildur, however.

They ignored the trumpet call and pressed on through the clouds.

"Stupid old fool," Gruloch spat. "He'll get himself and all the rest of them killed."

Alice watched on, unable to intervene, as the swirling clouds swallowed five dragons beneath them before they vanished from her view.

***

"There!" The Maji pointed, directing the attention of the twin girls to a small space above the centre of the city.

The dragons emerged one by one through the swirling clouds, heading directly towards the location of the palace.

The little girls focused their energy, fearing the wrath of their husband if they were to fail him. Their hands joined, fingers interlaced.

Their eyes shone white and bright, glowing like a cluster of stars, like the silver light of the moon.

The beasts dived fast.

With their heads pointed straight down, their wings tucked tight against their bodies, they fell faster than stones plummeting towards the ground below.

Five gigantic monsters moved in a controlled fall through the sky.

The soldiers standing by the palace doors watched, awestruck. Even General Versel felt her stomach tighten at the breathtaking sight.

"There they are," Takmel whispered into the girls' ears. "Kill them all."

Both twins opened their mouths as if calling, screaming.

They felt the power release from deep within, reaching through the frosty night air to bite a diving beast.

One dragon spread its wings suddenly in an attempt to slow its descent. It spiralled uncontrollably like a heavy leaf falling from a tree.

Toppling over and over, spinning round and round, the dragon screamed as flesh covering its shoulders stripped away.

A massive, leathery wing tore from the body, separated and thrown away into the sky.

Down it fell.

Down.

Down.

As the other four dragons unfurled their wings wide to level out their approach, the injured beast smashed into the earth with tremendous force.

A great cloud of dust and debris exploded from the surface as a deep rumble resonated over the city like distant thunder.

Four dragon riders, led by Haildur of the Traruk Clan, sped over the rooftops of damaged and burning buildings, leaving their fallen comrade behind. They directed their beasts to the impressive structure that overlooked Wintermarsh as they spread their formation out wide.

One beast made a direct line for a tower to the northern edge of the complex. A long jet of flame burst from its jaws and smothered the tall fortification. No sooner was the structure aflame, than the creature was whooshing over the Maji's head and out towards the ocean to the west.

Three soldiers manning the tower screamed in agony. One leapt from the structure and plunged down the face of the gigantic mound upon which the palace stood.

Another dragon hurried by and used its talons to tear a large portion of the palace roof away. A gaping hole at the apex of the main building opened, revealing broken timber rafters and an empty cavity beneath the slate tiles that covered the roof.

"There," Takmel shouted, pointing to the culprit that had damaged his home.

The girls turned to follow the beast as it twisted through the air, its rider peering to the ground where soldiers had gathered by the palace door.

The dragon turned sharply, directing its snout to the uniformed men.

Versel, standing a few paces from the Maji, saw what was about to happen.

"Move," she hollered to the soldiers standing in formation by the door.

Some men hesitated, not understanding what was about to happen, too busy watching other dragons making their approach.

Most of the men darted across the courtyard for cover behind raised garden beds or deeply recessed sections along the walls as a line of fire swept by the entrance to the palace.

Flames engulfed several men, turning to smoke and ash in an instant.

As the dragon swept by, the two little girls attacked.

Their eyes burned brighter.

Their mouths opened wider.

Versel could have sworn she saw something glowing from deep inside their throats, but with new flames flickering in the courtyard, she couldn't be certain.

The skin around the dragon's neck tore open, as if it was being rapidly eaten away by something unseen.

Deeper and deeper lacerations formed in its muscles and skin about its shoulders and jawbone. Blood spilled over the palace grounds, leaving a deep crimson trail in the snow covering the courtyard.

The dragon flew past the walls surrounding the keep and back over the city, but not before its head fell from its body.

The creature tumbled down the side of the mound, coming to rest in a mess of toppled houses far below.

Without being told, the twins turned their attention to another creature approaching from the north.

Holding hands tightly and staring with wide eyes, they tore ribbons of flesh from the creature's membranous wings.

A stream of blood filled the sky in its wake.

The dragon screamed in agony as it fought to keep itself airborne.

The rider, Tarnas of the Eranak, tried his best to keep his dragon level but to no avail. The poor creature fell fast and hard.

Haildur and the other rider accompanying him turned their dragons about to make a direct attack. They both swooped around the palace complex towards the south.

The sky sounded as if it ripped open, like a great canvas sheet being rent apart, as the beasts sped through the air.

***

"Look," Commander Zakhar said, pointing to the sky as the two dragons passed overhead before turning about. He pulled his bicorn hat from his head to wipe his brow with his sleeve.

"They're going to attack," Jendryng announced. A broad smile stretched over his face, making him look a little like an excited child.

Strewn bodies of white soldiers covered the street about them. Still, more of the enemy were running towards the palace to get away.

For now, the men of Woodmyst and Newholt had paused to watch the two dragons begin their assault.

A cheer erupted as the two beasts increased speed with a few flaps of their wings.

Only Captain Thornton and the Agrodien warriors watched with apprehension.

They watched as the two dragons drew nearer and nearer to the palace.

The space between the creatures and the giant structure closed rapidly.

Nearer.

Nearer.

Thornton gritted his teeth as both beasts crossed the sky directly above the tall wall along the southern edge of the palace grounds.

"Ursula is up there," he growled quietly, as the men about him were roaring, whistling, calling, clapping and chanting.

Yuri heard the captain of the Newholt forces through the din made by the men surrounding them. He reached his hand over and placed it on the old soldier's shoulder.

The dragons were over the courtyard of the palace.

One of them opened its jaws.

A bright orange glow emitted from its mouth.

The air near the palace suddenly burst into red and pink.

Thornton felt as if his heart had simply frozen.

He couldn't tell if he was holding his breath or if it had just stopped of its own accord.

"Q'Sharh!" Yuri hissed, his eyes wide with horror.

The cheering suddenly silenced.

All clapping and chanting had instantly ceased.

The men and Agrodien warriors watched in horror as portions of dragons sailed over the eastern wall and down into the city below.

***

It took every ounce of his energy to keep from screaming.

Dragon blood showered over him from head to foot. Great chunks of flesh smacked against the rock face about him, missing him by mere inches.

The blood covering him was warm, a slight reprieve from the harsh coldness he had experienced since starting the climb.

It made him feel ill, knowing that what covered him was once an ally.

With his breath shaking, and his hands trembling, Warren wiped the blood from his face as best he could. He let out a small groan as he felt tiny pieces of solid particles slip between his fingers, down his tunic, to slither along his spine. Even with his tattered cloak covering him, dead dragon juice had seeped into his clothes and soaked through to the skin.

There was nothing he could do about it but move on.

He checked the blade was still tucked away in his pocket.

It was.

Stretching to the next hold, he continued up the side of the mound towards the palace above.

Hand overhand.

Slowly and steadily.

It wasn't too much farther to the top.

Onward, he pressed, stained crimson and dripping wet.

***

"Good girls," Takmel said with a broad smile.

He kissed the twins on the tops of their heads and wrapped his arms around both of them, almost appearing grateful and loving.

Almost.

Saruun Versel watched, maintaining her composure as well as she could. She saw the girls' wet eyes as they fought back tears.

The light was gone from them now.

Her heart sank a little as she looked upon two children, distraught and scared.

She could also see her master's sincerity was nothing more than pretence. He was good at hiding who he truly was.

But not that good.

"I love you both so much," he said to them as he peered over at the general. "I'd like to see the prisoners."

"My lord?" the general asked, seeking further clarification of his request, concealing her concern for the girls.

"Bring them to me," he commanded. "Bring them here."

"Yes, my lord," she replied with a bow, before moving away to the barracks.

Twenty-Eight

Two soldiers dragged Walters through the wide boulevard to a platform, a large stage hewed into stone at the northern end. Raised garden beds bordered the broad area surrounding the stage with benches built into them. In summer, the gardens would have been a glorious spectacle, with birch, oak and maple trees stretching their long branches filled with leaves over the open ground. Flowers of all colours would spill from the garden beds as the thickest of green grass carpeted the ground from one side of the park to the other.

Minstrels would play festive tunes on the stage as children ran about. They would set markets up along the sides of the road where pedlars could sell useless, exotic trinkets from a far-off land that probably never existed. Stupid, silly young ladies holding onto the arms of stupid, silly young men would often be the sport of such merchants, enticing the eye of a girl with some sparkling gem that was nothing more than shaped and smoothed glass tied to a thin leather cord. Of course, the stupid, silly man would purchase such a trinket for the stupid, silly lady because he believed it would increase his chances of finding himself wrapped in her arms and legs later, when they were alone.

Now, in the deepest, darkest moments of winter, the area was dead. The branches of the birch, oak and maple trees were lifeless, gnarled limbs that twisted over the open ground. Snow blanketed the park instead of fertile grass. The garden beds were empty, and the music emitted from the stage was the shouts of soldiers.

Seated upon the platform, in two wooden chairs near a small fire, were two faces that Walters recognised. The soldiers brought him to the foot of the stage, each carrying him under the arms. Another followed them, Walters' sword and sheath in his hands.

Both men seated on the platform rose to their feet and approached the edge as they dropped Walters to the ground. They peered at him for a long time, paying particular attention to the swelling around his right eye, which had almost completely closed up, and the crooked angle at which his nose sat.

"Who did this to him?" one officer asked.

"A few of the men lashed out, sir," the soldier carrying Walters' weapons replied. He placed the sword and sheath on the edge of the platform.

"Find those men," the officer instructed the soldier. "Bring them to me. Inform them that Colonel Owen wishes to offer a reward for their success."

"At once," the soldier replied as he saluted before turning on his heels.

Owen looked at the two soldiers flanking Walters.

"You may leave," he ordered them, to which they also saluted and moved away.

"Good to see you again, my friend," the other officer said, crouching low.

"Coogan," Walters replied, acknowledging the other. "Forgive me for not looking at you with both of my eyes. It would seem your men thought I needed some readjustments on my face."

"Still of good humour, nonetheless." Owen smiled and took a deep breath as he stared at the injured man. "Why are you here, Walters?" His question was met with silence. "You are meant to be stationed to the north of the palace. Why are you here? Where's Larson?"

More silence.

"Is Larson dead?" Coogan pressed. "Did you kill him?"

"I didn't kill him," Walters was quick to reply.

"But you *did* kill one of our men," said Owen. "Why did you run? Where were you going to?"

Silence.

"You were running away," Owen continued. "Weren't you? You abandoned your post and left Larson to die."

Walters lifted his head and looked at the men. He offered a small nod. There was no reason to hide the truth from them. They would simply keep asking and asking until they got the answers they wanted.

"Why?" Coogan asked.

"Look around you," Walters replied. "The city is gone. Everything is burning."

"It's not that bad here," Owen told him. "A couple of smashed windows. Nothing a good lick of paint and some minor repairs won't be able to fix."

"People are dead all over," the other argued.

"Well," Owen replied, "that's your fault for not getting them out in time. We took all the women and children to North Keep before the first attack. What were you lot doing?"

"Are you blind?" Walters asked. He couldn't believe the blasé attitude of both men before him. "The entire city is in ruins. The dragons have destroyed it all. We can't recover from this."

"We can recover from this," Coogan answered. "And we will. It might take some time, but we can rebuild. We can repopulate."

"I'm looking forward to that part," Owen jested. "Besides, the dragons are done for. They've started attacking the palace."

"And this is good news?" Walters questioned, his brow creasing.

"Yes," Owen answered. "Our scouts informed us that five of the monsters came from the clouds and all of them were destroyed. Nothing can get near the Maji. He will defeat our enemies before the night is through and we will live on to fight and fuck for another day."

"But not you," Coogan put in. "You will need to be executed for your treachery."

As the officer spoke, three men approached, accompanied by the soldier that Owen had commanded to retrieve those who had beaten Walters.

"Are these the ones?" Owen asked the soldier. "Did these fellows beat this traitor into the state he is currently in?"

"We did, sir," one of them replied, quite pleased with himself.

"Come up here, lads," Coogan said, inviting them with a wave of his hand.

The three soldiers moved to the side of the platform, where there was a set of stairs carved into the rock. The other soldier, the one that had done Coogan's bidding, moved to stand behind Walters. He watched the three others climb the steps and move across the stage to the two officers.

Walters slowly lifted himself to his feet, stumbling slightly.

The soldier behind him placed a hand on his arm to help steady the injured man.

"Are you all right, sir?" the soldier asked.

"You're a good man," Walters told him. "A good soldier. Help me to the edge of the dais. I need something to lean against."

"Perhaps you would be better placed upon the ground, sir?"

"Too cold," said Walters. "I need to be on my feet."

The soldier nodded, his hands upon the traitorous officer's shoulders as he aided Walters to the edge of the platform.

"Well done, lads," Coogan said to the three approaching across the stage. Both he and Owen reached their hands out to shake the soldiers' hands in a congratulatory manner.

"He's a wily one," Owen added. "We've known him for years. I'm surprised you were able to capture him."

"He surrendered in the end," one of the proud soldiers answered as he took Coogan's hand in his.

"Surrendered, you say?"

"Yessir." The soldier smiled.

"And you still felt it necessary to beat my friend to a pulp?" Owen asked. "Even after he surrendered to you?"

The three soldiers looked suddenly dumbfounded.

Like a flash, both Coogan and Owen drew their daggers from their belts and slit the throats of the two men with whom they were shaking hands. The third turned to run.

At that moment, Walters reached for his sword resting on the edge of the platform. With a quick spin, he sliced the blade through the helpful soldier's neck, taking his head from his shoulders.

Owen threw his dagger at the third soldier on the stage, striking the man between the shoulder blades. The soldier fell clumsily to the platform, cracking his forehead open as it struck the stone.

Coogan, by this time, had noticed what Walters had done. He pulled his own sword free of its sheath and started for the edge of the stage towards the injured prisoner.

Taking a few steps backwards, away from the stone platform, Walters prepared for the attack.

So many things happened at once.

Coogan leapt from the stage.

Owen turned to see what was happening, reaching for his sword instinctively.

Walters brought his blade around in an arc from his shoulders, down behind his back and upwards by his side.

Coogan neared the ground, just in front of Walters. The other's blade met him, into his crotch, before sliding deep into his belly.

Owen sprinted over the platform, down the steps and around the side of the stone stage. "On me," he shouted. "On me."

All soldiers in close proximity heard the alarm. The sound of many footfalls filled Walters' ears. He knew he didn't stand a chance against all of them.

He also knew he would never leave Wintermarsh again after tonight.

"You won't escape this," Owen told him, his voice filled with rage.

"I know," Walters answered.

Two soldiers attacked from behind.

Walters reacted quickly, swinging his blade around his body with one hand to block their blows. He lifted his dagger from his belt with the other and dug it into one attacker's face. At the same moment, he plunged his sword into the chest of the other soldier.

Owen used that moment to lunge towards his old friend and begin his own assault. He raised his sword over his head, its point directed at the wounded man.

Walters heard the other approaching.

He ducked low, yanking his sword from the body of the dead soldier and swiping it wide.

The blade lodged deep into the soft tissue beneath Owen's ribs, cutting so deep that it touched his spine.

It wasn't enough to save Walters.

Owen had plunged his sword through Walters' flesh, between his neck and shoulders. The blade sank straight down into the cavity inside the injured man's ribs and deep into his body. Only the hilt and handle of the weapon stuck from his shoulder.

Both men crashed to the ground as a dozen men appeared around the edge of the garden area.

The soldiers watched in silence as the two friends closed their eyes and breathed their last breaths together.

Twenty-Nine

Thornton led the ground force to the sloping road that wound its way along the side of the great mound in the midst of Wintermarsh. Their intended destination was the structure at the top, surrounded by tall walls and several towers. If archers manned the structures, the men of Woodmyst, Newholt, Dendadia, and the Agrodien warriors would be easy prey.

Then, there were the guards posted along the road itself.

They had set stations up at intervals along the path. The only way past them was to overcome them. The ledge to the left was too steep to climb up, and the slope to the right too sheer to go down.

At least twenty guards stood watch at each posting. They armed all with long swords, protected with face-covering helmets and thick armour, and draped with white tunics.

The fleeing men from the plaza found revitalised boldness once they had reached the steep road. Passing the first guard post, a few yards from the base of the path, they reformed and waited for the invading army to approach.

"This'll be a bloodbath," Commander Zakhar stated.

"Theirs or ours?" First Officer Grady asked as they slowed their approach, following Captain Thornton and his men along a wide street that led to the rising, winding road.

Before any protest could be given, Yuri charged forward, the other Agrodien on his tail.

A sudden surge of arrows from a small band of archers, still retreating from the earlier skirmish in the plaza, flung through the air from the enemy in a desperate attempt to hinder the rapid approach of the nine warriors.

The reptilians leapt and dodged the attack. Most of the arrows struck the buildings in the street surrounding the men of Newholt, Woodmyst, and Dendadia.

"Shit!" Jendryng spat as a bolt brushed by his cheek, thudding harmlessly into a house wall directly behind him.

The same couldn't be said for several of their comrades, who were hit in their chests and legs.

"We're just targets standing here, lads," Thornton called. "Come on."

With that, he raced after the Agrodien, lifting his sword above his head.

A mighty roar went out as the men charged towards the rising road to the palace.

Yuri was already tearing into the men at the first guard post with tooth, claw, and blade. Nola'ee and Nakrah sliced their way through the archers before another barrage of arrows could be unleashed upon their allies. The remaining six reptilians charged up the hill after more fleeing archers.

Duga was the first to strike at them, using his own bow and arrow. His bolt struck deep into the back of an archer's skull, knocking the man hard to the ground.

Kavnu and Draav, with their blades held over their heads and pointed at the enemy, hacked into the backs of the stragglers.

Panicky breaths and cries of fear escaped the white soldiers as their pursuers closed in fast. There was no time to turn and fight, as a small few discovered. The Agrodien warriors simply cut them down as if they were crops for the harvest.

By the time Yuri had re-joined his warriors, Thornton and his men were running past the first guard post, stepping over dismembered bodies and through pools of blood.

"I hope they leave some for us," Sparrow jested, copping a strange look from First Officer Grady as they increased their pace.

It didn't look promising for the men.

The Agrodien had reached the second guard post and engaged in battle with the soldiers there.

Thornton could see Yuri's dominant form, silhouetted against a fire behind the post, swinging his giant arms and long tail about as his sword ripped through white soldiers as if made of rags.

"What's that?" Commander Zakhar called, pointing to a small object tossed from the guard post, hurtling high into the air before it bounced on the road.

It was a head still wearing its helmet.

It had been torn, not cut, from the neck. A short length of spine still attached at its base.

Zakhar looked on, a little sickened by the sight.

"Come on," Thornton hollered, quickening his pace.

As they reached the second guard post, the Agrodien started on for the next.

There was nothing left for the allied men to do here, so they followed the reptilians onward.

Yuri watched as Nola'ee reached the third guard post before the rest of them. She leapt high and brought her blade down deep into the white soldier's chest before ripping it free again, just in time to block an attack from her side.

Swinging her sword around her body, she cut into her opponent's leg, sending him to the ground as another raced at her with his sword held high.

She was quick to dodge the sudden attack, rolling quickly to her right across the frost. The assailant's sword struck the ground where Nola'ee had been before he felt the kiss of her blade in his ribs.

She is almost as good as the Kayl'sro, Yuri believed. *Perhaps not quite as quick.*

Nevertheless, no man's blade had come close to striking her. Not one soldier had been a genuine challenge to the female. Yuri also believed no Agrodien would pose a suitable test for Nola'ee, either.

Bein and Nakrah were next to join her side, finding challengers of their own instantly. The three Agrodien formed a circle of sorts, their backs towards each other as they fought off a small number of white soldiers, only twenty, attacking from all sides.

"Move on to the next guard post," Nola'ee shouted to Yuri as she plunged her sword through one of the white soldiers. "We have this under control."

Yuri gave a nod in reply and charged past. He turned to look quickly at those following. With a quick wave of his hand, gesturing them all to follow, and getting a look of confirmation from Thornton several yards behind him, he continued up the hill.

Thirty

"We lost Haildur," Gruloch called out to Alice, pulling alongside her. The dragons were regrouping above the clouds again. She counted them quickly. There were fifteen remaining, including Liana. "This tactic is no longer working. We must try something else. There are few of us left."

He was right.

The strategy was failing. More dragons had fallen within the past hour than any period during the battle.

Dark magic was pulling the beasts to the ground. Alice could feel it.

"There is nothing left but to either flee or attack head-on," the girl answered, calling over the howling wind. "I don't want to be responsible for the losses of any more Haigok or dragons. Take your people and go. Flee to a safe distance. I can't ask anything more of you, my friend."

"What of you?" he asked. "You must come with us."

"No," she shouted. "My family is down there somewhere. The men and Agrodien still fight upon the ground. I'll make a direct attack on the palace. I'm going to confront the Maji myself."

"That was Haildur's error," Gruloch reminded her. "And look where he is now."

"I know," Alice replied, as she urged Liana to turn towards the clouds swirling beneath them. "Take your people to safety," she shouted into the wind. "That's my last instruction to you."

With that, she dived out of sight and into the swirling clouds.

Gruloch pulled his dragon up to a halt where it hovered in place, over the area where Alice and Liana had vanished.

***

Willis stepped from the barracks and into the courtyard. The sound of men shouting and roaring from outside the wall was growing louder.

An army was coming.

"Gather your weapons," he shouted back to the doorway. "Put on your armour. Get out here now."

"What about the prisoners?" a voice called back from inside.

"They're in a cage," Willis hollered back. "They're not going anywhere. Get out here."

Within moments, a stream of men charged from the doorway. They moved as one, with Willis at their head, making their way to the large iron gates that opened onto the road that wound back down to the city below.

Willis was first onto the twisting path, running through the guard post at full pace with his sword high. His eyes fell instantly upon the men charging up the slope towards him. His fellow soldiers, guarding sections down the road, were already engaged in battle or being torn apart by sword and spear.

He quickly glanced up to the ramparts of the wall surrounding the palace grounds where he could see a few men standing in place. Each of them held bows and appeared to carry full quivers.

"What are you waiting for?" he called up to them as the rest of the men from the barracks spilled onto the road behind him.

The first few soldiers leaving the palace grounds pulled to a sudden stop. Their faces drained of colour as a deep fear gripped their hearts.

Willis was still peering up at the archers on the wall, wondering why they hadn't engaged in shooting the attacking army down.

"Load your bows and fi-ah..." he said before Nola'ee sank her blade into his throat.

He gurgled softly as a thin trail of blood trickled over his chin.

His eyes moved to her as she pulled the blade free. Dropping to his knees, he stared up at the figure standing over him with awe.

He didn't believe he had seen anything so remarkable. Taller than any man. Menacing, terrifying and strangely beautiful at the same time. Terror gripped him as he watched her raise her sword above her head, ready to strike again.

He tried to say something, tried to protest, only spurting a thick spray of blood from the wound in his neck instead.

Not even Versel could compare to this vision. There is nothing so majestic.

Or so Willis thought, until he saw another reptilian leap past him, high in the air with a blade held in both hands over his head.

The creature was larger, robust, and massive. It moved with a speed and grace that no trained fighter could match, turning and slicing into Willis' men effortlessly.

Nola'ee brought her blade down hard. It sank deep into Willis' skull, bringing instant death.

"Save some for us, Yuri," Nakrah called to the older Agrodien, who was engaged in battle with the soldiers by the gate.

"Perhaps you should try to keep up with me," Yuri replied as he blocked an attack from one soldier's blade with his own, kicking another white guard from the road at the same time. He flung the guard into the air and over the side of the giant mound upon which the palace stood.

***

Liana burst from the cloud with a tremendous roar. She spread her wings wide and directed herself directly towards the white palace.

Alice scanned the area quickly, searching for soldiers, allies, familiar faces.

She saw the skirmish near the gates, the army of her allies climbing the road.

Then she saw him.

Takmel.

He was standing in the middle of the courtyard that opened out upon the main entrance of the fortress. Near to him were two small girls, staring up at her.

"There she is," the Maji gasped. "Finally." He pressed his hands on the twin girls' shoulders. "Bring her down."

Their eyes turned a glowing white. Their stares fixed upon the rapidly approaching beast.

Closer and closer it drew. Its jaws widened as if in preparation to douse the area with fire.

At that moment, the three remaining queens of the Seven re-appeared at the palace door.

"Ah, my wives!" The Maji chuckled. "Just in time to see it all come to an end."

Takmel summoned Commander Versel with his hand, smirking madly all the while.

"Fetch the prisoners," he said. "I want them to see how this all ends."

"Bring them, now," she barked to some of her men gathered nearby.

Alice turned Liana away.

Shooting wide towards the sea, the dragon circled the palace at a distance. She had seen guards moving from the palace doors to another building nearby, that she presumed to be barracks. Either the men were gathering more soldiers, or perhaps one weapon that had taken many other dragons down was in position on the palace grounds.

As she flew out, high over the water, she looked for a scorpion weapon and saw none. There were no ballistae near the palace. Only Takmel, the brides of the Maji and soldiers.

The brides.

The two little girls by his side.

They were the weapons he used to bring Haildur to the ground.

Her heart sank a little as she considered the situation.

The girls were young, like her.

Alice wondered if they committed themselves to him, or if they did what they could out of fear of him.

In either case, she knew they needed to be stopped, not only because they were a danger to Liana and any other dragon in the air, but because the Maji drew his power from them.

She could sense they were very powerful indeed.

She urged Liana to straighten her approach, marking Takmel as the destination.

It was time to attack.

Hand over hand, the boy climbed.

The skin of his fingers was so numb, he couldn't feel the cold stone beneath them. His face felt as if it had frozen in place. His body shivered and trembled so violently that his muscles started to have strange fits of spasms.

Through the howling wind, he heard the din of battle above him.

Swords clashed.

Men cried out and an occasional mighty roar of an Agrodien filled the air.

He saw the top of the iron gates from his position. It wasn't very far away.

Creeping along the rock face, careful not to slip on the icy stone, he moved to the edge of the tall wall that surrounded the palace grounds. Slowly, he lifted himself to the road where he saw the battle taking place.

The white soldiers were fighting valiantly, but the Agrodien warriors were better. Soon the guards of the palace would be overwhelmed as more men of the eastern lands climbed the road, drawing nearer to the fight.

With a quick glance around as he crouched by the entrance to the palace grounds, he noticed all eyes fixed upon the skirmish.

Believing he had remained unnoticed, he started through the gates, keeping close to the wall.

He sneaked into the grounds, creeping behind the guardhouse and into the shadows, hoping to remain unseen.

Crouching again, he patted his pocket. The knife was still there.

He wrapped his arms around his chest and shivered uncontrollably, violently.

Here, between the guardhouse and the wall, he sheltered from the wind, but it was too little, too late.

The chill had penetrated through to the bone.

Alice watched several soldiers manhandling four women, pushing them into a line in front of Takmel and the two little girls. She recognised them instantly.

Catherine, Amicia, Ursula and her mother.

She panicked and tried to urge Liana back into the sky.

It was too late.

The two little girls had made contact with the dragon. White light radiated from their eyes as they stared directly at the beast.

Liana's great membranous wings were tearing open. Alice heard the wind whistling through the new wounds in the beast's skin. Ribbons of flesh tore away as blood sprayed out in a vaporous trail.

Liana roared from the pain as she fell uncontrollably.

Takmel laughed hysterically as he watched the dragon plummet.

"Tear the bitch to shreds!" he shouted, clapping his hands.

Emily struggled against her captor, screaming through her gag in agonised protest.

Turning on his heels, the Maji smirked at her. He looked back to the sky to watch the dragon fall as he quickly moved to Versel, taking a dagger from her belt.

The First Garrison Commander had no time to protest. Nor would she have.

She looked to him, a little confused at first, as he lifted the blade away, but resumed her posture as any good, obedient soldier should.

"An army at the gate," a voice called from the wall. "An army at the gate."

Takmel's expression immediately changed from elation to frustration. He turned to Versel and pointed to the falling dragon and the girl on its back.

"Take care of her," he commanded. "I don't need any interruptions."

"Yes, my lord," the general replied, pulling her sword from its sheath.

The Maji grabbed both of the twin girls by the scruffs of their necks, leaving four guards to watch the prisoners. He forced the twins over the courtyard a short distance towards the gatehouse. They both winced as his fingers dug into their muscles, causing intense discomfort.

"Here," he said to them both, coldly. He turned them both to face him before crouching to the ground. "Join hands," he instructed, manipulating their limbs with his fingers to make them do what he wanted. "Now, put your other hands upon me."

They complied, one placing her hand on his left shoulder, the other placing her hand on his right shoulder.

He placed his own hands on the ground and closed his eyes.

With a low, deep voice that seemed to rumble through the earth, he spoke one word.

"Rise."

Alice prepared for impact.

"I'm so sorry, girl," she said as the ground came up to them fast.

Liana hit hard, smashing through the southern wall that surrounded the palace courtyard. She slid on her stomach, breaking through a storehouse and several raised gardens, sending stone, dirt and snow spraying into the air all about her.

Finally, she came to a sudden stop after hitting the side of the stronghold. Alice came flying out of her saddle, through the air with both swords at the ready.

She heard the dragon groaning behind her as she landed on her feet.

Her rage was too strong to ignore.

Takmel was before her. Just across the courtyard.

Her mother, sister and friends, bound and gagged, upon their knees and guarded by only four men just a few yards away.

She started towards them, intending to free them of their bonds.

A thousand thoughts ran through her head. Most of which resolved in her joining with the other three of her coven and destroying Takmel once and for all.

It would soon come to pass, she believed.

Takmel and his two small brides were across the courtyard, away from his prisoners. It would all be over soon.

A flash of a blade brought her back to reality. She blocked the attack easily enough with a quick flick of her wrist to counter the blow with one of her own swords.

The sound of steel against steel rang out loud and clear as Alice focused her attention upon the tall, blonde woman dressed in dark armour.

"I'm afraid I can't let you pass," the woman said. "I am General Saruun Versel, First Garrison Commander of the Maji."

Alice maintained her silence as she quickly evaluated the woman by her stance and how she held her weapon. The girl was certain that the general was a great warrior, but nothing she couldn't handle.

Versel gestured to twenty soldiers gathering behind her, placing themselves between the four prisoners and herself.

"These men, and I, are charged with the duty of stopping you," the general explained.

"Stopping?" Alice asked, "Or killing?"

"The Maji's words were, *take care of her,*" Versel replied. "I personally would prefer stopping to be a sufficient resolution. But if killing you sees my orders fulfilled, then so be it."

With that, the general swung her massive sword over her head and down towards Alice's small body. The girl raised her left hand, using the blade she held to block the blow. Her right hand jabbed her other sword towards Versel, intending to plunge it into the general's gut.

It was knocked off course by the sword of one of the twenty white soldiers who had put himself between the girl and the armoured woman.

With a quick look about her, Alice saw the soldiers were surrounding her.

They intended to attack her from all sides.

She tightened her grip on her swords.

Her knuckles cracked loudly as they turned white.

"You could all just walk away," she told them, looking to Versel as she spoke.

"I must obey my master," the general told her.

Alice peered quickly over to the Maji, still crouched to the ground, his hands upon the snow. His two young brides were standing by him with their hands on his shoulders. Their eyes glowed brightly as they stared blankly into the sky.

Some terrible was about to happen.

She needed to get to him, to stop whatever it was that he was doing.

Turning her attention back to Versel, she corrected her stance and prepared to fight.

"When you are ready, then," she said.

Thirty-One

Captain Thornton stopped in his tracks. He was only a few yards from the combat between the Agrodien warriors and the white soldiers. Holding his arms out, he signalled the others under his command to halt.

"What is it?" Brook asked, pointing to their reptilian friends. "The fight is right there."

"Look," the captain said, pointing to the bodies strewn over the road before them.

Severed limbs, broken torsos, and dismembered pieces of flesh quivered and moved.

"By the gods," Commander Zakhar murmured as he watched a blood-soaked man rise to his feet. Much of the figure's face hung precariously by a few strands of skin about the cheeks and chin, baring wet flesh and bone for all to see.

Soon, more of the dead lifted themselves from the ground, blocking the allied men from reaching the fighting Agrodien near the gates.

A call resounded from down the line, near the rear.

"The dead are marching this way," a voice shouted.

Thornton peered back along the side of the steep mound to where the path hugged tightly to the rocky wall down the way. Sure enough, there were dead soldiers slowly making their way up the embankment, dragging swords and axes after them.

They were trapped.

"We can't kill the dead," First Officer Grady remarked as he watched the dead men before they start their approach.

"We fight until we can't," Thornton told him.

With that, the captain raised his sword and charged up the hill towards the enemy. Brook, Jendryng, Sparrow, and Vawdrey were close behind. Each of the men marked a foe as they drew nearer.

With a quick slash of their blades, limbs fell free of the dead soldiers. It wasn't enough to stop the assault, only enough to either disarm them or catch them off balance.

Thornton hit his blade hard against the side of his adversary. It caused the dead man to stumble and trip over the side of the road.

The white soldier tumbled down the embankment, bouncing off boulders and sliding down sheer rock faces until he came to a rest in a thick pile of snow collected on a small ledge. The dead man then pulled himself from the deep frost and started the long climb back up the rock face.

Thornton had no time to wait for the soldier's return. Another was already upon him, swinging a double-sided battle-axe towards the captain's head.

Ducking beneath the strike, Thornton rolled over the ground. He quickly swiped his blade at the figure's legs, removing one limb below the knee.

The axeman fell hard, dropping his weapon to the road with a loud clang.

Sparrow, engaged in his own battle with a dead swordsman, saw the battle-axe bounce on the ground near his feet. He kicked at it, sending it sliding across the road to Thornton.

The captain lifted himself to his feet quickly, sheathed his sword, retrieving the axe from the ground.

The fallen axeman, lying upon his belly, reached for Thornton with both arms. The captain raised the battle-axe and brought it down hard, straight through the axeman's spine. The sharp sound of iron striking stone resonated as the axe connected with the road beneath the figure.

Still, the axeman reached out to Thornton.

He lifted the axe again and struck the dead man through the spine over and over until the figure split in two.

With a swift kick, he sent the upper half of the man over the side of the mound to let it fall into the darkness below.

By this time, all the men were engaged in battle.

Thornton looked up the hill to the Agrodien warriors by the gate.

They were having as tough a time as he and the rest of his men.

The reptilians were having small victories, cutting down a foe, only to see the same man resurrected and ready to fight again.

"Q'Sharh!" Yuri roared as he planted his boot into the head of a fallen soldier. "Stay down."

The reptilian stepped away, ready to fight another soldier who was charging from his right. The white soldier swung his blade around from his side, intending to chop into the Agrodien as if he were a tree.

Yuri stepped out of the way of the attack, plunging his own blade into the attacker's belly. The man moaned loudly as the wind evacuated his lungs from the blow.

The Agrodien pulled his sword free of the soldier with one hand as he seized the man by the head with the other. With a great hurl, he sent the soldier into the air, out past the road and over the side of the mound.

"Why did you do that?" Nola'ee asked as she parried the blow of another white soldier's blade.

"They are coming back to life," he told her. "I saw Captain Thornton send them down the side. It is an excellent strategy. It will take them some time to make their way back up here."

Nola'ee sliced her blade through the belly of her opponent, tearing open both armour and flesh. Her gaze fell upon the man whose head had met a violent end by Yuri's boot..

The figure was pushing itself back to its feet, leaving its crushed skull and minced remains of its head upon the ground.

"You might want to send that one over the side, also," she said.

Yuri turned to see the dead man standing before him. The figure's lower jaw had remained in place, displaying a row of lower yellowing teeth that jutted up through a mess of wet, red flesh.

"Q'Sharh!" Yuri spat as he raised his sword.

Alice ducked beneath a wide attack from Versel's blade. Simultaneously, the girl kicked her left leg out as she spun on the toes of her right foot. She knocked the legs from beneath two white soldiers, sending them falling onto their backs.

Like a flash, she leapt upon them and plunged her blades into their chests. Three men rushed her, bringing their swords down upon her position.

She was too fast, tucking her legs as she crouched and rolled forwards out of harm's way. In one fluid motion, she was back on her feet and turning to face the three nearest attackers.

One, on the left, brought his sword upwards in a wide arc. Another, in the middle, swung his long blade over his head with both hands. The third, on the right, levelled his sword point towards the girl's body and lunged forward.

Alice blocked the arcing blade on the left with one of her swords. The sound of steel clashing filled her ears as she kicked high and hard with her right foot into the face of the soldier in the centre. Her body twisted in the air, bringing her left foot off the ground.

She used the sword in her right hand to knock the right-most soldier's blade out of his hand as her left leg snapped around to strike him on the side of the head.

All three crumpled to the ground as the girl landed on her feet.

Not giving the men time to recuperate, she stuck her blades into the necks of all three in rapid succession.

The remaining fifteen soldiers looked at her, surprised. Five of their own were on the ground, dead, and the girl didn't even appear to be breaking a sweat.

She was calm.

She was in her element.

"Don't just stand there," Versel said to them.

Four men nearest to the general were first to move. They ran at the girl as fast as they could.

Their armour was heavy, Alice saw. It slowed them down.

She crouched slightly as they drew near to her, leaping high into the air at the last moment.

Her legs twisted and her body rolled, turning the girl upside-down as the men passed beneath her.

She stuck two of the soldiers with her swords, plunging the blades deep into the soft flesh between their shoulders and necks.

Landing back upon her feet, she turned to the left-most man. He was already swiping his sword towards her.

She blocked it with her right-hand blade and stuck him in the belly with her left.

The last of the four attackers charged from behind her.

With a quick flick of her left wrist, she turned the blade around in her hand so that it pointed past her back. She pushed with her legs to lean towards the approaching soldier, sending the sword through his chest plate and deep into his ribs.

By now, the other eleven men were placing themselves into position around her.

Alice peered at the general. The woman looked afraid.

Nine men were down, and not even a mere scratch on the girl.

Versel's countenance changed from being scared to one of pure anger. She screamed in frustration and lunged towards Alice. Her sword chopped and hacked through the air as she drew closer and closer to the girl.

There was nowhere to go.

The white soldiers completely surrounded her. Leaping over them would only prolong the inevitable. She had to be rid of this warrior woman.

Alice stabbed her left sword back into the throat of a white soldier standing directly behind her.

What happened next occurred in the blink of an eye.

The soldier, with the girl's blade sticking from his neck, was still standing on his feet.

Alice lifted herself, using the hilt of the protruding sword, so that she could kick out with both feet towards Versel.

The general copped a hefty kick to the chest, which sent her flying.

As Alice fell back upon the pierced soldier, knocking him to the ground, Versel smashed into the palace wall with a thud.

The general fell limp on the ground, dropping her sword by her side.

The girl rolled back to her feet, flashed her blades back to her sides, and prepared to fight again.

The twelve white soldiers peered across the ground to their fallen leader.

Versel moved, murmuring softly and appearing extremely groggy.

All white soldiers turned their glaring eyes upon Alice. Not one of them looked happy to see their general laid out upon the ground.

Alice took a deep breath and tightened her grip on her blades.

The twelve raced forward and attacked as one.

The girl blocked and parried blows that came at her with ferocity, strength, and speed.

Liana roared, possibly in an attempt to scare the men away from her keeper, or possibly because she was in tremendous pain.

Alice wanted to comfort the beast, but the sight of flashing blades had her attention for the time being.

She kicked out with her right boot, connecting with the knee of one of her opponents. A sharp snap echoed from the limb as the soldier fell hard.

He screamed as he dropped his blade.

Alice let him writhe in agony as she continued the fight with the other eleven.

Blocking, parrying, slashing.

The throat of another opened, sending a fine spray of blood over her face.

It did not deter her.

Now there were ten.

She swept her left foot wide along the ground, knocking one man onto his back.

As she blocked the blow of one man to her right, she plunged her other sword into the fallen man.

Recoiling immediately afterwards, she turned and hacked her left sword into the side of another, where the chest plate separated near the hip. There was only a thick layer of leather in that spot, not thick enough to stop her blade.

Eight.

They regrouped before her, in a line. They now stood between her and her mother, sister, Ursula and the queen.

Alice glanced over to Versel quickly. The general was unconscious.

One soldier suddenly lunged.

The girl was too quick for him, removing his head before he could make contact with his blade.

His body slammed into the ground beside her.

The seven enduring soldiers stood in place, catching their breath.

They leered at Alice, but there was fear in their eyes.

Each of them knew they couldn't beat her, but they had their orders.

One moved.

Alice tensed for another bout.

Suddenly, the soldier stopped.

His attention fell upon the area immediately behind the girl.

"Oh shit," another said, stepping backwards slowly.

Soon, the other men edged away cautiously.

She looked at them, confused at first. Then she heard the slow clunking sound of movement behind her.

The seven retreated away, faster and faster, keeping their faces towards the scene behind her.

She turned.

Liana gave a soft chirp.

It wasn't the friendly noise she usually gave. There was a hint of uncertainty in the call.

The bodies of the fallen thirteen soldiers were moving. Rising. Crawling. Reaching for weapons.

Alice quickly looked over her shoulder to the Maji.

His hands were resting on the ground. The two little girls still had him by the shoulders. Their eyes, brightly illuminated, were staring into the sky.

"Bastard," Alice hissed, as she turned her attention back to the dead.

Thirty-Two

Throughout the city, the dead rose.

Thousands of the slain, soldiers and civilians, buried and lying amongst the devastation of Wintermarsh, crawled, walked, and slithered through debris. Slowly, gradually, they made their way into the streets, striking terror in all who witnessed their resurrection.

Charred corpses hobbled from the wreckage of dragon fire. Crushed mothers and their children clambered from toppled structures. Fallen warriors picked themselves up from the ground and limped along the streets of the city.

Every one of them made their way towards the palace.

They had heard the call of their master.

"By the gods," a sailor standing by a window muttered.

He was guarding the door to a tiny house by the side of the plaza, keeping watch as others tended to the wounded inside.

"What is it? Captain Rashiid asked, seated by the stove, nursing his own bandaged knee where an arrow had struck him.

"The dead," the sailor replied. "The ones that the Agrodien tossed from the windows."

Several of the wounded suddenly bore worried faces.

Upon hearing the word of his people, *Agrodien*, Rabor, lifted his head and peered at the sailor. The reptilian pushed his hand against the puncture wound in his thigh, the tight bandage stained with a small spot of blood, wincing as he swung his legs over the side of the table.

"You should stay where you are," Rashiid told him.

"Agrodien," the other said, pointing to the door.

"No," the captain replied, shaking his head. "No Agrodien. Just the dead."

Rabor rose to his feet and shuffled to the sailor's side.

Sure enough, there were no others of his kind to see as he peered through the window, but he could clearly see the archers that had been torn and tossed into the court moving away. Some crawled, having their lower limbs ripped away. Others walked, but they lacked an upper appendage or two.

"They're leaving," the sailor reported. "They're going towards the northern end of the plaza."

The wounded throughout the room relaxed their countenances.

The dead were not coming for them.

"They go to Maji," Rabor said. He appeared agitated, coiling his tail and making a fist with one hand. "They go for Yuri. They go for Kayl'sro Alice."

Rashiid nodded as the Agrodien turned to face him.

"We're in no state to fight them," he informed the reptilian. "We can't defeat the dead. Not like this. They will win."

"I die for Kayl'sro Alice," Rabor replied, standing tall and defiant.

"And then you'll be one of them," the captain explained. "You will die and then come back to fight your Kayl'sro."

Rabor took a moment to absorb the other's words.

Eventually, he lowered his head with a small nod and accepted what he had been told. He turned back to the window and peered through, watching a white soldier, devoid of everything below his ribs, crawl across the snow, trailing after the rest of the dead.

Thornton kicked another of the white soldiers over the side of the steep embankment. The warrior bounced off several of the dark stones on his way down before knocking another, who was crawling back towards the battle, from the rock face and into the darkness below.

The din of clashing swords close by intermingled with similar sounds coming from afar.

The captain moved his gaze down the road, where he could see the cavalry near the end of the line. The dead surrounded them.

More and more figures appeared from along the path, streaming from the city's streets and moving together like a slow herd. For every one that a living man cut down, ten more would arrive, then the one cut down would rise again.

As Thornton watched one horse get pulled to the ground, its rider torn apart, he realised it was a lost cause.

They couldn't win.

Not against this horde of ghouls.

He looked to the Agrodien fighting a few yards away, up the embankment.

They were facing similar odds.

The dead were clambering from over the sides of the road and back into the fight quicker than the reptilians could deal with them.

"This is it," Thornton growled, not intending for his words to be heard.

"Fight until we can't," Sparrow said, lopping the head off his opponent. He then pushed his sword into the torso of the dead man, who was still swinging his own blade wildly, and steered him over to the edge of the road. With a forceful nudge, Sparrow sent the headless figure tumbling down the side of the mound. He turned to face Thornton. "That's what you would always say to us. Fight until you can't."

"I fear this may be the day when we find out what that means exactly," Thornton replied, allowing his sword to find a challenger of its own. He hacked the blade through the arm of another white soldier, causing the dead man to drop his axe on the ground.

Commander Zakhar turned from the road's edge, after sending another corpse over the side, and thrust the point of his sword into the temple of Thornton's opponent.

The figure's face contorted, rolling his eyes up into his head as he curled his lips and bared his teeth.

"I like that," the commander told them. "Fight until you can't."

First Officer Grady reached over with one hand, grabbing the same dead man by the back of his tunic, between the shoulders. As both Thornton and Zakhar retrieved their blades, the first officer tossed the figure over the side of the road.

"This is a last-ditch effort on the part of this Maji," Grady said before peering over to Yuri. The large Agrodien was tossing two of the dead soldiers over the cliff, one in each hand. "My guess is that their queen is in there beating the living shit out of him, one way or another. We should try getting in there to lend a hand instead of dancing around with this lot."

"Charge the gate," Brook reiterated, looking to Thornton. "Make the call."

"We won't all get inside," the captain told them, looking back along the road to the growing throng of the dead. "We'll lose some of our people in this mess if we don't stay focused upon the enemy."

"The enemy is in there," Brook replied, pointing to the wall behind him. "These are just his puppets."

Thornton nodded.

"You're right," he said. "We're wasting time out here and getting nowhere fast. Call them up. We're going in."

With that, Thornton moved to the middle of the path, with Jendryng and Sparrow on either side of him. Together, the three men hacked through several living corpses as Brook gave a loud, crisp whistle for all to hear.

He attained the attention of the living men fighting along the way.

"Charge the gate," he called to them.

The order echoed along the line.

Within moments, the men of Dendadia, Woodmyst, and Newholt moved as one.

The horses barged through the throng of the dead as the foot soldiers dodged and elbowed their way along the road as best they could.

The dead, slow at reacting, could still take a few of the living down as they made the charge.

"Charge the gate," Thornton barked as he raced towards the Agrodien.

Yuri turned to see the advancing men racing up the hill.

The reptilian gave a tremendous roar as he raised his sword, calling his warriors together.

Closer and closer to the open gates they drew, hacking and chopping their way through the dead.

Limbs fell to the ground. They tossed bodies over the edges of the road. Men fell, both living and dead.

Closer and closer.

The allied forces regrouped near the top of the road, slicing their way through the white soldiers, stepping over pieces of flesh and through pools of blood.

Closer and closer.

A great creak and ear-shattering shriek resounded as the gates shut, slamming with a loud clank.

The guards inside the palace grounds had locked the allied forces out.

"Q'Sharh!" Nola'ee roared, standing only inches from the barrier.

"Shit," Thornton spat, peering back along the line.

The swarm of the dead was upon them, creeping from the city and along the road.

They were trapped.

As the clash of swords ensued from the rear of the line, Thornton felt his heart drop.

"This is it," Brook said from his side, echoing his own sentiments.

First Garrison Commander, General Saruun Versel, slowly lifted her head. The throbbing ache in her temples made her feel as if her head was about to burst.

Her eyes remained shut as she tried to remember what had just happened.

Carefully, she lifted her body from the ground to sit up, sliding her back along the stone wall. The metal armour covering her shoulders scraped against the surface, making a grating sound that shook the insides of her head violently. The ache intensified.

She ran her fingers along her right cheek to the pounding spot just to the side of her forehead. The sensation was cold and chilling to the touch. She couldn't feel anything in her fingers at all, only icicles against the skin of her face.

It took her a moment to realise that she still wore her steel gauntlets on her hands.

Her thoughts reformed into a logical sequence.

She had been in a fight.

A fight that she had obviously lost.

A fight with a little girl.

The sound of clashing blades grew from a soft echo to a din of clarity as she opened her eyes.

Blurry forms, shadow and light, surrounded her.

The flicker of flames high in a row and dotted about her. Some close by, others a short distance away.

She remembered she was in the palace's courtyard.

As her vision became clearer, she could determine that the row of flame across the way and high above came from torches lit on the defensive wall surrounding the grounds.

Shadows moved before her. Some sluggishly. One; she believed it to be one; moved like the wind.

The form was smaller than the others.

Faster.

It leapt and turned about the other forms with such an incredible speed that Versel supposed it to be a piece of cloth caught on the breeze.

As her vision became sharper, she saw the two swords carried by the figure. They flashed and twirled, slicing through the other shadows relentlessly.

Confusion swept over the general as she witnessed one form, clearly wounded by the smaller form, continue to fight without as much as a murmur.

Then she saw why.

The larger figures were her own men, all dead. She now saw the large gaping wounds in each of them, caused by the girl's blades.

Still not ready to rise to her feet, feeling groggy from being thrown against the wall, Versel watched the girl hack one of the dead soldiers apart with strengthened savagery.

The general had noted how the girl had killed her men. Merciful strokes of the blade, strikes to vital places that induced a quick death.

What the girl did now was almost frightening.

She hacked limbs away, took heads from bodies, cut the dead soldiers into small pieces.

Versel could understand the brutal approach. After all, the men were not staying down.

Even with legs or arms missing, even without their heads, the soldiers continued to reach for the girl, swing their blades in her direction.

The general peered over at the four prisoners kneeling on the ground. Each of them watched the girl with agonised frustration.

The mother wept as she watched on, helplessly.

Versel tried to stand. Her head spun about and black splotches appeared before her.

She let herself relax, moving her gaze past the prisoners to the Maji.

He was still pressing his hand to the frost. His two little brides stood beside him, touching his shoulders as they stared at the sky with mouths agape and eyes glowing white.

The agitated call of the girl's dragon captured the general's attention.

She turned to see the wounded creature bleeding upon the snow at the far end of the courtyard. It eagerly watched the girl leaping about. Versel surmised the beast wanted to join the fight.

Outside the gates, Zakhar slammed the heel of his boot into the mangled face of a white soldier climbing back upon the road. The figure tumbled over the side, taking several other dead men with it.

He quickly peered down the sloping path to see a multitude of movement, the living and the dead, in battle.

Farther down the way, more corpses were making their way up the embankment, either along the road or clambering up the side of the mound. He saw white soldiers, women, children, the elderly, charred shapes that resembled oddly formed bones held together by ribbons of black and burnt flesh.

The screams of men seemed to be endlessly filling his ears as the dead pulled more and more of his allies to the ground to be slaughtered, only to rise moments later and join the ranks of the enemy.

They dragged horses to the ground, shrieking in agony as the fiends tore them asunder. Their riders desperately called for aid, only to silence suddenly as the blades and fingers of the horde dug into them.

Fight until you can't, he told himself over and over. *Fight until you can't.*

As the dead drew nearer and nearer, the commander surmised that his fighting days would soon be done.

Five of the dead soldiers scrambled to their feet and started for the girl, raising swords above their headless bodies.

The girl plunged her swords into the back of a legless torso. The body flailed its arms about, reaching around for the young huntress.

With a great thrust, the girl flung the torso from her blades and into the five dead men, sending them sprawling to the ground.

Like a flash, the girl swung about as she sheathed one of her swords on her back. Quickly, she took a dagger from her belt, crouched low as she faced the four prisoners, and threw the knife as hard as she could.

Versel thought the blade was going to strike the auburn women, the girl's mother. Instead, it flew past the woman's head, by the side of the guard holding her in place, and over the courtyard.

The Maji screamed as the blade plunged into his back, just below his right shoulder blade.

The twin girls closed their mouths, and their eyes dimmed as they took their hands from their husband's shoulders.

At that moment, the dead surrounding the girl fell to the ground and came to rest.

Thornton was bringing his sword downwards, intending to strike his opponent in the head with the edge of his blade. Instead, the white soldier fell to the ground before the captain's weapon came close to striking the corpse.

The sound of armour clanking, swords and axes falling, and bodies thudding to the ground reverberated along the road to the palace.

The living men gave up a mighty cheer.

Not willing to celebrate yet, Thornton turned his attention to the gates, still closed.

"Can you break it down?" he asked Yuri, who was already peering at the blockade.

Without a word, the Agrodien leader ran at full speed through the gates.

The other eight reptilian warriors joined him, pushing with all of their strength.

"Get in there," Thornton commanded the surrounding men.

The captain of the land forces, the commander of the fleet and twenty other men charged into the iron barrier.

Their feet slid over the frosty ground as they pushed with all of their might.

Versel pressed a hand to the wall as she forced herself to her feet. She watched the Maji rise to full height, wincing as he turned to face the girl.

"You little bitch," he cried, reaching over his back to retrieve the dagger. It was beyond his grasp.

Suddenly, the clouds opened above the palace as fourteen winged beasts burst into view.

"Look," the guard holding Ursula in place bellowed, pointing to the sky.

Takmel moved his gaze to the clouds.

"No," he gasped upon seeing all the remaining flying monsters coming straight for the palace. He looked at the twins, who were glancing about, frightened out of their wits. "Kill them." Takmel pointed to the sky. "Tear them all apart."

Too afraid to disobey, the little girls sobbed as they turned their attention to the approaching dragons. White light emitted from their pupils, intensifying as they focused on their targets.

Thirty-Three

Thornton swore out loud as he watched five white guards run into view, each carrying long pikes. The guards levelled their weapons towards the men and Agrodien warriors, pressing themselves against the heavy iron bars.

"Push," Zakhar hollered, as they all pushed with as much strength as they could muster.

The gates creaked and groaned.

The guards raced forward, pushing the tips of their long spears through the bars, piercing five men on the other side.

Nakrah reached through the gate and snatched a pike in his leathery hand. He tilted it to the sky and pulled it to himself hard and fast. The guard, gripping tightly to the weapon, came along with it, within reach of Bein, who seized the soldier by the neck and squeezed tightly.

A loud snap ensued. The guard released the pike, dropping it to the ground before Bein let the body fall to the ground.

"Push," Zakhar called again as the remaining four guards lined up to begin another attack.

The sharp points of the pikes grew larger and larger in Thornton's eyes, one of them coming straight for him.

Yuri let out a mighty roar. He put his head down and pressed his hands against the bars near the middle of the gates.

The iron beam securing the gate in place bent with a long groan before snapping in two.

The gates buckled and came away at their hinges, tearing part of the stone walls away with them.

The white guards dropped their pikes and fled back into the palace grounds with one hundred men and nine Agrodien in hot pursuit. They didn't get very far, racing a short distance towards the barracks with the reptilians, catching them before they could reach the safety of the structure.

As Yuri and his warriors made quick work of the four guards, slicing through them with their swords, Thornton peered to the sky, where he saw several dragons pass by overhead, almost within arm's reach. The noise of the beasts cutting through the air was deafening. The sudden gust following the animals almost knocked him to the ground.

He turned his attention back to the way before him and directed the men to the left of the broken gates, towards the main doors of the palace, where he could see a gathering of sorts in the courtyard.

"There they are," he called, running towards the scene.

"Kayl'sro," Yuri bellowed upon seeing the girl across the way, immediately charging after the captain.

Takmel, still with the dagger sticking from his back, moved to Emily. He winced with each step, the blade feeling as if it was grating against bone as he walked.

Taking a handful of Emily's red hair in one hand, pulling at it so hard that her head was almost facing the sky, Takmel leered at Alice, taunting her, urging her to approach.

Anger and fear swept over the girl, to the point of being overwhelming.

Her mother was in danger, tied and gagged, defenceless.

Without hesitation, she did exactly what the Maji wanted her to do.

Alice charged towards him, sprinting as fast as she could.

Takmel drew a dagger from his belt. Versel's dagger. His face contorted from pain as the muscles in his back moved about Alice's blade, still stuck in place. He then pressed the edge of Versel's dagger against Emily's throat.

The message was clear.

The girl skidded to a halt.

"I just need a little time," Takmel told her calmly. Sweat had formed upon his brow. He appeared nervous, glancing over his shoulder at the army of men and Agrodien warriors approaching.

Alice held her hand up to them.

Stop.

Yuri was first to comply, looking anxious as he came to a halt, his tail coiling wildly.

Nola'ee's hands trembled as she momentarily locked eyes with the girl. A silent understanding passed between them. The reptilian wanted to attack and take the Maji down. She knew she could do it. A step or two, a quick leap into the air and then swords, claws, daggers and teeth. It wouldn't matter which weapon she used. He would be dead.

The tear streaking down the girl's cheek was enough to dissuade her.

Alice reiterated her instruction, keeping her hand in place until all men and Agrodien had ceased their advance.

"I know you will never be mine," Takmel said slowly. "So, I need to be sure you are never so foolish as to stop me again." He pressed the blade against the auburn woman's skin just hard enough to draw a little blood.

"No," Alice protested.

"Then surrender," he said. "I'll make it quick for you. My general is the best swordsman of my entire forces. She'll be precise. You won't feel a thing. I promise." He pulled Emily's hair tighter, forcing the woman to groan. "Don't, and you'll watch her die."

General Versel moved into Alice's view, hobbling slightly as she carried her sword limply in her hand.

The girl looked at each of the four women.

With their gags in place, and hands bound, their abilities were hindered. Words needed to be spoken. Power needed to be shared through touch.

Catherine wept uncontrollably as she looked at her younger sister.

"Will you let them go?" Alice asked through her own tears.

"Let them...?" Takmel almost laughed. "So they can attack me again? Are you mad? Your coven is mine. They will never be free for as long as I live. But they will live, Alice. I promise.

"Your commanders will be imprisoned," he continued. "The men under their charge will be put to work in our mines, upon our docks, on our farms, and will rebuild this city to its former glory.

"The entire land, from here to Newholt, will be mine. I will stretch my fingers over every city, town, farmhouse and passing caravan before I tighten my grasp.

"I will burn your beloved Woodmyst to ash," Takmel explained. "Its inhabitants... Your beloved husband... All of them will be taken and placed according to my will. I won't kill them, Alice. I won't even torture them, but they will never be free. Never. I promise."

Alice looked over at Versel and saw tears building in the general's eyes. The tall, blonde woman couldn't keep her gaze on the girl, looking down at the ground in shame.

They will never be free. Never.

Alice bent her knees and lowered her blades to the ground.

Emily sobbed as she watched her daughter surrender.

Alice placed her swords on the ground by her feet. She stood to full height, continuing to shed tears.

"Do it," the Maji commanded his general.

In silence, Versel moved towards Alice.

"I'm sorry," the blonde woman whispered as she drew close to the girl.

She placed a hand on Alice's shoulder, guiding the girl to her knees.

"Keep her on her feet," Takmel instructed. He looked over his shoulder at the gathered army from the east. "I want them all to see. And I don't want her to be within reach of those swords ever again."

Versel was apprehensive, her breath escaping her almost like a stutter.

Alice sensed the uneasiness.

"It's all right, General," the girl assured her. "Do your duty."

A deep frown built upon the general's face. A tear spilt over her cheek as she raised her sword.

Liana let out a great, remonstrative cry.

Versel prepared to swing her blade.

Alice lifted her head high.

Her braid moved upon her shoulder, dangling to her breast to touch the iron claws resting upon her bearskin cloak. A soft chime rang out, filling her ears as she shut the world out, keeping her gaze fixed upon her mother.

"I love you, Mama," she said with a smile. "It's all right. I go to be with Papa now."

Alice saw Versel moving in the corner of her eye.

The blade was on its way.

Takmel immediately slit Emily's throat without warning.

The smile on his face was enough for Alice to know that he intended to kill her mother all along, a final display for the girl to see before she lost her head. His timing, however, was careless.

Alice dropped to the ground.

Versel's sword swept by, barely missing the girl's head.

Catherine screamed through her gag as she watched her mother fall to the ground, blood spraying from the wound on her neck.

Alice retrieved her swords, tightening her grip as she charged, running faster than she ever had before.

The guards watching over the four prisoners turned to flee, suddenly forgetting that an entire army was standing between them and any means of escape.

At that moment, Christina, the Gold Queen, and Sarah, the Lilac Queen, bolted from the palace door. They raced across the courtyard, snatching the twin girls into their arms, twisting the girls to face away from them.

The Maji was too busy to have noticed the bold move made by his wives. His attention was upon Alice, who was getting closer and closer with each drawing breath.

Bursting from the shadows by the wall, Warren, the stableboy from Erimoor, sprinted over the ground. He moved to Catherine and cut at her bindings with the dagger he had earlier taken from Akasati's body.

Tendrils of smoke expanded from the Maji's flesh as he started his transformation. The blade stuck in his back fell to the frost as his flesh transformed.

He saw Alice getting closer at a very rapid rate. She leapt into the air, both blades directed towards him. His eyes widened in fear as he considered whether his conversion to his vaporous form would be quick enough, or whether she would strike first.

He stepped away, but he was too late.

She was upon him.

Her blades moved deep into his chest.

He smiled menacingly as she came to land.

A look of confusion and hatred swept over her face as she realised that his body had turned into a swirling mass of smoke.

The Gold Queen lifted a carving knife from her cloak and plunged it deep into one twin's hearts. The Lilac Queen dragged the sharp, serrated blade of a bread knife across the other child's.

Both of the little girls showed expressions of relief as copious amounts of blood spilled over their scarlet and black gowns and upon the snow at their feet.

Catherine, free of her bindings, reached her hand out towards the Maji.

"Absorb," she uttered.

Takmel instantly converted into his solid form. Power drained from his body.

Alice's blades were still in his chest, sticking out of his back.

He turned his head to look at the two little girls, their blood spilling upon the courtyard. His eyes widened with horror.

Weaker and weaker, he became. The colour in his face drained away.

He looked at Christina and Sarah.

They leered at him as they dropped the two little girls into the frost. Rich, thick blood had soaked into their fine clothing.

Without explanation or any words of malice, they slit their own throats open.

"Why?" Takmel whispered as he watched them fall beside the twins.

Alice twisted the blades in his body. Tears streamed over her cheeks.

He felt immense pain and winced as he moved his gaze to hers.

His skin was becoming sullen. A white, mist-like essence escaped his form and drifted to Catherine as she drained his life force away.

"Why?" he said again.

"Dear husband," Isabel said, stepping from the palace door. "It's simply our time. None of us can bear you any longer. None of us can live with the guilt of what you have made each of us do.

"You stole us from our lives," she continued. "You took away everything we loved. We are simply returning the favour."

He reached his hand towards her, a loving gesture as he wept.

"Come," he pleaded. "Come to me, my love."

Isabel stepped down to the courtyard and started towards him, slowly.

"Come closer," he groaned, his strength slipping away. "Give me your power."

She gave a small grin as she lifted a meat cleaver from her gown and thrust it, with brute force, into her own skull. Her eyes rolled into her head as she fell to the snow, twisting and jerking slightly.

He cried out. The pain clearly intolerable.

Alice pulled her swords from his flesh.

Blood spilled over his chin. He grinned at her before dropping to his knees.

"I still have one wife," he slurred, looking over to Catherine.

She lowered her hand, ceasing her action of draining him, becoming a blubbering mess. "You're still my wife," he bellowed, spraying blood over the ground at Alice's feet.

The girl shook her head. "Not after today, she isn't," Alice told him.

With that, she used both blades like a set of shears to cut his head from his body.

He fell. The last of his life force spilt from his neck to form a pool of thick blood.

The girl turned to Versel, preparing for another confrontation.

Instead, the tall woman dropped her sword to the ground and lowered herself to one knee.

"My queen," she said. "My sword is yours."

Alice looked on as the remaining guards followed their commander's example. The archers upon the wall lowered their bows and quivers.

The battle was over.

It was all finally over.

"Heal her, Alice," Catherine sobbed, crouching by her mother's side.

It was too late.

Emily was gone.

Alice, suddenly weak, dropped to her knees beside the auburn woman.

"I can't," she replied, almost unintelligibly through her tears.

The elder sister knew this to be so. She reached over and placed her hand on her sister's shoulder.

"She's with Papa," Catherine sobbed.

Alice nodded before lowering herself to kiss her mother on the forehead.

Thirty-Four

Alice tended to the wounds on Liana's wings as the other three women of her coven carefully cleaned Emily to prepare for a pyre.

The men of the east had collected the timber, who weren't having their wounds tended to, and piled in the centre of the courtyard, before the entrance into the palace.

Thornton had volunteered to retrieve the bodies of the Erilian women and Captain Schoenbach from the hillside to the south of the city. He took his four most trusted men and several horses with him to see the job done. Yuri sent Mralner, Kavnu and Duga along for the ride, instructing them to return to the plaza where Rabor and Zakhar's men were sheltering.

"Take the wounded to the docks," Queen Amicia instructed the captain and his men. "Bring our dead back here."

"There may be too many for one trip," Brook told her.

"Then, do the best that you can, Lieutenant," she replied, placing a warm hand on his arm.

The troop mounted their steeds and set off through the broken gates, back to the city below.

Yuri and Nola'ee, guarding their Kayl'sro, watched curiously as Alice ran her hands over the split flesh of Liana's wings. She had been at it for a long time.

"She may not fly again," Gruloch told the girl, crouching by her side. "A dragon without wings is like a horse without legs."

Alice looked to him coldly. She perceived his meaning.

"That's not going to happen," she said sternly. Her eyes were red from crying and her countenance was weary. "If I can get her to one of the ships, I can tend to her wounds on the journey home."

"Woodmyst is far inland," the other reminded her. "There is no wagon large enough to take her to the docks here, let alone overland from Newholt, or wherever you plan to strike land, and then onward to your home."

She ignored him and waved her hands over one of the large cuts in the membranous wing, whispering soft commands for the beast to heal.

"Alice." He placed a hand on her shoulder. Nola'ee touched her claws to the hilt of her sword. "My heart is breaking right now," the Haigok told her, ignoring the Agrodien threat. "I saw this one hatch with my own eyes. It does me great displeasure to tell you that putting her down would be best for her."

"I can't," Alice sobbed, trying to focus her power on the dragon. "I can't let her die."

"She's in so much pain," Gruloch told her, listening to the beast groan.

"She's laden with eggs," Alice told him quietly.

"What?" The other rose to his feet and stepped back, a look of surprise upon his face. "How could you know?"

"I know," she replied. "I know, just as I know I carry my son in me. I just know."

Gruloch stared at her for a long time. She continued to stretch her hand out to the beast, waving it slowly over the wounds.

"How can I help?" he asked, eventually.

***

They set a large pyre in the courtyard before the palace.

Catherine and Alice held one another tightly as they watched the flames engulf the shrouded bodies of those who had travelled with them from Woodmyst. They each said their farewells to Akasati and Karlena, the last of the Erilian women, and Captain Jeremy Schoenbach of the *Adelandria.* They spent most of their tears on their mother, Emily.

"Now, she rides alongside your father in the realm of Grolle," Amicia said to them.

"There is no Grolle," Alice replied coldly. "There are no gods."

Yuri looked away from the flames and to the Kayl'sro. His eyes glistened from the tears he had been crying. Even now, while she farewelled her mother, she remained insufferable towards the gods.

He said a quiet prayer for her, on her behalf, hoping that Q'Sharh would be forgiving towards him for talking to the gods of others.

"Gods of Woodmyst," he whispered under his breath, in his own tongue. "Give them safe passage home."

Nola'ee, standing to his side, heard his words. She reached over and took his hand in hers.

Yuri turned to see another fire burning just as brightly at the far end of the yard.

There, Commander Saruun Versel stood under the guard of eight men of Newholt. She was devoid of her armour and weapons, watching the bodies of the Maji, three women and two little girls burn away.

She too, had been shedding tears.

Yuri just couldn't tell for which of the dead upon the pyre she was crying.

***

The night became morning.

Many in the city continued to mourn during the day. Others tended to the wounded while the crewmen of the fleet prepared the ships to leave.

Supplies were taken to the docks, and some personnel had boarded, along with the cavalry horses and supplies from the wagons.

The vehicles, Alice decided, would remain behind in Wintermarsh. They had served their purpose, and there was no longer any need of them. Nor could they fit securely upon any vessel, with all the men, supplies, and horses taking up so much room.

By the early hours of the afternoon, barely anyone had had any rest. Alice had spent most of the night and the next day in the courtyard nursing Liana. The dragon was showing some improvement, but still had a long way to go.

Strength had returned to the beast's limbs, enough for her to move about, but the tears in her wings were still prevalent and needed more time to heal.

Alice took some time to enter the palace, moving down into its belly to speak to Commander Versel, her wrists and ankles chained inside a small cell.

"I will leave soon," the girl said, approaching the bars of the tiny prison.

Versel looked up to her with sodden cheeks. She was leaning against a thin cot upon the floor, half-hidden in the shadows.

"Will you take me with you?" the general asked. Her voice was soft and expressed a tiny amount of fear.

Alice shook her head. "No," she replied.

"You intend to kill me, then."

"I probably should," the girl said. "I have destroyed your city. I have killed your Maji. I have left little here for you to cling to. If I let you live, there is a chance that you will seek revenge. So, I probably should kill you."

"You have my sword," the golden-haired woman told her. She had said these words before, when surrendering to Alice. "I am yours to command, my queen."

"How quickly your loyalties have changed," the girl said.

"I need to serve," the woman said, a deep frown forming on her face. "I need a purpose. Take me with you."

"No," Alice answered. "But I will give you a purpose."

Versel peered at Alice, both curiously and fearfully. "What purpose?" she whispered.

"You will serve Woodmyst," the girl told her.

The prisoner furrowed her brow and looked at her captor oddly. "Then you will take me with you?"

"No," Alice answered. "You will serve Woodmyst from here."

"I don't understand."

"Wintermarsh will, by every definition, be an extension of Woodmyst," the girl explained. "You will obey the laws, customs, and leadership of Woodmyst. You will keep a treaty with Woodmyst and her allies. You will broker treaties with Wintermarsh's allies to form new alliances with Woodmyst and her allies. You will do your part to ensure that peace is kept across the entire lands from the Western Sea to the Eastern Sea by submitting your forces to the control of Woodmyst.

"I will place here an envoy representing Woodmyst in Wintermarsh," Alice continued. "Their office will be established here, inside this palace. I will expect them to live and work here, govern the people with a fair and just hand, and protect the people against any enemies that might try to take advantage of a city rising from the ashes."

"And you want me to protect this envoy?" Versel asked, lifting herself to sit on the cot as she wiped her tears away. "I'll do it, my queen. If that is what you command."

"No, Saruun Versel." Alice smiled. "I want you to be this envoy."

The general felt a lump form in her throat. More tears welled up. "Me?"

"Correct," the girl responded. "And your first duty is to find suitable accommodations and ongoing care for an individual in desperate need."

"Who?" Versel asked.

Thirty-Five

Gruloch met her on the dock. He had already seen the others of her coven aboard and waited until she arrived. When she did, she had all ten Agrodien warriors surrounding her, Rabor limping to the rear using a crudely fashioned walking stick.

"Alice," he called. She met him with a thin smile and reached her hands out to him. He took them gently. "I must leave. I have already sent the remaining Kazrekh riders home. Tarnas and his last rider, as well as the last two of the Traruk Clan, have decided to accompany me to the land of the Nrarukh. We need to find out what happened to Ganda, why he didn't return."

"Then this may be goodbye," she said.

"It may be, yes," he replied. He pulled her in close to him and wrapped his arms around her. "It would disappoint my father for making a friend with a daughter of man. But to hell with him and his old ways."

"I think my father would have been proud that we could forget our pasts," she told him. "I think he would have loved to have seen this bond between us build as it has. I will miss you."

He stepped back to look at her.

"One day," he said, smiling, "we may see one another again. You are always welcome in my home, Kayl'sro Alice of Woodmyst."

"And you in mine," she replied with a smile and a small bow. "Gruloch, Lord of the Haigok."

With that, he turned and offered a feigned salute to Yuri before striding along the dock.

Liana, perched on the quarterdeck of the frigate moored nearby, let out a loud chirp as the Haigok walked away. She spread her wings wide, displaying the small holes and tattered edges that hadn't completely healed over.

***

As they sailed away, Alice stood by the dragon, stroking her snout gently. She peered back to the tall white palace, to a balcony high upon the tower's side that overlooked the western quadrant of the city.

There, she could see a tall, golden-haired woman dressed in her formal uniform with a small boy standing to her side. Both waved to the parting ships as the wind filled the sails.

Alice waved back, but she was certain they wouldn't have seen her from such a great distance.

It didn't matter.

Saruun Versel still served a purpose and Warren, the stableboy, now had a home with fine linen and a decent bed that didn't smell like a horse.

Behind the palace, she saw several beasts rising into the air. They moved towards the east at first, towards the rising sun, before banking slowly to their left as they lifted higher and higher into the morning sky. Soon, they vanished into the clouds as they started their journey north.

"It's done," Catherine said from behind her. Alice turned and smiled at her sister. "I don't feel him any longer. It's really done."

"Almost," the younger girl said. She looked to Yuri, who was holding to the banister tightly in the middle of the port side of the main deck. A look of queasiness lay on his face. "There are still a few small things to take care of when we reach home."

***

The eagles carried their axes high above the quarterdecks of the thirty-one vessels speeding southward, a few miles off the coastline. With the wind behind them, and their sails filled to the brim, the ships of the fleet were making tremendous distance over a short period of time.

A little before sunset, they had reached within eyesight of Erimoor. During the night, they passed Blackshore. The morning light of the next day revealed the Griralith Pass to their left.

All the while, poor Yuri had stayed on deck, coping with the icy cold sea spraying over his face as he stayed by the port side of the boat. Alice had noticed him hurling the contents of his stomach overboard several times. She had taken it upon herself to see to his needs, bringing him fresh water and bread, which he wasn't able to keep down for long.

"The boat people are strange," he told her in his tongue. "This is not the right way to travel."

"Most people get used to it after a while," she shared, crouching beside him to hand him a mug of water. He gulped it, keeping one hand on the rail at all times. "You can't stay awake the entire journey. You should find a place to sleep."

"I don't like boats when I stay on top of them," he replied. "I think I will hate it more if I were to go below."

"Commander Zakhar believes, if the wind continues like this, we will be at our destination in perhaps three days."

"Three more days?" the other questioned with wide eyes. The vessel rose and fell over a deep wave. Yuri felt his stomach roll over and over. He hung his head over the side of the deck and ejected the water he had just taken.

Alice rubbed his back. "I'll fetch you some more water."

She started across the deck and was met by Zakhar, who had been watching the Agrodien on and off during the journey.

"How is he faring?" he asked with concern.

"Not well," Alice replied, fondling the mug in her hand. "The sooner we can get ashore, the better it will be for him."

"We will pass Dellmoor when the sun is at its highest, or thereabouts," Zakhar informed her. "We could anchor there and take some time on solid ground if you wish."

"No." She shook her head and looked over her shoulder at the reptilian, who was now lying prostrate on his belly, with his hand hanging over the side of the ship. "I don't think the people of Dellmoor are ready to welcome us just yet. They will need more time to mourn their queen, I think.

"Pryholt would be a better choice," she continued. "But I think we should continue onward to our first designated stop."

"Oldcastle it is," the commander replied. "We'll try to make the trip as quick as we can for his sake.

"In the meantime," he continued, "I have a fermented mixture made from parsley and rosemary in the galley. I always keep some on board for those who experience uneasiness upon the waves. It helps to settle the stomach; something I learnt when I was a young lad first recruited into the navy.

"I've held off, because it is meant to be taken when the vomiting has subsided, but he just has not eased up in the slightest. I then thought that perhaps the Agrodien digestive system might be different to ours, so I kept it where it is."

"I think anything is worth trying at this point," Alice replied. "I was on my way to fetch him some water. Perhaps I will get a mug of this…"

"It doesn't have a name," he said. "The men just call it *chuck juice*. Ask the men in the galley. They know where it is."

"Chuck juice?" she replied with a smile.

"I know," he said, grinning. "We should've come up with a better title for it than that." He turned to watch Liana. She had her head high and wings unfurled so that they stuck out far beyond the sides of the ship. "Funny how others seem to enjoy the experience of sailing."

"I think she's pretending to fly," Alice replied, looking at the rips in the dragon's wings. "It's possibly as close to doing so as she will get for quite some time."

***

By nightfall, Bein had taken up position with Yuri. Both reptilians sat with their legs dangling over the side of the deck. Alice let the two remain alone as they were both engaged in quiet conversation and had been for some time. Now and then, she saw the older warrior place a gentle hand on the other's back.

She moved to Liana, who had lowered her head to the deck where she half dozed. Alice lifted a large rolled-up canvas from the deck and carried it to the dragon's side, where she unfurled it. Some men working the decks looked to her amazed, as it was something that would have taken two of them, perhaps three, to move.

She spread it over the beast like a large blanket. It was proving difficult with the wind constantly blowing it this way and that.

Catherine appeared on the deck. She saw her sister's plight and approached.

"I'll help," she said, taking a corner of the canvas and walking around the great dragon.

Liana craned her neck about wearily and watched the older girl, offering a friendly chirp.

Both sisters drew the canvas over the creature and tucked it around the wings.

"Thank you," Alice said, looking at her sister. She noticed the other gazing thoughtfully towards the bow. "What is it?"

"Look." Catherine gestured with a nod.

The stars were brightly covering the sky ahead of them as the clouds separated. Standing on the foredeck, arm in arm, near the bowsprit, stood Nola'ee and Nakrah. Their tails coiled around one another's as they looked out to the twinkling lights in the sky.

"Do they know?" the elder sister asked quietly.

"I'm not sure," Alice replied, stroking the dragon's nose as it drifted off to sleep. "I told Commander Zakhar today. He has offered his help."

"Ursula spoke to Thornton some time ago," Catherine put in. "He was hesitant, but he understands. Amicia claims she has nothing to hold her to Newholt any longer. You're all I have left."

"Arthur and I have discussed this at length already," Alice said, stepping to Catherine's side. "I'm not sure about David. Aunt Linet and Uncle Lor might protest. Alan will be heartbroken."

"They should be part of this," the auburn girl suggested.

"You should see to that," said the other.

"Me?"

"It's been some time since they have spoken to you," Alice explained. "You should bridge that gap."

Catherine nodded. It felt that she had not been a part of her own family for a long while. She needed to repair what damage had been done.

"It's him I worry about the most," Alice said, looking to Yuri. "I think he will take it the hardest."

"You haven't told him?"

"I did," she replied. "A long time ago, it seems. So much has happened since. We almost got into a fight over it. I put it off since. I think he expects that I have changed my mind."

"Speak to him, Alice," Catherine said. "He needs to know."

The girl watched the large reptilian, still clinging to the rail with one hand as he spoke to Bein.

"Not now," she replied. "It's not the right time."

Thirty-Six

Two more days passed by. The winds subsided somewhat as the vessels followed the coastline to the east, entering the Sea of Lunkhul. Pryholt moved by during the first night, Greyrose and the scorched forest by the sea, during the early morning hours.

That evening, they dropped anchor as close to the shoreline as they could to the ruins of Oldcastle. From there, several passengers went ashore in longboats as ropes carefully lowered steeds into the water so they could swim to land.

Thornton and his four men, along with the Agrodien warriors, were first to place boots onto the dry land. They set up a perimeter, holding flaming torches as they guarded the approach of other long-boats and horses paddling through the water.

Alice was last, amongst those departing, to leave the frigate, taking her time to say goodbye to Liana.

"You will take care of her?" she asked the commander, looking over to Liana who still perched upon the quarterdeck, flapping her wings excitedly.

"You have my word," Zakhar assured the girl. "I'll feed her a goat each night from now until you are reunited."

"Just don't let her get fat." Alice smiled, a tear welling in her eye.

"She'll be fine, Alice," the other said, placing a friendly hand on her shoulder. "I swear it."

"Thank you," she said, embracing the man.

He wrapped his arms around her. "You should get going before they leave without you," he whispered into her ear.

She climbed down the rope ladder hanging over the port side of the vessel and got into the last longboat. There, the other three of her coven waited for her.

The crewmen rowed the women to shore and assisted them from the boat, where several of the men that had travelled with them from Woodmyst met them.

The troop remained on the edge of the sea to watch the thirty-one vessels sail away to the south, the wind in their sails again.

"How long before they reach Newholt?" Jendryng asked.

"A few days at most," Alice replied, keeping her stare on the dragon. "The northern winds will slow them down when they round the horn at Bellmore."

The beast craned her head, about to look at the girl, letting out a long, despondent call that echoed over the water.

Alice wept.

"Come, Kayl'sro," Yuri said softly, placing his hand gently upon her arm. "We should go."

***

The moon rose high in the cloudless sky, full and bright, with a deep blue haze surrounding it. A contrast against the dark sky accompanied by countless twinkling stars, it hung precariously above the mountains to the east, seeming to cast its light over their way home.

Alice and the Agrodien led the troop, as their eyes could see the worn and weathered road more clearly in the strange light cast by the moon. By the time they reached the edge of the Lunkhul Forest, the silver orb had climbed to its highest point.

"We could make camp here," Alice suggested, "or we can continue into the forest. We will be at the West Gate by dawn if we do."

Ursula peered at the dark passage made by the trees, stretching their twisted and gnarled fingers over the road. The shadows were deep, their way veiled in blackness. She shivered slightly, pressing herself against Thornton.

"I don't want to go in there," she whispered to him quietly so that only he could hear.

"I think we should continue," Amicia said. "I'd rather walk through the night and get to Woodmyst on the morrow, than spend another night in a tent."

Ursula let out a long sigh. Thornton kissed her brow and hugged her tightly.

"Funny thing about that, Your Majesty," Jendryng began.

"We didn't bring tents," she finished for him.

He shook his head, no.

"We should just keep going then," Catherine put in.

The trees groaned as they swayed in the wind, a mournful song with a macabre dance.

"I'm not sure," Ursula said softly, her voice shaking as she held her hands together fretfully, placing them up to her chest.

"Don't worry," Thornton told her, keeping an arm around her shoulders. "I'll be with you every step."

"Come on," Alice said to the horse she was leading, tugging on its reins. It seemed to hesitate, twitching its ears about before moving forward.

The group continued into the shadowy tunnel. Splotches of silver light touched the ground in places around them. It was visually confusing to most of the travellers, as shadow and light played tricks upon their eyes.

Again, the men and women put their trust in Alice and the Agrodien warriors, as they appeared to see the path ahead.

They were well into the journey, far into the forest, when Alice commanded them all to stop.

The branches stretched over the path like enclosing fingers, swaying gently as the breeze sweeping from the mountains swam through the trees. A soft hiss encompassed the troop, drawing a faint whistle on the air, and the occasional protesting moan from the forest as the wind pushed a little too hard against a pine or leafless oak.

Someone coughed along the trail.

"Shhh," Alice hissed.

"What is it?" Catherine could hear her heart racing in her ears.

"Shhh," the girl repeated, cocking her ear as she lowered her hood from her head.

They could hear twigs snapping from their right, along with something shuffling and crunching through the snow to their left.

Alice pulled her swords free. The reptilians followed suit.

"Alice?" the elder sister whined.

"Quiet, Catherine," the younger retorted with gritted teeth and a low voice.

More shuffling came from the north of the path. A growl muttered from the south.

Alice was the first to see them.

Two shining eyes glared at them from the middle of the road ahead. They moved forward slowly, towards a patch of silver light streaking through the twisted branches above.

A large, black paw came into view, followed by another. The shiny orbs filled out, revealing a large, box-shaped head with long teeth.

Catherine instinctively reached her hand out to it.

"Absor—"

"No," the young girl snapped. "The others might attack."

Catherine lowered her arm and looked about at the darkness surrounding them.

"How many?" she asked, clearly frightened.

"Too many to fight," Nola'ee reported, watching the forest to the south of their position.

The rukyul in the road stepped a little closer. Its hackles raised as it bared its teeth to Alice.

The girl lowered her swords and stared into its eyes.

She steadied her breathing, slower, slower.

Her heart eased.

She made herself calm.

Carefully, she took one step towards the creature.

It tilted its head slightly, studying the girl.

Its curled lips eased and fell gradually to hide its fangs.

Alice took another step.

The rukyul closed its mouth and sniffed at the air between them.

It looked the girl up and down. It relaxed its posture and turned, leaping off the road and racing into the shadows to the south.

Several more creatures raced after it, brushing past the soldiers on the road before vanishing into the night.

"I think I just shat myself," Vawdrey shared.

"Me too," Amicia whispered.

***

It was first light when they arrived before the West Gate.

Alice had never been happier to see the tall stone walls surrounding Woodmyst in all of her life. She couldn't bear waiting much longer to see her beloved Arthur. She so wanted to go to the Warde house where she was raised, fall onto her bed and rest in her husband's caress, even if it was for only a short while.

"Who goes there?" a voice called from the parapet above the gate.

"Alice," the girl replied. "Alice Gyfford."

"Alice?" the other, an elderly man dressed as a guard, called back excitedly.

"And Catherine, my sister," the girl continued. "Queen Amicia of Newholt. Ursula Wadham of Whitekeep. The warriors of the Agrodien nation. Captain Thornto—"

"They're back," the old man cried out merrily, ignoring the list that Alice gave of others accompanying her. "By the gods, they're back. Someone fetch the magistrate, and bloody well open this gate."

With a loud clunk and creak, the gate opened.

Another guard, perhaps older than the other, ran out to greet them. His steps were clumsy and comical to perceive. Alice wasn't sure if she was laughing because of the strange sight, or because she was happy to be home at last.

"My goodness!" The second elderly guard clapped his hands. "We've been hoping you would return soon. Welcome back. Welcome back."

As they moved towards the gate, Yuri looked towards the north.

"We should return to the glade, Kayl'sro," he said in his own tongue, gesturing to the other Agrodien. "I need to see my wife and children."

"I would prefer it if you stayed and got some rest first," she replied in kind. "But I understand if you want to leave."

"What's that?" the old guard asked. "What's he saying?"

"He wants to see his family," Alice explained.

"They're here," the old man told her. "All of them. They've all moved from the caverns."

"Here?" Yuri asked, glaring questioningly at the old guard.

***

News of Alice's return travelled quickly through Woodmyst. People had come from all parts of the city to see her moving along the street even before the troop had reached the market square at the centre of the community. They lined the edges of the road, cheering as she walked by as tall as she could manage, waving and smiling.

Inside, she was tired and only wanted to be left alone. She so desired time for herself and her family.

Andris' was the first face she recognised. He met the troop near the Assembly Hall.

"Good to see you, Alice," he said.

"And you," she replied, looking at the thirty soldiers he had brought with him, neatly lined up in three columns. "Can you escort us through this?"

"That's why I have come," he replied. He signalled the squad, who responded by stepping forward. "These men will show the Agrodien to their homes. Their families are waiting for them."

Yuri looked at Alice in question.

"Go," she told him. "I'll see you later."

Yuri bowed slightly and growled, "Kayl'sro."

She watched them move away, towards the east.

"These men," said Andris as he turned to another group, "will escort our soldiers and horses back to the barracks. Captain Thornton and his men are welcome to join them. There is hot food and beds at the ready."

"Thank you. I'll stay with Ursula," Thornton replied graciously.

"Begging pardon, Captain," Brook interjected as Sparrow tugged on his sleeve. "But I think the men and I will take that offer, if you don't mind."

Thornton looked at the four soldiers that had gone so far with him. He gave them a tired smile. "Go on then," he replied.

"Thank you, sir," they all said.

Soon, only the four women and Thornton remained standing before Andris and the last column of men.

The crowd gathered in the market square chanted Alice's name over and over. She offered a quick wave of her hand, which was answered with a deafening cheer.

"Come on," Andris yelled over the sound. "Let's get you home."

***

The walk seemed long and arduous.

The crowd appeared to follow them, chanting the girl's name over and over, to the point of it becoming unbearable.

Never had Alice believed the streets of Woodmyst to be so long.

Never had she known Woodmyst to be so large in its size.

Eventually, when Andris opened the door for her, she thought perhaps they were at the wrong house, but the crowd suddenly fell silent for her when she saw him.

She knew they were still calling her name, but she couldn't hear them.

All she knew was Arthur.

He stood at the door, his smile broad and wide. Tears streamed down his face as he held his arm out to her.

She ran and fell into him.

"You're back," he whispered. His voice filled her ears.

She pressed her lips to his and cried.

Thirty-Seven

David sat at the kitchen table with his face in his hands, sobbing profusely. Amicia and Becka sat on either side of him, consoling him as well as they could.

Since hearing the news of Emily's death, he had turned into a blubbering mess. It was enough to break all of their hearts.

"I can come back at a more appropriate time," the magistrate, Stephen Latham, said from near the front door.

"No," Alice told him. "We need to speak."

"He's taking the news rather hard," the magistrate said. "Isn't he."

"For him, the Maji has taken three wives," Alice replied.

"Poor fellow," Latham said, shaking his head.

Alice led him inside and offered a chair positioned by the fire in the sitting room. The older man accepted, sitting down and holding his palms towards the flames.

"Thank you. It is cold outside." He smiled at her as she sat next to him in a seat of her own. Latham looked over at David again. "Are you sure you don't wish for me to return later?"

"Quite sure," Alice answered. "I have plans to sleep a little before nightfall."

"Nightfall?" the magistrate questioned. "What happens then?"

"A town meeting in the Assembly Hall," she replied.

"Town meeting?" He looked to her quizzically.

"I want you to organise a meeting," she replied. "Nothing fancy. Just get word out and arrange seats on the platform for Amicia, Ursula, my sister and me."

"Are you planning to become the new council of Woodmyst?" he asked. "Like the Seven before all the horrible mess that we have just endured?"

"No," she answered. "Not like the Seven. Not like that at all."

He looked relieved. She understood his concern.

"Takmel is dead," she assured him. "The Maji is gone. The Mirikin are gone. None of them remain."

"I know," he said. "It's just…"

"You worry my coven may pose a threat to the people here," she finished.

"I don't mean to offend," he said apologetically.

"You're not," she assured. "Set up the assembly. It will all make sense after tonight."

Arthur approached, holding a steaming mug in his hand.

"Tea, Stephen?" he said, offering the drink to the magistrate. "Warm your insides up before you go back out there."

"Thank you," the other replied, relieving the boy of the cup. "Might also provide enough time to see some more of that crowd out there part ways. They all drummed me for information about you lot. Especially you." He nodded to Alice.

"It's cold out," Thornton put in, sitting beside Ursula on a sofa by the wall. "They'll return to the warmth of their homes soon enough."

***

After Magistrate Latham left, David moved to the sitting room to stare into the fire. When all those around him had thought that there were no more tears for him to cry, he suddenly started up again.

"You should get some rest," Arthur said, pulling Alice into the hall-way quietly.

"I was hoping you would come, too." She frowned.

"So was I," he replied. "But I think he needs me a little more."

She agreed with a nod.

Reluctantly, she made her way to bed. Within an instant, she was behind a closed door, out of her clothes and beneath the covers. Her eyes closed, and she was asleep before her head had barely touched the pillow.

When she awoke sometime later, the sun still filtering through the window, she noticed another's arm draped over her waist and soft breathing against the back of her neck. Naked skin pressed against her own.

It wasn't Arthur.

She was still half asleep, and very confused.

"Catherine?"

"Mmmm," a drowsy mumble responded.

"Why are you in my bed?"

"Amicia is in mine," she groaned. "Ursula and Thornton are in Mama's. I had nowhere else to go."

"And why are you out of your clothes?"

"Why are you?" the older sister enquired.

"Mine are dirty," Alice answered.

"So are mine," Catherine told her.

Alice considered that for a brief moment. It made sense. She still felt odd and uncomfortable.

She wanted to ask how David was, but her exhaustion overtook her and she drifted back to sleep.

***

Night came and the meeting at the Assembly Hall began.

The Four sat upon the platform and priority seating was arranged for their families and close friends, including the Agrodien.

The hall filled to the brim. Some had to stand around the edges of the benches, and a crowd had gathered at the door.

"We've never seen this many at one time," Latham said, whispering into Alice's ear. "Shall we begin?"

She nodded.

Latham moved to the edge of the platform and held his hands up, a signal for the crowd to quieten.

"Woodmystians and fellow guests," he began. "It brings my heart a great warmth to stand before you today and declare that the Maji and the Mirikin have been defeated."

The audience roared.

The magistrate held his hands up again. The crowd took a little longer to get over the excitement.

"Yes," he said as the room became a low murmur. "Good news indeed. Not only have we seen the end of a mighty terror, but we have seen the triumphant return of the daughter of the hero of Woodmyst, Tomas Warde, and the one we have declared Queen of Woodmyst, Alice Gyfford."

The room erupted in raucous shouting and applause.

"Kayl'sro Alice," the Agrodien chanted over and over. Soon, the entire room had joined in.

Magistrate Latham gestured to her. A wide smile beamed from his face as he beckoned her to the edge of the stage. He moved away to the side, giving her the floor.

She rose to her feet, wearing the bearskin cloak with the Iron Claws of Agrodia about her neck for all to see. She copied the magistrate's example and held up her hands to silence the people.

"People of Woodmyst," she began. "Old Woodmystians, here before I was born. New Woodmystians who have come from far and wide." She looked over the reptilians that called her leader. Sitting amongst them were the northern families, who had given refuge in the glade.

They were all there.

All together.

A tear rolled down her cheek.

"We have lost some great people along the way," she told them. "Brothers. Fathers. Sons. Husbands. Sisters." She choked a little upon saying the word. Her thoughts turned to the Erilian women. "Mothers." She almost burst into tears.

"We have made great alliances also," she said, swallowing the pain and trying her best to keep composure. She looked to Arthur, sitting in the front row beside his father. He silently offered support, nodding to her. "Woodmyst will forever have friends in the Haigok. We owe them a tremendous debt for the losses they suffered during the battle of Wintermarsh. We have allies in faraway lands, such as Dendadia, who came to our aid with her ships. Let us not forget Newholt, who has been by our side from the very start of this conflict."

The crowd offered supportive applause as Alice waved a hand to Amicia first, then to Thornton and his men seated near the front of the room.

"You have appointed me your queen," the girl continued. "I am overwhelmed and grateful to have been given such an honourable position. I accept the role with a reverent heart."

Some in the crowd cheered, repeating the chant again. *Kayl'sro Alice. Kayl'sro Alice.*

She held up her hands to them.

"I also say, with a heavy heart, that I intend to announce my successor this night and abdicate the position of Queen of Woodmyst."

The entire Assembly Hall almost fell silent with soft echoes of gasps and whispers.

"We chose you," someone in the room shouted.

"I know," she replied. "I know. But I hold the right to choose a successor. And I do not do so with a light contemplation. I've thought this through for a very long time, even during a time before you considered me to be your chosen leader.

"I thought about who it was that could lead my people if anything were to happen to me," she continued. "I thought about who would make a better leader than I ever could be. And now, when I have been appointed your queen, I considered these things again. And the answer is the same still.

"I will not be remaining in Woodmyst," she told them. "I will leave at dawn to travel to the lands past the Eastern Sea."

A rumble erupted in the auditorium. The crowd shared looks of despair and confusion, also shared amongst friends and those she considered family.

"I cannot lead you," Alice explained. "But there is one who can."

The room gradually fell silent again.

"He will guide you with a loving hand," she said. "He will support you and guard you as if you are one of his own children. He will embrace you and hold you in times of hurt. He will fight for you and keep you safe when enemies come. He will give you words of comfort when you need them the most, and words of courage when you are doubtful. And he won't be afraid to put you in your place if need be.

"I know this," Alice said, a tear sliding over her cheek, "because that is what he has done for me."

She looked down at the crowd, her eyes meeting those of the only one who could be the true leader that Woodmyst needed and deserved.

"Yuri," she said, holding her hand out to him. "You are the Kayl'sro we need."

His heart leapt into his throat. His breath hitched and became shallow.

A thick quiet hung in the air as the crowd took their time to contemplate what Alice said.

Thornton suddenly jumped to his feet and applauded and cheered. Gradually, others followed, beginning with the other men of the captain's squad.

With shaking legs, Yuri lifted himself from his seat, with a little helpful push from his wife Galonia. He looked down to Koryn, his elder son seated on the bench, and Donhran, his little one, sitting upon his mother's lap. Neither seemed to understand what was happening, but Koryn smiled at his father in any case.

His eyes moved to Corandra, his daughter, his firstborn. She was holding Bein's hand and weeping cheerily, laughing between the tears.

The room erupted in a thunderous clapping.

By the time he had turned around, Alice had removed the iron claws from her neck. She held them out to him in both hands as he climbed the steps to the platform.

"Kneel," she said to him when he finally stood before her. "I can't reach up that far."

He bent his knee and bowed his head so she could tie the Iron Claws of Agrodia around his neck. She took the bearskin cloak from off her back and draped it over his shoulders. "Now stand, Kayl'sro Yuri. King of Woodmyst."

He did so, looking at her with sodden eyes.

The crowd chanted his name. *Kayl'sro Yuri.* Over and over.

The Agrodien wrapped his arms around the girl in a warm embrace and lifted her from the platform.

"I don't want you to go," he whispered in her ear as the crown continued to roar. "I should go with you."

"Your place is here in the home of your ancestors," she replied. "You are the Kayl'sro and you wear the Iron Claws of Agrodia."

"The Iron Claws of Woodmyst," he said, gently lowering her to the floor. She gestured for him to speak to the assembly. He was hesitant, afraid to do so.

She urged him to approach the edge of the stage, holding her hand up to signal the crowd to lower their voices once again.

"I..." Yuri began. He paused and swallowed hard. His throat had never felt so dry. "I no speak common words good," he said. "I still learn. Kayl'sro..." He looked to Alice and remembered that he now wore the claws about his neck. "Alice teach me. She learn my words quick. I slow student." There were some low chuckles emitted around the room.

"I am happy..." He paused again to find the correct words floating about in his thoughts. "I am thankful. You take my people into your city and give shelter and food. You show kindness to me by giving kindness to them. Now, you my people and we your people.

"Alice say I good leader," he continued. He shook his head slowly. "I just try to help. I will do my best. But I need your help.

"We one people," he said, holding up a thick, leathery finger. "We Woodmyst together."

Thirty-Eight

Alice could still hear the roaring approbation from the night before as she rode a light-coloured steed through the South Gate. Arthur was beside her, seated upon the chestnut stallion. The horse was truly his now; she thought.

She had offered to saddle the beast for Arthur earlier in the morning, but the stallion had continued to shake the seat from its back as she attempted to loop the strap through the buckle. Funnily, when Arthur stepped in to do it, the horse stood rigid and waited patiently for him to complete the task.

The sun breached the eastern horizon, sending a warm golden glow over the mountain peaks. Trailing her were twenty armed riders of Woodmyst who surrounded the rest of Alice's party.

Catherine, Ursula, and Amicia were followed closely by Thornton and his four men. Behind them, riding upon a wagon laden with tents and supplies for the journey, were David, Lor and his wife Linet with their son Alan.

Alice turned in her saddle to look back at the walls of Woodmyst.

Standing upon the parapet above the gate were several people she believed she would never see again.

Andris and Sevrina, who held her newborn son in her arms. Ruttger and Courtney beside them. Nola'ee, who was clearly crying, and Nakrah holding her tightly. Corandra was still holding Bein's hand. Alice believed she would never let him go again.

Yuri towered over them all, raising one large arm above his head while holding his wife around the shoulders lovingly in the other.

Alice could see the Iron Claws of Woodmyst, twinkling in the new day's sunlight as they rested upon the Kayl'sro's chest.

She raised her hand and waved back to them for as long as she could.

***

The journey took three days to complete.

The troop stopped for the first night on the Twisted Road, high in the mountains at a campsite they had used before. So long ago, it seemed.

It was a long and arduous climb to the top of the range, with icy patches along the road that caused the horses to slip a little here and there.

The next day was mostly downhill. Even this proved to be slow going, as the way was unsteady and the turns were tight. The horses needed to be walked most of the way, and the wagon evacuated of its passengers on several occasions as the soldiers helped navigate it around twists and turns, steep dips and slippery rises. By the time they reached the open plains of the south, the sun was below the western horizon and camp needed to be set up.

The final day of the journey went with no complications. The way was straight for the best part. Their only problem was thick snow patches where the cart often bogged.

Very late in the afternoon, they came upon Newholt.

Even from such a far distance, they could see scaffolding surrounding the palace, small cranes positioned over structures throughout the city, and roughly forty ships anchored offshore. Another five moored at the newly constructed docks.

Amicia wept as she took in the sight.

Alice edged her horse forward gently as she noticed a band of six riders leaving the edge of Newholt, riding towards them.

"We have company," she told the others. "Slow going from here. Let them come to us."

It wasn't long before the riders met up with the troop.

"State your business," one of them said. There were no uniforms. They dressed in the clothes of workers and storekeepers. All of them, however, carried swords sheathed upon their hips.

"I'm Alice," the girl answered. She gestured to Arthur. "This is..."

"My queen," the lead rider gasped, looking at Amicia. "I apologise. We weren't expecting you so soon."

"It's quite all right," the other answered with a smile, wiping the tears from her cheek on the back of her sleeve.

"You look different in riding attire, my queen," another stated.

"Perhaps that's why you didn't recognise her," Thornton suggested to him, sarcastically.

"Who might you be?" the second rider asked.

"Captain George Thornton, at your service," the old soldier replied, moving his cloak to display the hilt of his sword. "Who might you be?"

"Terrence," the rider answered.

"Terrence," Thornton repeated.

"Yeah." The other nodded. "Terrence."

"Just Terrence?" Vawdrey questioned with a cheeky grin. "Mama didn't know who Papa was, then?"

"He's nobody," the first rider interjected. He turned to the other rider. "Shut up, Terrence."

"Yeah," Vawdrey added. "Shut up, Terrence."

"We'll escort you to the palace, my queen," the lead rider announced. He looked to Alice. "My lady. If you would like to follow us." As they started towards the city, the lead rider ordered two of his companions to race ahead and inform the guards of the new arrivals.

By the time they reached the palace gates, a welcoming party had gathered in the courtyard before the entrance.

Sub-Commander Landon Wake and Sheriff Nathaniel Monteacute stood side by side on the steps leading into the palace. Behind them were three women.

Ursula recognised them instantly. Before anyone had time for introductions, she was off her horse and racing across the ground towards them.

"Monty," she called. "My girls."

All five huddled in a warm embrace. They shed tears and shared unintelligible words amongst their sobs.

Alice moved her gaze to the end of the courtyard, where she had housed Liana during her last visit to Newholt. The space was empty.

"Welcome back, my queen," Wake said, stepping down from the stairs and making his approach.

"Thank you, Sub-Commander," she replied, waiting for him to fulfil the protocol of helping her from her horse.

Alice didn't wait for such a ceremonial act to be performed. She dropped from her steed and handed her reins to her husband, still seated upon the stallion, before approaching the soldier.

"My lady," the one-eyed man said with a polite nod.

"Sub-Commander," she acknowledged. "Any news from Commander Zakhar?"

"Uh…" He looked at Amicia and back to Alice. "Yes. I thought you might like to freshen up and have something to eat before we discussed such things."

"My travelling companions would appreciate that," she replied. She waved a hand at the twenty soldiers that had journeyed with them. "These men of Woodmyst could also benefit with accommodation for the night."

"I'll see to it immediately," Wake replied.

"News?" she questioned.

"Of course," he answered. "Commander Zakhar is aboard his frigate, moored at dock two." Alice turned and started towards her horse. Arthur readied to hand her the reins back. "But your dragon is not on board," he continued.

She turned and gave him a questioning look.

"Where is she?" She stepped towards him. "What has happened to her? Is she hurt?"

"We had her moved to the new warehouse," he explained. "The weather took a turn for the worse one night and her canvas sheet blew away out to sea. We've taken the best care we could, offering her meat to eat, but she seems to have gone off her meals. She hasn't eaten for three days."

Alice leapt onto her steed, taking the reins from Arthur. In an instant, the two were charging side by side through the palace gate and back towards the city.

Twisting and turning along the streets, they dodged and leapt, barely missing people and obstacles in their way.

Eventually, they came upon the docks.

They saw Zakhar's frigate tied to the pier. Next to it, moored to a neighbouring dock, was a larger ship with the word *Gypsy* engraved upon its hull.

Next to the vessels, just a few yards away, was a large construction that reminded the two of an oversized stable house.

"That must be it," Arthur said, steering the stallion along the boardwalk.

They raced their horses to the structure and through the large open door to its side.

The room was immense. Arthur considered the enormity.

They pulled their horses to a stop and absorbed the scene before them.

"You could fit the Assembly Hall in here," Arthur muttered. "Two, or three times over."

There were crates and boxes, piles of cargo neatly stacked against a wall to their left.

Alice moved her eyes to the right.

Curled in the far corner was a giant lump of a creature with its head tucked beneath its wing.

The butchered carcase of a sheep or goat lay untouched upon the floor not too far from it.

A deep, sad whine emitted from the beast as it let out a long breath.

Alice dropped to the floor and started across the room towards the creature.

"Liana," she called gently. The beast didn't move, except to let out another long whine. "Liana, it's me."

The dragon craned her neck about and stared at the girl, lifting her head high.

As Arthur watched, he wasn't certain whether the dragon recognised his wife anymore. The beast just seemed to watch, as if measuring the person approaching.

The dragon let out a deep growl, tilting its head curiously as the girl approached slowly, cautiously.

"Liana." Alice held her hands up to the beast.

Suddenly, a soft, friendly chirp emitted from the dragon.

"It's me," the girl said again. "Come on."

Liana let out another chirp and lowered her head.

Alice rubbed the beast's snout.

"I missed you, girl," Alice said, pressing herself against the dragon's cheek.

Liana chirped over and over again, producing a deep, guttural purr as the girl rubbed her palms over the dragon's coarse skin.

Arthur smiled as he watched the two reunite.

"Amazing relationship they have," said a voice near the warehouse door.

He turned to see a woman leaning against the frame. She wore a wide-brimmed cavalier hat and had a rapier sticking from beneath her long coat.

She started across the floor to him, reaching her hand out.

"Captain Davine Staiger," she said, introducing herself. "You must be Arthur."

They shook hands.

"How do you know my..."

"Yer Alice's husband, correct?"

"Yes." He furrowed his brow. He glanced at his wife. "But how do you know her..."

"And she's the dragon girl, right?"

"I suppose," the boy replied.

"Then," Staiger said with a smile, "she's Alice and yer Arthur."

"All right," he said, still confused.

"That's my ship," she told him, pointing through the door. "The *Gypsy*. And you, yer wife and yer dragon, will be my guests for the voyage to Dendadia."

"We will?" He looked to Alice, who was still petting Liana, no doubt listening to the conversation.

"The *Gypsy* has a larger deck space than any of those other frigates," Staiger explained. "We decided it would be better for such a creature to have a little more room to spread her wings, so to speak."

"So to speak." Arthur nodded.

"I just don't know how to get her on board," the captain shared. "She was easy enough to get in here. What with the wind and sleet, she wanted to crawl off the ship and into shelter. A little coaxing with a ram, and she was tucked away. But getting her back out and onto the *Gypsy*? I don't know."

"I'll take care of that," Alice called from across the room.

"She can hear me from way over there?" Staiger smiled. "Good ears, yer girl."

"Amongst many other things." Arthur grinned. He liked this woman. She seemed friendly and warm-spirited.

"Ah, look at him!" Staiger laughed. "Dirty boy. And so young, too." She started away. "I'll leave both of you to yerselves. I suggest you might want to load what you need to take on board tonight. We leave in the morning. Enjoy one night in a palace bed. The cots onboard aren't as plush. I'll see you at dinner."

"Dinner?" Alice questioned.

"At the palace," the captain replied.

With that, Captain Davine Staiger was gone.

Thirty-Nine

A large number gathered around the enormous dining table.

Alice and Arthur sat at one side with Catherine, David, Lor and Linet with their son Alan along one side. On the other sat Ursula, Thornton, and the four men under his direct command. Seated at the far end of the table were Sheriff Monteacute, Sub-Commander Landon Wake, Captain Staiger and three Whores of Whitekeep.

Amicia stood at the head with a glass of wine raised. She looked sorrowfully to the empty seat beside hers. Jonathon was no longer there to hold her hand or kiss her cheek.

"To loved ones lost," she said.

The guests held their glasses high as they remembered those that had fallen along the way.

Amicia took her seat and looked over at all the faces gathered around. "Tomorrow will bring a new beginning to all of our lives," she stated. "Some of us will leave these shores for a land far away. Others will stay to rebuild this one into something beautiful, I think.

"But I will be on one of the ships to Dendadia come dawn. And this city needs someone to care for her." Amicia looked along the table to Sub-Commander Wake.

"I would gladly take the responsibility, my queen," he told her. He moved his gaze to the woman seated beside him. "But I will also be travelling with you. Davine and I wish to start a life together in the lands to the east."

"I too will leave," Thornton announced. His men looked at him with perplexed faces. "I'm not one to give long speeches, so, Brook, you have command."

"Thank you, sir," the other replied, mystified. "I think."

"That must mean that you're leaving, too?" Rose asked Ursula, her green eyes becoming moist.

She responded with a solid nod.

"I am bound to Alice," she replied. "The four of us to one another. I must go with my prime. Besides, you don't need me," she said, glancing over at the three women by the sheriff's side. "What you did here is commendable. The four of you have rallied this city together."

Amicia nodded, agreeing with Ursula's words.

"She's right," the queen agreed. "The four of you led the uprising. You freed Sub-Commander Wake from captivity. You're the leaders this city needs."

"I don't know about that," Monteacute objected.

"You are." Ursula smiled at him. "You especially, Monty."

Monteacute downed his glass of wine as the gravity of his future struck him hard.

"We'll do our best," he said to the gathering before turning to face Amicia. "We'll try not to let you down, Your Majesty."

"You'll do just fine, Sheriff." She smiled.

There was a long silence as the others sipped from their glasses.

"I won't be joining you," David said eventually.

Alice and Arthur shot him a questioning look.

"Why?" the boy asked.

"I love you, son," the large man replied. "But I lost three wives here. I feel closer to them here. I can't come with you.

"You have proved to be your own man time and time again. You don't need me. It's time for you to make your own way. Start afresh with your wife.

"I'll be returning to Woodmyst tomorrow, but not until I see you off on your journey."

Alice sobbed. "David," she moaned.

"I wish I was better to you," he said. He looked to Catherine. "To both of you."

Both girls leapt from their seats and moved to embrace him.

Amicia moved her gaze to Lor and Linet. Both were wiping tears from their eyes.

"We just came to see our nieces off," Lor put in.

Linet gave him a playful slap across his thigh.

***

With the ships loaded, anchors raised and sails unfurled, they started out to sea. The eagles, with their axes gripped in their talons, flew high upon the masts.

David stood upon the end of the pier to see them off with Lor, Linet and Alan by his side. They waved their arms high, Linet a blubbering mess as she held a white kerchief in her hand.

Catherine and Alice both clung to Arthur as they sobbed and waved from the stern of the *Gypsy*.

Ursula blew kisses to the three young women, whose business she had once managed, and to the sheriff, who had been her best customer. Thornton kept his arm around her waist as he raised his hand to farewell the four men he had travelled so far, had so many quests with.

"You still owe me six gold coins," she whispered to him with a playful grin, her hair being tossed in the breeze.

"Presently, I am without employment," he told her. "So, I suppose you will have to take it out of me by means of hard labour."

She giggled, running a hand over the whiskers on his cheek. "Oh, I will," she replied.

Queen Amicia stood near to them, watching her city grow smaller and smaller as the wind pushed them farther out to sea. She felt a sudden and deep sense of loss. Everything she was, and everything that had made her who she was there, back on the land she was leaving.

"Don't be so sad, my queen," Landon Wake said from her side. "Yes, we are leaving loved ones behind, living and otherwise, but we are entering a time of excitement. An adventure awaits. This is a good day. May there be many more to come."

She smiled.

"Amicia," she said.

"Sorry?" He looked to her, a little puzzled.

"My name is Amicia," she explained. "I'm not the queen of anything. Not after today."

He nodded, and touched her gently, comfortingly, on the arm before moving to Captain Davine Staiger's side in the wheelhouse.

"How are they holding up?" First Officer Stalekk Rank'sku asked him as he stepped into the tiny room.

"Fair," Wake replied. "I'd say we'll have a few more tears shed between here and Dendadia."

Staiger sensed the small amount of heartache in the man's voice. She reached out and took his hand in hers.

"It'll all be fine," she said cheerfully. "You'll see."

He smiled and put his arms around her, forcing Rank'sku to grab the wheel as Wake planted his lips against hers.

"All right," the first officer said, moving into position as the others held their embrace. "I guess I'll take over."

Amicia scanned the city slowly. The scaffolds and cranes were a sure sign that Newholt, and the land beyond, would rebuild and start anew. Already, there was a welcome change in Woodmyst where they appointed an Agrodien leader and welcomed as so.

She turned and looked at the sea ahead of them. Before them lay uncertainty. Mystery.

An adventure awaits, was how Wake had put it to her.

"A good day," she said, repeating his words as she moved her eyes to the others gathered about the stern.

Liana stretched her wings over them as she felt the salt spray against her skin and the sun upon her face. She let out a guttural cry as the *Gypsy* rolled gently over a shallow wave.

With the wind in her sails, and not a cloud in the sky, the *Gypsy* sprinted towards the rising sun.

Epilogue

It was dusk and velvet and crimson draped the clouds covering the sky as the sun dipped below the horizon. The snow fell gently upon Woodmyst and a deep sense that all was well had enveloped the city.

Yuri wrapped his arm around Galonia's shoulders as they strolled by the Assembly Hall and market square. Both had thick cloaks wrapped about them to keep warm as they moved slowly towards the West Gate.

People passing by offered friendly nods or quick waves with their hands. Sometimes, these gestures accompanied a soft utterance of "Kayl'sro," or "my lord".

All in all, and for the best part, it appeared that Woodmyst was warming to their new leader and his kind.

Still, four armed men, dressed in armour and wearing long swords on their hips, followed a short distance behind, ready to defend their new king.

They continued westward along the road, stopping briefly to look at small things that others took for granted. Stonework. Peat bricks. Neat and square little gardens. Stone walls and fences.

Yuri and Galonia came to a stop outside of such a location bordered by a high iron fence. The empty ground inside, blanketed in snow, seemed to beckon to the Agrodien couple.

The covering snow subsided a little, moving in a straight line beneath the closed gate and into the large yard. It was a path beneath the frost.

Through the bars of the gate, Yuri saw something that grabbed his attention. He stepped over, with Galonia still wrapped in his arm, and pushed the iron gate open.

It swung inward with a soft squeak.

Galonia didn't question his action, leaving him to believe that she saw it, too.

"Wait here," Yuri told the guards softly. The men instantly, and instinctively, took up position on either side of the gate as their new leader and his wife entered the grounds.

The reptilian couple walked guardedly along the path, crunching the snow under their boots. Their eyes fixed upon the object that had their complete interest.

Closer, they drew to the centre of the enclosed land, right to where the great oak tree had once stood.

Yuri crouched and peered curiously at the ground.

It was a strange thing to behold.

Four tiny green leaves with serrated edges, stretched out upon a single stem, had pushed its way through the snow.

It was not the season for fresh growth.

In fact, they were still at the height of winter.

Yuri cocked his head and lowered his brow as he studied the sprout. His heart thumped rapidly in his chest as many thoughts swirled around in his head. Most of them filled with uncertainties.

He pondered what such an occurrence could mean.

Was this a good omen or bad?

Lowering herself beside him, Galonia ran a gentle hand over his back, the other around his waist at his front. Her head rested upon his shoulder as, she too, considered the tiny growth.

She turned her head slightly to whisper softly in his ear. "Kill it."

THE END

Acknowledgements

I thought I'd wait until I completed all ten books of The Woodmyst Chronicles before I included any Acknowledgements. I know most authors include one of these in every book they write, but really... I don't know that many people.

First, I thank my family for their support. Not just for this series, but for the many times when a simple word or two helped to encourage me in this endeavour. To my father and sister, there were a few times I thought I was wasting my time giving this writing thing a go. Then, something you said, without even knowing my thoughts, would put me back on track. I'm very grateful.

To all my friends, work colleagues, ex-students and acquaintances; thank you for lending me your ears, offering advice, patting my back and kicking me in the arse when needed. Many moments with you kept me grounded and helped me to keep achievable goals instead of setting my sites too big.

An extremely big thank you to my editor, Sally Odgers, my manuscripts' fairy godmother. No matter how many times I ran my words through grammar checkers, spell checkers and online bots that supposedly use artificial intelligence to correct any piece of writing, nothing beats the human touch you supplied. Thank you, thank you, thank you!

Another massive thank you to Dee Dee for the outstanding, amazing, tremendous work you did with designing the covers for this series. I was completely blown away by the beautiful cover for the first book in the series, The Walls of Woodmyst, with each successive book cover eclipsing the previous. You are a master at your craft.

To the good people at Whitekeep Books and Ingram Spark. Without you, these books would not have made it to print, or into the hands of readers everywhere. I'm eternally grateful for that.

More thanks to the writing and reading community on social media. Without your reposts, retweets, likes, pokes, smiley face emojis and kind words; others may have missed the news of these books. You are a very tight community and I love all of you for your enthusiasm, inspiration, encouragement and patronage towards books. You're all exceptional!

Last, but not least, I'd like to acknowledge the many sources of inspiration for my embarking on this journey. The obvious writers (in no particular order); Stephen King, Margaret Atwood, George R. R. Martin, James Patterson, J. R. R. Tolkien, Dan Brown, C. S. Lewis, J. K. Rowling, R. L. Stine, Matthew Reilly, Tara Moss, Jane Caro, Neil Gaiman.

Special thanks to John Flanagan, Ahn Do, Oliver Phommavanh and Nathan M. Farrugia, who all gave great advice or answered silly questions in passing (whether on social media, emails or as this teacher ushered you through the playground to the staff room for biscuits and tea after you spoke at a school where I once worked).

I'll never forget Mr Flanagan's advice when I told him I was considering writing a novel (which I'm sure he will never remember as it was a fleeting moment many, many years ago) and I pass it on to others who may consider doing the same.

"Give it a go, and see," he said.

So, I did.

And so should you.

Robert E Kreig

About the Author

Robert E Kreig was born in Newcastle, Australia and grew up in its outer suburbs.

He has always had a love for books, particularly well-told stories involving action, adventure and fear.

Some of Robert's favourite authors as a young reader included J. R. R. Tolkien, Stephen King, Orson Scott Card, Ray Bradbury and Frank Herbert. As he grew into adulthood, the list continued to lengthen, adding more influential writers such as George R. R. Martin, Matthew Reilly, Nathan M. Farrugia, Dan Brown, James Patterson, Michael Connelly and Lee Child just to name a few.

Inspired by movies like Star Wars, King Kong, Jaws, Jason and the Argonauts and other great adventure pieces, Robert listened to the voices in his head and entertained the strange visions dancing through his mind to assist him with writing his fantasy series The Woodmyst Chronicles.

Robert has penned ten books for the series which follow the lives of many characters, particularly focussing upon a family who must face many trials before the epic conclusion. Clashing swords, strange creatures, flying dragons and sorcery inhabit the world surrounding Woodmyst.

Robert has also written a standalone book, Long Valley.

Robert currently lives in Canberra, Australia where he hopes to one day become a full-time writer.

Other Books By This Author

THE WOODMYST CHRONICLES

From a faraway land...
...comes a new adventure.
The Woodmyst Chronicles is the story of a small community that faces the hardest of trials in a world filled with darkness, violence and magic.

Books In This Series...
THE WALLS OF WOODMYST
THE SONS OF WOODMYST
THE HEIR OF WOODMYST
THE WARLORDS OF WOODMYST
THE HUNTRESS OF WOODMYST
THE SHADOW OF WOODMYST
THE BRIDES OF WOODMYST
THE GODS OF WOODMYST
THE WEAPONS OF WOODMYST
A FAREWELL TO WOODMYST

LONG VALLEY

In the small community of Long Valley, nestled comfortably beneath snow-capped mountains, people quietly go about their business. Everybody knows everybody and there are no worries to give mind to.

But something has awakened.

A tragic accident near the valley's army base sparks a number of terrifying events, placing the local civilians in mortal danger.

A contagion is subsequently released into Long Valley, infecting pets, livestock, wildlife and people.

It's up to the local law enforcement and a small band of citizens to try to keep the town safe.

In the end, it becomes a struggle for survival as the people of Long Valley are overcome by the urge to feed.

THE CALM VOICE

No one in the remote town of Edwards Hill could have known that she was capable of such carnage.

Least of all her parents, the first to die.

Driven by the gentle words of The Calm Voice, she inflicts a barrage of carnage and death, leaving a trail of blood in her wake.

Her goal is to bring death to all who have hurt her.

All she needs to do is listen to The Calm Voice.

All she needs to do is just focus...

Just focus...

Focus...

The Calm Voice is a dark psychological novel surrounding the actions of one girl on a fateful morning in April, 2017. Kristin Matthews is fed up with her life, her oppressive parents, and her bullying schoolmates. She is compelled by a soothing voice thrumming in her head to seek revenge on those who have wronged her. At the top of her list is a trio of girls who have taunted her to breaking point. After careful planning, she embarks on a deadly rampage through Edwards Hill State High School, bent on destroying all her pain one final time. What follows is a haunting description of the day's events, culminating in an ending no one will expect.

www.robertekreig.com

www.whitekeepbooks.com